THIRST TRAPP
Wedding

Also by Christina Hill:

Thirst Trapp Farms
Tips Up
Love at First Flight
Love has a Name (#1)
To Love Again (#2)
Love Finds a Way (#3)

THIRST TRAPP
Wedding

CHRISTINA HILL

ISBN: 979-8-9857199-7-0

Book Cover by Erika Plum

Edited by Tracey Barski

To the ones willing to take that risk.

"Sometimes, if you're lucky, someone comes into your life who will take up a place in your heart that no one else can fill, someone who's tighter than a twin, more with you than your own shadow, who gets deeper under your skin than your own blood and bones."
—Snoop Dogg

One

Tilly

"You've got to always go back in time if you want to move forward."
–Snoop Dogg

I wouldn't do this for anyone else but her, my best friend, the woman getting married in a week, and the new mother of two, rambunctious kids...of the goat variety.

I blow a piece of hair out of my face. "Avery, we've been in this position for long enough."

Sweat builds on my brow as I do my best to balance in a table-top position with one leg extended backward and a yoga mat beneath me. Oh, and a goat on my back, which Avery named Vincent Van Goat. I will scream like a rabid animal if his cloven hooves dig into my spine one more time.

Avery lets out a slow breath, careful not to move quickly. "I'm afraid to move. I don't want to hurt ScapeGoat."

Honestly, I passed concern and care a long time ago when Vincent Van Goat head-butted my leg while I was in a downward dog position. If he doesn't kill me, this hot summer day in Big Timber, Montana will. Bismarck, the city I'm from and where Avery and I met in high school, gets hot, but only for the five minutes of summer we get every year. Otherwise, it's ball-freezing cold, like my heart. Just how I prefer it now.

I've been visiting Trapp Farms for the last two summers since Avery decided to move here and start a low-key spa for visiting guests. Not only do said guests get a facial, but they also have the once-in-a-lifetime opportunity to hug a cow for an hour. In between lying with a smelly ogre and a foot soak, Avery decided to fall in love with a sexy, bearded farmer, which explains why I'm here: it's wedding week.

Also the week I've been dreading. Not because her fiancé, Wyatt, is stealing her from me, though I have had words with him about this. But because this week is all about the power of two people falling in love and reminding me I'm no good at it.

I lower my leg and drop into a few cat-cow stretches, providing unstable footing for the wannabe tap dancer on my back. Eventually, he decides this rollercoaster ride is his worst nightmare and jumps off. But not before his bony hooves dig into my skin and make me scream like a wolverine.

I sit back on my heels, grabbing at my back as if I've been stabbed—it would probably hurt less. Coaching myself through a few deep breaths so I don't murder the livestock here, I ask, "Remind me why we're doing goat yoga in their pen? Can't we just do it in the farmhouse? You know, where the cool, conditioned air lives."

"Tilly." Avery grunts just as ScapeGoat jumps off her back. "You know Wyatt isn't a fan of having the animals in the farmhouse."

I rotate my neck side to side, working out the extra kinks I absolutely blame the goat for putting there. "That's never stopped you before."

She places a finger to her lips as she sits up on her knees. "Shh! Don't say that so loudly. Wyatt could be lurking. He can't know Mother Clucker spent the night indoors that one time."

I furrow my brows and push myself to stand before slipping my sandals back on. "You said it was twice."

She peers around us, looking for eavesdroppers. "Three times. But only because Wyatt was meeting with his new financial advisor for the farm in Billings, and I was lonely."

I tip my chin up and cross my arms. "Right."

She rocks back on her heels and stands in one fluid motion. "I told Wyatt that if we got goats, I'd teach them yoga so when guests come, they can enjoy—"

"Stabbing pain all over their body?" I fill in. "How about the smell of their—"

"You really aren't an animal person, are you?" she asks, shaking her head at me.

"I don't hate-hate them. But loving them is weird." Love is weird. Period.

Attaching yourself to one person and hoping they'll reciprocate those feelings for all of eternity? Weird. It doesn't help that my parents are divorced. My list of grievances about love was ten pages long by the time I turned sixteen.

She narrows her eyes at me. "It's my wedding week. You have to do everything I say."

I throw my hands up, then bend to roll up my mat, which is now covered in what I'm going to tell myself is dirt and *only* dirt. "Since when does becoming a bride mean I have to exercise with animals and do whatever else you've romanticized in your head? It's not written in that rulebook you gave me, is it?" The one I had to confirm she didn't need me to sign a blood oath just to read.

She shakes her head and bends to grab her mat, too. "If you had read my wedding planner I gave you, then you'd know it wasn't a rulebook. It was a carefully written list of instructions, details, and my color scheme."

I tuck the rolled mat beneath my arm and shoot her a glare. "Isn't your color scheme called *nature* since it's outdoors?"

She closes the small gap between us, tucking her somewhat rolled-up mat under her arm, too. "Yes, with pops of red to match the barn."

The sound of a shovel sinking into gritty earth steals my attention, and I turn toward the noise before I can respond. What fills my eyes first is pure rage, and then memories of two summers ago, followed by a falling sensation low in my belly as Ronny's arms flex with every dive his shovel makes into the dirt. I know just how strong those arms are since he held me, standing upright and suspended in mid-air as he plunged—

"Ronny, do you know where Wyatt is? I thought he was with you?" Avery asks, completely oblivious to the thoughts just racing through my head.

I adjust the mat under my arm and grind my teeth like I want another scolding from my dentist as Ronny—Wyatt's farmhand and annoying neighbor—stops flinging shit everywhere and meets my eyes. They're so damn...pretty—dark brown at the edges of his irises that lightens as it closes in on his pupil. But he'll never hear that from me. At least I won't tell him again. I've sworn off all things Ronny, and if it weren't for my best friend—who is marrying his best friend—I would have sworn off farms, too. But I can't do that since Avery insists I visit her at least every couple months. So, I'll just have to suck it up for another whole week and keep the past where it belongs: in a meat grinder.

He spears the shovel into the ground and rests his hands on top. "Haven't seen him in at least an hour. Try the horse barn."

He tips his chin behind us toward the big, red barn that will serve as the backdrop for the outdoor wedding in exactly eight days.

Avery nods, then looks at me. "I'll catch up with you later. I'm going to go see what day Wyatt's family is coming to settle into the cabins."

I open my mouth to say something, but her back is already to me, the word *BRIDE* spelled out across her shoulder blades. This is her second day wearing that shirt, and I don't see her taking it off anytime soon.

My gaze slowly swivels back to Ronny, and I make a fist at my side. "Ronny."

He uses his tongue to shift his toothpick to the other corner of his mouth with a sly smile. "Tilly."

I want to snap that toothpick in half, throw it in his face, and then kiss that full mouth of his. Instead, I hike the yoga mat higher under my other arm and glare at him.

He leans further into his shovel and tips his cowboy hat back, revealing more of his dark-toned skin that feels as soft as it looks. At least it did two years ago. "You did something new with your hair."

I resist the urge to touch my newly cropped hair. The first time we met, my wavy locks reached my mid-back, and I'm sure he remembers that since he held a fistful of it in...never mind. It's a shade darker than my usual basic brown, but I treat my hair as an accessory and change it often to mix things up. I'm a hairdresser; it's what we do.

I wave a hand in front of him. "I see you're still the...same."

My voice catches on the last word. His wide shoulders, narrow waist, and scruffy jawline are all as I remember from a few months ago when I visited Avery, but it's what he's packing beneath his T-shirt that looks new. How has he developed *more* muscle tone? It makes me hate him more. I'm a mixed bag of wanting to rip the buttons on his shirt and hitting him over the head with the shovel he's leaning on.

He studies me through a squint. "I like consistency."

I give a pinched laugh and take that as a diss. Everything Ronny says to me might as well be. "Yeah, okay."

He stands straighter, wrists still stacked, one on top of the other, holding that damn shovel. "Is there a reason that's funny to you?"

Two years is a long time to hold a grudge. But no one ever blamed me for being mild-mannered. I'm as batshit stubborn as they come. I will die on this molehill before I let this man best me. Once upon a time, for two blissful months, we were great together. Electric and wild, fun and spicy. It only took one conversation to change my mind, and now, I can't stand him.

"Hilarious, actually." I push out a hip. "Don't you have work to do?"

"Don't you have goats to annoy?"

I scoff. "Don't you have shit to fling?"

He lifts the shovel and drives it into the ground at his side. "Don't you have wedding things to stress about?"

I take a step closer, and so does he. "Don't you have chickens to lasso?"

His smirk drops into a frown. "You don't lasso chickens."

"Whatever." Another step, and I'll be in his personal space so hard, he'll hate it. But my brain is struggling to think of a good retort when we're this close. My eyes have never left his except for now when they dip to admire his new muscles up close. "Don't you have tractors to bench press?"

He steps closer until our noses are almost touching. "Are you offering to spot me?"

I go mute. Thoughts are hard, words are harder, and Ronny's biceps are the hardest. I open my mouth to say something, but nothing comes out.

He pulls out his toothpick and sticks it in the front pocket of his flannel, grazing my shoulder since both of us refuse to leave these tight quarters first.

It's at this moment Vincent Van Goat decides to take his shot and head-butt the back of my knee with his empty skull, shoving me forward into the brick wall of Ronny's chest.

Arms circle around my waist, gripping me tightly and threatening not to let go. And for a split second, I believe those arms will be everything they once promised they would be. Protective, loving, safe, *home*.

I peer up at him as he looks down at me. Those lips were as familiar as my own once. The havoc they created on every inch of my skin is felt now like it happened yesterday.

But it didn't.

This doesn't work; we don't last. He told me that two years ago.

I shove myself out of his arms, looking more like a bird who accidentally flew inside and is trying to get out.

I spin around and point at Vincent Van Goat. "You."

He could give zero fucks right now as he makes one of his many irritating sounds while the goatee on his smug little chinny-chin-chin moves, too. I'll be searching the internet for goat-roasting recipes later.

Ronny snickers from behind me, and I whirl around and point at him.

He holds up one hand in surrender, then walks to the side of the small outbuilding Avery called the Hooves Hotel, where he leans the shovel against it. Sliding his hands in his jeans pockets, he stares back at me.

"It's good to see you again, Till."

The fumes coming from my ears at the usage of my nickname on his lips could start a forest fire. My brain barely registers the *it's good to see you* part since I know those words are lies before he even says them.

He turns, opens the gate, and exits the pen, strutting—yes, strutting—off to go plow something. Or someone. I loosen my grip on the yoga mat. The possibility of Ronny finding someone else is there. It's been a reality for me, too. I just never found anyone. I've dated, as I'm sure he has—you don't look like Ronny and possess as much swagger as he does and stay home on a Friday night. But nothing has stuck. Love doesn't work for me like it works for other people. I've tried.

I rub my forehead and pull my hand away with dirt smeared there. Just great. The first time I've seen Ronny since my last visit and the longest we've spoken to each other since *that day*, and I've got dirt on my forehead.

Vincent's throat vibrates with another sound.

"Shove it, goat!" I yell loudly, scaring a flock of birds that take flight from a nearby tree.

I need a shower. Cold first, then piping hot.

Two

Ronny

"It ain't no fun if the homies can't have none." —Snoop Dogg

How many more fences are you going to mend?" Wyatt asks, impatience leaking from his mouth.

I look over my shoulder and sneer at my next-door neighbor. *Next* meaning a quarter mile away. We've been best friends since we were kids. He spent summers and occasional weekdays at his grandparents' farm while I grew up out here every day of the week.

We caught fish in the creek running through his property, climbed trees until our hands were sticky with sap, and conducted races from one part of the farm to another. No medals were given, just the promise to do the other person's least favorite chore. I hated having to muck horse stalls, but I didn't have to do it nearly as often as Wyatt had to tinker on some old equipment Pop was convinced would run again.

I would do anything for his family because I know they'd do anything for mine. When Wyatt's gramps passed a few years back, Granny struggled to keep the farm moving. Being older than he was, she was in no position to sit atop a tractor and harvest the alfalfa they grew. So I hired a part-time crew at our farm so I could help her out.

I have no regrets. I'd do it all over again if I had to.

"It would go faster if you got off Axel's back and helped."

He pats his horse's neck, and his tail swooshes with the touch. "There are two kinds of people, Ronny," *here we go,* "ones that fix fences and ones that tell you when your work sucks."

I know for a fact it doesn't suck. He sucks. "Let me guess which one you are," I start.

"You really need to pull them together more if you don't want to be doing this again in a few weeks," he finishes.

I gesture toward the fence. "Show me how it's done, then."

"I could." He pauses. "But I'm really just here for one thing."

I scoff and grab the pliers stashed in my back pocket. "Does this *thing* have a loud mouth and fire coming out of her ears most of the time?"

"Maybe."

I can tell he's trying not to laugh as he covers it with a cough. Being friends for so long means I know him as well as the boundaries of my own family's farm—Adler Farms. I know he sucks at Connect Four, still owns a pair of his fancy city-slicker boots, and loves his family more than anything. He also had a rough go of it a year back after his cuckoo for Cocoa Puffs ex decided to show up as he was starting to move on. Her eggplant-colored athletic wear only stirred up trouble and offended everyone's retinas. What a piece of work.

With the two wires stretched taut, I use the pliers to crimp and secure the sleeve over them to keep them in place. My pop taught me how to do this before I could see over the fence or stretch my hand wide enough to hold the pliers. I grew up to find I rather enjoyed the quiet, repetitive work. But not today, when Wyatt's bringing up the woman I have to do multiple cold plunges a day not to think of.

I could use one now. The sun is at its highest, and the number of times I've used my gloves or forearm to wipe my brow is higher than Granny's Bunko winnings. The start of this summer has been unseasonably warm, and it's only mid-June, which apparently means nothing to Montana.

"I'm guessing Avery sent you here to talk to me?" I ask, separating and wrapping the wire ends.

"Granny heard you two fighting in the goat pen this morning and told Avery she thought Tilly was about to smack you with a shovel." He clears his throat as Axel shifts on his hooves. "Avery just wants to make sure everyone will play nice this week."

I should have known approaching Tilly would have come back around to bite me in the ass. It always does. Staying away isn't exactly easy when it comes to her. Like being on a diet and pretending quinoa tastes the same as chocolate cake.

It's not the same.

The goat pen should have been a safe place to get our first greeting out of the way since the last time she visited Avery months ago, but I guess not. There's no privacy with that family. Wyatt and Avery might be the only ones living in the farmhouse since Granny moved in with Wyatt's folks, but that doesn't mean they don't have regular visitors nearly every day.

Granny especially. She still comes multiple times a week to heckle us about not posting so many thirst traps on social media. I'll believe her when she stops sharing my videos to every granddaughter across the state. Doesn't matter if she knows them.

"I'm offended Granny thinks Tilly would have been able to hit me." I would have fended her off. I'm taller and stronger; I've lifted her enough times to know. "I'll play nice. You don't have to worry about me." Standing straighter, I walk back over to my horse, June, and tuck the pliers into my saddlebag. "But I can't promise the same from her."

"Avery's gonna talk to Tilly." Wyatt rubs his forehead. "Look, I know you two have—"

"Had," I correct. The last thing I need is anyone thinking there's anything present tense about Tilly and me.

I might know how her skin tastes or how many brightly colored pairs of underwear she owns, but that's the sum of us. Two months shouldn't have been enough to upend my life, but it was. And then there was that time last summer before Wyatt and Avery got engaged where I tried talking to her and ended up with my mouth on hers. She shoved me away before things could go further, and I'm glad she did. I shouldn't have done that, but Tilly has this way of making me feel I'm a breath away from caving like a barn made of toothpicks.

If I could scrub her name from my memory, I would, but I can't.

"You two *had* something going on; I don't know why you can't just tell me what the deal is. Maybe it would help me understand. Hell, maybe it would make sense why we can't have both of you in the same space for more than a few minutes, or you'll draw blood."

I stab a finger at him. "That was an accident. Tilly didn't listen to me about pocketknife safety."

"Yeah, yeah."

Willful woman.

Slipping my foot into the stirrup, I grab the saddlehorn to fling my leg over June's back with a grunt like an old man. Twenty-nine isn't old by any stretch, but there's nothing like the talk of a woman I kind of dated to add more gray hairs on my head. There's a reason I haven't brought up our short but passionate history. Wyatt's been sweet on Avery since she first came to start the spa at Thirst Trapp Farms two years ago. It wasn't long before her BFF Tilly surprised her with a visit. One look at those long legs, Daisy Duke shorts, and heels, and I knew I'd be taking them off her that night. I was right. But the thing about taking heels off a woman is that eventually, they put them back on.

A farm is no place for heels.

Better I remember that.

June starts back toward the barn before I even have to urge her. Seems someone is just as eager to get out of this heat—and this conversation—as I am. Wyatt leads Axel beside us. "Tilly and I had some good times." No one has ever left the kind of nail marks on my back or hair in my shower drain like her. "But we come from different worlds. We're two different people. She's a heel-wearing firecracker, and I'm just a guy wanting to mend fences and spend time outdoors. It would've never worked."

I've recycled this lie enough times, I'm starting to believe it. But my life looks a hell of a lot different now than it did two years ago. I have more responsibilities than ever and no time for screwing around with women like I used to. Granny can keep her list of granddaughters.

"Is that why you pushed her away?"

A sound comes from the back of my throat I have no explanation for.

I rest a hand on my thigh while loosely holding the reins as if this idea is ludicrous. It's not—I *did* push her away—but hell if I'll admit that. "I didn't push her away." Wyatt leans forward to try and catch my eyes. I don't let him. "I just didn't sleep with her again."

Tilly's the kind of woman you quit cold turkey before you wake up and realize her name is permanently inked on your bicep, and you're helplessly addicted. I'd end up promising her my whole life, and I couldn't do that. I couldn't risk it.

"You two might come from different worlds, but love can find you at the most unlikely times in the most unlikely people."

The sound of our horse's hooves clopping against worn earth and rock is the only thing resounding between us. I slowly turn my head and glare at him. "Are you fucking serious right now?"

"What?"

"You sound like page fifty-six of a romance book." I angle the reins to get closer and punch him in the arm.

"Ouch!" he cries, rubbing his bicep. "Maybe I deserved that. Those old rom coms Avery has me watching are starting to get to my head. I think I just blacked out."

I wave him off and keep my distance so none of that happily ever after bullshit gets on me. I need a woman who wants this life. Not one who thinks she does. Just because Wyatt ended up hiring the love of his life doesn't mean mine has more shoes than I have cattle.

He offered Avery the job sight unseen after leaving the hiring process to me. Well, turns out Avery had never run her own spa before, but she was licensed in massage and was our only applicant, landing her the summer gig. She rolled up with all of her things to move into the two-bedroom cabin built by Wyatt's gramps to live and run the spa out of.

"You know I've got your back, but this is my soon-to-be wife's best friend. If it weren't extremely important to her that you two get along, I wouldn't be here. But it is. We want this week to be drama-free, and I don't know, maybe even *fun*," he says with a short laugh. "You get that, right?"

I adjust my Stetson hat with the curled sides and custom leather braid around the center, perfectly formed to my head after years of wear. It was my grandpa's before it was mine and there isn't a day I go without wearing it. "Got it. I'll be a perfect angel for your perfect wedding week."

He lets out a sigh. "Thank you. Now, a couple more things..."

I grip the slack reins in one hand even tighter. June may not need me steering her to where she already knows where to go, but I need something to hang on to. It's not that I'm not happy for Wyatt and Avery. They deserve all the celebrations, but I like my routine. The work I wake up doing and fall asleep thinking about. A week of festivities like this comes with expectations I don't want to worry about—conversations I need to have and don't want to.

Wyatt drones on about all the events, big and small, dinners and brunches, bachelor and bachelorette parties, some other things I can't remember, and...

"Tilly's cooking dinner for everyone?" I ask in surprise.

Wyatt looks straight ahead, resting one hand on the saddlehorn and one on his thigh, the easy gait of our horses making this conversation still possible. "Yeah, tomorrow. Haven't you been listening?"

"Mostly. But why?" Last I knew, Tilly couldn't cook anything without giving it a good char first.

He rolls each of his flannel sleeves up. "Said she wanted to host a family dinner as a *thank you*."

The horse barn is in sight now, and pretty soon, we can call it quits on talking about Tilly, and I can escape her again. She visits on and off a few weekends a year, but now I've got an entire week around her with all of these scheduled activities. I didn't exactly leave things in a good place, pissing her off worse than a farmer trying to catch a mole. I'll be lucky to make it out with my dick still intact.

"What time?" My tone is short and to the point.

"Be at the farmhouse at six."

I click my heels into June's side, already eager for lunch and another cup of coffee. "I'm not dressin' up."

He laughs and matches our pace. "I wouldn't expect you to. But you know Granny won't let you wear that hat at dinner. Might as well leave it at home."

I resist adjusting my hat. It's a part of me I often forget is there. Until Granny or Mama scolds me about it, that is. "Fine. But you know Granny or Mama are the only ones I'd leave it off for."

"Oh, I know," he drawls. "Leave the pocketknife home this time, too. Avery doesn't need a horror scene to keep her up at night. I'll see you tomorrow morning; it's your day at the farm, right?"

To hell with that, I think since I never go anywhere without my knife, but I nod and pull back on June's reins when we reach the trail from Wyatt's house to mine. He'll have another ten-minute ride before he makes it back, but it's a beautiful one. All cleared trails and high grass banks with trees hovering along each side. If he's lucky, the huckleberries might even be ripe. I've been checking them nearly every day. "I'll be there first thing."

He nods once and steers Axel toward the trail.

I peer out across our farm to see if there's anything else I need to add to my neverending list. On top of keeping everything running here, I've been helping Wyatt start his venture of giving people a farm experience they won't forget. I thought he was insane when he wanted to start a spa, renovate the cabins his Gramps built, and rent them out to individuals or groups who haven't seen a cow before. But he's done well. Enough to sustain the farm and appease the bank. Enough to put some extra cash in my pocket to convince my folks I can take care of things.

To start that legacy I'm set on creating.

Pop does what he can, but fixing equipment, tending to the cattle, and sitting horseback most of the day isn't an option for him anymore. He's getting older, tired. Mama, too.

And there's only so many guests I can watch hug a damn cow before I lose my mind. I'd never think of doing that with our cows. They're raised for meat, not snuggles.

I'm not convinced Wyatt thought that activity through, but the guests sure love it.

I click my tongue as my heels squeeze June's middle. She trots, picking up her pace so I can check in with my folks, eat a piece of pie I know Mama made, and drink that second cup of coffee I've been thinking about before heading back to the fields to move cattle. It's the kind of work that never ends, and while most days look the same, there's always something that changes: a sick animal, broken equipment, stubborn heifers, and even more boar-headed ranch hands I've got to look after. At least a native old-timer, Ernie, keeps those few boys in line for us most of the time.

Apart from the occasional trip into town to drink a beer at the Thirsty Hippo, that's most of the excitement I've seen in the last two years. There isn't time for socializing, let alone dating, when I'm too busy moving our grass-fed beef from one pasture to the next, testing soil, and scheduling them for processing to distribute to our customers. It was Pop's life work, and now it's mine.

Leaning forward in the saddle, June picks up our speed to a gallop. We don't need to race back for anything other than the fact I like the fast clip. The rush I feel when we eat up the ground of the fields isn't like any other, but some things have come close. Tracking and killing a buck, finishing a project, or sleeping with women—*one* woman, that is.

The wind whipping at my face is a fresh reprieve that sobers me. I can't be thinking like this. Not when said woman is a ten-minute ride away and staying in one of Wyatt's guest cabins. The same one Avery lived in and continues to operate the spa out of when guests are here.

I hold onto my hat so it doesn't fly off and push the thoughts of warm, supple skin and piercing brown eyes out of my mind.

Instead, I imagine her holding a pitchfork, which seems to help a little.

Three

Tilly

"Dizzle fo shizzle mah nizzle fo rizzle." —Snoop Dogg

Flopping back onto the bed, I yell, "Why me?"

This bed is so annoyingly soft and plush, the way it cradles every slight and exaggerated curve of my body and gives me unmatched lumbar support. At twenty-eight, I can't say this is anything I've thought about until this bed. How am I supposed to go back to my lumbar-cracking mattress now?

But I can't even enjoy it since I'm utterly screwed for leaving my salon in North Dakota.

I continue shouting other obscenities at the ceiling fan like it has personally offended me. And it doesn't make me feel better.

"What happened?" a voice cuts in. "I thought I heard you yell *why me.*"

I snap my head toward the bedroom door. "Avery."

All of the healing power of this mattress is undone in one quick look. I now have a crick in my neck like I'm eighty-four. I should also mention I've started watching Jeopardy and eating pie after dinner. Hanging out with Granny so much is starting to rub off on me. Maybe that's my problem here.

Avery's hands slide into the front pockets of her shorts. "I tried knocking, but I'm not sure you heard me over all the wailing."

My head falls heavy on the pillow, arms splayed wide. "I'm not crying, I'm just..." I don't know what I am. Tired? Overwhelmed? Wishing I could do at least *one* thing right.

I'm normally a positive person, but today, I want to feed all the positivity to the cows.

She tip-toes through my color-coordinated rows of heels toward the end of the bed. "What's going on?"

My head is spinning, but I keep my eyes on the ceiling. "Suzanne is dead set on making all of my blonde clients brunettes and handing out perms and bangs like they're part of a buy-one-get-one-free sale. One person even left with blue highlights they didn't ask for. How does that even happen?" I should have bumped my few appointments to next week instead of allowing my boss—who does better running the salon—to step in. Normally, I'd take vacation time, but she assured me she had it under control. Well, she's unhinged with a pair of sharpened scissors in her hand. "It'll take weeks to revert those kinds of mistakes. That is if those clients decide to return to the salon."

She sucks air through her teeth, wincing. "As a natural blonde who has never had her hair colored, I can only imagine the shock of seeing blue hair in the mirror."

I lull my head to the side with great effort and point at her. "My clients pay good money for hair like yours." I drop my hand. "At least, they did."

"Did I mention how grateful I am that you're taking a week off work to be here?" she asks tentatively.

"Roughly ten thousand times. Today."

"Okay, good." The room is silent until Avery speaks in a low voice. "I thought you were yelling because of how upset you were seeing Ronny earlier."

It makes sense since I've kept thoughts of Ronny shoved in the back closet of my mind since *that* summer—the one where I put my heart out there, and he whacked it with a fly swatter like it was a pesky insect. Of course Avery would pick up on this. She's my best friend. But her fiancé is best friends with Ronny, creating a weird, convoluted friendship circle I can never get out of.

"I wasn't that upset."

"Granny said you had a shovel in your hands?"

I cross my arms over my chest and stare down my nose at her. "He had the shovel in *his* hands!" I yell back at the messenger. "Tell Granny if she's gonna spy, she needs to wear her glasses."

Avery curls her lips in to suppress her laughter. It's not working as she wants, and a few giggles slip through.

"I'm not upset about seeing Ronny again." Met one asshole, you've met this one. "But remind me to put worms in his food tomorrow night."

I'm smiling like I'm going to do this.

Maybe I should.

After the chaos of taking off work for an entire week, hashing out details for this wedding from afar, and stressing over spending a week in Ronny's bubble where I might trip and fall on his lips, I'm going to humor myself where I can. Messing with him is the highest form of humor I've got in my life right now and the only way I can keep space between us.

"Well, " she starts, "that's what I wanted to talk to you about."

"About putting worms in Ronny's food?" I push up to a seated position, promising myself a hot compress to ease the strain in my neck, then pull one leg in. The other dangles off the side as Avery sits on her bed—*my* bed. The bed? God, I'll never remember she isn't living in this cabin anymore. Her life is changing so fast; I'm just trying to keep up.

"No, nothing like that. The opposite, actually." She rubs the back of her neck and sits across from me. "Though please don't do that. Wyatt's whole family will be there, and since you're my only family representative until my parents arrive later this week, I want it to go well."

"Fiiiiine," I say in an exasperated tone. It's not like I'd really touch worms to put them in his food anyway. "Just spit it out then."

"It's about Ronny," she blurts.

I can't help but roll my eyes. It's an automatic response anytime I hear his name. That and an involuntary gag reflex I'm still working on. "What about him?"

"I know how...hard it's been to be around him."

I'd liken it to a root canal on all my teeth, but whatever.

I didn't always think this. But the man who gave me foot massages at the end of the day, combed my hair with his fingers while we watched movies, and danced with me like no one else was watching when they were doesn't live in his body anymore. He was taken over by foreign life forms and hasn't been the same since.

She continues: "And I know you're basically going to be in each other's vicinity for a whole week, so I just wanted to say...thank you."

"Thank you?" My brows high-five my hairline.

She shrugs. "Well, yeah. Thank you for putting up with your arch nemesis for an entire week just for me."

I sit up taller. "You're welcome...I guess. But Avery, I'd do anything for you. Ask me to walk over hot lava rocks, and I'm there. Invite me to skydive with you, and I'll find us a reputable place on Yelp with at least four stars because I know how you are about those things..."

"I would never go skydiving."

"You might...one day."

Her expression says she definitely won't.

I snap my fingers. "I'd even babysit Vincent Van Goat for you."

She purses her lips and twists them to the side. "But this is Ronny."

A stray hair falls across my forehead, and I blow it away, waving a hand toward her. "Yeah, but you're...you."

"I know, and while I want to pile-drive him into the ground with my elbow for what he did to you, I can't. He's Wyatt's best friend-turned-best man, our neighbor, and part-time employee. It's...messy." She puts her hands out as if pleading with me to understand.

And I do.

Mainly because there's no way Avery would pile-drive him. She'd probably just write him a scathing letter and mail it to him anonymously. She's not one for confrontation, even on her sassiest days.

I stare at the paisley-patterned bedspread and trace the oblong shape with my finger. The bright red shade I painted my nails yesterday was called *cajun shrimp,* which has nothing to do with anything Avery just said except for maybe how I feel: small and almost transparent with a bit of zing. I guess I've been letting how I feel, or don't feel, about Ronny get in the way of a lot.

"Avery, I promise you won't have to worry about any fights or issues between Ronny and me. We can be civil for a week." My tone is impassioned, and I almost believe myself. "We'll have plenty of other things to keep us busy."

She exhales. "Thank you. And you never know. Maybe this is the trip you'll bury the hatchet."

She said this last time, too. Let's just hope I don't mistake Ronny for said hatchet I'm supposed to bury.

"Fitting," I snicker. "Good thing I already know where the shovel is."

She reaches across the small expanse to grab my knee. "In truth, what you had with Ronny was…"

"Avery," I warn. "We don't have to get into it. This is your week. I promised to behave, not fan an old flame."

On the hard days, when I remember how warm and safe that flame felt, I try to think about how it quickly turned into a house fire that ate up everything it touched. Eventually, there were only ashes left in place of those memories.

She stares at me with her sea-glass blue eyes that see through me like a crystal ball she knows how to read. Glad one of us does. "You can't let your parent's divorce ruin your love life—"

"I'm not!" I retort, louder than intended but much too squeaky to be convincing. I clear the high-pitched tone from my throat. "Sorry. It just hasn't been as easy to find love as it has been for you. I've put myself out there, but it doesn't matter. I'm the girl you have fun with one night at the bar." Cue Ronny. "Not the woman you take home to your parents. That's just how it is."

If Ronny's parents weren't so close to Wyatt's family, I'm sure I would have never met them, either.

She grips my knee tighter and then pulls her hand away. "I don't want to see you stop risking. It's okay to put yourself out there."

Oh, I'll put myself out there.

I'll still swim with sharks, travel to remote places I can't pronounce the names of, and eat sketchy food *I* didn't cook—I have boundaries. What I won't do is fall in love with Ronny a second time. Once was enough to ruin me for a lifetime.

The phantom kisses on my skin when the lights were turned off and his body was tucked close to mine are etched all over me like carvings on a tree. They don't go away. They just live in me like the cruel and unusual punishment they are.

Tears pool in the backs of my eyes, but I already know I won't let her see those. Not now—not this week. I prefer it when I'm her human diary, not the other way around.

"You sound like the inspirational quotes on the inside of the Dove chocolate wrappers." I laugh, blinking back any tears. "Next, you're going to tell me to *hug the sunlight* or *live your dreams*."

We both start laughing and get distracted talking about the rest of the week, including her final dress fitting in a couple days. I haven't seen the dress since we went shopping six months ago, and while I have pictures to reference, I know seeing it fitted will be like an out of body experience.

Avery eventually stands from the bed to leave, admiring all the shoes I brought neatly lined up against one wall. I take better care of them than the rest of my things. "You can use the closet and the dresser to put your clothes in if you want."

I follow her gaze, noting the piles on my bed, suitcase, and top of the dresser across from the door. Unpacking is going as good as it looks. "But if I do that, how will I know where everything is?"

She shakes her head and then stares at the ground by my feet. Her smile completely fades, and she looks almost...pale.

"Avery?"

She jumps back with a scream. I look down at the slip-on wooden clog platforms I kicked off beside a few outfit options I didn't go with this morning. Nothing seems out of the ordinary. Until I spy something dark—forest green or maybe black—sticking out from under the bed.

I scream louder.

She yelps.

Now, we're both screeching.

"What is that?" She clutches the door frame while I yank my legs up so fast my knee connects with the bottom of my chin, rattling my teeth.

"It's not moving." She steps closer and squints at it.

"Careful!" I yell, rubbing my jaw. "That's what it wants you to think. Once you get closer, it will come to life and attack you."

She doesn't listen and starts squatting to get a closer look.

"Stop! It's going to eat your face off."

She glowers at me, then grabs my hefty sandal with a real, natural wood sole and prods it. We both jolt, but the tail only flops like it's made of...

"Rubber," she says, nudging it again. "It's a rubber snake."

She picks it up with her bare hands like Steve Irwin on *The Crocodile Hunter*, balancing it between her thumb and pointer finger.

My mouth gapes, and my legs relax into a criss-cross. "I can't believe you used my shoe."

She hands me the heel, and I clutch it to my chest while she inspects the rubber snake. "At least now we know it's not real. I'm guessing it didn't sneak into your suitcase, so how did it get in here? I never had any rubber snakes when I lived in this cabin. Neither did Wyatt. Actually, I've never had one *period.*"

I'm silently grateful there are no kinks of the rubber snake variety she'll need to tell me about. I would be an eager listener, but I wouldn't like it one bit. Okay, only a little.

The slimy thing is somehow still jiggling even though Avery's hand isn't moving. I have an idea who did this. Someone who wants to mess with me without getting in trouble. Someone who is both immature and too sexy for his own good. Someone who might actually have a snake kink.

The seething tone I use in my head is damning.

Ronny.

Four

Ronny

"I'm not rapping, I'm conversing. It's just a conversation between me and you." —Snoop Dogg

Outside the horse barn, I tie June up when I hear a door slam. Turning, I don't see what I expect to, yet it's nothing I haven't seen before.

Tilly thunders down the steps, heading toward the farmhouse with some kind of green, bouncy...is that a snake in her hand? She's got on those devilishly short shorts she likes to torture me with and a red cropped shirt that might as well be a sports bra. It feels like maybe this isn't the time I should be staring, but I can't stop.

Good thing she isn't looking over here.

She keeps marching her way over the short gravel walk to the porch of the farmhouse, pounding five times with a heavy hand. Only one person has earned that much vitriol from her, and it's me.

Dogged woman.

"Tilly!" Avery calls after her while I stay firmly planted beside June, wondering if I can slip out of the area unnoticed or disappear into thin air.

This doesn't end well for me.

"Tilly, no one's there!" Avery yells, cupping her hands around her mouth. "He's not here!"

Tilly whips around on the porch, and it's like I'm watching an old Western drama play out before me. I doubt there'd be half-dressed women in flip-flops sans guns, though.

Wait, does Tilly have a gun? I sure as hell hope not after the pocketknife fiasco. Double-checking wouldn't be a bad idea.

"Where is he?" Tilly fires back to Avery.

That tone is out for blood.

Avery is halfway to the farmhouse when June decides to sneeze. *Shit.*

Both women snap their gazes in our direction. I've been spotted. I give a small wave and tip my hat because what else am I supposed to do? I guess I could run, or hop on June and ride back to my farm. But I just got here. Mama needs more eggs for all the baking she's been doing, and I'm not about to leave here without them to face a different woman's wrath.

"You!" Tilly sets her feet to stompin' my way.

"Tilly, just wait a minute. I'm sure there's an explanation," Avery tries to convince her. "It's just a fake snake."

I square off with the woman rushing toward me, thunder in each step, flames coming out of her eyes, and short hair riding the wind. I'm not going to back down. The moment she senses weakness, she'll devour me. If I give her an inch, she'll take fifty miles. It's a basic theory I've put to the test many times in the past.

With one hand on June's shoulder and one tucked in my front pocket, I wait until Tilly is standing in front of me. Except she does more than that. She gets right up in my face, her chest nearly grazing mine, and waves the rubber snake between us.

"What the hell is this?"

The coiled toy springs wildly in her hand, and I shrug. "Looks like a rubber snake to me."

"You put it in my cabin."

"Did I?"

She dangles it in front of my face. "Yes!"

I unfold my hand from my pocket and grab part of the snake, inspecting it mostly so she won't slap me in the face with it or fashion it around my neck like a noose. I never put this in her cabin like she's claiming, but that doesn't mean I didn't fall asleep some nights smiling at the day Tilly would have a run-in with a slithery creature. I just hoped I'd be there to see it.

This is close enough.

"You think I put this in your cabin?" I twirl the tail between my fingers.

She finally lowers her voice to a pitch that won't make my ears bleed, but she hasn't let go of the snake.

She tugs it closer to her. "I *know* you put this in there."

I peer over her shoulder to see Avery shaking her head. She mouths an apology with a shrug of her shoulders.

Focusing back on the woman nearly stepping on my toes, I say, "And how did I get this in your cabin without you knowing?"

She pulls back a little, eyes still stormy as she strangles the snake. "You put it in there before I got here."

I purse my lips and nod. There's tension on the snake now, but hell if I'll let go first. "So I went into town, bought this rubber snake, and came back here to plant it somewhere in your cabin to find." I ignore the lightning crackling around her like an orb. "Where did I hide it?"

She pushes her chest out further, and fuck me if I don't notice that perfect little v-shaped dip at the center. "Under the bed."

I slowly shake my head, staring down at her face this time. "I wouldn't have hid it under the bed."

She scoffs and tugs on the snake. "And where would you have hidden it?"

"*In* the bed." I yank it back.

Her eyes heat with something I swear isn't all hatred. It's familiar in ways that wake up my body to possibilities I'd long since impaled with a sharp object. But her expression changes, morphing back to her shield of anger faster than I can catch up.

"Give it back," she demands.

"No," I say.

"Tilly," Avery warns from behind us.

Tilly shakes her head but steps back and jerks harder. "What do you mean *no*?"

"You said it was my snake," I clarify, holding it firmly in my closed fist. "So, I'll keep it."

"But you left it in my cabin," she retorts.

"Left it?"

"Planted it!" she corrects.

My eyes slip only for a second to the tight line of her jaw and the long, linear column of her smooth neck. I can see her start to swallow, but I lift my gaze back to her brown eyes—that look almost black right now—before she notices me watching her like the damn fool I am. "Then let me get rid of it for you."

Instead of letting go like a grown man might, I circle my other hand around it, like this really is a rope and not a snake, and pull harder.

Tilly's heels pop off the ground as I draw it in, forcing her closer. Gravel crunches under her feet as she plants them, and if I didn't hear Avery's small, strangled sound, I definitely saw her slap a hand over her mouth. Tilly puts her other hand on the snake, too, and pulls. It's only made of rubber, and I know what she can do when she's determined. She'll rip this thing clean in half and take my pride with her.

The snake doesn't stand a chance, but I'm more worried about me.

I angle the snake so it's at my hip, and we're chest to chest again with barely a hair of space between us, just like we'd been yesterday when she first arrived. The smell of her takes over my senses—something floral and lemon, sweet and bitter, just like her. I can feel her breath on my neck. I'm sure she can feel mine on her face since she's a four-inch heel shorter than me.

Tilly loves her heels. Blue, purple, silver, gold, I've seen her wear every color in the rainbow and then some. They rival the colors I wake up seeing on the horizon, which might be why a painted sky always reminds me of her. That and the times we woke up to it together when she'd come to visit the farm. It peeked through the window of her cabin while our legs were still intertwined.

That heated look is back in her eyes. She's either going to knee me in my junk or kiss me. Either way, I'll be feeling something.

She doesn't get the chance to do either.

Avery finally saves us all and clears her throat. This shakes Tilly out of whatever trance she's in, and she immediately lets go of the snake and takes a step back. She looks at the ground, then Avery, and shakes her head. "Have it."

The snake is fisted in my palm at my side as Tilly pivots on her heel—flip flop—and walks back to her cabin with a little less stomp than before. I watch her the whole way until she's safely back in her cabin, where I can't reach out and pull her into me like I want to.

"Nice one." Avery nods.

I finally look at her, forgetting she watched that all play out, when I catch sight of what she's wearing. "New shirt?"

She looks down at the oversized T-shirt she has on where Bob Ross appears to be painting a landscape picture of Thirst Trapp Farms. The sign hanging above the drive in the painting says as much. That was all Wyatt's doing—changing his family's farm name to attract a younger demographic. It mostly worked except for the few who expected shirtless men at their beck and call. But no one by the name *Magic Mike* lives here.

"It's a new one I just added to the online shop. The pre-order has been doing pretty well," she says like she didn't just witness whatever *that* was with Tilly. As if this is a normal conversation we might share any other day. And on any other day, it would be. But after what just happened here, I'm on edge. I can't pretend I'm not affected by her best friend.

I give June my back, and Avery shifts on her feet, kicking up dirt and rocks. I'm not sure how to transition this, so I choose to say little. But she doesn't. "Great weather we're having."

Talking about the weather is a safe bet, even though I hate it. Living in a small town has given me enough practice to talk about cloud formations I'm no expert on and a minimum of a seven-day forecast in case we need more conversational material.

"It's too hot." And I mean that in more ways than one.

"It's late afternoon; of course it's hot. But it'll cool off by next Sunday for the wedding."

Sunday is the day Wyatt and Avery met, and they don't let anyone forget it.

"Mhm," I mumble. I'm still trying to figure out what just happened or didn't.

She hooks a thumb behind her. "I'm gonna go check on her."

I pinch the bridge of my hat and nod once.

She scurries off back toward the massage cabin—*Tilly's* cabin—while I'm left to figure out what to do with this rubber snake. It wasn't me who put it in her cabin, but someone did. With enough digging, I could probably figure out who.

Or I could keep it.

Yeah, I'm keeping it.

I stuff it in my saddlebag, staring at the dust stirring after the tornado that just blew through unexpectedly. A small smile lifts the corner of my mouth as I think about all the possibilities this snake just gave me.

Five

Tilly

"Anytime you're with somebody, you become a reflection of that person." —Snoop Dogg

What in the blazes is that racket?" Granny asks. "Is something on fire?"

I'm quickly trying to hide the disaster that is the stovetop at the sound of her voice. "Granny!" I put the lid on the cast iron pan and lower the heat before facing her. For good measure, I rest an elbow on the fridge with my back to the stove, blocking it from view. "You're early."

She sticks up her chin a little higher. "Well, I'm never late."

The kitchen has always been a two-butt space with partial renovations going for it, like the painted cabinets with new hardware, wide farmhouse sink, and matte black faucet. There are also only a few places left to display more chicken paraphernalia. A window above the sink to look at the chicken pen wasn't enough for Avery. She needed to dedicate an entire room to those little peckers. Wallhangings, towels, small figurines, magnets, and a cooking timer all match the feathered creatures my friend has become obsessed with.

But those lucky bastards outside, and their inanimate shrines inside, don't have to worry about messing up a perfectly good Dogfather recipe in the cookbook Avery got me for Christmas last year. It's supposed to taste like a warm hug in your stomach.

The ash currently simmering in the pan is more like a heavy stone no one will be able to swallow.

Avery appears from the other room, sidling up beside Granny. "Everyone's here and very, *very* hungry." She raises a brow like she's waiting for me to announce dinner is ready.

It's ready...just not edible.

"You never answered my questions." Granny shuffles closer across the terracotta-colored tile. "And who's yelling at us over that speaker?" She points to the portable Bluetooth device on the opposite counter.

I glance at it while shifting my body so she can't see the disgraced chicken breasts I mutilated. "He isn't yelling. He's rapping."

"It's Snoop Dogg," Avery answers.

"I don't want to know what any of that means." Granny waves us off and starts walking to the formal dining room.

My shoulders lift to my ears, looking at Avery. "It's just his rap name."

"She probably thinks it's something dirty." Avery brushes it off. "How's dinner coming?"

Can she smell it? Does she know? She can't know. I turned on the small vent fan when the sauce on the top of the meat started crusting on the bottom. I thought I aired it out, but with only one small window above the sink, maybe the evidence is still lingering.

I'll tell her it's the zest.

Having no idea what the *zest* of lemon was, I just added the whole thing. Things went downhill from there. Damn you, Snoop Doggy Dog. Yardie Yard Bird jerk chicken should not be this hard!

I press closer to the fridge. "Great. Just fine. Putting the finishing touches on it now. I probably only need fifteen more minutes."

"Sounds good. I'll get everyone set up at the table," Avery says before disappearing down the hall.

"Use the nice China!" I call after her.

"Got it!"

Use the nice China?

These rocks marinating in the pan will *break* it.

"Shit, shit, shit!" I turn back to the counter by the stove and then maniacally scan the cookbook recipe to see where I went rogue. "What the hell did I forget that made this look like cardboard with a dirt garnish on top?"

Now, I just need to figure out how to make something else in fifteen minutes, or we might just be eating Granny's fine China. I've never professed to be a good cook. I can't even bake. One time, I baked a cake for my half birthday, and it disintegrated before I could frost it. My parents were too busy working, fighting, or divorcing to teach me any skills in the kitchen. By the grace of a quick metabolism and the convenience store down the street, I survived off anything in a package. But reading a recipe shouldn't have been this hard.

"Everything alright in here?"

I whip around, my back to the stove once again. But this time, I'm pointing a pair of tongs at the burglar who just came through the backdoor. My teeth knock together.

Ronny.

The hair currently stuck to my sweaty face isn't very convincing, so I brush it away, resting both hands behind me on the oven door handle after discarding my weapon. "Everything's fine."

He gives me an assessing look.

So I give him one.

Damn, he looks good tonight. We haven't seen each other since Snake Gate yesterday, but it's like he's another human entirely. He isn't wearing his cowboy hat, giving the world more access to those endlessly dark brown eyes. His hair is nearly black and pushed off his forehead, while the ones at his nape curl and hang over the collar of his infamous pearl snap button-up shirt that is practical in all the ways. Easy on and even easier off.

Wyatt describes him as a darker Jonas brother minus the singing talent and often calls him the farm *Pretty Boy*. He's plastered all over the Thirst Trapp Farms social media pages, topless, which is just as racy as it sounds.

Avery says he looks like Aladdin with a cowboy hat. I say they're both right. But I happen to think he also fills out a pair of Wranglers pretty well. He'll never hear this from me though.

Meanwhile, I must look like I just hiked Mount Kilimanjaro.

Because I pretty much did.

Avery and Wyatt invested in air conditioning after moving into the farmhouse last summer when Granny moved out and sold Wyatt the farm, but the stress of cooking is no match for this level of sweating. I can feel the small hairs sticking to the nape of my neck and behind my ears, not to mention the T-shirt I had to ditch after mixing the first few ingredients. I'm now in a mildly suggestive white tank top with food splatter. Thank God for the apron with Granny's face on it reading *I Love My Granny* which hides most of the offending stains.

Ronny's eyes take me in, and I jump in before he can make any snide comments. "I'm not really in the mood for," I wave a hand down the front of him, "*you* right now."

After almost losing one of my hoop earrings in the pan, I don't have any patience left. I mean, I did lose the hoop, but I was able to fish it out with the spatula before it cooked alive with the chicken. Obviously, I couldn't put it back in my ear, so now I look like a pirate.

His eyes journey from me to the stove, so I shift my body to cover it, but he's moving too fast. He's around the opposite counter, trudging straight for the disaster I concocted like a crazed scientist with too many glass bottle potions at my disposal. Salt, pepper, cloves, dried parsley, paprika, cinnamon, and a sprinkle—or *zest*—of star anise. I couldn't help it. They looked so pretty, like actual stars.

I hold up my hands to fend him off, but he easily grabs either side of my waist. My body—she's such a traitor—is prepared for him to lift me onto the counter and pry my thighs apart with his body so he can kiss me good and hard like he used to. Instead, he hauls me to the side to focus on a towel.

Not just any towel.

The one that I must have left too close to the gas flame and is now on fire.

I cover my mouth, pressing my back closer to the sink. "Oh *no.*"

He says nothing but grabs an oven mitt to tamp out the flames in seconds. A few lasting sparks singe the flour sack towel enough to leave holes and burn marks all over it.

Turning back around, he tosses the oven mitt on the counter and quickly brushes his hands over my bare arms and hands. "Are you hurt?"

I don't know how to respond. I'm stunned. He's touching me like he used to—like a part of him remembers he used to care about me.

There goes my body again, wanting to melt into him like a fudgesicle, but my brain knows better, so I yank my hands back. "I'm fine."

Now he looks shocked. But it doesn't last long when he looks at me dead on. "You're welcome."

His snarky tone is not working for me. "*Not* thank you."

"Really?" He crosses his arms with his back to the fried chicken, which is quite literally *fried.*

I point at my chest and lean forward. "I'm trying to cook dinner, and you're here doing God knows what. You're probably in here to distract me, so I'll ruin everything and make a fool of myself in front of everyone."

He scoffs and scratches at his shaved jaw. "You know what, Tilly?"

I cross my arms, waiting for him to say *anything.* I'm ready. I've been building my defenses against him for two years. The amount of sandbags guarding my heart is staggering. It's an actual fortress.

His jaw locks tight, and he stares without blinking.

I'm not sure how he's doing this, but I stand taller and stare back, machine guns ready. My eyes twitch the longer I try to hold them open.

He slowly shakes his head and then breaks eye contact. "Never mind."

What? I blink rapidly.

He strides out of the kitchen, clenched fists at his sides, albeit with a little more sass than when he walked in.

It doesn't matter, though. I'm still surprised by how the conversation ended. Where were the cannons and drawn swords? The rocket launcher? A squirt gun at the least. He didn't yell or swear or bend me backward and lick my neck. I barely got that clenched jaw from him. I hate it even more. I wish he had told me *what* then I could have told him *what,* and we'd be trying to keep our voices down instead of letting things drop like a hot potato.

But maybe it's for the best. He was starting to look too serious, and we aren't serious.

He doesn't care, and neither do I.

Huffing, I turn back toward the stove, assessing my burnt offering in the frying pan and Snoop's cookbook on the counter.

Time to start over.

Six

Tilly

"This is for my G's, this is for my Hustlas." —Snoop Dogg

"Even though I'm eternally grateful you made dinner for all of us tonight," Avery whispers as she leans closer to me, "what the hell is this?"

A fair question. "Tacos."

Avery leans over to Wyatt. "It's a taco."

It should be a soft shell flour tortilla, but they only had pita bread in the pantry. I warmed them in the oven, but I forgot they were there, and now they resemble pita chips.

"Ahhh." He lifts the corner of his jerk chicken delivery vessel and then scratches his dark beard.

I whisper to Avery, "In my defense, operating that oven is like launching a space shuttle. Why are there so many buttons, dings, and lights?"

She holds up a hand. "I'm sure they taste great."

One of us is mostly confident in that. I made sure everyone's glass was filled to the brim with homemade lemonade since I surprisingly had a few lemons left and in case they needed to wash it down. At least that didn't take a four-year degree to figure out how to make.

"Ew!" Jack, Wyatt's nephew, yells from down the table. He might be twelve, but he isn't short on opinions. "What is this s—"

"Language!" Granny yells.

Even though Gramps no longer has a physical seat at this table, and Granny already entrusted the farm's success to the next generation, they are both in every fiber of what happens or doesn't happen here. We all know who's really in charge.

"I was going to say *stuff*, Granny." Jack sits back in his chair. "I think you forgot the sugar." He can barely open his eyes past a squint as he twists his lips into a pucker.

Stace, Wyatt's sister with the brown pixie cut I commented on after three seconds into meeting her the first time, leans closer to Jack to shush him while Granny wags a finger.

Apparently, you *can* add too much lemon.

They are definitely not going to like the chicken then.

Annie, Stace's ten-year-old daughter with a brown ponytail, pushes the burnt crisps of chicken I salvaged from the pan around her plate. "Are you sure—"

"Just don't ask questions," Stace cuts her off.

"Thank you so much for the dinner," Wyatt's mom, Deb, says to me with a cheerful smile while her husband, Carl, continues chewing. I'm not sure he's stopped since he took his first bite.

Deb's brown hair is the same shade as Wyatt's, but her eyes are lighter and softer, like his sister's. Wyatt's height was definitely inherited from his dad, though, since Deb is shorter than everyone in the family.

They all have only ever made me feel welcome. They're a real family. One that sits around a table every Sunday, or skips the phone calls to come over and invade your space with prying questions and something fresh from the garden. I've rarely seen Stace come to the farm without a bunch of something in her hands.

I might talk to my dad every few weeks, but Mom is too busy living her second-chance life apart from us to make time for things like family dinners. Being welcomed by what I consider a *real* family means more to me than anything, which is why I wanted to thank them by cooking dinner. Instead, I might poison them.

Avery didn't have a family like this either. Her parents aren't mean or anything. They've just been shells of themselves since their family imploded. I'm happy that Avery gets to experience a tight-knit bunch, but it reminds me of what I'll never have. A husband, kids, a house with a porch swing just like the one here at the farm, and a parakeet named Oswaldo.

Okay, scratch the parakeet. Birds scare me.

Granny pipes up from the head of the table, "Can't say I've ever eaten food from a taco truck."

Shoving fallen pieces of chicken back into the fake taco disintegrating in my hand, I gape at her. "Oh no, I made—"

Avery grabs my arm and speaks out of the side of her mouth like a ventriloquist. "Better not explain too much in case she learns of the towel incident. Granny got that for Wyatt's birthday."

And I sent it up in flames. Great. "I'll keep my mouth shut."

"So, Tilly," Ronny says from a few seats down the table. My shoulders slump with a sigh. "What kind of seasoning is in this?"

Clearly the high road he decided to take while in the kitchen is good and gone. I bounce my gaze. "Avery, will you please tell Ronny that the seasonings can be found in the cookbook I used if he's curious."

"Which cookbook?" he asks.

Stace pauses mid-taco lift and nudges Bryan beside her. Their kids, Jack and Annie, are too busy batting pieces of chicken around their fine china like hockey pucks. A better use for it, I'm sure.

I continue talking to Avery. "Tha Boss Dogg's cookbook."

"The boss who?" Granny asks.

"I'll explain later, Gran," Avery adds.

Ronny picks up a loose piece of cut-up chicken—even the inside looks charred—and bites into it, letting the flavors steep on his tongue. Finally, he lifts his brows, fixing me with a stare. "Is that...star anise I taste?"

Screw his freaky-good taste buds and my need to go off-script.

"Avery, will you let Ronny know that I hope he breaks a tooth?"

Deb sucks in a breath and holds it while Carl releases one beside her.

Ronny makes a show of swallowing. "Wyatt, tell Tilly she needs to rinse the canned beans before putting them in the food."

"Uh..." Wyatt does not indeed say anything more.

I grab my silver special occasion butter knife for protection. "Tell Ronny they aren't beans."

Stace sets down her pita something and grabs the utensil right out of Annie's hand before she can eat the bite she had speared on her fork. "Hey," Annie protests, but Stace only gives her a tight shake of her head.

Ronny wipes his fingers on his cloth napkin and squints at me. "Tell Tilly she has to turn the stove off at some point."

"Tell Ronny I know he hid the snake under my bed."

Wyatt's brows dive together. "Snake?"

Avery sighs. "I'll explain that later, too."

"Tell Tilly I don't own any rubber snakes."

"Rubber snake?" Jack adds.

"Tell Ronny I don't believe him."

"Tell Tilly she needs to get over it."

I glare back at him. "Tell Ronny he can go suck—"

"Hold it right there," Granny scolds me, "or you'll owe me your slice of pie again tonight for the language, Tilly." She pins me with her hard stare, then shoots it across the table at Ronny. "And you'll be mucking stalls for the next month."

I slump back in my chair and loosen the grip on my knife. Ronny shoots me one more pointed look.

Annie determines this is the best time to wail on the hockey puck bite of chicken she'd been batting around her plate like an All-Star Pro earlier. Her aim and force are impeccable since it hits Wyatt square between the eyes.

"Ouch!"

Avery stands to try help him, but the tablecloth somehow gets stuck—

"Avery!" I try to save her glass and plate, but they go where the tablecloth goes and clatter to the hardwood floor with an ear-splitting crash. There goes the fine china.

The entire room is silent.

Stace's mouth is open. Bryan is holding back a laugh while Annie looks between Wyatt and the mess on the floor. Deb just grabs Carl's shoulder and says, "I'll get a towel."

"Don't!" I scream, my voice hoarse with desperation. I didn't have time to hide the beloved towel I mutilated beyond recognition—kind of like the dinner. "Let me get something."

I rush into the kitchen and search every single drawer for a different, less-ruined towel, but all I find are silverware, glasses, pantry items, and a coffee mug with Granny's face on it. How is she doing this? What website is she using?

I'll ask her later.

All of my thoughts get devoured when I hear, "Looking for this?"

I whip around to face Mr. Star Anise himself. Without answering, I tread toward him and snatch the towel on my way back to the dining room. Everyone has already started helping Avery pick up the mess as I mop up the sticky lemonade.

Deb grabs another plate, but Avery holds up a hand. "I'll just share with Wyatt. I'm not all that hungry anyway."

Wyatt rubs the space between his eyes, effectively removing the smudge of seasoning while each of us takes our seat.

I. Feel. Horrible.

Avery was technically the one to pull the plate off the table, but I made the chicken that was launched at Wyatt's head. Guilt licks the back of my neck while I scoot my chair back to the table. This dinner is *not* going the way I'd planned.

Stace claps her hands once. "So, Avery, are you ready for tomorrow's final dress fitting?"

Avery waves off the offer of my lemonade. "Y-yes, and I'm bringing the veil and jewelry to try on with it, too."

"Which reminds me," Wyatt starts, "Ronny, I picked up our suit jackets."

Images of Ronny in a fitted jacket bombard my mind, and I combat them by picturing him finding a certain rubber snake I hid for him. I sneer deceptively behind my glass of lemonade that has now become my dinner.

Just kidding, I can't swallow this. I spit it back in the glass.

I wonder if he's noticed the missing snake in his saddlebag. I'm sure he thought I'd just let him have it after walking away, but really, I just marched back to my cabin to spy out the window and see where he stashed it. June didn't even bat her amazingly long lashes when I stole it back while Ronny was chatting up the ladies—a.k.a. the hens.

The table falls into easy conversation, ranging from how to keep the chickens out of the ceremony space to the cinnamon rolls Helen, the town bakery owner, and her daughter, Mabel, insisted on making for the wedding party. I'm too distracted watching Ronny eat his taco-lookalike and not choke on it.

He peers over at me, picking up one of the *fake* beans and smashing it between two fingers. Looks like he's figuring out what I did—had to do—since there was nothing else in the pantry. Chickpeas are a legume but have a similar texture to cooked beans. So, ha.

He doesn't stop staring but scoops a forkful of taco innards up with his bare hand and shoves it in his mouth, licking the tips of his fingers afterward. The wasteland between my legs quivers just watching him do this, and I despise it—*him*.

His face gives nothing away, but I know for a fact how bad it tastes.

And that makes me smile.

Seven

Ronny

"An older guy, he's going to show you things that a young man can't show you. He's going to show you how to stay alive." —Snoop Dogg

I can still taste Tilly's tacos after brushing my teeth and three rounds of mouthwash when I get into my truck—Gertrude—the next morning. I'm not sure what possessed her to add canned chickpeas to tacos, but biting into them was torture. Only second to the crispy chicken that was more crisp than chicken.

Don't even get me started on the sin she committed by adding star anise to taco meat.

Giving her the satisfaction of how much I disliked them wasn't an option, so I ate every bite of that damn taco. Swallowing was the hardest, and I drained the entire glass of pure lemon juice she made just to do it. But I made my point. And the point was...

Shit.

There was no point.

But she would have eventually killed me off with her cooking if we stayed together, whether on purpose or accident. I'd never know since I'd be dead. I was right to break things off and almost told her the real reason why last night after the towel incident in the kitchen. I'm glad I held my tongue in the heat of the moment. It was nowhere near the right time for that. She would've set me on fire like she did the towel.

My body reacted without me wanting it to when I went straight for her arms and hands to see if she was okay. I had to coach myself down with a well-placed *down boy* just to get out of that moment unscathed by touching her again.

Even when she's driving me mad, she can still somehow pull a smile out of me. As I was getting ready to leave last night, I slipped my feet into my boots, only to find something squishy under my toes. I immediately pulled my foot out and dumped the boot upside down.

Tilly didn't hide her laughter as a rubber snake fell to the floor. She must have taken it back when I wasn't looking and shoved it in my boot.

Damn woman.

"I'm gonna turn around and head through the other pasture," Pop says from the cab. "You good?"

"Yup," I call up to him from the bed, where I loaded two water troughs that needed moving and filling.

It's our morning routine. Every day, I pour Pop his coffee, fire up Gertie, and he drives us around so I can fill the water for the cows. I'll have to do another check and fill later since we have a few troublemakers who like to tip the stock tanks. Little asses.

Unlike Wyatt, we don't use our cows for hugging therapy or photo ops. We're a beef supplier, providing high-quality, grass-fed cuts. We have a few milking cows that give us some of the thickest cream, too. But that's only for us and for trading through our local co-op.

It takes a lot to keep up with the standards our meat distributor sets, but being a part of a distribution line is worth it. I get to farm and do all the work with my hands while someone else sells it. It took Pop some convincing to go this route, but he came around after learning the benefits of sustainable farming.

I've got a small group of people who help run the farm on the daily, which comes in handy when I'm helping Wyatt. But it's starting to weigh on me as if I've got an actual cow on my shoulders. The amount of work that needs to be done here if we want to continue to scale—along with everything going on in my personal life—is only increasing while Thirst Trapp Farms is starting to create a name for itself on the Experiences R Us website. More people are reserving cabins to visit every day, and the last time I asked, Wyatt said they were booked a year out.

I need to talk to him about this, but there hasn't been a right time with the impending wedding. But I'm running out of ideal opportunities to bring it up. It's not like I'm planning to ditch him, but I need to start giving Adler Farms the attention it requires.

I want Pop to see how serious I am to inherit his life's work. I'm not about to give that up like it's trivial. Belonging here, in this family and to this land that raised me as much as my parents, is close to sacred for me.

The sun is just starting to crest the tops of the Crazy Peak mountains, casting shadows on the clouds and painting the sky in muted tones. It's a view I've seen my entire life, but judging by my surprised reaction, I still wake up each morning without remembering what it looks like.

The barn creaks and snores with every passing gust of wind from age and use, but hearing it whip through the tall grass and trees is a sound I fall asleep to. It's better than any sound machine. The smell of manure doesn't bother me either since the promise of ripened fruits warming in the sun is worth the added fertilization every single year.

Mornings are still cold enough in mid-June that my hat and jacket are a necessity when the sun isn't anywhere to be seen. I sit back on the edge of the truck chewing on my toothpick as Pop navigates to the next field where our few milk cows stay like pampered princesses. They're all tagged in case they get mixed, but we try to make sure that doesn't happen.

Hopping down, I unlock the gate for Pop to pass through, shut it behind him, and jump onto the lowered tailgate, letting my legs dangle. He carefully drives over divots and earth mounds to the water spigot. Unloading the plastic stock tank, I position it and start filling.

"They getting ready for the wedding over at Trapp Farms?" Pop asks, leaning out his window.

Even though Wyatt changed the name from Trapp Farms to *Thirst Trapp Farms* a couple years back with a new sign hanging over the front drive, Pop still refers to their land as he's always known it. His friendship with Wyatt's family goes back a generation to the first wedding held at the farm, which his parents, my grandparents, attended: Granny and Gramps'. Later, more like forty years ago, Wyatt's parents were hitched out in the fields, then Stace and Bryan almost fifteen years back. It's a place with a history of forevers and I do's.

I kick the plastic bin with my steel-toe boots. "Yeah. Dance floor gets delivered today, and Wyatt plans to string lights from the barn. I'm sure I'll be helping with that."

If I sound tired, Pop doesn't mention it. He nods and stares off across our land. The same land he's been plowing for ages. Removing tree roots and stumps to fencing off portions for horses and cattle. There was a time we had chickens, too, but now we get all our fresh eggs from Wyatt and Avery. It's become Avery's pet project, quite literally, since she's named all them chickens like they're her pets. Dora the egg-splorer, Mother Clucker, Hilary Fluff—I've always just preferred the name *chicken*.

"Have you seen Tilly yet?" he asks.

My posture sags. "Yesterday. At dinner."

"And?"

I check the water level again. "And there's nothing more to say."

She's still the woman I drove miles to Bismarck to see for a weekend, who squeezes all the joy out of life and me. The one who considers lime green a neutral color and harnesses a confidence fit for a queen.

But I'm no king, and I wasn't in the right headspace to become one.

He rests a lazy hand on the steering wheel. "Don't wait until the last minute to tell her, son. She deserves to know."

I say nothing more, and neither does he. I know he's right. Waiting this long was never part of my plan. But I've kept quiet for so long, it's hard to get it out now. There's so many times I wanted to tell her, so many times I almost did.

But I don't want to hurt her anymore than I already have.

The running water drowns out my thoughts. Sometimes, when the world is mostly quiet like it is right now, I try to see the farm like Pop. He's always got a corner of his lips turned up when I see him taking it in like he can't help it. His sweat and blood helped build this place—more blood than anything—and hell if I'll let it go to rubble as he gets older. He's roughly the same age as Wyatt's parents, but he had his knee replaced due to a motorcycle accident in his twenties that never quite healed right, forcing him to walk with an obvious limp.

Farming may not have been the life I was supposed to be born into, but when my parents adopted me at only a few months old, I inherited it. I won't for one second let them down. I stepped into a different family history that had already started. But my parents always said I came at the right time. I believe them, but that doesn't mean it's always easy when I still have so many questions.

After morning chores, we head back to the house, parking old Gertie my pop has probably owned my entire life beside it. We both use Gertrude now for runs into town or hauling trailers and equipment, but I'm the one who named her. We spend enough time together; she's as good as a nagging farmwife, and I love it.

"I heard there were biscuits and gravy on the menu this morning," Pop says, shutting his door. It squeaks at the hinges, and I make a mental note to oil it at some point today.

I take off my beanie and run my fingers through my hair before seating it back on my head. My stomach is already growling at the thought of my favorite hot meal. "Let's eat then."

Pop pats my shoulder. "You doing alright?"

I stare back at him. The lines on his face have only become more pronounced, and his jeans more worn. The farm somehow adds ten extra years to a person.

"I'm fine, Pop. Just thinking," I reply.

He pats my shoulder with a smile. "Always thinking."

I wish that weren't true. Mostly because of the kinds of things occupying my mind. I'm thinking about Tilly in that apron last night or when she took it off before dinner, and there was a stain over her right breast. I don't think she noticed. The fact she only had one earring on, and I kept picturing myself taking it off for her wasn't good.

"It's nothing important." And I mean that because thoughts of Tilly aren't real life.

They're like a vacation I took years ago and still recall. A bright light that tans your skin and offers you piña coladas for breakfast, lunch, and dinner. The memories are the salt in your hair and on your skin after a full day of swimming in the ocean that never seems to go away despite the numerous showers you take. The delicious food and fruit you gorge yourself on because calories don't count when you're on vacation.

But in real life, they do count.

In my life, they definitely do. So I do my best not to remember.

We walk to the side of the house where the steps are. The shingles are dark green but have been a few different colors over the years: blue, white, tan, and a peculiar shade of brown that didn't last the spring. It's where I've lived my whole life and is as familiar to me as the worn pair of pants I slide on every day.

I easily jump up both steps, but Pop takes each a little slower. He built them along with the rest of this small but functional house. The day where he can barely walk up them is getting closer. A ramp would be more his speed, but if I built it for him, he'd just balk.

In the mudroom, we toe off our boots and hang our jackets. The last thing Mama wants is dirt tracked through her home. It may be small, but she takes great pride in keeping it orderly. She also has a strict *no-hat* policy like Granny that she never forgets about, so I yank off my beanie and smooth down my disheveled hair.

"Mama, we're back," I say so I don't startle her.

"Wash up and sit down. Breakfast will be ready soon," she instructs, rinsing her hands.

Pop kisses her briefly on the cheek before we both take turns washing our hands in the large, white sink set into laminate countertops that are as non-aesthetic as they get. Mama plates the food and carries everything over to the breakfast nook. We don't have a formal dining room like Wyatt's farmhouse has. His Granny wanted a place for the whole family to gather, but our space is plenty big for the three of us.

"Ronny, will you say grace?" Mama asks.

I hold out both hands for them to grab, and we bow our heads. "Father, bless this food that it would nourish and strengthen our bodies. Amen."

"Amen," they repeat in unison.

I didn't eat anything when I got home last night, though it was the only thing I could think about as I was falling asleep. I was starving. But this meal is worth the wait. A cream base with salted sausage and an extra heap of pepper to give you a kick in the teeth. Mama knows how to cook, and biscuits and gravy might just be the way to my heart.

"I'll stay and help with dishes," Pop says, head bowed over his plate.

This is code for *I won't be going back out in the fields today.* I've gotten used to it. Very rarely is he out there with me and the crew these days. He's taken over the management and paperwork while I shoulder most of the physical labor. That is until he gets tired of being behind a desk and comes to see what we're up to outside.

"I'll be around most of the day and can take care of things," I murmur around a mouthful. "Gotta get a few things done at Wyatt's, like I said, but I'll be back."

"If you see Granny, tell her to pick up her cell phone every once in a while." Mama cuts into her biscuit. "I know she knows how to use that thing. Lord helped us all when she figured out the internet."

Pop just chuckles behind his coffee mug.

Mama and Granny are best friends and have been for years despite their age gap. Days spent on the porch swing drinking the south's version of homemade ice tea—bourbon—and chatting away like hours didn't matter.

"Granny says Tilly is staying for the whole week." Mama steals any feeling from her tone.

It doesn't take much to figure out what she isn't saying. "She is."

My parents didn't exactly agree with how I ended things, but they were understanding.

"Sounds like she's giving everyone haircuts tomorrow." Mama reaches over and ruffles the hair on my head that's grown over my ears. "You should get one, too, before the wedding."

The last thing I want is to be at the mercy of Tilly's clippers. "I'm good. I'll go into town or something."

"Nonsense. She's right there. And she's a professional, in case that's what you're worried about." Mama lifts her coffee mug to hide her smile.

Too bad I saw it.

"I'll see if I have time." I'm worried about a lot of things when it comes to Tilly, especially a pair of scissors in her soft, strong hands. It's a combo I'd rather not try.

She nods once. "Good. And we need to go into town so I can get more ingredients for the pies I'm helping Granny make for the rehearsal dinner. Merv, why don't you come with me."

We both know it's as good as done when Mama asks.

She adds, "Do you have something nice to wear, Ronny?"

"Wyatt picked them up already," I say, barely recalling what the suit looked like. This is an outdoor summer wedding, though. Not the church-dressing kind.

"And what about Camila? Is she coming to the wedding?"

I knew she'd ask sooner or later. "She doesn't feel right about coming."

All eyes would be on Camila if she decided to come. Questions that would demand more of an answer besides *mind your own damn business*.

Mama nods and then prattles on about wedding plans and all of the things she's helping Granny with. Pop listens with his head bent over his plate while I wish for my days to look different. I want to put my head down and sweat out thoughts of Tilly and a different life, a different time.

Instead, I can't stop thinking about the rubber snake stashed in my coat.

Eight

Tilly

"Sometimes, a loss is the best thing that can happen. It teaches you what you should have done next time." —Snoop Dogg

Avery, you look..." I shake my head, covering my mouth while the bangles on my wrist slide down my forearm and clank together. The words to describe how stunning she is, how bodacious her ass looks, and the way her golden hair seems brighter next to the white all condense into one: "Beautiful."

She runs her hand down her slim hips covered in the silk, tapered fabric. It hugs every part of her until it reaches her knees, then flares out slightly before hitting the floor. The back plunges to the middle of her spine with a trail of buttons leading all the way to the hem. It's subtly classic and hot and—

"What kind of underwear you gonna wear with this?" Granny tips her head to the side, assessing the situation as if she's wearing x-ray vision glasses and not bifocals.

Avery looks at us behind her through the mirror. "Uh, maybe...well, I don't know."

But I know. This is the kind of dress you wear cheeky lace knickers with a garter under. Something devastatingly risqué hidden beneath its modest silky drape. I'm not sure if saying so would corrupt the delicate sensibilities in the room, though, so I keep my mouth shut. I'll let Avery open the ones I bought her in private later.

"What shoes are you wearing, Avery?" Deb asks from beside Granny and Stace, expediently changing the subject before Granny moves onto bras.

We're all here today, having made the one-hour drive into Bozeman—except for Avery's mom, who plans to show up the day of the wedding like mine. Avery had to convince her mom to come dress shopping the first time. But not these three women. So far, Deb, Stace, and Granny haven't missed a thing. Dress fittings, veil try-ons, favor shopping, and cake tastings, even though Granny and Deb are making an assortment of pies. It didn't stop them from suggesting it was a necessary step they *all* needed to partake in.

"I already have the shoes." Avery lifts the hem of her gown that was sitting heavy on the ground. "Tilly, can you hand me that box?"

I pick up the familiar box beside me and hand it to Avery. She opens the lid and slips out a block-heel platform sandal from Bella Belle I bought for her. They are light blue and covered in flowers stitched in gold thread. I splurged on them, but these heels were too perfect for someone who would never buy them for herself. Someone who has basically kept them locked in a safe since I surprised her with them.

Stace gasps and cradles either side of her face. "It's your something blue!"

Granny waves. "That's hogwash."

"What do you mean, Gran?" Stace levels her with a look only granddaughters can get away with.

"The girl can wear whatever colors she wants. Some traditions are a load of shi—"

"Langauge!" Deb pipes up. "Remember?"

Granny's brows stay woven together as she shakes her head.

Avery catches my eyes while the three debate tradition and hands the shoes to the alterations woman I keep forgetting the name of so she can help slip them on. They're three-inch heels, putting Avery almost at Wyatt's height but short enough to still be comfortable for long-term wear. I did my research. The painstaking job of trying them on myself was easy. The fact I bought three of the potentials, hurting my meager salary, was not.

Avery slowly spins to face us now that the hem isn't pooling on the floor, locking eyes with me. "I love them."

"I knew you would." I bounce my crossed legs while twisting the gold and black bracelets around my wrist. I'm really trying to keep from crying, but it's hard seeing her like this. Days away from committing to the man of her dreams forever. Hours away from Miss to Mrs. I didn't think it would make me so emotional, sentimental, or maybe just left behind somehow.

I always envisioned this day coming, Avery getting married and me...not. The closer we've gotten, the harder it's been to stomach the fact I won't be doing any of this. The dress, the cake testing, the family, the something blue. All of it is an alternate universe that I'll never be a part of. Zombies are more likely to take over the earth.

My parents had the big, fancy wedding with all of the guests witnessing what was supposed to be their forever. But it didn't work out for them, and it hasn't worked for me.

I've put myself out there, but nothing has come of it. It's not like I've avoided dating and been closed off to the idea of *more* with someone else, but it hasn't happened. Al and Bill, Chuck and Basil—yes, that was his real name—never worked out. I thought I was fine with that until right now.

"Will you put my veil on for me?" Avery draws me out of my thoughts.

I nod and stand on wobbly legs; the wind chimes I decided to wear on both arms are loud in this serenely quiet space.

Picking up the long, sheer veil, I use the time with my back turned to get it together. The soft, white tulle reaches the floor and then some, providing a dramatic length that I can already picture going down the aisle—or grass.

People will gasp or cry, probably both.

It's me. I will do these things.

Stepping up on the podium, I tuck the comb clip at the back of her head to secure it, fluffing the white tulle like I'm on an episode of Say Yes to the Dress, and I'm prepared to do anything for my bride. I will stitch her a new veil myself or raid the stock in the back of the store if she hates this one.

The women behind me exclaim as they see the full vision come to life. She isn't just the friend I spent countless hours on my cordless house phone with when we were in middle school or the woman who lived through the sudden death of her brother, straining the relationship with her family. The girl who will drop anything to be there for other people, or the human who owns more graphic tees than Hot Topic. She's *Avery* and is all of those things wrapped together and even more that can't be quantified.

I press fingertips to my tear ducts to ward off the waterworks I'm nine seconds from.

Avery smooths her dress again while pursing her lips. "Don't you dare cry."

I fan my eyeballs. "I can't help it."

"Watermelon." We all look at Granny, and she shrugs. "It usually works if someone's about to sneeze. Thought it might work for tears, too."

I sniffle while Deb dabs at her cheeks. Stace has already cried twice and doesn't hesitate to jump into the deep end a third time.

Avery extends her hand for me to grab. I know she's always called me her human diary, but if that's true, she's my middle-of-the-night emo blog. The one where I ask the deepest philosophical questions like *what even is love?* without reservation because it's safe. I can tell her anything. She's the one person in my life I can say this about.

As an only child, I didn't grow up with a brother or sister to roll eyes with at the ridiculous things our parents said. I barely even had parents to my name.

But I have an Avery.

She hugs me and points at the mirror beside us while the rest of the women chat with the alterations manager. "This will be you one day," she whispers.

My expression falls off a ten-foot building, hitting a garbage can on the way down. "This might be as close as I get."

"I thought you wanted to get married?"

I shake my head, opening and closing my mouth. I pivot and face her, still gripping her hand. "Wanting to doesn't mean I will." I shrug one shoulder. "I've pictured the kind of wedding I'd have, but I'm not in any rush to make it down the aisle."

"What does your day look like?" She pries because she knows she can.

I swallow and look around the bridal shop. Honestly, the kind of wedding I pictured for myself looks nothing like puffy dresses and sweetheart necklines. There aren't rows and rows of chairs for people I haven't talked to in ages or an aisle I'll most likely trip down. It's small. Elopement-small with a strappy dress, bare feet, and so entirely simple, a five-year-old could plan it, making for an intimate exchange between me and...him.

Whoever *him* is.

I take a deep breath and point at the dress I've been stealing glances at. "It looks like that dress."

Avery follows my finger to a dress hanging on the end of one of the racks. "That one?"

I nod and swallow again. That's it. Simple and sexy.

She lets go of my hand and gathers a fistful of her dress in her palms, stepping off the platform. She's heading straight for the dress.

"Avery!" I snap, wishing I had suctioned myself to arm.

She waves me off before plucking the dress right off the rack and striding back over to me. She holds it out, garnering looks from everyone in the process. "Try it on."

She's delusional, hyped up on happy endings, chocolate cake, and wedding aesthetic Pinterest boards.

I haven't stopped shaking my head since she grabbed the hanger. "I can't," I protest.

Stace stands and feels the silk texture of the dress I pointed out. "It's beautiful. You should definitely try it on."

"Isn't that against the rules?" I ask like this will get me off the hook.

The alterations manager speaks up, "It doesn't matter to us. I can help you get into it and clip it in the back if you need."

My eyes are wide. I don't think I could have thought up something more frightening than putting on a wedding dress for a day that isn't going to happen. "This has to be bad luck or something. I don't think I should. Granny, tell everyone it's hogwash!"

This is worse than chanting Bloody Mary repeatedly in the bathroom mirror when I was younger. Her ghost has obviously gone rogue and is haunting me at this very moment, telling me of a future I'll never have.

Why are there so many mirrors in here?

"I'm with Avery on this one," Granny says. "If you don't try it on, I'll be forced to and nobody needs to see that, dear."

"Tilly." Avery tilts her head and puts her hand on her slim waist. "Come on. It'll be fun. It's not like you're going to buy it and walk out with it. You're just trying it on."

Stace takes the dress from Avery and holds it out to me. "It's like playing dress up."

I *do* like dressing up, and I've never tried on a wedding dress before. The way I'm actually considering this right now is startling. It's not like this is any different from some of the other nice dresses I've worn. It's just shockingly white.

So, so, so...white.

I twist my mouth to the side as I consider. The puppy-dog eyes Avery is shooting me are pathetic, but she knows they do the trick. I hold out my hand. "Okay. But only for a second."

Avery and Stace start clapping their hands while Granny leans close to whisper something to a smiling Deb. Seems like everyone is more excited for this than I am.

"Alright. Here I go."

My feet are dragging as I step onto the platform and disappear behind one of the curtains. There's a small seat to set my clothes and a tall hook on the side wall for the dress. I hang it up and quickly strip down, removing my striped T-shirt dress, platform sneakers, and all of my bracelets. This isn't the kind of dress you'd wear underwear *or* a bra with, but in case the dip in the back goes too low, I only take off my hot pink bra. It doesn't exactly go with *white*.

Slipping each foot into the dress, I slide it over my hips. The feel of the fabric is smooth against my skin as the slinky straps relax over my shoulders. The cowl neck bodice curves around my breasts perfectly as the mermaid fit hugs every line on my body before hitting the floor. It's a little big in the back, but that could also be because my entire spine is exposed to the very top of my underwear.

At first glance, I worry this was a mistake.

On the second one, I note how *sexy* I look.

The white plays nicely with my darker complexion, and the slight sheen of the dress makes my skin appear as though I've used a stick of highlighter. I'm glowing. Actually *glowing*.

"Ready?" I ask everyone. I'm the only one who might not be.

"Ready!" They all yell.

I push back the curtain, and the open-mouth reactions are worth the cost of this free activity. The alterations gal helps tighten the dress at my waist with clips, and what's left in the mirror is a woman I don't recognize.

"Wow," I whisper. Pure shock floods me, and I can barely take my hands off the silk.

Avery steps onto the platform in her dress, putting her hands on the sides of my arms as she rests her chin on my shoulder. "You. Are. Stunning."

Deb and Stace reiterate the sentiment.

Granny squints. "Is your underwear...pink?"

"Granny!" Stace scolds.

I just laugh, which eases some of the tension in my shoulders. "Maybe."

Granny shakes her head and points. "There's a rip."

"It's supposed to be there, Gran," I say. The slit in the front goes to the top of my thigh, and the slinky fabric drapes down to the floor, curling around my feet and leaving enough length for the colorful heels I'd pair with this.

Tears start to press at the corners of my eyes, but they aren't welcome here. No emotions are because I'm a brick wall who doesn't *need* a white dress. "I'm gonna take it off now." I don't move toward the dressing room.

It's like I'm stuck staring at this person in the mirror. I don't want to forget her, but I also want to rinse my eyes with bleach and remind myself why this was such a bad idea.

"Let me take a picture first." Avery steps off what I now refer to as my stage to where I was sitting next to her purse.

"No!" I whip around, nearly tripping on the lengthy fabric.

Avery rifles through her things while I beg. "Avery, please. We really don't have to do this. I tried it on, and now I'm going to take it off."

"Why? It's not like you have to show the picture to anyone. You can just have it saved so one day, when you're looking for dresses, you can remember this style."

I swallow and look down. Forgetting this dress would be impossible now that I'm in it. There are certain things I've put on that I could never forget. Like my first pair of heels, the red sweater my mom got me on

Christmas before she told me about the divorce, or the jean shorts I live in every summer.

This dress has been added to the list.

But it's too late to protest since Avery already has her phone camera pointing straight at me. There's never been a photo I didn't enjoy posing for, so I bend my knee so the purposeful slit rides all the way up my leg, one hand long beside me and the other on my hip. I push the sadness out of mind and hope no one sees its lingering effects on my face.

"Smile," Avery says.

I give her a sultry smirk instead. This dress doesn't say sweet smiles and light pecks.

It says, *I'm sexy, and I know it.*

Nine

Ronny

"Whatever it is you do you have to master your craft." —*Snoop Dogg*

"What are you two looking at?"

Avery quickly stashes her phone behind her back, like I didn't already see her showing it to Wyatt, and stands in front of him. "Nothing."

She's hiding something, and I don't like it.

Wyatt points at Avery. "What she said."

I pause at the bottom of the porch steps of the farmhouse, peering up at them and the bullshit they're spewing. But I'm not about to ask. For all I know, it could be Wyatt in a position I don't need to see. "Alright then."

I start to walk up the steps, but Avery blurts, "I shouldn't show you."

My foot is propped on the bottom step, and I'm calculating the distance it'll take me to pass them and go inside. "That's fine."

She looks back at Wyatt. "But maybe I should."

"You shouldn't," Wyatt confirms, shaking his head emphatically. "We're supposed to be helping them play nice."

"But I could."

Wyatt looks at the phone and then at me. "You could."

"It might help them admit their feelings and be more civil," Avery adds.

They're having a whole ass conversation in front of me. I could do without the commentary. Whatever's on that screen has something to do with Tilly.

My brows pull together. "I don't want to see. I'm just here for a haircut."

I caved and asked Wyatt to add my name to Tilly's list today since there aren't any other times available with the barber in town before the wedding. Driving to a neighboring city to find someone isn't what I want to spend my time doing, either. So I'm here.

As much as I don't want that woman's hands on my head, I also do.

"Tilly's just finishing up Carl's cut." Avery's still clutching her phone. "I could show you the picture if you swear not to say anything."

Nothing good ever comes by swearing these kinds of things. "No."

Avery stands straighter. "What do you mean *no*? Don't you want to know what this picture is?"

"No," I say again flatly.

She squints down at me. "Trust me, you want to see it."

I do kinda want to see it.

"It's nothing bad, just..." She tips her head side to side, looking for a way to describe the mystery photo on her phone screen. "It's different. Something you've never seen before."

I laugh because there are few things I haven't seen between birth and death. Living on a farm makes sure of that. "Then show me."

She pulls her phone to her chest. "Maybe I shouldn't. Wyatt?"

He sighs and puts a hand on her shoulder. "Just do it."

"Do it?"

Wyatt nods.

"Someone just show me the damn photo!" I say with more intensity than I planned. Apparently, seeing this photo is a top-five experience I need to have.

Avery gives me an assessing look. I half-expect her to tuck the phone in her pocket and be done with it, but my curiosity has won out, and I want to see what's on that screen.

I *have* to know.

"Fine." She flips her phone and steps down so my eyes are level with the picture filling her entire screen.

It isn't big enough.

White dress, tan legs, and dark-cropped hair make my mouth run dry. It's Tilly. But not like I've ever seen her before, and I've seen her in a lot of ways. This is new, and Avery was right...nothing I've ever seen before. Dreaming this wouldn't even do her justice.

"That's Tilly," I state for the record because it's been too many seconds of quiet. I needed to say something to prove to everyone, including myself, that I was still breathing, still alive.

"That's her," Avery confirms, the sound of amusement in her voice.

The slit in Tilly's dress rides all the way up to the apex of her thigh, and her legs look like they go on forever. The silhouette hugs her in all of the right places, and Lord help me if I don't note the peaks of her nipples under that ruched neckline.

It reminds me of the suck-your-soul-right-out-of-your-body red summer dress Tilly wore one time back when we were seeing each other. She surprised me with it when I came over to the farm to take her dancing, but we never got further than the living room. That red was far from the stark white in this photo, but I don't have preferences when it comes to Tilly.

I rub my chin and force my eyes away. "Why is she wearing that?"

"Because I made her try it on."

So it's Avery's fault I'll be dreaming of this tonight.

I relax some, knowing there isn't some guy out there ready to put an engagement ring on her finger. At least none that I know of. My hands form into fists at the thought, and it makes my stomach plummet. Of course, Tilly is going to date. Of course, she'll attract someone else with her vibrant personality and even brighter smile. The tall heels she likes wearing, the way kissing her feels like a tease. Of course, someone will come along, and I'll be forced to forget all of her. Every damn memory we have together.

But Tilly isn't the kind of woman you fuck and forget so easily.

I know because I've been trying.

I clear my throat just as Carl opens the screen porch door and walks outside. Avery yanks her phone back to her chest to hide the photo I'll never be able to unsee. My curiosity is a damn traitor that now has blackmail on me. I never should have looked, given in to that small voice that sounded a lot like Avery's.

Carl starts talking with Wyatt and Avery, smoothing the back of his hair. I'm on autopilot and don't say hello or goodbye. I just walk up the rest of the steps, fling open the screen door, and slip off my boots like I've done so many times before. The faint voices outside are nothing compared to the sound of running water then a broom swishing across the terracotta tiles in the kitchen. My body is hyper-aware of every noise she makes.

Are we alone? Or is someone else here? I'm not going to say anything about the picture since I told Avery I wouldn't. *Damn secrets.* I'm definitely not going to imagine her with the red dress pushed up her thighs. But seeing Tilly in person, knowing *her* like *that* exists...shit. I should have stayed outside longer.

This is why a year ago, I couldn't help kissing her again when she showed up for our walk along the creek. Too many memories of us, our short but packed history, the way her crop top skimmed the high-waist of her leggings. I feel like I'm walking straight into another trap today with white and red coloring my thoughts.

I need to put the images out of my mind. For the next fifteen minutes, my head will be in the hands of a woman who hates me. She doesn't give me sexy smirks like she was in that picture. And she won't be standing in a way that catalogs every single part of her. The woman inside that kitchen scowls and crosses her arms. She makes snide comments and would absolutely cut my ear if I stepped out of line. Pretty sure she'd slice me no matter what. I brought a few Band-Aids in case.

I take a deep breath and walk to the back of the house and into the kitchen.

Tilly stops sweeping. "You."

Her eyes lower to slits as she studies me. I shove my hands in my pockets and study her right back. She looks different. The air feels charged. Maybe I'm somehow different after seeing that picture or remembering too many times from *before*.

Well, I'm fucked.

I lift my hand to say *hi*, but it turns into a point when I recognize a large belt buckle looped through her jean shorts. "Where'd you get that?"

She doesn't look down. "A store."

That's a lie. "No, you didn't."

"Yes, I did."

I look at the mountains etched into the oval-shaped buckle with white snow caps and a big, blue sky in the backdrop I've lived under all my life. That's *my* belt buckle.

"You stole it." It's not a question.

She leans the broom in the corner of the counter. "You left it."

"I want it back."

"Too bad. Didn't you just hear me when I said you left it? That's a cardinal rule. If you sleep with a woman, whatever you leave behind belongs to her," Tilly says, organizing her scissors on the counter like she's choosing which weapon will work best to get the job done.

I grind my teeth together. The woman in white is now the woman in my belt buckle. I won it after a ring toss game at the fair a few years ago, but it's become as good as irreplaceable now that she's wearing it. I thought I lost it, and I guess I did, but it's here now, feet from me. Though it might as well be miles.

She leans her hands onto the back of the chair in the middle of the room. "Aren't you here for a haircut?"

I was. Now, I'm not so sure I want to sit down, knowing my belt buckle is hugging her waist. But I'm not leaving here without this haircut.

I'll get that belt buckle back another time. In a way that won't involve sleeping with her.

I stalk over toward the chair and turn to sit, showing my frustrated resignation. She drapes a black cape around me, pulling it tight before snapping it around my neck.

"That's too tight," I tell her, clearing my throat.

"Good."

Why did I think this haircut would be anything different than every other interaction I've had with this woman? I reach behind my neck and adjust the snap to loosen it.

She starts spraying my hair with water to wet it, and a deep sense of dread fills my gut. I shouldn't have come here. Being in this chair, it's close to putting my life in her hands. Those delicate but deadly hands. I take a deep breath. It's fine. It's not like she's going to really cut me. But the thought of walking out of here without hair crosses my mind.

"Just a trim," I say for clarification.

She mumbles under her breath as she combs—a.k.a. rakes—through my hair. The spray bottle is back, aggressively drenching my hair, neck, and now T-shirt. This cape isn't seal-proof.

"That's a lot of water," I venture to say.

"You have a lot of hair." More spraying.

Having enough, I reach up and pluck the spray bottle from her. "I'll hold that for you."

The kitchen turns quiet, apart from the patterned snip of her scissors. I need to start a casual conversation so she sees me and my hair as less of a threat.

"Thanks for returning the snake." Wrong choice.

She's quiet before saying, "I was disappointed you didn't yell, *there's a snake in my boot.*"

I scoff. "Why would I say that?"

"Haven't you ever seen Toy Story?"

I shake my head. "No."

"Head still," she demands, gripping either side of my face in a near headlock.

My back goes rigid. "Yes, ma'am," I mutter.

"If you ever call me *ma'am* again…" She doesn't finish that thought.

The buzz of the clippers starts up in my ear, and I jump. I didn't mean to, but the damage has been done.

She grabs the top of my head with her hand to keep me steady. "A little jumpy are we?"

I clear my throat and dig for another topic. "Where are your heels?"

Her hand is steady as she moves the clippers rhythmically from the base of my hairline to the crown of my head, working in vertical lines from left to right. "What do you mean?" There's an edge to her question.

"You haven't worn your heels since you've been here." It's purely an observation. Tilly isn't exactly known for her flat footwear. I've simply noticed that we aren't at eye level anymore, and I have to look down. It's an inconvenience, really.

"Same reason you aren't wearing yours," she says, turning off the sheers.

I let the jab slide, hiding a smile. "All the shit on the ground?"

"Exactly. I brought a few heels, but I have other shoes specifically for when I visit. They're more platform or wedge than heel."

Of course, she did. The woman has more shoes than could fit in the back of my pickup.

Thankfully, she sets the clippers aside after cleaning up my neck and continues to work with her comb and scissors, blending the shorter sides with the longer hair on top.

Her hands are steady as she cuts. I can feel the confidence in how she handles herself, moving quickly, trimming, and brushing stray hairs away. I don't have a mirror to look in, but everything feels normal enough. It's not like she's giving me a mohawk or anything.

In a matter of seconds, she stands in front of me, eyeing the sides and front of my head to make sure it's even. I'm not prepared for this—for her. The photo is haunting me. But Tilly in front of me *in the flesh* puts her eyes on display, her lips at a dangerous distance. I only notice them because she's chewing gum, drawing my attention straight to that mouth of hers. The feather earrings that skim her shoulders and move with the motion of her head act as pendulums, forcing my eyes to fixate on their movement next. My body wants her, and I hate how much.

We're completely alone.

I could reach out and drag my hands up her thighs or tug her to straddle my lap and kiss her neck while she finishes trimming my sides. I could slip a hand up her coral tank and feel the ragged breaths expanding and contracting her lungs, the curve of her tits.

I could do a lot of things.

But it's been my good sense that won't let me act again.

This isn't exactly the first haircut she's ever given me. I wasn't a stranger to her salon chair the one time I went to visit her in Bismarck, but this time is different because we aren't those people anymore. The Tilly that smiled at me in the mirror or purposefully leaned close enough for me to kiss as she snipped the hair hanging over my forehead isn't the one avoiding my eyes now.

Visions of white come barreling back into my mind's eye. Sleek and tight, curvy and sexy. Avery should have never shown me that picture. I should have never asked her to.

But I did.

I saw it, and now I can't stop thinking about it—*us*.

"Done." She finally meets my eyes, though briefly, and stands taller. I swallow back my thoughts as she grabs the underside of my chin, tilting my head from side to side. "Do you need me to shave your face? You're looking a little shaggy compared to your usual baby face."

"Just because I don't have a beard like Wyatt doesn't mean I can't grow one."

She snorts. "Prove it."

I won't be proving it.

She stares down at me, hand still holding my chin, as I delay giving her a response—mostly because I can't think of what to say. I wasn't expecting this cut to end so quickly.

I yank my chin from her grip, irritated with how weak I feel. "No, I know how to shave."

She rolls her eyes and walks to set her tools on the counter. "You can leave now."

Stop being a jackass. "Thank you," I say to smooth things over.

"Don't mention it," she mumbles from behind me.

I don't think things are smooth.

Wyatt's words from the other day come back to me—*play nice*—mingling with the vision of Tilly in that damn dress I should have never seen. Maybe there's a way to quit this animosity between us. Just because we didn't work out doesn't mean we can't be nice to each other—friends even. It might help to get on neutral footing before I tell her what I need to.

I unsnap the apron, shaking it out on the floor before standing to drape it over the chair. All of the fine hairs I imagine stuck to my clothes get shaken out, too, as I try to think up how to save this.

My hands are back in the safety zone of my pockets. "Do you have any other haircuts today?"

She turns to face me, leaning back on the counter. Her arms are crossed, and she's scowling in that perpetual way of hers. "No. You were the last."

I know for a fact she doesn't scowl at everyone. Something about that thought makes me want to see her teeth more. If white or red are off limits, maybe a smile isn't.

Grabbing the back of the chair, I pull it up to the sink and flip the faucet on. I point at the chair. "Sit."

She scoffs and crosses her arms. "Yeah, right."

I shoot her a stern look. "Come on. Let me wash your hair. You've been doing it for everyone else."

So much for neutral territory. I skipped right over that and went straight for somewhere in the realm of *show me what's under your shirt.* Washing a person's hair is intimate. In reality, I know scrubbing shampoo into her scalp isn't going to start something, but maybe it'll end it. Wyatt wanted us to be friends anyway. Doing something nice for her would show everyone that I'm trying.

"No." Her jaw is rigid. "Why would I listen to you? You'll probably bleach my hair, or release a family of spiders to make their home on my head. No way."

"You didn't do any of that to me."

She stares at the ceiling. "I would never get that close to a spider."

"See," I drawl, flipping on the water. "I'm not going to do anything other than wash your hair. Promise."

Her gaze darts to the water rushing over my hand. The softening in her eyes tells me she's curious.

"Are you afraid? It's not like I have scissors in my hand." I hold my hands up just to prove my point.

She glowers at me.

"What if I say please?"

She pushes off the counter, taking two strides toward the chair. "Say it," she demands. "Say, *please.*"

I don't have to say it. I could end this right here and leave on a pleasant *thank you.* But I don't want that, and the way Tilly seems to be entertaining this is enough for me to add a bit of sugar to my voice when I say, "Please."

Giving in, she pivots to sit down and leans her head back. But before she rests her head on the sink edge, I grip her neck and slide a small kitchen towel underneath so she's comfortable.

She fixes me with a stare then closes her eyes. I tell myself it's probably because she doesn't want to look at me since she seems anything but relaxed. Her shoulders are crowding her ears, and her hands rest in closed fists on her thighs. It makes me want to see her loosen up some.

I use the sprayer nozzle to wet her hair. Slowly convincing her as I comb through the dark strands that I'm not going to spray her in the face or unleash insects on her, which I'd never do, for the record.

"See? Not so bad."

"Whatever," she spits out. Slowly she lifts one lid, peeping at me. "Why are you making that face?"

"What face?" I relax my brows. This isn't as easy as I was expecting it to be. I hope my face gives nothing away as to how I'm really feeling: totally fucked. "Where's the shampoo?"

She points to the side of the sink. "Over there."

I grab it and squeeze a generous amount into my hands, then lather it into her hair, using the tips of my fingers to massage her scalp.

She lets out a small moan at the back of her throat. If it was once, I could ignore it. Twice, I'd consider it a fluke. But three times, it startles me enough that I stop massaging her head and grip the side of the large, white farmhouse sink. "Damn it, Tilly," I mutter. Is she making these noises on purpose? Is she trying to make me lose my mind? The answer is always yes. Maybe friends don't or shouldn't wash each other's hair.

Her eyes close again as she smirks. "What?"

"Never mind." I sigh heavily and start to rinse out her hair. The point has been made. I'm not a dick. We can be cordial acquaintances, and I can haul her against the fridge and search for that moan with my mouth.

Wait, no. That's not friendly, either.

"All done." I grab another towel and work on drying her hair.

She snatches it from my hands and sits straight in the chair, squeezing the excess water from her hair. "Thank you," she whispers, glaring up at me through her lashes.

I dry my hands and pretend those two words don't heat my blood like they do. "You're welcome."

I've never held fire before, but I imagine this is what it would feel like.

Ten

Tilly

"If the ride is more fly, then you must buy." —Snoop Dogg

I don't see why I have to go," I say, leaning against the fence while Avery brushes Axel beside me.

Axel blows air through his nose and startles me. "Bless you."

He doesn't say thank you. Rude.

"Because you're my maid of honor," Avery reasons.

"So?" She's used this excuse for everything. Last night she reminded me when it came time to do the dishes after dinner. "Can't you have Stace or Deb go with him?"

She shakes her head. "Deb and Carl are both working today, and Stace had to take her kids to the doctor for checkups."

"And Wyatt? Why isn't he going?" I'm not ready to be done with this.

"He's in town getting feed for the animals."

"Granny?"

"She hates car rides."

The one day I need someone to be stuck in a cab with Ronny for the afternoon, and they aren't available.

I lean further into the fence, propping a foot up on the wooden rung. "I'm not going."

Her shoulders slump. "Please?"

"No." Hard pass.

"It's not like you guys have to talk. Ronny's just going to pick up the boarded horses at the other farm while you get the leather keychains for the wedding favors," she explains. "You'll be there and back within a couple of hours, tops."

"Why can't he get them?" I ask. "His legs aren't broken. Can't he just walk over and get the favors when he's done picking up his beloved horses?"

She fires a look at me. "You'll save time and get back sooner if you go."

I cross my arms over my chest and pout. "When are we leaving?"

Ronny's blue and white old beater of a truck comes rolling up the drive with the obnoxiously large logo on the back indicating he can haul shit.

Avery stops brushing Axel to crane her neck. "Now."

"And what if I kill him?" I ask with a straight face. A valid concern.

She looks from me to his truck. "Then at least hide his body in a good spot."

I kick off the fence and point at her. "You have a really twisted sense of humor sometimes."

"You started it." She shrugs. "Love you. Make good choices."

"I always do." I flip my short hair and stride toward my cabin, bypassing the old truck and horse trailer parked in front of the barn.

He slides out of the driver seat, booted feet hitting the ground as I pass. "Tilly."

"Ronny." I keep walking but peep over my shoulder at the back of his head since he's without a hat today. "I see you fixed your hair."

He sets his jaw in a firm line. "Cut the rat tail you left me with right off with kitchen scissors."

"Too bad." I shrug and face forward. "It looked good on you."

He grunts in response.

I knew Ronny was nervous about me cutting his hair yesterday, and for good reason. Just not for any of the ways he thought. Being in those close quarters again wasn't easy, so I decided to distract myself by leaving a little patch of hair in the back middle of his head. It's harmless fun and did the trick of ignoring how delicious his mouth looked. Lucky for me, he had no idea the extra hair was there when he left the kitchen.

Walking up the porch steps, I open the door and walk inside my cabin like it's any other day, any other time. But it's not. Today, a giant snake dangles from the ceiling in front of my face. My screams can likely be heard for hundreds of miles, waking up people on the other side of the world with how shrill they are.

The rubber is a dead giveaway, indicating it's dead. Lifeless. *Fake.*

I grab it in my fist and turn back to stare across the gravel drive to where Avery and Ronny are standing. His smirk is visible from here, but Avery's mouth is wide open, and she stops brushing Axel.

I stab a finger toward him. "You!"

"Ronny," he calls. "The name's Ronny."

He hides his laughter behind his fist as I storm into the house and slam my door. I look at the rubber snake in my grip and then around the room. There's a small living area just off the kitchen and a bedroom Avery turned into the spa with a short hallway leading to a bathroom and my room. I need a place to hide this thing so Ronny doesn't get his hands on it again. Not until I'm ready to offer him payback.

I shove it under the couch cushion then sit on top of it. I might be stuck going to Greycliff with Ronny for wedding favors, but I'm going to make him wait. I have things to do that need to happen.

Right. Now.

I roll my shoulders back and jut out my chin, making a list in my head.

***

"WHY ARE YOU picking up horses anyway? Don't you have enough?" I ask Ronny from the passenger seat.

The windows are down since the A/C doesn't work. It must be an old truck thing because Wyatt's truck A/C is broken, too.

He doesn't answer, so I peer over at him. His jaw is clenched shut, and he's staring straight ahead with one arm slung over the top of the steering wheel as the other rests on the door. Up close, Ronny's features are always more startling. His nose is straight, his jaw is squared and angular, and his skin has a creamy dark complexion. Looking at him feels like a physical ache behind my ribcage.

"Oh, come on. Are you going to be pissed the whole trip?" Sighing, I reach for the radio to turn it to a different station.

He swats my hand away like it's an annoying gnat. "Yes."

"Just because I took a little while to get ready?"

"A little while?" He glares at me and then back at the road. "You spent an hour in your cabin doing Lord knows what while I banged on your door and paced the driveway."

I study the fresh coat of red paint I added to my nails. It turned out better than expected because I didn't rush. "I needed to shower and touch up my nails." And organize my shoes by color from darkest to lightest while finishing my audiobook. "This little trip was sprung on me when I already had plans for today."

The way he's gripping the steering wheel has me afraid for its nonexistent life. "And painting your nails couldn't wait until later?"

"No!" I yell, the sound reverberating off the wind whipping through the cab and tangling my hair. "I couldn't do it later. They were horrendous."

Everything else went to the top of my priority list when I realized how much it would probably annoy him. But he had it coming. The snake prank was...unexpected. I don't like that he got a reaction out of me, even if it was screamed curses. Except now, I'm stuck with his sour attitude for the afternoon.

"Let's just try to have a good time." I reach for the knob again.

He shoves his hand between mine and the radio, turning it off.

I grind my teeth together. "I love silence."

"Good because no one touches my radio," he says with a bite.

I laugh, but he doesn't like that.

He shoots glances at me. "What?"

I continue laughing like it's really that funny.

"Spit it out, Till."

The nickname stops me cold. All of my laughter dies a slow death. "Nothing."

"Tell me."

Raking fingers through my matted hair, I sigh. "You make it sound like people who touch your radio are trying to touch *more* than your radio."

He shakes his head, not so effectively ignoring my comment, and recommits his tight grip on the wheel. "You're wearing my belt buckle again."

I fist it proudly. "Feel like a real cowgirl with it, too. Might wear it every day."

He's like a bull ready to charge, breathing in and out through his nose.

I look out the window and smile at the fact he gets ruffled so easily. He might as well be a Sour Patch kid. Sour at first with a sweet, gummy center. It might have been short-lived, but yesterday in Avery's kitchen, when he washed my hair, I saw that sweet side of him. The one that made me want to purr like a cat and curl up in his lap in front of a sunny window. He was the same man who once taught me how to ride a horse and drive an ATV with enough patience to fuel a trip to the moon and back.

But not today.

Today, he's all tight-lipped and pucker-faced.

We've been in this truck for twenty minutes already, but Avery forgot to inform me that we'd be the slowest people on the road. Apparently, old trucks towing horse trailers bring you to roughly turtle speed or below.

"Are we there yet?" My voice is whiny because I know it will irritate him that much more. It's not like I haven't already asked twenty-five times.

"No," he says in a flat tone. No emotion, no feeling. Just a word.

This is going to be a long day.

The front windshield reveals the exit Ronny is slowing down for. *Liar.* We're already here. He pulls off and navigates down a long road running parallel to the freeway before eventually crossing under the overpass. The place is nothing like I expect since it's right off the highway, and apart from a few houses, it's the only sign of life around here.

A cabin-style home sits across a looped gravel parking lot from what looks like a newly built, two-story building. Behind the house there are a few silos and other cabins further away and tucked against the hillside.

"What is this place?" I ask. Ronny turns right and continues down a different gravel drive in front of the new building. As we pass by, I note a pond out front and a large mill rotating in circles on the outside. "Why are we here again? To buy more horses?"

His sigh goes on for minutes. "You ask too many questions."

I mouth *you ask too many questions* back to him while my face is glued to the window. "You don't offer enough information."

He says nothing as we drive under the archway and pull up in front of a small, red barn. With the window down, I can already smell the foul odor unique to all areas with livestock—except in rural Montana. The smell lives in the air at all times. Oddly enough, I'm starting to get used to it.

I go to open my door, and Ronny rushes to grab my arm in a quick motion. "You can stay here. I'll only be a few minutes."

I look down at his hand gripping my arm—bare arm—and then back at his steely gaze. "Are you forgetting I came here to do something, too? I need to get the wedding favors."

He pulls his hand back. "Just wait a minute, and I'll go with you."

So much for saving time.

I cross my arms and huff while he gets out of the truck, leaving me to stare off in boredom. "I'm hungry."

"Don't eat my truck."

I roll my eyes. "And what am I supposed to eat? All the food you brought?"

"No eating in my truck, either. There's a water bottle on the ground." He points under my feet and then slams the door.

I reach for the half-full bottle. "Water isn't food, dumbass."

He rounds the hood and shakes a guy's hand who looks barely a day over eighteen. The young boy has a cowboy hat like Ronny usually wears though not today. Today, Ronny chose to wear nothing. His head is naked.

I mean, apart from the fantastic haircut I gave him. He rarely goes without some kind of hat, whether it's the annoying cowboy hat he likes so much or a backward *Thirst Trapp Farms* baseball-style one. All of my trim work from yesterday is on display, and while I know my work is solid, it's annoying me how good those sharp lines look on him.

They both walk back to the horse trailer, and I wait. Ronny took the keys with him. A smart choice since he knows I'd probably turn the truck on just for the radio, but instead, I'm listening to silence.

I really don't like silence.

It's too...quiet.

Too boring.

I prefer loud noises and even louder voices. It's one of the ways I resemble my dad. I never had to guess whether he was home because his voice was as loud as an entire construction site every time. Mom was the quiet one. Maybe that's why she couldn't stand him. Or maybe that's why he couldn't stand her. If there was one thing they were united on, it was that they were getting a divorce.

They said little would change, but everything did. I lived with Mom in her new apartment on weekdays, Dad on weekends, and the occasional vacation time my mom took to travel. Both seemed content. But I couldn't help blaming Mom for being the one to leave. She always appeared more relieved than Dad to be done with their marriage. Maybe that's why my relationship with her has been more strained.

This is exactly why I hate quiet. My thoughts always take roads I don't want to travel.

I unfold my arms and curl one of my feet behind the opposite knee. I have to adjust the belt buckle I got from Ronny so it doesn't stab into my stomach.

More silence.

I can't even scroll on my phone since there isn't any service in the middle of nowhere, Montana, so I look out the window. There's a fenced pen and a cow grazing just outside near a small red barn, but I'm about as unexcited to see her as she is to see me.

A full garden and greenhouse are directly outside the front windshield with lush green plants and rows of other vegetables with green, leafy heads or intertwining limbs. Avery's garden isn't nearly as large as this one, but hers has more flowers.

God, I'm so bored.

I'm thinking about gardens now, which I can assuredly say has never happened before in my life. I'm usually stuck on thoughts of extreme adventures. Could be because they're the only activities that allow me to *feel*. I can feel the wind in my hair, the splash of water on my face, the way my stomach folds over on itself.

Carrots and cauliflower can't offer any of that.

Grabbing my purse at my feet, I remember the granola bar I stashed in there for the dress fitting the other day. Hangry is really not a good look for a bride, so I've been carrying it around in case I needed to deploy it for Avery. Looks like I'm the one who needs it now. I rip open the package and take a bite, my whole body relaxing with a satisfied sigh.

I note the glove box in front of me. A slight tingle races up my spine, but I can't tell if it's a warning to keep it shut or open it.

I'm going to open it.

There's no way I'm not.

It'll give me something to do, and Ronny wanted me to stay in here. He knows I'm nosy and still decided to leave this perfectly good, perfectly *closed* glove box unattended. I reach for the small lever, expecting it to be locked like everything else in Ronny's life, but it pops open easily. Papers are stacked in a heap, hiding everything else inside, so I carefully remove them and set them on the bench seat beside me. I unbuckle my seatbelt to lean further forward and push around a few pens, coins, and a random hair brush I'm instantly curious about.

There's nothing exciting in here, making my shoulders slump in disappointment. I don't know what I wanted to find. Maybe a diary or scandalous letter to a long-lost lover. That would explain why he shut things down with me so quickly. I would have preferred finding letters, honestly. Knowing he was in love with someone else would have been easier to choke down than *this isn't going to work*.

I mean, it was his loss, after all. I'm great. A little loud and eccentric at times—most times—but when we first met, he liked that about me. He told me so. And even if he didn't, I love that about me. I'm the only person I've gotten better at loving over the years.

Before, we had been electric. Every touch between us, and there were plenty, sent trills up and down my body. We danced and slept together the first night we met, which felt like similar activities. When I moved, he moved. When I ran my hands down his chest and wiggled my hips against him, he gripped me tighter and pulled me closer.

Now, I just want to break every one of his fingers like a toothpick. Like when he washed my hair yesterday. I'm not above a good hair wash. It's always the best part of going to the salon. And I admit a part of me was interested if he'd be any good. But by the end, I was more irritated by how fantastic his hands felt twisted in my hair. I was one scalp massage away from hauling him back to my cabin. See, *annoying*.

I take another bite and rifle through the papers I had set beside me, finding nothing of importance. Car insurance, the title to this vehicle, and a truck manual that has to be at least forty years old. Then, I find a piece of mail sandwiched between everything that has Ronny's name on it. The white, rectangular envelope is already opened, so it's not like I'm ripping into it. I just pull it out.

There's a letter and another official-looking document from a medical facility behind it, but I start with the letter, reading it from start to finish and then over again.

"Is this real?" I whisper to myself, flipping the letter over to try and find any clue it's a fake, sent by someone in another dimension because the contents indicate as much.

There's nothing.

It's real.

I can hardly believe what I'm reading, and as I start to scan the second document behind the first, my mouth falls open. How did I not know this? It's surprising, like finding out you somehow put your shirt on inside out and wore it all day that way.

Ronny is private. I knew that when it took multiple dates to get him to open up about things. But this feels more than private. Maybe I shouldn't have snooped, but now I know.

"Ronny's adopted."

Eleven

Ronny

"You don't get respect if you don't deserve it." —Snoop Dogg

Those shorts. They were the worst choice for today. What the hell was she thinking?

It's hot outside, topping close to eighty, and Gertie's A/C had an unfortunate encounter with an opossum—don't ask—but it's not *that* bad.

I stalk behind Gabe, the ranch owner who boards some of our horses. He leads me to where they're at in the small front pasture, nostrils flaring in sync with my heavy breathing.

Damn threads hanging loose down her shapely thighs, looking light-washed and innocent, while the vixen wearing them came outside strutting like she was on a runway. Granted, there are few situations that woman has been in that she doesn't treat as such.

She got in the truck, and I almost ordered her back inside to change. Not because I don't fucking love those shorts, but because keeping the promise to myself to leave Tilly the hell alone is close to melting in this heat. But I didn't do that. Instead, I bared my teeth the whole way here, giving me a tension headache from all that stress.

I'm not some masochist who enjoys this form of torture. Tilly just hasn't worn anything yet that I don't like. Except for one thing: my belt buckle. The way it spans the front of her waist, reaching over the rise of her jeans and dipping low over her zipper, makes me want nothing more than to grab her by it and rip it off.

I had to consistently remind myself she spent over an hour in her cabin doing things I came to find out were nothing more than silly little tasks. Her front door might have been locked, but I was close to going around back and scaring her half to death just to teach her a lesson about teaching me a lesson.

"Did you say something?" Gabe says over his shoulder.

I tear my eyes from my boots, kicking up dirt with every step, following right behind him. "No, sorry." I must have been mumbling to myself.

"I brought all the horses up here," Gabe says, pointing to the four familiar ladies and gents. "I'll help you load them up."

I've worked with Gabe for the last few years, boarding our horses over the winter to cut down on feed and maintenance costs. Our cattle herd has grown, making it easier to offload some of the burden where we can. He and his family are good people, having built this place from the ground up. It was a raw piece of property to start, but with the help of his parents and extended family, they've really made this place something. Not to mention a couple of the downtown businesses they've been able to revamp.

One by one, I stand with my back against the rear door of the trailer while Gabe brings each horse over, and we load them in. I've been picking them up in groups but this is the last one. Using the lead rope, I point in the direction of the empty space I want them to go, and luckily, I'm not dealing with any first-timers. Staggering them and offering fresh hay and water for the ride back, they're all content when I secure the rear latch.

"That does it," Gabe says just as my phone starts ringing.

I slip it out of my pocket to see who's calling.

Camila.

I'm sure she's probably calling to talk about the details this weekend, but it doesn't feel right to answer her call when Tilly's only feet away in my truck. Time is running out on having all the conversations I need to have before this wedding. This isn't the kind of thing you surprise someone with, especially Tilly. It will change everything.

The whole reason I agreed to have Tilly along today was so we could talk, but so far, the words aren't coming out of my mouth. All I've got is, *Hey, Tilly, remember two years ago when I said we wouldn't work well together?*

I tilt my head back and close my eyes. I have to figure my shit out soon.

Checking my wristwatch, I note the twenty minutes it's been since leaving Tilly unattended. I made it clear my truck was a no-eating zone. My stern, expressionless face must have indicated I wasn't joking. I should probably feed her, water her, take her outside. God, what am I even saying? It's not like she's a puppy or a houseplant.

"Pleasure doing business with you, Gabe." We shake hands. "Will I see you at the wedding?"

His cheeks turn crimson. "Mabel invited me, so we'll be there. Together. It's a date."

The corners of my mouth lift. *Say it isn't so.* "Mabel from the bakery?"

There aren't many establishments in our downtown square, but I like to think the ones we have are quality. Helen's bakery might have been one of the first to open on Main Street, touting mouth-watering cinnamon rolls as big as your head that never disappointed. She wasn't wrong. To this day, even with an expanded breakfast menu, her bakery brings in all the gossip a small town can offer, which is more filling than the roll itself.

It wasn't long ago that Mabel's mom, Helen, was trying to set her up with Wyatt. Not that it would have made a difference. Avery had already moved to the farm by then. Helen's attempts were futile. Mabel just seemed embarrassed.

I love to hate small-town drama.

Gabe nods. "I think I gained a few pounds since asking her out. I was in the bakery a good deal."

There isn't a chance Helen would have let him leave without biting into one of those prized cakes. "I'm sure you did. It only takes one."

"I'm pretty sure I'm fifty deep at this point.

"Well, good for you."

"Thanks, man," Gabe says, smacking his lean belly. "Helen only has her working there a couple days a week now. The rest of the time, she's making food and espresso drinks here in the cafe." Gabe's face is bright with pride, and hell if I don't notice how he stood straighter and pushed his chest out a bit more.

Happy endings aren't really my thing, but for the likes of Gabe, I'm glad.

"See you Sunday then." I go to tip my hat and realize I'm not wearing one. It's only one of many things that have irritated me so far today. "And sorry again I was late today. It's been a hectic week."

He waves me off. "Don't worry about it. I'm sure there are a lot of things to get ready over at the farm, especially since it's outdoors."

Yeah, and hot flings that turn sour and look for any excuse to annoy you. "Something like that."

"Could you use any help getting things ready for Sunday?" he asks. "By the way, do you need anything? Extra tables, chairs, linens..."

I purse my lips. "They're renting most things, and we've got the rest covered. But if we need your help, I'll be sure to call."

He nods and walks off toward his four-wheeler in a hurry. Likely off to send dirty texts to Mabel. Or maybe that's just what I would do if I were sweet on someone.

Young love.

It knows nothing.

I shake my head and walk back toward my truck and the woman inside, who is as impossible as they come.

I open the driver-side door, and she mumbles, "Finally. Took you long enough."

Her legs uncurl and drop to the floor as she sits up straighter. The water bottle I left that was half-empty is drained and sitting crumpled on my seat is a wrapper, along with—

"Are those crumbs?"

Twelve

Tilly

"Stay true to who you are and what you stand for, and you'll go far in life." —Snoop Dogg

I look at the evidence on the open bench seat between us. "No."

He climbs in and inspects the seat, picking up what is, indeed, a crumb and pinches it between his thumb and pointer finger. "How is this not a crumb?"

I had already folded the letter and tucked the envelope with the other papers back into the glove box before he made it back. The last little bit of time was devoted to coming up with stories about Ronny's family.

Maybe he's royalty, but his teen mom's pregnancy caused a stir, and she wouldn't be able to keep her crown if she went through with it. Or his dad was in a mafia motorcycle gang, his mother some rich debutante, and their parents forced them apart after the adoption.

The need to know what actually happened is clawing at me.

"How do I know it isn't yours?" I toss back.

"Because I *never* eat in my truck."

"Oh really?" I cross my arms. "Never?"

"Never."

I can feel the blood in my body rising, and my cheeks flush. I'm not sure why that one word feels like a scolding, but that's my reality. It could be because I'm on thin ice knowing what I know now. Can he tell? Can he see it in my dodgy eye contact and avoidant body language?

Even I can tell!

Reading those classified documents made me hungry, and I might have shoveled it into my mouth faster than necessary. And, sure, Ronny might have said not to eat in his truck, but he locked me in here by myself for who knows how long. I wasn't going to starve.

I swallow my guilt and hope he doesn't see my throat move with the motion.

His head tilts to the side, and then he does the unthinkable. He eats the crumb. "Hm. Chocolate chips?" His eyes widen. "Do you know how much chocolate smears, Till?"

So we're back to the nickname. "You were gone for a long time, okay? A couple of chocolate chips weren't going to hurt anyone. What is this? Some kind of inquisition? Do you want to handcuff me and take me down to your town jail, where I'll be forced to pay the price for eating a chocolate chip protein bar in your old ass truck?" I put both of my hands out, wrists side up. "Well, cuff me then. But you should also know I didn't save you any."

"Because you had to eat the evidence."

I shake my arms for extreme emphasis. "Apparently, not all of it."

The mention of handcuffs was the wrong direction. Now, all I'm thinking about is Ronny using a pair of handcuffs for a very different reason than taking me to jail.

He isn't entirely immune to such thoughts, either.

His eyes darken, but he quickly shoves the keys in the ignition and says, "I'm driving over to the main building first, and then we'll go to the leather shop."

"Why would we go to the main building?" I cross my arms, willing an answer out of him while convincing myself I won't blurt out what I know. I still have a job to do here, which is to remember the wedding favors. I've forgotten at least five times.

He puts the truck in gear and starts slowly rolling forward. "It's where the cafe is. They have food, and since you ate in my truck but didn't save me any, I'm hungry."

He pulls around the circular gravel drive we passed on the way in and parks near the edge so the horse trailer doesn't take up too much space. I slide out of the truck, relishing the feel of the sun kissing my exposed skin. Shorts were the perfect choice for today.

We stride up the short staircase and walk inside in more silence. The entirety of this place is made of wood. Walls, floor, ceiling, shelves, everything is made of some kind of tree. It smells nice, though, like the outside just waltzed in and made itself comfortable. The tall beams on the ceiling support large industrial metal fans, and old wine barrels are being used as table bases. The entire place looks like it could be in a magazine. Rugged, strong, and ethereal, all in one mental snapshot.

The mill rotating in circles on the outside is really grinding what looks to be flour inside, dumping the grainy powder into a small bucket on the floor. The smell of freshly baked dough is bombarding my senses.

"Isn't this quaint?" I say to no one since Ronny darted to the register. This rural, small-town stuff is starting to grow on me. Not like fungus, but like gray hairs that you learn to make peace with.

Ronny is up at the counter ordering, then meets me beside the roped-off mill. "I heard they sourced this mill from France."

I nod. "Impressive."

"It's a fairly new building. Same with all the others, but they're unique. Not every day you find a cafe, leather shop, barn, and livestock all on the same property."

Who died and made him the social media marketer for this place?

I've never heard of anything like this before, and while I'm truly in awe, I'm most surprised by how many words Ronny just said to me without any snide comment thrown in. I hardly know what to do or say. This easy conversation hasn't been *us* in a long time.

My phone starts to ring in my pocket, interrupting the thought, and I whip it out. I answer without looking to see who it is—my first mistake. "Hello?"

"Matilda."

She's the only person who uses my full name. "Mom, hi."

I step away from the noisy mill and walk toward the back of the space where floor-to-ceiling windows cover an entire wall, looking out toward the bluff that towers above.

"I finally had reception and needed to call you," she says in that direct way of hers. Little feeling and even less interest.

"And you didn't want to text?" You know, like normal. We rarely talk on the phone, and it's...weird.

"Too unreliable. Look, I'm not going to be able to make the wedding this weekend. I'm stuck in the Caribbean and don't think I'll make it back in time."

Which is code for *I'm extending my trip and not coming home.* She does this often enough I know how to speak I'm-retired-and-I-know-it. I'm not a stranger to spending holidays or special occasions, like my birthday, without her. After the divorce, she decided to throw herself into the world of travel and hasn't looked back, quite literally, since.

"And Dad?" I ask.

"Oh," she starts. "I have no idea what his plans are. You'll have to call him."

I roll my neck out. "Okay."

"You sound mad."

"Nope." I shake my head just to reinforce that I won't be and walk around the space, the wood planks groaning beneath my feet.

She doesn't spend a second longer acknowledging or analyzing my answer further. "I'll be back in a couple of weeks, and we can eat at that one restaurant you really like," she promises.

"Sure." I'd bet money she doesn't know which restaurant is my favorite.

The shelf in the back corner has all different kinds of soaps, lotions, and facial potions. I pick up a couple bars and smell them, seeing if they match what their labels say they smell like.

"Reception is getting rough, so I'm going to let you go. Love you." She doesn't wait for me to reply with my own sentiments and hangs up immediately.

I bow my head and tuck my phone in my pocket. I can't say I'm not a bit relieved she won't be coming. Sometimes it's more effort to be around her than not since we no longer have Dad in common. Now I'll be able to enjoy the wedding without the guilt of needing to talk and spend time together.

"You good?"

I turn around to Ronny, who snagged a barrel table with a glass top by the window and has an assortment of pastries in front of him.

"Just my mom." I take the seat across from him but sit on the edge of the chair, not quite committing to the spot. "I thought you were hungry?"

He cuts into a cinnamon roll. "I am."

"So you got pastries?"

He takes a bite and mumbles, "Yeah."

I laugh and lean back in the chair.

"Is your mom coming to the wedding?" he asks through a mouthful.

I twist my lips to the side and shake my head. "Not anymore. It's fine. She wouldn't have been much fun anyway."

"You still aren't close to her?"

I peer over at him, and his steady gaze is ready to catch mine. It's a lot, this look he's giving me. Intense and direct but not like the bullshit my mom just dished out. The weightier kind you can feel more than see since he knows my family history. "No, I'm not."

"And your dad?"

I sigh and stare at my lap. I've seen my dad more in the last year; he's personable and fun—much easier to talk to—but I'm not sure that makes us any closer. He's just as distracted by his own life but in different ways. He spends most of his time with his bowling league—Balls to the Wall.

"Not really. Maybe? It's complicated." There really isn't a better way to describe our relationship.

In many ways, Avery and I have similar relationships with our parents—hers got quiet, mine got distant. But the aftermath was the same: we could only rely on each other.

He doesn't say anything but scoots a plate with a blueberry scone across the glass-top table.

I stare at it and then at him. "What's this?"

"Yours," he says through another bite.

"I didn't order that."

"No," he agrees. "I did."

I squint at him. "You ordered this for me?"

"Yes, okay. Now would you stop asking questions and eat the damn pastry?"

I try really hard not to smile and pull the small plate even closer. "Fine." I should say *thank you*. It's what I would have said to anyone else in a situation like this one. But this is Ronny. And this is me. So, I don't say anything as we finish eating our pastries.

In silence.

Thirteen

Ronny

"You can teach an old dog a new trick if that old dog listen." —Snoop Dogg

It should be under Avery Trapp. Or maybe Wyatt Trapp," Tilly says to Mariella, the woman in the denim apron holding a knife. She has good reason to since this is a leather shop after all.

The real problem here is she can't find our order.

While Tilly searches for a photo on her phone, I make my way around the darkened room located in one of the buildings near the cafe and above the cheese shop. There are strips of different natural-toned hides, more tools that are akin to torture devices, and a large work table with barstools circling it at the center.

I've always appreciated work done by hand. Not the fast, assembly-line way of things, but the slow, methodical work that's created one stitch, carve, or curse at a time.

"Let me check with someone else about this," Mariella says. "You said your name is Avery Trapp, correct?"

Tilly pauses and says through a cough, "That's me."

I snap my gaze up from the stool I parked myself on. Did she really just tell that woman she's Avery? The hammer makes a loud thud on the table when I drop it, stand, and move closer to the corner of the room where Tilly waits outside the curtain the woman disappeared behind.

I bring my face parallel to hers, my chin hovering over her shoulder. "What are you doing?"

She rears back like she's been caught, chopping a hand through the air. "Geez. You don't need to scare me just to say words. I'm getting the wedding favors. You know this."

I run my tongue along my top teeth, thinking. "You just told her you were Avery."

"Yeah, I know."

"But you aren't."

"Well, duh," she says quietly. "I panicked, okay? I wasn't going to take the risk of her saying she wouldn't let me take them because I wasn't Avery. We've come too far to turn back now, and I promised to secure the favors. It's my job."

I lift my brows as she lands one last karate chop in the air. "Alright then."

Mariella exits with what I'm assuming is a paper bag full of small leather goods. "I found your order in the back—one hundred keychains. My partner put them on the highest shelf." She opens the bag for Tilly to peer in and see for herself.

Tilly picks one up, pressing a palm to her heart. "She's going to love these."

I elbow her, and she looks up at me before realization strikes. "I'm going to love these." She shakes her head. "I mean, I do love these."

The poor woman's smile is frozen, looking to me to supply an explanation I don't have, and then hands Tilly the bag, confirming she (Avery) had already paid for them.

"Congratulations on your upcoming wedding!"

Tilly gives a small nervous laugh.

I correct Mariella. "I'm just a...person."

Now I'm panicking. We tried friends when I washed Tilly's hair and had to hide my hard-on leaving the farmhouse, and *lovers* hasn't been us in a long time. I don't really know who I am to her.

"Oh," the woman says, "sorry for the confusion."

Tilly's piercing gaze finds the side of my face, and I shrug while giving her a side-eye. Maybe she wanted or even expected me to play along, but that isn't happening. I'm not Wyatt, and she's not Avery. We're two people just trying to get through the week without killing each other. Or fucking.

"Did you get a chance to see the finished honeymoon silo yet?" Mariella asks Tilly (a.k.a Avery).

"Honeymoon what?" My face contorts even more than it already is.

"The silos made into cabins that were just finished yesterday." She points to Tilly (a.k.a Avery). "You have it booked for next week, but I know you haven't seen it yet because...well, no one has seen them yet!" She laughs to herself, chipper for suggesting it.

Tilly peers up at me with wide, questioning eyes. I search her face for any indication that we can escape this moment without seeing the cabin Avery and Wyatt will be spending their honeymoon in. Everyone knows what happens on a honeymoon. The last thing I want is to go see where my best friend and his lady are going to be doing it. I don't have time for this, either.

But Tilly has this problem saying *no*. "Yes. We'd love to see it!"

***

ONE BUMPY RIDE and a short but in-depth history lesson about this farm, and we made it to the silo grain bin turned rental cabin.

The cliffside has been dug out to make room for the rentals and situated just high enough above the rest of the ranch to be able to admire it like a pirate searching for treasure. From this vantage, I can see it all. The valley below decorated with gardens and animals, the freeways cutting right through it, and even my truck and trailer parked in front of the cafe.

Aside from the view, this area must have taken a lot of work. There's just enough space to park a car and accommodate the small fire pit, but they had to dig out the hillside to make it happen. The silo is made of silver metal, so sunbeams bounce right off it, forcing me to look away and wish I brought my sunglasses, but the trim around the windows and door sport a cedar wood to warm it. The craftsmanship is admirable, giving me ideas to tuck away for future plans. There's even a spiral staircase around the side that leads to a small portico perfect for watching the sunrise or sunset.

I didn't know Gabe and his parents had any of this planned, but apparently, they'll be renting them out on Experiences R Us as Wyatt did. I guess Thirst Trapp Farms was part of their inspo board. I've never made one of those before, considering cows and grass would be the only things on there. Maybe dirt.

"Wow," Tilly says under her breath, stepping out of the small golf cart with duct tape and a prayer holding it together.

I step out, too, and lower my voice from beside her. "Are you referring to the silo or the ride we almost died on?"

"Definitely the ride," she says without skipping a beat.

I stretch my back, though it's not all for show. They'll want to level out that drive and fill in the potholes before guests arrive—before Avery and Wyatt do. He told me they were staying local, but this is right down the road. It's closer than close. Granny could walk here for brunch if she wanted to, considering how near it is to his parent's place.

"I have to get back to the shop, but just use the code 5789 to unlock and lock the door," Mariella explains, sliding across the worn white leather seat of the cart. "There's a short trail over there that leads to the cafe." She backs out and heads down the hill.

Someone's in a hurry.

I look back up at the looming silo and then Tilly. Glints of gold are highlighted throughout her hair, and the soft curves of her shoulders reflect the little bit of light that's left. It was a much later start than I wanted today, but with the sun preparing to be swallowed up by the mountain ridges, it isn't so bad to spend it here like this.

Tilly hasn't moved, so I say, "We don't have to go in."

She glares at me. "I'm going in."

"Alright," I drawl.

She walks a few steps to the door and starts punching in the numbers. The door immediately flashes green and unlocks. Tilly slowly pushes it open and steps over the threshold onto the cement floor, holding the door for me like she expects me to follow.

I do, but only because I'm not about to let her go inside alone and end up kidnapped. But the prospect of being in the honeymoon suite with her is enough to make me feel like I should run home in order to burn off the amount of steam percolating in my body. Alone with Tilly has never ended well for us.

I let go of the door, and it shuts with a bang that makes us both jump. Tilly stands in the middle of the room since there isn't one stitch of furniture in here. It's a small enough space that I can't easily avoid her. There's only so much square footage in a refurbished grain bin.

She slides open a tall barn door leading to what looks like a three-by-three bathroom and walks in. I breathe slowly then scratch the bottom of my jaw. I need to get a grip. Women never plague me like this. But even as I think this, my mind is producing combative words ready to pick a fight: *this is Tilly.* The history and passion we have are enough that I should've begged Mariella not to leave me here.

But I don't beg. I'll just suffer through this as best I can.

She comes back out of the bathroom, her feet scuffing along the cement floor. "So, you're adopted."

I almost don't register what she says since it's so out of place. Here I'm trying to keep my thoughts pure with a woman who is actively upheaving them with a backhoe, and she's asking about my family history.

I cross my arms over my chest, widening my stance. "What did you just ask?"

She glances up from the floor, and I try to find any sort of pity in her eyes. People tend to do that. They hear I'm adopted and think I must have been born to a woman in jail for some heinous crime, but really, my birth mom was just a woman who found herself pregnant by her boyfriend and didn't have the means to care for me. I know their first and last name but nothing more.

No photos. No family history. No memories.

She clears her throat. "You're adopted."

It's not like I keep this fact hidden, I just don't broadcast it. I live with the thoughts enough in my head, putting them on display has never been how I want to be defined. Especially with Tilly.

"You never said anything."

"No. I didn't." It's not as easy as talking about the weather.

Thoughts of our first night together bombard my mind. Tilly told me everything. At least most of it. She told me her favorite color down to the hang-ups she had because of her parent's divorce, all while my mouth was on her neck, fingers curled around pieces of her hair, or her tucked in close with my chin on top of her head.

There were plenty of opportunities I could have told her. I talked about my parents, the pressures of the farm, even the beginning of my friendship with Wyatt. Truth is, I shared more with Tilly than anyone else who has or hasn't shared my bed.

"Why?"

Hell if I really know. Telling her I was adopted back then would've been like scraping open wounds that hadn't fully healed—tender and all too honest. I don't think they ever will. Not when there are still so many question marks. I only offer a shrug. "It didn't feel relevant."

She crosses her arms and scoffs. "Okay. Right."

"What's all that about?"

She glares at me. "What?"

"All the huffing and puffing you're doing. Why is knowing I'm adopted such a big deal to you?"

She sighs. "It's nothing."

"It is something, or you wouldn't have brought it up," I say, egging her on. Is it surprising to her? Does she think less of me? "How did you even find out?"

Her eyes look everywhere other than mine, and she doesn't answer right away.

"Till," I say with an edge of warning.

"Don't call me that!" she snaps.

I hold up both of my hands in surrender.

She lets out a breath. "In your truck...there are official-looking papers from a doctor's office. An envelope and a letter..." Her voice trails off as I try to piece things together.

"There's a letter in my truck saying I'm adopted?" I can't seem to think of what that would be since I rarely go to the doctor—a blood test maybe?—but I'm relieved that's all she found or else we could be having a completely different conversation. One that was forced instead of me being able to control it.

I have to tell her.

She nods. "A detailed physical, maybe?" Her shoulders drop. "I don't know, but it had a different name listed under your paternal parents. The letter from the doctor said they were missing your background medical information."

Of course it's incomplete because I don't know any of those things about myself. I don't know if cancer runs in my family or if early onset dementia will take me out like a Nerf gun bullet to the eye. I don't know if my birth parents still live in Montana or moved to a commune to grow cilantro. Hell, I don't even know if I have any siblings. All of these facts stoke my anger.

I clench my fists at my side and grind my jaw. "You went through my stuff? You read my private medical documents?"

She kicks at nothing on the ground. "What else was I supposed to do in your truck?"

"Not go through my things!"

"You were gone for a long time," she retorts.

"It was twenty minutes." I shake my head. "And that doesn't even matter. You shouldn't have gone through my things."

She uncrosses her arms and squares herself off with me. "Are you really that upset about me going through your things? Or are you just upset that I found out you were adopted after lying to me about it?"

"Both," I answer before I can filter my response. I drop my chin to my chest.

She makes a smacking sound with her mouth. "That's what I thought."

Her tone is soft, but the words are like a magnifying glass into my soul.

"I didn't lie," I defend.

"You didn't tell me the truth."

Am I really that upset she went through my things? Yes, because I'm a private person. But maybe it's less about the rifling and more about the fact that now she knows. Being adopted hits a place so deep inside me, I wonder how I can still feel it so strongly after all these years. I've tried to bury it, but that hasn't worked either.

I didn't tell Tilly because I didn't want her to walk away. I was terrified of losing her even in the moments I was holding her. Finding out I'm adopted could have changed her mind. Right now, I still don't even know if it has.

"I'm sorry for going through your things," she says just above a whisper. "You being adopted doesn't change—wouldn't have changed anything between us, you know. It just feels...big. Like you couldn't share something like that with me when we were...close."

She's hurt.

I hurt her.

Again.

I bite the inside of my cheeks hard and stare at the ground, saying nothing. *Shit.* If this is how she feels about finding out I'm adopted...

She shuffles toward the door to leave, but I'm still standing in front of it, so she has to reach around me for the door handle. But when she grabs it and jiggles it once, it doesn't open. I turn and face the door, giving her space to yank on the handle a few more times.

It's not opening.

"Here, let me try." I step forward.

She blocks the door. "I've got it." I stare at the back of her head as she keeps trying. Nothing she does is working. "We're locked in."

"Can I try now?"

She steps out of the way and waves me forward to try.

I grip the lever handle tightly and tug it down. It doesn't move. I pull it up, but it doesn't budge. I jiggle, and kick, and shove my shoulder into the door, but it doesn't open. "Damn it," I mutter under my breath. "It's locked. What's the code again?"

"I told you it was locked," she says with a sneer. "And I don't remember. That was at least five minutes ago."

I glare back at her. "Just great."

Silence stretches as we both start thinking. I'm not just thinking about the door, though, I'm thinking about the woman on this side of it. With me.

Fourteen

Tilly

"Life is about growing and evolving." —Snoop Dogg

He's probably wondering what I'm doing in this bathroom. Who cares? Not me.

I stopped caring after the first ten minutes of being stuck in this silo together.

Knocking on the door did nothing since the cabin is set into the mountainside and far enough from any other cabins and civilization that no one could hear us. Add that to the fact I still don't have any service—*thanks, nature*—and Ronny left his phone in his truck.

We're screwed.

And also, if I have to share a space with this man any longer, he will be, too. Screwed, that is. God, why is his shirt so tight? And those jeans. They're unnecessarily snug around the half-moon shape of his ass.

Two soft knocks rap on the door. "Mind if I use the bathroom?"

I roll my eyes even though it's wasted since he can't see me. Obviously, my plan of staying in here until someone comes and rescues us, or we die, is clearly not going to work. I sigh heavily and stand from the closed toilet seat.

I unlock the door and slowly open it a crack. "Yes?"

"Can I come in?"

I assess his intentions through the small slit, then open the door wider.

"Thanks," he says as I slip by him, careful not to bump, touch, or grind. That last one wouldn't be a problem if we hadn't already been in that position once or twice before.

"Did you check the windows?" I ask before he can shut the bathroom door behind him.

He nods toward the front of the silo. "I tried all the ones I could reach, but none would open."

"Dang," I whisper. "And the patio porch up above?"

He twists his grip on the bathroom door handle and shakes his head. "We'll figure something out," he assures me, even though it feels like an empty threat.

"We're not going to find a way out of here! We will shrivel up like vegetables without any nutrients because there is no food and water in this place. By the time they find us, they'll be filming a Dateline episode and reminding people to never go into cabins with coded locks on the front door."

"Tilly."

I hold up a flat hand. "Don't give me any more encouraging platitudes like *we won't die in here* or *it's only a matter of time*. You don't know that!"

He shifts on his feet just inside the bathroom. "I wasn't going to say any of that."

I roughly tuck the same piece of hair behind my ear that I've been dealing with all day. If there were scissors available, I would snip it off right before using them to chisel a hole in these cement floors. "Well, then...what were you going to say?"

"I've had to pee for an hour."

My mouth gapes. "You have a real way with words, you know that?"

"I do. Now, go get a glass and fill it from the tap and enjoy some of the leftover fruit and hoagie sandwiches the workers must have left in the fridge," he says before closing the door to the bathroom with a slight slam I'm totally reading into.

So maybe we aren't going to starve, but I could contract a deadly disease by drinking tap water and die. Who knows where it's really coming from? A well in the back pasture? A hose off the leather woman's house? But if I don't drink anything, I'll die.

I'm taking my chances.

I walk into the small kitchenette on the other side of the circular room and fill up a glass of water before guzzling it down like I'm a freaking camel with maximum storage space in my humps. I fill it again, then open the mini fridge beneath the counter and spy the sandwiches Ronny mentioned. I'm not even that hungry since it's only been an hour and some change since I devoured that blueberry scone, licking every last crumb from the plate, but I eat it anyway.

I'm halfway through a turkey and salami on wheat bread when Ronny comes out of the bathroom and strides into the kitchen like he owns the place, or at least commands it. So what if he actually does? I'm not going to tell him that and give him an ego boost he doesn't need.

He's been out here far longer than I have. While I was rubbing toilet paper between my fingers to guess what ply Avery and Wyatt will be enjoying, he was clearly doing the work of foraging to make sure we don't starve.

"Not so bad, right?"

I turn the sandwich over in my hand and talk with my mouth full. "The bread's a little soggier than I prefer, but it's good."

He smirks and shakes his head.

I stand straighter, knowing there's more to his reaction. "Just say it."

He takes a wide stance across from me. "I've just never known you to like turkey."

I finish my bite and swallow. "I'm also not a fan of dying young, so I'll take my chances on deli meat and tap water, thank you."

He fills up a glass in the sink and takes a few sips like a calm, well-adjusted human, while I attempt not to notice that he remembered something small and unimportant about me. Why would he do that? How dare he try to impress me by bringing up a very minute detail about my preferences.

I hate the way it makes me feel. All warm and cozy-like.

"I think we've tried everything we possibly can at this point," he says.

I lean against the kitchen counter. "So you're just going to give up?"

"I never said that."

My next bite is too big for my mouth, but I try to talk around it anyway. "You might as well have."

"I'm taking a break," he says. "Plus, Mariella will notice my truck and trailer are still here if she hasn't already. Eventually, someone will come looking for us."

*****

Two Hours Later

"WHAT WAS THAT about someone coming to check on us again?" I roll over to my stomach and stare at Ronny, who is leaning against the curved wall with his feet kicked out and ankles crossed.

"You just had to come in here."

Is that blame I'm sensing? "You didn't have to follow me. And if my memory serves, you were the one who let the door close behind you."

He rests his head on the metal wall. "You forgot the code right after you used it."

I want to laugh maniacally. Instead, I sputter a sound that resembles a hyena *and* a chimpanzee. "I'm sorry my pea-sized brain can't hold all those numbers at one time." There's a sarcasm in my voice I can't hide.

He shakes his head. "That's not—"

He cuts himself off, then stands abruptly and strides purposefully toward the door again, giving it a good shake like he's testing whether he can break it with the sheer force of his frustration. I have no doubt he could at least inflict some damage on the handle or by shoving a booted foot through the glass panels.

"No one has even so much as walked by here!" he says through a grunt.

Unsurprisingly, the sharpness of his gaze can't cut glass and free us, either, considering how intently he's looking at the door.

I roll onto my back on the hard ground I'm pretending is a plush bed. "At least we have half a sandwich and tap water to get us through. But don't think for a second I won't eat you if it comes down to it."

"You're disgusting," he says and, after a short pause, adds, "You wouldn't be able to eat me before I ate you."

I raise my brows. This conversation has taken a turn, and now I'm not sure what we're talking about. Eating each other or...dropping it is my only course of action here.

He comes back and slides down the wall with a heavy sigh. "I'm going to have to break that door or at least a window at this rate."

I rest my hands on my stomach and count all the industrial screws used to hold this silo together. "Calm down there, Thor. No need to start vandalizing property. This is going to be Wyatt and Avery's suite in a few days."

"There's not even a bed."

"I hadn't noticed." My spine is only stabbing into the concrete below.

He scoffs. "I'm surprised you haven't tried to break a window yet. You were more freaked out than I was earlier."

I shrug one shoulder. "We're taking turns. You've got this round." I yawn deeply. "I'm getting too tired to care." I check my phone for the time again, and it reads: 7:12 p.m. The sky outside doesn't even look all that tired yet. We've probably got another couple hours of light, though muted. "We could tell jokes to pass the time," I suggest.

"I don't joke," he's quick to say.

"Are you too manly for jokes?"

"No," he says flatly, pulling his knees up and resting his forearms on them. "I just don't like them."

"I don't believe you."

He turns to look at me at the same time I angle my head back to look at him. He's upside down to me, but it doesn't make him look all that different, unfortunately.

"And why don't you believe me?"

I stare back at the ceiling when looking at him makes my stomach do too many pirouettes. Believing him hasn't exactly been easy since our last real conversation where he rejected me the day after he told me how excited he was to see me. What kind of evil person has the ability to yo-yo between vastly different feelings like that? I promised myself I wouldn't let him see how much it hurt me. How heartbroken and devastated I really was to know everything I thought and felt was a sham. I've always prided myself on being open and hiding nothing, but what Ronny said *hurt*. He won't get the power to do that again.

I bulldoze those thoughts out of my brain and decide on something much less personal. "One word: snake."

He gives a low laugh. "You started it."

My gaze snaps to his. "Did not! I found it under *my* bed, remember?"

"I never put it there," he says, locking eyes with mine. "Swear."

His gaze turns intense, and it scares me enough to want to turn away. But I don't. He tracks my face, studying other parts of me he used to. There's an indifferent look in his gaze most of the time, except for right now. His features are softer, brows relaxed, and there's a curve to his lips where I'm used to seeing a straight line.

Speaking of lips, I'm sure he will take great satisfaction in the fact my eyes track to his mouth. But if he notices, he doesn't say anything.

With Ronny, there's always been this draw. Like we're somehow the north and south poles of a magnet all at once. Sometimes opposing, but other times...not.

Don't give in.

"You put that snake under my bed," I say, though my voice is only a whisper.

He peers at my lips again before licking his. "I didn't."

My neck is completely exposed—*too exposed*—while lying on my back, head tipped back just enough. There isn't a more uncomfortable position except when Ronny told me we were over. I was standing outside the farmhouse, car door slung open while he leaned against it. It was right before I was leaving to go home after another weekend on the farm when he bombed the world I'd been living in.

I thought we were there together.

I guess not.

Moving my feet after that conversation was like asking Wyatt to shave his beard—impossible. My legs were filled with sand, making lifting and lowering my feet to the pedals difficult, so I pressed down on the gas, speeding all the way home and back to safety. Back to a place where Ronny's rejection couldn't reach me. But it did because I replayed it in my head until I felt physically sick.

We're too different.

We want separate things.

You aren't good enough for me, is all I really heard.

Every emotion rushed through at once, causing me to vibrate with all of them: anger, sadness, relief, embarrassment, murder.

Fine. Not murder. The only one who can push me that far is Vincent Van Goat.

Sure, I'm still attracted to Ronny, and I can tell by the heated way he looks at me that he feels this tie we have, too. But I know things will never go further than this. Never further than hot nights with slick skin and friction...so much friction. We had an expiration date, just like every other guy I'd been with.

It's my brand of curse.

I use a rougher tone this time when I say, "You did."

His eyes narrow. "I swear to you, I didn't."

"And I'm supposed to just accept that it was someone else?" I retort.

"Yes!" he says quickly. "Tilly, back then, after you came to visit me...I didn't mean to hurt you the way I did."

The snake is long forgotten, and I fear we've entered a different kind of gauntlet. The one where we talk about *that day*.

Hot tears fill the backs of my eyes as a tingling sensation climbs my nose. *I will not cry*. Not in front of him. He's taken too many of my tears already because he *did* hurt me.

"I wanted to tell you so badly, but it wasn't...I couldn't..." He rakes rough hands through his hair. "God, I'm not making any sense."

He's not, but it's too late anyway. I look back up at the ceiling, breaking the rickety bridge between us. "Well, it was a long time ago." And trusting the words that come out of his mouth isn't something I do anymore.

He says nothing more, and neither do I.

There aren't any words to say to the guy who helped me build a brick wall around my heart.

Fifteen

Ronny

"When you're dead, you don't breathe, you don't see, you don't feel, you don't love." —Snoop Dogg

F inally," I murmur as headlights shine through the windows. "Someone's here."

She pushes to stand as I hop off the floor, a renewed spring in my step, and rush to the door. If I need to start pounding, wave my hands in the air, or remove an article of clothing just to get their attention, I will.

I'll have to save it for the next time I get stuck in a cabin with Tilly for three hours since Mariella gets out of her golf cart and strides to the door. She's no longer in a hurry at all, but I am. Spending more time in this cabin would break me.

There have been too many near misses. The last time I came out of the bathroom, Till had been lying on her stomach, and the slight curve of her ass and toned thighs was the final straw. Even my thumbnail stabbing into my palm wasn't helping.

Tilly materializes beside me while Mariella waves and punches in the code we forgot. It works, and she goes to push it open, but I'm already pulling.

"Thank God," Tilly says under her breath, gripping the side of the door frame.

"What are you two still doing here?" She looks between us. I look at us. Tilly's hair is askew from rolling around on the ground like a bonafide temptress, and I raked my fingers through my hair enough times, I'm sure it looks like I was electrocuted. She glances behind us to see if a bed somehow materialized. I wouldn't need a bed to muss Tilly's hair like that. "You two weren't..."

"No!" I bark abruptly. "We got locked in here right after you left and couldn't get out. All of the windows were sealed shut—"

"Yeah, they don't open," Mariella says with a wince. "Sorry about that."

Since when do windows not open?

Tilly crosses her arms. "We figured that out."

"And there was no other way out," I finish saying. "The keypad must lock from the outside."

"We're still working out the kinks. At least you helped us figure that one out!"

Mariella takes us back to my truck in her golf cart where she apologizes again and says something about things happening for a reason. I didn't hear her all the way since I was too busy starting up my truck so we could get the hell out of there. The horses need to be let out.

I need to be let out.

The ride back to the farm is a quiet one. Neither of us had much to say after everything that *was* said—or almost said. I felt like a mumbling idiot. Add that to the fact I was hungry and tired for more than just food, and I needed a shower and the familiar coolness of my bed sheets to put this experience behind me. My bed is going to feel a hell of a lot more empty tonight though after spending hours with Tilly.

Thirty minutes later, I pull up to the barn at Adler Farms, and Tilly jolts awake.

"Don't take me!" she screams.

I conceal a laugh and speak in a hushed voice. "It's late, but I didn't want to wake you. I still have to get the horses out. I'll unhitch the trailer afterward, and you can drive my truck back to your cabin. I'll pick it up tomorrow."

There's a slightly wet sheen on her lips from her drool, but she swipes it away and arches her back in a stretch.

I tear my gaze from her before my blood turns molten. "Sound good?"

"Fine, I guess." She yawns and settles deeper into the seat.

Hightailing it out of the cab, I trudge toward the trailer with heavy feet.

Tilly is the most vibrant person I know, but I've noticed that light dim a little. Hearing her put into words—or close to it—how much it crushed her and how she doesn't trust me made me rethink my jackassery. It's not like I needed confirmation. It's just going to make what I have to say even harder. I should have gone about everything differently. When I told her we would never work, it was brash because I didn't want to leave any hope. That's a dangerous thing in the hands of a woman who was two squeezes away from owning your heart.

But, damn it, I hate that I hurt her.

I hate she doesn't trust me.

I hate that we can't stand being around each other.

I hate that our best friends are getting married, and we're not.

And if I don't hurry up and get these horses unloaded and get into a shower before bed, I'm going to fall asleep while standing up, which is never a good look. I'm not used to going to bed past nine since I wake up before the sun, and worrying isn't going to change the past.

One horse, two horse, black horse, blue horse.

No blue horse. That's just the flickering light outside the barn acting up again and making our all-black mare named Black Beauty look like she has blue highlights.

Settling the four horses into each stall I readied for them, I check their water and hay before locking up for the night. The barn doors slide together with a thud, barely audible over the truck's engine still going so Tilly can stay warm in the cab.

I hate that I care so much.

I grunt while unhitching the trailer from the truck. I'll need to move it again tomorrow, but I'll do that when there's more light, and I can properly back it beside the barn without screaming expletives as a lullaby for the animals. My sweat-stiff clothes chafe along my ribs, and my mouth is so dry, thanks to my truck's idling exhaust, I'm craving water.

I'm so close to being done. Tilly can be on her way, and I'll be one step closer to sleep. Maybe it'll give me the perspective I need for how I tell Tilly everything.

But by the time I open the driver's side door again to give Tilly proper instructions for driving Gertrude, the cab is completely empty.

She's gone.

***

"YOU WERE SUPPOSED to stay in the truck."

I'm seething. Jaw clenched, hands fisted at my sides like I mean to do something with them. Maybe I do. This woman makes me want to punch a hole through my own damn wall.

My breathing is erratic after taking the outdoor steps along the side of the barn two at a time. She looks up from behind my fridge, as in the one in *my* studio apartment.

"I was hungry. Again."

Her words are muffled behind the bite of a banana she's currently chewing, the bulk of it pressing into her cheek. My words are even more clipped. "You could have been home by now, eating your own food."

"But you have bananas. I don't."

Steam is probably wafting off me. She's preventing me from becoming one with my pillow. "Then buy some of your own."

She shuts the fridge door, holding her half-eaten banana in one hand while the other rests on her hip—

Wait a minute.

I point at her bottom half. "Are those my sweatpants?"

She looks down, then back up to meet my heated gaze like it's akin to an ice bath, not an inferno. "My legs were cold, and I've been wearing jean shorts and that giant belt buckle all day, thanks to you."

"How is that my fault?"

"I don't know!" she yells. "It just is."

The space up here is small, but now, the few pictures on the walls, the white cabinets, and the minimal furniture are all closing in on me.

I peer over at my bed, where she decided to discard her shorts.

I shake my head. "So you just thought you'd put on my sweatpants?" Those are *mine*. The same pair I wear every single night. It gets drafty in this loft sometimes, and I like how loose they are while still perfectly snug on my waist after years of wear. I was planning to come up here and put them on.

"I'll take them off when I go."

"You're going *now*." I might already be sleep walking.

She takes a bite, eyes on me.

I watch.

She chews.

I keep watching.

She takes another bite of her banana—*my* banana. "I will after I finish this."

I shift awkwardly on my feet, facing the kitchen in my four-hundred-square-foot barn loft apartment. The bed, two chairs, and barstools pushed against the kitchen counter are all visible at once, no matter where I stand.

She takes another slow bite.

I swear she's doing this on purpose.

"Almost done?" I ask through gritted teeth.

"Nope."

My jaw stays clamped while I look at the ceiling before announcing, "I'm going to shower."

I leave her standing in my kitchen, eating a banana, while I storm off toward the only place in this loft with a door and some privacy. But Gwen Stefani might as well be singing directly into my head:

B-A-N-A-N-A-S.

Sixteen

Ronny

"It's hard to say goodbye to the streets. It's all how you do it." —Snoop Dogg

I'm out of the bathroom, and her banana is no longer in her hand. I just hope she had the good sense to put the peel in the compost bin, not the trash.

However, she's now sitting on my side of the bed, feet kicked up and crossed at the ankles, reading the book on my nightstand. "You're into some weird shit," she says with a whistle. "Dragons. Really?"

I stare longingly at my sweatpants on her body. It's a good thing my dresser is in the bathroom for easy access to the rest of my clothes. The area is probably the biggest space, and for purely practical reasons, I keep my clothes in there and was able to throw on some joggers. Second only to my sweats.

"It's called fantasy."

"Yeah it is," she mumbles, thumbing pages.

I roll my eyes, using the towel to dry my hair.

"Nice lamp, by the way." She sets my book down and jabs a thumb toward my nightstand. "Did you kill it?"

I side-eye the lamp in question. Three elk legs, cut off below the knee, are propped tent style and hog-tied together with a lampshade to finish it off. The hooves provide solid footing for the lamp to stay upright...literally.

"I found it."

She rolls her lips in before asking, "Where?"

"A store in town." My response is bland, hoping I'll bore her enough to leave.

"Did you pay money for it?"

"Yes."

"Why?"

I lob a question at her. "Do you have to ask so many questions?"

"Yes, you know that."

"Do I?" I have her exactly where I want her.

Kind of.

Where I really want her is pressed against my—

"I thought you were going to say it was a family heirloom," she says before my thoughts run off like wild horses.

I aim for the laundry hamper by the bathroom, throwing my towel in and making it. "I don't have enough family to have heirlooms."

The loft is quiet as she absorbs my words. They weren't manufactured for our back-and-forth but rather conjured from the slight ache I've lived with and always will. The one that was dredged up this afternoon when Tilly went snooping.

There isn't a day that goes by that I don't think about my birth parents. Mama and Pop are my parents in every way, but that doesn't mean I'm not keenly aware my life wasn't supposed to be this. I just don't know anything different. Maybe that's why I've always lived with that pang in my chest because it's more of a longing to understand—belong.

She tucks her legs beneath her, shifting to sit on her heels. The sincere look in her expression almost appears real. "You have Merv and Esther."

"I know," I say, barely audible.

"Do you ever think about them? Your birth parents?"

Them didn't need an explanation. The stories I've come up with over the years just to explain why I'm here and not...wherever they are, are equal to pi—not the strawberry rhubarb kind.

My knee-jerk reaction is to say *no*, but something about Tilly, this moment, my exhaustion, and seeing her in my sweatpants on my bed makes me feel a tug to say *yes*. But the words are stuck in my throat, so I nod and stare at the ground.

"It's okay that you think about them. It's normal to wonder," she says. "I know it's different, but I still dream about what my life would be like if my parents were together."

Being locked in the silo really did us in, apparently. It's been more talking than we've done in a long time. But it's still not enough. It's not all of the talking I need to do.

A part of my heart constricts at the thought of having someone like her to come home to every day. To share the things that are unshareable in most company. Even just this sliver is enough to crave the whole thing. I want to stay here a bit longer.

"Do you ever feel guilty?" I ask. "For thinking about it."

"Sometimes," she replies. "But then I realize it's just how I'm working through it. If you don't understand what you lost, I don't think you can fully appreciate what you have."

The words hit with a thud in my chest, releasing a sigh I must have been keeping pent up for years now. Two, to be exact. I needed her words, if only to remind me being adopted isn't the sum of who I am now. But maybe it's time to start accepting that piece of me, especially if someone like Tilly can.

Looking up at her, I study the parts of her face that aren't shadowed by the dim, hoofed lamplight in my room. The pout of her lips even when they're closed and the endless expanse of her dark irises. They climb every part of my body without ever leaving my face. The deep tone of her skin is darker thanks to the summer sun. But the lighter tone beneath her askew tank top strap makes me think she's lived in that one shirt all summer. Are there more tan lines on the rest of her body? What about under my sweats? She's a little unkempt after nearly four hours locked in that cabin, and maybe that's why she still looks hungry. Starving, actually.

This is the Tilly that grabbed my attention after the first few seconds of meeting her. I couldn't keep my eyes off her then, and I'm struggling to do it now.

I *have* to tell her.

But I can't when she isn't hating me. I want to live here for a minute and remember what I fall asleep thinking about sometimes. There was a time, a place, a summer when she liked me.

She unfurls her legs and stands up from the bed, crossing her arms like she's trying to hide. She's never been very good at that, though. "Why are you looking at me like that?"

I blink rapidly but keep my eyes on her. "Like what?"

"Like…" Her voice trails off.

She chews on her bottom lip, and it's then I feel it. A dangerously strong urge to be the one to sink my teeth into that full lip of hers. My voice is gravelly when I ask again, "Like what?"

She steps closer to the front door like she's going to make a quick escape, and her back presses against the smooth maple finish. My hands have been on every inch of this apartment loft as I renovated it, just like they've been on every inch of her. The overwhelming desire to flatten my palms on either side of Tilly, box her in, and remind her of all the ways we worked and forgetting why we didn't, become unbearable.

Lessons from my mistake last summer be damned.

I'd kiss her roughly the way she likes, the way I like. I'd gather her body to fuse with mine. I'd hold her long enough to remember, but not nearly as long as I'd like.

She has one hand on the door handle—a warning. "Like you did. Before."

My hands flex at my sides, and I repeat, "Before."

Before I broke it off.

Before I told her she wasn't right for me.

Before I walked away and didn't look back.

Before I shut her out completely. It's what I do. It's what I've always done—or tried to do—to focus, find purpose, move on from the past that still haunts me.

It's never been about not being able to stand Tilly. Sure, it's what I made her think, but it's not the truth. No, the truth is that it terrified me she'd wake up one day and realize she hated this life—hated me. I wouldn't be able to watch her leave first for reasons I couldn't control.

I don't hate Tilly.

I've just always hated the thought of her walking away.

But maybe I can avoid that. Instead of promising her marriage and forever when I don't know what that looks like yet, maybe this could just be what it was *before*. It could be a summer fling, something short-term that has an end date. We were good once. We could be good again. We don't have to remember all the ways I fucked up. We could just forget. Maybe this could help us.

My damn feet take a step closer until we're toe-to-toe. "Like this?"

Her throat moves as she swallows. "Like that."

She drops her hand from the door handle, so I lift mine and place it on the doorframe beside her head. "How about now?" I whisper.

Her chest rises slightly, and I'm close enough now that I can feel her breath on my face as she stares up at me. Both of her hands are trapped behind her back, but she doesn't move. She stays exactly where she is, as if posing for a still life. A picture I want to handle and study, touch, commit to memory.

"Just the same. You look like you want to kiss me," she finally says without blinking.

Her gaze drops briefly to my lips, and it's enough to stir my blood, light it on fire with moonshine and a match. "I want to do more than that."

"More?" she asks.

"Yeah." I lean closer until my lips hover near her ear. "Like the things you enjoy."

Still, she doesn't move. "What things?"

A laugh rumbles out of me. "So many damn questions."

She lets out a small exhale. "We don't do that."

"But we could. Just tonight," I say through a rough voice.

I pull back slightly, but the scent of that perfume she likes, which I can never remember the name of, pulls me back down. Angel this or number that, I have no idea what it's called, but it forces me closer again. To run my nose along her jawline and inhale the fresh lemon and lavender of her.

I slide my hand from the frame, following one finger across the strap on her shoulder, down her arm, and then her waist before hunting for every dive and swell of her stomach. She inhales slightly, making me dip my head lower to catch all of her sounds like butter-flies in a net. "This."

"Mhm," she mumbles. "And?"

I move my finger up her stomach, between her breasts, and up to her collarbone. "This."

She doesn't say a word, trailing my fingers back down again and skimming my lips over the pulse at the top of her neck.

A small gasp leaves her mouth, and then her hands are gripping the front of my shirt. I hold my palms up like she's got a gun to my chest instead of fistfuls of my T-shirt. Seconds pulse between us, our eyes locking while she asks even more questions without saying a word.

Her lips are in a hard line when she grinds out, "I hate all of those things."

The corner of her mouth twitches. I know she's lying, but I have enough will to risk grabbing either side of her waist and hauling her closer to me. "No, you don't."

It's not enough to have her like this. So close, but not quite enough. There's a reason we fell into bed with each other the first day we met. With her, it's always been easy to get here. My body wants hers, and the way she's practically trembling from restrained want, tells me all I need to know. I'm already hard inside my joggers, the throb unbearable knowing she'd know exactly how to fix that.

"You're right, I don't," she says then yanks me around, pivoting us so the door is at my back, and she's kissing me.

It's rough and wet, our mouths open wide like we're consuming one another. Tongues and lips collide in a fierce battle of wanting. My vision starts to spin behind my closed eyes, but all I care about is stifling every sound she makes with my mouth, eating them up before they ever pass her lips. I grab her ample ass I've been staring at all night and haul her up enough so she has to stand on her toes. She releases my shirt and rakes rough fingernails through my hair.

Her breasts press close to my chest in a deliberate and familiar way that makes me want to rip her tank off and explore them. Are they the same? Different? I swear I can't remember. I have to know. I *need* to.

I walk her backward and flip us until she's pinned against the wall beside the door. Her mouth pulls away from mine, and I waste no time kissing down her neck, tasting her sweet scent on my tongue and lapping it up like the Tilly-dehydrated man I am.

Her hands are still woven in my hair at the base of my neck, pulling me closer and breathing hard against my temple. "This...happens...once," she manages through her panting.

"Once." I nod as my lips devour the dip of her collarbone.

"Once."

I rub my erection into her, and she pushes back like this is a game of toss.

She looks at me through a haze of lust. "I still hate you."

I keep pressing into her, satisfied by the way her hips buck and search for purchase. "I know," I say. "But you don't hate *this*."

Her breathing is erratic. "You're right; I don't."

It's a wonder those two words don't make me come right here.

You're right.

Seventeen

Tilly

"If you stop at general math, you're only going to make general math money." —Snoop Dogg

I haven't forgotten how he tastes.

It's nostalgic in the same way he sounds and how he responds to my touch.

I flatten my hands on his chest and push him backward like a lineman would, not a petite woman who doesn't crest his shoulders without my heels.

His shins hit the side of the couch, and he instinctively circles an arm around my waist. If he's going down, he's clearly taking me with him. I only wriggle my hips and roughly kiss him to approve this message.

He rights himself, then dips his fingers in the waistband of my—*his*—sweatpants. "Did you wear these for me?" he murmurs against my lips.

"No." I give him a peck, and he throws me a coy grin. "I wore these for me."

His finger slides back and forth. "Headstrong woman."

"They're comfortable," I add, muscles tensing with each swipe.

"I know."

Stumbling slightly, he grabs the back of the couch while keeping me close to his chest, and we continue taking all the kisses we haven't had for too long. His hand slides easily down the back of my pants, getting a handful of my bare ass.

I whimper and tug him closer, pulling him away from the couch, or at least trying to, when he rams into the coffee table. "Damn it!" he yells when he hits the metal leg. He yanks his hand out of my pants.

I stop kissing him, panting hard. "You good?"

My skin feels flushed, and if his hair indicates how mine looks, I'm sure it's standing up after he raked his fingers through it.

He doesn't let me go. "I'm fine."

"Good." I cradle his face and place a lingering kiss on the corner of his mouth. One that makes me all too aware of how hard he feels against my stomach.

I've missed this—the crazed moments of getting caught up—the way he knows his way around my body already. This is what I needed.

Without wanting to take a chance on another injury, or because he likes the stability the wall provides like I do, he walks me backward again with a wide stance to keep us balanced. My back connects to the firm surface, and a breath rushes out of me. His mouth finds mine immediately. The feel of his pliable lips on mine and the way our tongues tangle mercilessly is the most heady feeling I've experienced in a long time.

This is who we were.

And I never forgot that regardless of how hard I tried. Maybe it didn't get this far last year because he didn't kiss me in the privacy of his loft like he is now.

I twirl us around and shove him into the wall. His back hits with a thud, but this time, the one framed picture beside him falls off its hook, crashing to the ground. Neither of us cares enough to look. No glass shatters, only plastic cracks on the floor.

His shoulder blades press together, and he winces. I remember just how rough we can be. He'll have bruises tomorrow. I'm counting on it. I want his body to be marked by me if only to prove this really happened.

"Take your shirt off," I demand, lifting at the hem.

He snatches it back from me and takes his time, slowing everything down to a crawl while I'm ready to press my foot down on the accelerator. He fingers the neckline of his shirt just behind his neck and pulls it off. My hands are on him before he can even get it over his head, exploring all the places he's worked hard to maintain.

"Where did these come from?" I ask, kissing his pec.

He's breathing hard. "What do you mean?"

I trace his stomach muscles, and they instinctively flex. "The biceps, forearms," I swat his midsection with the back of my hand, "the abs. They've multiplied."

He grumbles. "From manual labor and long days, stepping up and down tractors and carrying salt licks like medicine balls. You know, cowboy shit."

My hands are greedy to hold all of him at once. "Cowboy shit."

He snatches my hands as they wander the plains of his broad chest. "Your turn," he says. "Take your shirt off."

I comb my fingers through the curls of hair on his chest, then follow them with my mouth, mumbling against his skin, "You take it off."

He suddenly grabs behind my neck and lower back and flips us around until I'm pressed against the wall once more. My moan is loud, and he devours me, kissing and sucking on my bottom lip as he drags his hands down my sides, his calloused hands scraping the exposed parts of my skin in a potent way.

Reaching the edge of my tank, he pulls up, managing to get it over my head, then realizes, staring at my chest..."You took your bra off?"

"I was never wearing one."

He swallows, and I push my chest out, itching for him to touch me. "All day?" he asks.

I shrug a shoulder. "It has a built-in one."

All of my exposed skin makes his mouth fall open. He can't manage many words, though he tries. "But this...you..."

I loop a hand around his neck and pull him to my mouth. He willingly comes but takes a handful of my breast with him. Our skin this close, this warm, and nothing between us, I feel so much of him. The way his stomach contracts with heavy breaths against mine, how his thigh feels straddled between my legs as he pistons his hips, and how taut my nipples feel, grazing his chest. It's all provoking me to a brink I can't see or stop myself from barreling over. I don't think about anything that got us here, only that we are.

I don't think about last summer when he kissed me, and I pushed him away.

I don't think about the wedding this weekend, or our best friends.

I don't think about how we aren't right for each other.

I don't think. At all.

I just *am*.

He pulls me off the wall but keeps me tight against him as he walks us toward the bed. I'm too focused on kissing his bottom lip to walk, so with a huff, he nips at my lips, grabs behind my thighs, and lifts. My legs wrap around his waist, arms circling his neck, and I bite the top of his shoulder.

He yelps and pauses halfway to his destination. "You bit me."

"You bit my lip first."

He can't seem to keep his eyes up. "Not as hard."

"How would you know?" I ask. "It hurt."

He flattens me to him, pressing light, forgiving kisses across the swell and dip of the top portions of my breasts that he can reach. I arch my back, forgetting what day it is, where I'm at, what happened earlier, two years ago, or even five minutes ago that led to this.

He lightly drags his teeth across my chest. "You like it when I use my teeth."

I throw my head back, and my moans tell him how much.

While he kisses every part of my neck that his tongue can reach, I say, "Lay down. Right there."

He looks where I'm pointing: the middle of the bed. Without wasting another second, he tosses me to that exact spot. I scream in shock while flailing back on the bed. "What the hell?" He scans my face in the dim light, second-guessing the decision to toss me until my hands go straight for the waistline of my sweats. Or his. I can't decide if I'm giving them back yet. "You were supposed to lay down first," I bark. "Get over here."

He smirks. "Why?"

"Because. I was going to take your pants off first. But if you're offering." I wiggle the waistband so he can see the edge of my bright blue underwear.

"Wait." He stands beside the bed and points at my hands, fisting the sweats. "Don't you dare take those off."

I look at where he's pointing. "And why not? I know you're not shy, Ronny. No need to pretend when I know exactly what you're capable of."

"I'm not—" He swallows, rubbing the underside of his chin. "Just don't take those sweats off."

"Is it because they look better on me?" I ask with a devilish smile.

He doesn't deny it. "Because I'm going to do it."

"Just get over here."

"Yes, ma'am," he drawls.

I scowl, but it doesn't deter him.

He might like risking his life.

Eighteen

Ronny

"When I'm no longer rapping, I want to open up an ice cream parlor and call myself Scoop Dogg." —Snoop Dogg

I don't know how much more of this I can take.

I'm so damn thirsty and hungry; I want to tear every stitch of clothing from her body and lap her up like the mirage in my desert.

She drags her hands up her stomach and over her breasts, touching herself in all of the places I was going to.

I grunt and bite the insides of my cheeks until it hurts. "Keep doing that." Then, I shove down my pants until they're at my ankles, her eyes glued to where I'm straining against my briefs. I've never felt this hard in my life. I want to simultaneously do something about it while also living in this in-between so it never ends.

Tilly doesn't know, and will never know, that there hasn't been anyone else. She isn't a woman I could just get over, especially when I saw her enough weekends throughout the year when she visited Avery. She was always right in front of me but never in reach. Even with handfuls of her now, she could easily slip away.

Her fingers move in rhythmic circles around her pert nipples, then she drags them down and up her stomach again as she watches me watch her. "Like this?"

I can't even speak to confirm or deny. I'm just moving closer, placing flat hands on the bed, crawling over until I'm hovering beside her body so I don't crush her. There are so few clothes between us, and I kiss her like

I won't get another meal. And in truth, I won't. This is only happening once. Tonight is all we get.

I'm painting a mural on the side of her hip, stomach, chest, and collarbone with my hand and fingers, dipping under her curves to memorize their shape. I trace where our lips connect and press myself further into her leg, the thrum of my erection desperate to feel her. Be near her—in her.

I've been in this woman's bed before, and I wasn't just blowing smoke when I said I knew what she liked. She doesn't want to go slow or hear long lists of compliments. She wants rough and disheveled, rumpled, and a little wild.

We roll slightly, and my belt buckle on her discarded shorts makes a clinking sound.

I reach and hold them up while kissing her collarbone. "I want this back."

"No." She digs her nails into my back. "Those shorts won't fit you anyway."

I toss them aside, forgetting they even exist. Her body is warm and lithe as I prop myself on my elbows above her. She only grips my hips harder, rolling my weight fully over her.

"I haven't slept with anyone since...us," she whispers, fingers now digging into my ass as my hips rock slowly.

Her words are a slow drip as I replay them in my mind. She hasn't slept with anyone, either?

Two whole fucking years.

My face is only inches from hers, but it's close enough to see how her breathing slows. Her eyes dart between mine, likely trying to gauge what I'm thinking.

Should I tell her I haven't slept with anyone in just as long? Haven't thought of anyone like I've thought of her? It feels like I'd be admitting more, revealing to her that no one could compare to her. It's true. No one has. But once I say it, I can't take those words back.

My mouth opens, ready to say it. "I—"

Someone knocks on the door, and we startle. "Ronny?"

It's Pop. "Just a minute."

I scramble off Tilly like a teenager hiding a girl in my room and toss her the shirt she was wearing until a few minutes ago. She quickly puts it on, the sweats hanging low on her hips, her nipples pushing through the fabric, making me angry over the interruption. My shirt goes on after I slip my joggers up my thighs and needy dick, which I do my best to hide before stepping toward the door.

My breathing is erratic, so I take a minute to calm down, then open the front door a crack. "Pop."

"Ronny."

The stream of light escaping my loft highlights his body, so I flick the porch light on, and he comes into full view. "Did you need some-thing?" I pat down my hair with one hand when I see his eyes track up.

"Saw your truck out front, but you forgot to turn it off."

Shit. I can't believe I forgot about my truck. The plan was to come up here and fetch Tilly. What I wasn't planning on was...everything that came after that.

"I, uh—"

"Ronny kept it running since I had to use the bathroom." Tilly steps closer to the door, forcing me to open it further. I glance down at her tank, expecting to see how turned on she is, like my swollen dick I'm hiding behind the door. But instead, she's wearing one of my favorite blue and black flannel shirts she found and her shorts. How the hell did she have enough time to change out of my sweats? "Thanks again for letting me use your bathroom," she adds, smiling at me.

I don't know what my expression is, but it sure as hell doesn't wear a smile.

"Hi, Tilly," Pop says with a nod and grin. "Do you want me to drive you back?"

We both glance at each other in the second it takes before I say, "I'll take her. I was already planning to."

Pop looks between us. "Right. Then I'll head to bed. Be safe out there." He turns to walk down the steps he helped me design, holding onto the guardrail. "Be safe in there, too," he adds, though I'm sure he doesn't know I can hear him.

I close my eyes briefly, then wave a hand for Tilly to exit first. She passes in front of me, but I don't bother moving since I want to smell her again. We didn't have enough time for her scent to be permanently stained on my sheets, and I won't hide how ticked that makes me.

"That's my flannel." I don't mean for my words to come out so gruff, but they do. Our one night was supposed to be a full night. I didn't even get to do a quarter of the things I had worked up in my head.

"Easy, cowboy." She pats my shoulder, giving me a wary look. "Might need to deal with that *hard* problem of yours later tonight."

"I plan to," I snap back before realizing the admission. I try to channel a softer tone than how I feel right now. "I need to get my shoes. I'll meet you down at the truck."

"See you in a minute," she says, already walking out my door. "And thanks for the flannel."

My jaw gnashes together. "You're only borrowing it."

"Sure," she adds over her shoulder, descending the steps. "Whatever you say."

Nineteen

Tilly

"Hip-hop is what makes the world go around." —Snoop Dogg

I woke up like I have every other morning.

Except this one was different. There was a man in my bed. And not just any man. The one who told me we'd never be more than sex and is currently taking up half of my mattress and making every one of those painful statements real.

If only the actual sex had happened.

But it didn't.

By the time Ronny pulled up in front of my house, ready to drop me off and say goodnight, his truck died. After idling for a long enough time, *Gertrude* decided she was tired and ready to go to bed. Instead of walking back or looking for a jump from Wyatt so late when the farmhouse lights were clearly off, I offered him my couch.

To which he replied, "I'm sleeping in the bed."

I didn't argue because I suspected that might be some indication he wanted to pick up where we left off. But the man was a freaking saint the whole time I brushed my teeth and hair, changed into my tank and favorite satin shorts that give a little extra cheek, and slipped under the covers. I thought it was a little odd he stayed quiet the entire time, but it's because he was already passed out with his arm slung above his head.

Whatever.

I'm not *that* upset.

We just wasted our one night together, and hell if I'll agree to a rain check now that the morning sun is peeking through the old blinds in my cabin. It's amazing what a new day can bring: clarity.

In hindsight, it's best that we keep things as platonic as possible. Sex would only complicate things further, kind of like the kiss last summer, which involved far less hands than last night. This was not that. I couldn't see past the haze he put my head in when he did things to me I can barely think of today without breaking out into a full body flush.

What was I thinking?

Even making out topless on his bed was too far. When his hands dove into the back of my sweatpants like a torpedo and his heated gaze tattooed the word *mine* all over my body, I swear I wouldn't be able to stop for anything. Turns out his Pop's interruption was enough to do it.

But as I was climbing off the bed to change into my shorts again, I saw something poking out from under the bed: a pink feather boa. There's nothing else in Ronny's apartment even remotely feminine. It was so out of place. Is he sleeping with someone? He never got the chance to say anything else when I told him I hadn't been in anyone else's bed. Maybe he has. Or maybe she's been in his.

Oh no. Did he make out with her on his bed, too? Is she hot? Do they go on ice cream dates in town and cuddle up on his couch to watch his favorite Marvel movies? Maybe she lives on another farm, growing beets and tending...bees. She probably bottles and sells her own honey down at the farmers market and spends her hard earned money on flour to make fresh biscuits for Ronny that won't break his teeth. She knows how to cook, likes cleaning, doesn't mind walking in poop all day, and uses coconut milk to wash her hair.

She's perfect.

She's perfect for *him*.

I can't explain it, but I've always felt this deeper inclination there was someone else; he just wouldn't tell me about her. Ronny is like a bullet-proof security safe that requires facial recognition and a thumbprint scan to get into, so it isn't unbelievable that he wouldn't mention another woman he was in love with. He's definitely more of a player than anyone else I've ever dated. Granny and Wyatt have said as much.

Shit. Is she his lover? Or wait...am I?

I roll over to my side, facing away from him and looking around the room. The accommodations here are modest and nothing like my small house back home. For starters, my room has a hot pink accent wall, while these ones are varying shades of neutral white. It feels sterile and foreign when all I really want is the comfort of my neon palm tree light hanging in my room.

I have to get out of here.

This minimalist space is starting to close in on me and point a shaming finger at how screwed I am for kissing him last night. His girlfriend likely owns a shotgun, or she'll just sick her bee colony on me. Why did I do that? After raising every reason I'm angry at him for how blatantly he rejected me, and I still took my top off.

AND WHAT ABOUT THE FEATHER BOA?

Sliding out from beneath the beige three-hundred thread count sheets, I pad softly across the cold floors toward the door, grabbing Ronny's flannel shirt I stole (a.k.a. *borrowed*). I open the door slowly, but the damn hinges are louder than an Elk's mating call. I only know that because I can't stop watching videos of the Elk in Yellowstone, who's about as desperate as me to find someone to love—or fuck—him.

Ronny is still asleep when I peer back at the bed. His arm now slung over his chest, and the sheets are draped over his legs and waist, leaving nothing to the imagination. He's so infuriatingly *hot*, I want to punch him and jump on him.

Nothing makes sense.

Finally, I slip out of the room and walk swiftly on my toes to the living room, deeply exhaling when I don't hear any noises following me. He's asleep. But that doesn't stop the memory of last night from waltzing into my mind and asking me to dance again. His hands, the shadow of stubble along his jaw, and those damn hips of his are all ingrained in my mind in ways I won't be able to forget. But I also have to.

I have to because I can't let him back in.

I won't be the other woman.

I can't get hurt like that again.

We can't do any of *that*, or more. Or even less. God, what's wrong with me?

I'm well past over my head with this one. I just want to pretend this never happened and move on with the rest of the week until I can get home and slide between my purple silk sheets. Ronny will be my past again, and I can move on with my life, doing other people's hair until mine turns gray.

The urge to pack up all my things and leave now comes and goes, but I can't stay in this cabin, sharing air with him. What happens when he wakes up? I'm not about to stay and find out.

The tank and shorts I'm wearing aren't going to be a viable option outside of this space, so I push my arms through the flannel shirt sleeves and start buttoning. It hits mid-thigh, and while it's not the raciest thing I've ever worn, I'm sure it will raise some eyebrows if anyone sees me. Which means no one can see me. I just need to get to the farmhouse so I can borrow some clothes from Avery and return to this cabin when Ronny has vacated.

Sneaking closer to the front door, I make sure my steps are lighter than a fox. The sun practically stabs me in the eyes as I quietly step onto the porch and shut the door behind me, forcing me to blink several times until I'm convinced the sun isn't attacking me. The wood grain porch under my bare feet promises slivers with one wrong move, but the gravel of the driveway is even more unforgiving as I make it off the last step.

"Shit! Ouch. Ow!"

If Ronny didn't have some kind of hold on me, I wouldn't have to sneak out of my own cabin at some ungodly hour of the morning to seek shelter and a place to hide.

Just make it there without being seen, I tell myself.

"Ah!" I yell after a jagged rock stabs the sole of my foot and the soul in my body.

I wince with every step, and my knees buckle with every other one. It's like walking over coals, except they aren't hot, just I-have-the-power-to-bring-you-to-your-knees sharp. I'm clutching the flannel at my chest with one hand and staring down at the ground to make sure I don't make a wrong turn and end up with a rock piercing through the soft flesh of my pinky toe.

I don't notice the woman's voice until it's too late, and she says, "Tilly?"

I stop moving. And breathing.

"What are you...wearing?" Of course Wyatt's sister would be galavanting around at this hour, and if I had looked at a clock, I would have known what hour that was.

I've learned that people will respond to my confidence in a situation. If I act like walking across rocks barefoot in the man's shirt you're supposed to hate at a time when roosters haven't crowed—*did they*?—is normal, it will be. So, I stand straighter and paw at the front of my shirt. "Stace, hi. Um, this is my new flannel. Isn't it great? It's so comfortable, too," I say. "Here, feel it."

I navigate over the rocks with minimal wincing for her to cop a feel. She raises her brows while touching the soft blue and black patchwork. "I guess it's pretty nice, but I've just never seen you wear flannel. I thought you said you hated it?"

"What? No!" I chuckle loudly. "Did I say that? I love flannel. It's so...stylish. I just got it."

"Uh-huh." She appraises me before leaning closer like she's sharing a secret. "Are you wearing any pants?"

"Shorts." I hurriedly lift the flannel. "See, I'm wearing shorts."

She nods slowly, probably because they barely pass for that, and then shakes her head. "We just got here last night and are staying in cabin two right next to you."

Lovely. "Oh, that's great!"

It's not that great.

Did they already see Ronny? Does she know he's in my cabin?

She shrugs. "I know it's silly to be staying in one since we only live fifteen minutes away, but for the sake of old times, we thought it would be fun. It's what Gramps built them for, so why not?"

Gramps. The legacy holder of Thirst Trapp Farms. Well, before it was *Thirst* Trapp Farms, anyway. "I'm sure it means everything to Wyatt to have you all here to celebrate with them." I run my fingers up the buttons to ensure I didn't miss one.

Her lips curve, and she starts walking backward. "By the way...have you seen Ronny? I see his truck, but I haven't been able to find him. I need to ask about the dance floor being delivered later today."

My bones turn to ice and melt right out of me. "Nope. Haven't seen him." Blatantly lying has never been my thing, but in this situation, telling her the truth is not going to happen. *He's in my bed* doesn't have multiple meanings even if I tried explaining. I'd just make it worse.

I go for something more subtle. "Maybe try the goat pen. He likes them."

Maybe not so subtle.

I hate those little conniving creatures. And I'm supposed to teach goat yoga as an official bridal party event. I'll do it, but I won't like it.

"Good idea." She wags a finger and heads in that direction.

"Bye!" I release a breath before it chokes me once I'm well past her and have a chance to think about what was just said.

I just got it?

Feel it?

I can't believe I said any of those things. But at least she bought it.

Finally, I reach the first step on the porch when a male voice stops me. "Is that you, Tilly?"

No, it's your other fiancée's best friend who also slept with—next to!—your best friend and possibly regrets it, but maybe not because it was pretty fantastic falling asleep with—next!—to each other.

I brush the hair out of my face and peer up at Wyatt, who must have just come out of the farmhouse. "Yes."

He looks at me. I look at him. "Okay..." he says, drawing out the word. "Is that yours?"

I clutch the flannel. "Yeah, why?"

"I could have sworn Ronny had one similar."

My blood turns to ash. "Nope. This is mine." Not a lie, since I'm keeping it, but not the whole truth, either. If he gets any closer, he'll smell Ronny all over this shirt. I don't smell like freshly cut grass and dirt. I'm the homemade floral soap you buy on Etsy. The kind with pieces of flowers stuck in it for a little extra grit for exfoliation.

He eyes me suspiciously. I strike a pose, hoping I don't flash an eager butt cheek.

"I'm gonna go to the horse barn now," he says slowly. "Are you doing alright?"

My smile is saccharine when I reply with, "Peachy."

He strides down the porch steps, acting like I'm the Loch Ness monster. "I'll see you later then."

I throw him an exaggerated thumbs up, my mouth in a freeze-tag position until I'm facing the farmhouse again. I can't keep having run-ins like this where I have to pretend everything is alright. I'm going to crack eventually. There's a grown cowboy with a happy trail and muscles in my bed right now!

Relief aches in my feet after getting off those rocks. I peer behind me just in case there are any more surprise visitors. I really should have checked what time it was before planning my great escape, I might know where and what everyone was doing right now, but I didn't. I free-balled that breakout with zero thought.

The screen door, being held together by zip ties and years of love, creeks as I push open the always unlocked front door. A large moose head looms above the small entryway—*Moosifer,* as Avery calls him. A cross between Lucifer and a moose. I wasn't as terrified of him as Avery was. Probably because I added a few Mardi Gras beads to his antlers a while back, making him look ready to party rather than attack you from beyond the grave.

The house sounds quiet, so without delay, I take the opportunity to shut the front door, trying as hard as I can so it doesn't make a peep, and tip-toe toward the stairs. Still no noise from anyone, so I put my foot on the first step and look around for any signs of human life.

There's no one.

I exhale and continue to the next one, except it decides to screech at me, causing me to wince and hope no one hears it. I just need to get upstairs to Wyatt and Avery's room so I can get some clothes. From there, I'll hold a stakeout until Ronny drives back to his farm. He has to wake up and leave at some point.

Instead of taking my time and drawing any further speculation, I take the stairs two at a time, letting them squeak their little hearts out as I do. Making it to the top, I turn left and rush into their bedroom and shut the door behind me.

Quiet left my body at the bottom of the stairs.

But, unfortunately, that isn't my biggest problem.

I realize I'm not alone when Avery screams and sits up in bed like a mummy.

It startles me, but I'm more worried Wyatt or someone else will be summoned upstairs, so I rush to her bed, cup a hand over her mouth, and whisper loudly, "It's me, it's me. You have to stop screaming!"

With wide, fearful eyes, she finally stops screaming and nods.

I drop my hand away from her mouth and sigh.

"What are you doing here?" she says in shock.

I look down at my flannel and then at the sheet she has clamped at her chest. I point at it. "Are you naked under there?"

She pulls the sheet higher toward her neck. "Maybe. You didn't exactly catch me knitting now, did you?"

I hold up my hand. "Wait." Wyatt just left the farmhouse, which means... "Did you just have—"

"Sex with my fiancé?" she says in a biting tone. "Yes, I did, if you have to know."

"Of course I do." I'm her best friend. I smile broadly and snap my fingers a few times. "Get it, girl."

She shoves my shoulder. "Thanks for having the worst timing ever."

I laugh. "I think the worst timing would have been if I walked in and saw Wyatt's ass. I'm not sure I could stay for the wedding after that. I'd have to drive home immediately and forget all about you and the wedding—kind of like my parents did—and watch every crime documentary known to man in order to forget it."

She rolls her eyes and asks, "Did you talk to your parents then?"

There's a sinking feeling in the pit of my stomach. "Yeah. Mom is extending her trip and won't be back in time and my dad finally texted back that he has a bowling tournament; they aren't coming."

She reaches for my hand and tugs me to sit on the bed in front of her. "I'm sorry, Tilly. I know you wanted to see them. I really thought the wedding would be enough to bring them back."

"I guess not."

I don't hide the disappointment in my tone. Not with Avery. She knows how it's felt to go from having a family to having it all taken away. The divorce changed everything for me forever, and asking both of them to come to my best friend's wedding wasn't enough to get them here.

"It's a wonder Dale and Elaine are coming," she says. "My parents refused the offer to come stay on the farm, though. So, they'll be driving in the night of the rehearsal dinner and leaving after the wedding."

I shake my head. "Dicks."

"Tilly!"

"What?! You were thinking it, too. I just said it."

Her shoulders dip an inch, and she squeezes my hand, which is still gripped in hers. Eyes dropping low and picking up slow, she finally notices. "What are you wearing?"

Confidence. "My new flannel shirt."

"You don't wear flannel anything."

How did Avery *and* Stace remember this?

I scoff. "Yes, I do."

"No, you don't," she says matter-of-factly, like she knows me better than me.

She drops my hand and reaches for my collar, trying to pull it back. I swat her hands away. "There's nothing under there!" she yells.

"Yes, there is. See..." Pulling it back, I snap my tank top strap.

She lowers her eyes at me. "Tilly, whose shirt is that?"

I bite my bottom lip. "Would you believe me if I said I got it at a cowboy store?"

"No," she says with a laugh. "Because they don't exist."

I give a mock gasp. "Cowboy stores are real! They sell hats, belt buckles, and bottled pheromones at the register. You know what I'm talking about. It happened to you! And there's that one place..."

She cocks her head and glowers.

I sigh. "Fine. I stole it."

"From who?"

My leg starts bouncing without my say. "I could have stolen it from the cowboy store, you know."

She glares again, widening her eyes.

"Alright, alright. Stop with the looks; I'll tell you," I say. "I took it from—"

"Ronny!" She howls and almost drops her sheet.

I widen my eyes and try to shush her with my hand again. Even saying his name that loud might wake him and call him over here. "Keep your mouth shut!"

She avoids my attempts at covering her mouth and says, "You slept together! You did it! You're dating!"

I unseat myself from the side of her bed and climb on top of her so she'll stop spewing nonsense. "We didn't sleep together!"

"But you're dating?"

"No!"

"But you kissed him." She's stronger than she looks and is somehow able to roll me off her while keeping her plum-colored sheets hiked to her clavicle. "It was the trip to Greycliff wasn't it? I'm such a genius."

"How do you know I kissed him?" I ask, out of breath.

"You have a hickey, my friend. Right..." she jabs the base of my neck with her pointy finger, "there."

That means I've been walking around all morning with it. So much for being sly.

I relax back into the pillow before remembering they just had sex, and the likelihood of it being in this bed is as good as 99.9% odds, so I leap off, grasping my flannel for protection. It's doing very little of that, however. "Was sending us to Greycliff together your idea? I thought you needed me to go?"

"Yes and no..." she says. "It was Wyatt's idea, too."

"How? Why?" I ask, leaning against the wall beside the bed.

"Wyatt told Ronny about the wedding favors," she clears her throat, "suggesting you go, too. That's it, I swear. Then Ronny told him he'd swing by to pick you up."

"Why?" I ask. "Why'd you do it?"

She leans back against the headboard behind her with a muted thud. "You and Ronny have been at each other since two summers ago. But I know you, and it's not because you really hate him."

I swallow but keep my eyes on her. "I do."

"You don't," she says in a more direct tone. "You hate that it didn't work out because you really wanted it to." Her voice tapers off at the end to a quiet whisper.

The floor doesn't have any better answers than what Avery just said, but I look down at it regardless. If it was as easy as getting what I wanted, she's right; Ronny would have been in more than just my bed. He would have been more to me. But I didn't get what I wanted.

I got what I deserved.

Twenty

Ronny

"You can take your boy out the hood, but you can't take the hood out the homie." —Snoop Dogg

She just...disappeared.

I woke up and stretched my arm across the bed, knowing exactly who was there, or who was supposed to be. But she was long gone since her side of the bed was cool to the touch. The bathroom was empty; the kitchen, too, and after going back to the bedroom to get my boots, it wasn't easy to find them, either, since it looked like a shoe store exploded. The only thing missing were sale tags and the salesperson ready to measure your foot with a medieval metal contraption.

Finally finding my dark brown work boots with the loosened laces and steel toes, I slip each one on. Surprisingly, they're the only things I took off last night. Staying over wasn't my plan, but Gertrude can be temperamental at times.

Reminds me of another woman I know. One that is very absent right now.

Getting out of here without being seen is going to be a chore since everyone else is likely already up for the day. Stace and Bryan should be here, too, since they planned to stay in one of the cabins for the next two nights to help out. I'll have to say I got here extra early to avoid any questions about my truck being parked outside.

Checking my reflection in the mirror, I settle my curled-edge hat back on my head and choose the backdoor instead of the front. The cabin has a small porch off the back that I helped Wyatt replace a few boards in last year as well as the large soaker tub he created from a feeding trough for Avery. From what I understand, it still gets used plenty by the guests who stay here, but I prefer to keep my nature and bathing separate.

I should keep my women and my work separate, too, but we can't all be perfect.

Last night probably shouldn't have happened. I don't regret it because I've learned regrets are easy to come by and harder to shake, but I do need to talk to Tilly. We can't keep going on like this, whether bickering or sleeping together. It isn't fair to her. I've already crossed every road block, hazard sign, and warning bell when it comes to us.

There aren't any people outside the farmhouse when I scan around the side of the cabin. With work, wedding prep, and chores, I'm hoping everyone will be preoccupied long enough for me to sneak to the barn and get the electric jump for Gertrude. I'll need to head back to our farm soon and get chores done. I'm not supposed to be working here until tomorrow when I'll help Wyatt light the gazebo out back for the reception and carry the arbor toward the barn.

Plus, Camila is supposed to come by this evening. She'll want to know the plan for the wedding on Sunday, and I still don't have an answer for her.

With it clear, I walk through the grass until I hit gravel, and then I pick up my stride. My truck is halfway to the barn, and I'm just about to pass it when—

"Ronny."

I keep my head down. Maybe I can pretend I didn't hear him.

"Ronny!" Wyatt calls louder.

Not a chance. I look up with a small wave just as I reach the tailgate of my truck. "Morning."

He walks up with a smirk on his face. "You're here early."

"Maybe you're late."

"I live here."

I furrow my brow but say nothing.

"Anyway..." Wyatt starts, "I meant that you're a whole day early for work. You aren't supposed to be here until tomorrow." He leans an elbow on the edge of my truck. "What have you been up to?"

He's fishing. But he won't find anything. I don't like the kind of bait he's trying to catch me with, either. "I was looking to see if the backyards of the cabins needed to be mowed. You've got a lot on your plate, and Ernie's got things covered at my place, so..." I couldn't help noticing the lawns were pretty long while back there, but I have no intention of mowing them right now. I've got help at our place today, but it's because we're supposed to do some calf branding and need the extra hands.

"Great. And?" he asks.

I hook a thumb toward my truck. "Have to go back for my weed-whacker first. Forgot it."

"I have a weedwhacker." He crosses his arms.

I cross mine. "I don't like yours."

"Beats making a trip all the way back to your place."

"It's five minutes away."

He nods and assesses me. We grew up crossing the trail leading between our two houses almost every day. But despite him being my best friend, we also tend to act like siblings. Exhibit A...

"I'll be back in a bit. I have to check in with my parents," I explain. "Oh, and I, uh, need a jump, too."

He nods, looking me up and down again. "I saw Tilly this morning."

"Alright." So she didn't magically disappear. "Good for you."

He laughs. I don't. "She was wearing a flannel and was barefoot."

I try not to laugh. The flannel was—*is*—mine, and she obviously wanted to get out before I woke up.

"And why are you telling me? Tilly can wear whatever the fuck she wants." I can't keep the clip out of my voice.

He notices and holds up both hands. "Just wondering if you knew anything about it."

Wyatt knows our history, what I said, and everything I didn't. He has his opinions, and while he has a right to have those, I don't agree because he doesn't know the whole story. The last couple of years he's been busy with Avery, so it was easy for me to keep to myself in order to hash out everything that exploded in my personal life. But with Camila finally feeling more comfortable, it's now up to me to open my damn mouth.

I can't keep putting this off.

"I have no idea," I say with a shrug. "You should ask her."

"Or you could."

"Can't," I say and take a deep breath. "Because I need to tell you something."

He drops his arms and puts his hands in his pockets. "Alright."

Maybe he heard the shift in my tone, or how I'm struggling to look him in the eye, but he's quiet now, waiting for me to continue, not giving me anymore lip.

Getting this out needs to be my only goal for the day. I can't leave here without saying something, so I shift on my feet and start somewhere. "I haven't told anyone this. The only people who know are my folks."

His spine straightens. "Oh shit. This is serious. Should I get the whiskey?"

"Probably. But I just have to get this out."

He rakes his fingers through his beard. "Shots after, then."

I nod and take my time to gather my thoughts. I should have rehearsed this, but how do you tell your best friend you've been keeping something from them for the last two years? I didn't mean for it to go on that long, but Camila and I needed to figure things out first.

"I need to tell you about something—*someone*," I correct, shifting my gaze from the ground and back at him. "I need to tell you about Gianna."

***

MY FOOTFALL IS heavier while walking to the barn to grab the electric jump and carry it back to my truck. The process only takes a few minutes, something I convinced myself it wouldn't late last night, but once my truck is started, I open the door and climb in.

The whiskey shot Wyatt insisted on roils in my gut. It was a crime not to sip and savor it.

Now, I've got to get back to the farm to check in, get my weedwhacker, and come back to mow the damn lawns here. It's the last thing I have time for, but I can't get out of it now without admitting things I'm not ready to. Bringing Tilly into the conversation after telling Wyatt about Gianna—Gia for short—would be the doings of a damn fool.

I've already had one honest conversation today, and another might do me in.

Wyatt took the news of my four-year-old daughter surprisingly well. Better than I did when Camila showed up one day with a then two-year-old sporting my eyes and tanned skin and told me what I never expected to hear. There was a paternity test to follow because even though I remember sleeping with her, I needed to know for certain. I needed to know if that little girl was my heart walking outside my body.

She is.

But I knew before I ever got those results she was mine, and it's changed my life forever.

Wyatt's mouth fell open wider the more I talked. Once I got started, I couldn't stop. I filled him in on everything that's happened the last two years in under five minutes. By the end, he grabbed and hugged me. I can't remember the last time he'd done that—gripped me so tightly I was ready to pass out. We don't make a habit of it, but it felt a hell of a lot better than the slap I probably deserve when I tell Tilly.

The old, familiar bench seat inside Gertrude melds in all the right places. I've been driving this truck since I was twelve and got my license early. Living on a farm in Montana has its perks.

I know all of the random places I've stashed spare coins and straw wrappers. The cigarette tray being one of them. I know how to adjust the cassette tape so it'll play without skipping. And the only place to stash my sunglasses without them falling on the floor is hanging off the side on the visor.

But when I pull it down, something falls in my lap, and I throw it off me so fast, flinging it across the cab toward the window. I accidentally honk my horn, too, startling me even further. My heart rate is high as I realize just what tried to attack me:

Tilly.

Or the rubber snake she planted. The little minx had the gall to sneak this into my truck.

I look through the windshield just as the curtain in the front window of the farmhouse falls closed. She was watching. Makes sense since she has the perfect view without having to face me. Normally she'd love a chance to gloat, but after last night and finding her cabin empty this morning means she probably doesn't want to face me right now. But the fact she's still playing her games has to mean something, and having any part of Tilly is better than none.

I grab the offender that almost tried to kill me from the passenger seat. The snake looks the same as it did the last time I had it—dark green on top with a light green belly. I smile to myself and spend the five-minute drive home, plus the next hour doing chores, thinking of how I want to return it.

She might be trying to erect her walls to safely hide behind again, but I think she left a window open for me. Here's to hoping so.

Twenty-One

Tilly

"Be your own leader, be your own self, step out of my shadows and be your own person." —Snoop Dogg

Mother Clucker!" Avery yells, charging toward the chicken trying to stick its head through the wire fencing. "Don't you dare get stuck again!"

Remarkable creatures, really, I think to myself.

She rescues her prized hen from making poor choices and continues scattering seeds. "Just grab a handful and shake it out of your hand onto the ground."

I do as she says, but it feels wrong. "Do they really enjoy a dash of dirt with their breakfast?"

"They don't mind."

I raise my brows. "Can't say I would."

"Should we hunt for eggs?"

I stare at her like she's gone mad. There was a time when we were hunting for men in bars, and now we're searching for chicken eggs on a farm. "Isn't this place like hundreds of acres?"

"One hundred and fifty," she says. "But these ladies don't roam that far. Come on, grab a basket, and let's start by the barn."

"Why don't we start back here?" I point to the area around the pen directly behind the farmhouse. Ronny was still in the driveway, having a moment with the snake, which means I still can't go back to my cabin.

"Are you planning to hide from him all day? You're going to have to see him eventually."

My stomach churns at the thought. "I know. I'm just giving it some space. I'll wait until tomorrow."

She shrugs and grabs two baskets, handing me one before we open the small gate under the arbor and let the little cluckers roam. Taking my basket I start searching the ground. "Where are we supposed to look?"

"Everywhere," she replies. "They go for safe, quiet spots. I've found them under the deck, in piles of hay, and even in the wheelbarrow beside the coop with dirty bedding."

I nod and walk to the back porch off the kitchen of the farmhouse. "I feel like we're searching for Easter eggs."

"Basically."

"And you do this every day?" I ask, kicking at the grass.

Avery let me borrow a pair of black rubber boots, a T-shirt, and jeans. I wrapped Ronny's flannel around my waist due to the irrepressible thought that he'd somehow track it down and steal it back before I'm ready. It smells nice.

"Yup. Every day. I love it, though."

"Why?" I hunt around the edge of the porch when the question flies out of my mouth. "I meant to say it's just so different from anything you ever planned."

I've never lived outside of North Dakota, but I've traveled enough on my own that living outside the main metropolis where I grew up hasn't ever been a desire of mine.

"It's not like I had this on my vision board," she says with a repressed laugh.

"Oh my gosh! I remember that." I bark out a laugh. "The one you spent so much time clipping pictures out of magazines for?"

"That's the one."

"Don't forget the inspirational quotes you included that you wanted to write on the walls of the spa you'd open one day."

She bends to grab a couple eggs from a lawn chair beside the patio. "Yeah, I had a lot of plans once. Starting a spa for people who want an immersive farm experience wasn't anywhere on that board. Not even close."

There's a beat of silence as we pass under the kitchen window, eyes on the ground, but it's anything but quiet. Out here, you don't hear car horns or traffic noise. You hear wind rustling through blades of grass, clucking chickens as they follow us, lowing cows out in the pasture, or sometimes Granny yelling for Wyatt. But other than that, it's peaceful in a way I didn't think it could be.

"It's not like it was easy to get used to. But I love it because I didn't know *home* could have a name," she starts to explain. "Wyatt, Granny, Deb and Carl, Stace, Bryan and the kids, even Ronny's family...they're the ones I've made my home in, and regardless of the learning curve to actually live on a farm, they're my family."

I stop walking and look around a few bushes, pretending to search for eggs. But really, I'm absorbing every one of her words and clinging to a small glimmer of hope that still lives in me to have a family like this. To wake up knowing you are someone's world and not just a planet that orbits theirs.

Avery searches the wildflowers at the corner of the house when I spot a light brown speckled sphere that blends in with the rock beds.

I quickly bend to pick it up and hold it above my head like a prize. "I found one!"

"Yay!" Avery cheers. "Your first egg! Should we eat it?"

I look at the egg and back at my friend. "Doesn't that just feel wrong? I mean this could be your next chicken bestie."

She shakes her head and loops her arm through mine, steering us toward the back porch stairs. "We have enough hens. I bet this one tastes delicious. Our eggs are the best in town, and everyone knows it."

I scrunch up my nose while holding the delicate egg in my palm when we're interrupted.

"What's that on your shirt?" Granny asks, leaning over the railing.

The shirt Avery gave me isn't exactly what I'd choose for myself, but my options were limited. Rather, they were limited to a vast array of graphic tees. I look up at Granny. "It's a succulent."

She squints to look at it. "Why does it have arms?"

I shake my head and climb the stairs, Avery trailing me. "I have no idea. Ask Avery."

Granny shakes her head as Avery says, "Gran, why don't I get you set up at the breakfast nook to pack favors."

"That's why I'm here."

We all head in, and Avery sets the supplies on the table for Granny to start organizing and packing. She offers to cook up the eggs we found, but I tell her I'm not hungry. I'm starving, but I just can't eat that baby chicken. I opt to stay inside with Granny while Avery heads back out to find more eggs and other farm chores people do.

Before she left, Avery asked me to make sure nothing extra got slipped into the favor bags. I have strict orders to remove anything Granny may have monogrammed her face on since she has a knack for doing this.

"Can I help?"

Granny doesn't look up. "Do you have two hands?"

"I do." I wiggle my fingers and grab a transparent mesh baggie and sit while she shows me what to include.

A packet of wildflower seeds, the leather key chain with the farm's logo stamped on it, a few pieces of chocolate, and a small thing of tallow hand lotion that Stace made. Little touches of *them* for every guest. I put a few together before deciding I should try the chocolate.

"Here." Granny tosses a few chocolates my way. "These were opened."

I grab them and turn them over in my hand. Little pieces of foil are snagged and torn, revealing the milk chocolate drops beneath them. "Aren't you supposed to throw away opened candy?"

She stops what she's doing. "I won't tell."

Shrugging, I set them down on the table in front of me and open the first one. Ten minutes later, I'm five chocolates in when Granny finally looks up.

"I thought you were going to help?" she says in a biting tone.

I wave my hand at the small pile of favors I did. There are four. "I'm eating all of the poisonous candy, remember?"

She shakes her head, still seemingly focused on her job. "You upset about something, Tilly?"

"No," I answer too quickly.

She isn't buying it and looks up over her glasses. "I'm good at listening."

"But nothing's wrong."

Her hands are busy stuffing. "Alright then. Pass me that box, would ya?"

I hand her a box with more seeds and return to eating my chocolate. It's not easy when the smooth melt-in-your-mouth flavor reminds me of how good this would taste eating it off Ronny. But then again, everything has been reminding me of him this morning—the shower's heat as it beat against my back earlier, the rough texture of jeans mimicking calloused hands, the chocolate, and the *pink boa*. I'm a mess.

I have no idea if he's really gone and after he caught me peeking out the window, I'm afraid to go check. My plan is just to stay here today. There are plenty of things to do to keep me busy. Avery gave me a list Deb and Stace put together, and I should probably show Avery a few of the hairstyles I'm thinking of for Saturday.

But focusing on a task right now is hard when all of my thoughts drift. This is exactly why I didn't want to complicate things even more.

"Tilly?"

"Huh," I mumble, looking up.

"You're either going to tell me what's bothering you, or I'm going to pull out the pie and then you're gonna tell me. What'll it be?" Granny asks, pinning me to the chair across from her. She removed her glasses;

now nothing is between me and her acute stare. Avery once said Granny has a way of knowing everything. I don't know if that's a *her* thing or an elderly person thing, but it feels like she can see directly into my soul, no bifocals necessary.

I open another chocolate and pop it in my mouth. "I met this guy." She doesn't need to know it's Ronny. "And we…" How do I explain this without using the word sex? "Liked playing cards together. A lot. We played a lot of cards the first night we met."

Granny nods, resting her forearms on the table, listening intently.

I continue: "We talked, too, and I loved our conversations. I wanted more of those, plus dates, commitment, and possibly forever together. I wanted more than to play cards with him."

I thought he wanted all of this, too; he just didn't know how to say it. I was wrong. He cut us off completely. But those slow mornings in bed when he'd kiss my forehead and tuck me into his chest, and the way he always asked when I was visiting the farm next like he couldn't handle it being that long told me a different story I wanted to believe.

"Well, did you tell him that?"

"Tell him I wanted more than just se—" I shake my head. "Playing cards?"

She starts stuffing favor bags again. "Yes. If he didn't know you wanted more than…playing cards, maybe he didn't know you wanted the same things he did."

I shift in my chair and open another chocolate. "I mean, I thought it was obvious how much I liked him…and playing cards. I would have played all kinds of card games with him if he asked. Bunko, King's Corners, Go Fish…"

Thinking back, I know I told Ronny I liked him. I showed him in every way possible. We talked on the phone after the first weekend I visited, texted constantly, and maybe sent a few just-for-our-eyes-only photos. The same day he told me he wanted to stop everything was the day I was going to tell him I loved him.

I felt it long before that visit, but I wasn't going to sleep on it any longer. I was going to tell him exactly how I felt—or thought I did—because I had never been with someone like him and wasn't about to let him go. He broke my heart in front of an audience. Sure, it was only in front of his horse, June, and my car, but it was enough to solidify my embarrassment—unrequited love is the cheapest kind.

"I think you should tell Ronny how you feel."

I snap my gaze to hers. "It's not Ronny." It absolutely is him. "It's...Card Guy."

"Mhm," she murmurs without looking up from her busy hands. "If he doesn't know how you really feel, maybe he's guessing. And guessing is the worst kind of truth."

I straighten in my seat. Telling Ronny how I feel won't change anything. He was very clear that day. *We'll never work out, you and I want different things, you aren't my type, we're good at sex, not a relationship.* The worst is that those words still feel like pinpricks in my swollen heart. I can't tell him how I feel and risk hearing all of those words again. It's why I couldn't stay in the cabin and wait for him to wake up and regret what happened.

The part that makes me physically ill is that he was right about all of it. I'm the girl that guys like to have fun with for a while. The one you date and play around with before finding the girl you'll bring home to your parents and start a life with. And maybe that's just who I am. It's not like my parents could figure things out.

What happened last night can't happen again.

"Speaking of Ronny," I start, tracing my finger along the wood grain of the table. "Do you know if he has a special someone?"

"Your Ronny?"

My mouth slackens, and I vigorously shake my head. "He isn't *my* Ronny. I'm into Card Guy, remember?"

She tucks her chin to her chest. "All I know is Ronny has never had a serious relationship since you."

I'm not even sure you can call what we had a relationship, let alone one that was *serious*, but hearing this makes me relieved all the same.

I nod slowly and purse my lips. "Good to know."

The pink boa is still a mystery. I didn't want to ask Avery about it today because then she'd ask Wyatt. And if she asked Wyatt about it, he'd go straight to the source, and it would get back to Ronny. It isn't that big of a deal. I let him kiss me, but that doesn't mean we're in a committed relationship where we totally love each other, and I want to have his babies any more than we were two years ago.

"Anyway, thanks for the advice with Card Guy, Granny. I think I know what I'm going to do," I say, standing up as the chair scrapes on the tile floor. I resist covering my ears. She doesn't. "I'm not going to say anything."

She peers up at me through a squint. "That's not what I said."

"I'll reestablish boundaries so no more card playing happens."

"Card playing...mhm," she mumbles.

"Cards will be a thing of the past, and both of us can move on," I say with a nod and then grab another chocolate from the bowl. "For the road."

I'm going to pretend last night never happened. So what would I be doing today if all of my thoughts weren't about Ronny? I'm sure Avery has something in her planner that has my name on it. My cabin could use a spruce up, and with goat yoga happening later, I need to mentally prepare.

The chocolate is already stuffed into my mouth, and I'm talking around it. "I feel loads better."

"I'm glad I could help." She smiles, but it's forced. "Does that mean you're leaving?"

I hang on to the back of the chair and wave her off. "I have a few things I need to do. Plus, I would just eat all the chocolate anyway."

"Right you are."

We stare at each other for a few beats before I snatch one last hand-ful—*I swear*—of chocolates and leave the farmhouse feeling better than I have since arriving.

At least I know what I'm not going to do: fall for the broody cowboy. Again.

Twenty-Two

Tilly

"Do what you feel is right, baby." —*Snoop Dogg*

Golden, glistening skin, low-riding jeans that show the elastic band of his black briefs, and the hat that rarely ever comes off his head, even in my daydreams.

He's totally thirst-trapping me.

I hate that it's working.

I've been staring out the window above the kitchen sink in my cabin for the last twenty minutes, and every single second has been worth it. Ronny's been weed-whacking the edges around the cabin and the outdoor tub sanctuary, meaning he's been close enough that I've had to duck down twice so he wouldn't catch me drooling—I mean, staring. The show will go on since he just started mowing, and there's a lot of grass back there.

Maybe he knows I'm here, perhaps he doesn't, but this feels intentional. Like he wants me drooling and begging and seeing everything I missed out on last night.

Sir, I don't need reminding.

The snake I hid in his truck must have really ticked him off to want to get back at me like this. That prank feels innocent compared to this. He's playing *dirty* and going straight for my loins. It's next-level payback, and I'm not about to sit around for the rest of the afternoon while he gets the upper hand.

Good thing I'm a master at playing games.

I can thirst-trap him, too, if I want. And I brought just the thing.

I rush back to my bedroom and rifle through my suitcase, throwing its contents on the ground until I find what I'm looking for. There are enough strings to make it look more like a shiny, gold slingshot contraption, but it's not.

It's a different kind of toy.

I strip down and pull it on, taking time to make sure my boobs aren't going to fall out, but also that they kind of do, then slip on my wedge heels that have no business going outside and reach for my sunglasses. Grabbing a bottled iced tea from the fridge and a book from the living room, I head to the backdoor and down the porch steps.

The lawn mower that looks more like an ATV is ear-splitting, but Ronny is wearing giant ear muff headphones to block out the noise, unlike me. I don't let it deter me. I walk carefully down the porch steps and toward the lounge chair near the side of the cabin. I have to tug it back on the lawn, but it isn't heavy, only awkward as I adjust the backrest to the right height and sit down, book in hand, ice tea on the ground beside me. I stretch out my legs and cross my ankles, making sure my entire gold bikini is visible—every last stitch on display.

On his next row, he cranks the wheel and comes back the way he came—my way—and the mower stops immediately. I pretend to be engrossed in my book and not to notice. But it's hard not to when flashes of tanned skin and low-slung Wrangler jeans are walking toward me.

He rips his headphones off. "What the hell are you doing?"

I speak without looking up, which is a feat on its own since he's casting beams of sexual tension left and right. "Sunbathing."

"In that?"

I set my book down with an exaggerated huff that could win me an award and look at him, grateful my giant sunglasses block my eyes. He isn't shy in pointing out the one-piece contraption I'm wearing. "Yes, in this. You're out here in..." I wave a hand toward his torso, *"that."*

He looks down at his chest. So do I. "I'm mowing the lawn."

I pick my book back up. "And, as I've established, I'm sunbathing."

He scoffs and rubs his chin. "Since when do you own a gold bikini?"

"Gold is my favorite color." It's not. Turquoise is.

His laugh is clipped. "Right. Well, I need to mow this area soon, so you'll have to move your sunbathing somewhere else."

I give him a sickeningly sweet, cavity-creating smile. "You can move it for me then."

This is the kind of thing that really gets him frustrated. He doesn't like when his work is interrupted. Too bad. He's mowing my lawn without a shirt on and expecting me to be okay with that. *Yeah right.* He can thirst-trap the whole internet, but not me.

He shakes his head, pulling his sunglasses down the bridge of his nose, then putting his hands on his hips. "Since when do you like reading about *Birds of Montana*?" he asks.

I don't register what he's saying right away until he points at the book in my hand. I resist looking at the cover while he's standing in front of me. "I'm trying to learn more about the wildlife."

"About birds?"

"Yes, about birds. I'm twenty-eight now, if you've forgotten, and birds are quickly becoming a new hobby of mine." I shift my focus back to my book, which has a photo of a black, white, and blue bird on it. Something called a Magpie.

He laughs, then without saying anything else, he stalks back to his riding lawn mower and starts it up again. He's upset I'm encroaching on his work time. Or maybe it's the fact we haven't talked since he left my cabin and found the snake earlier. Things feel different. His eyes were like two hands touching me everywhere. We were supposed to go back where we started—where we belong—instead, it's all different, and I played right into his trap by coming out here. But now I'm in this race whether I've trained for it or not.

When I lift my eyes to watch him through my sunglasses, I find him already looking my way. I try to ignore him and refocus on the birds, but it's hard. His gaze feels like it's scalding me, leaving marks to remember him by. He's not even looking where he's going, just like me.

I shift in my lounger, not loving how much power he has over me. The way my body reacts whenever he's around. So much for setting boundaries if my lady parts are screaming at me not to. Now we're both wearing less, and my cabin is *right there*. It would be easy to disappear inside for a while.

No.

Stop it!

I'm not doing that again. *We* aren't doing it. Not anymore. Not with Ronny. But being out here, with him getting closer with every row he cuts, is making it hard to remember why.

By the time he finishes the last row and puts his mower in park, I'm a frazzled mess of want and have created my own mental burn book for him, using phrases like *fugly* and *so not fetch*. Too bad it's not working.

I pick up my iced tea for protection and start guzzling it as he strides over.

"Time to move," he says sternly.

Ugh. Don't tempt me. He knows I love a commanding tone.

"I'm almost done." I go back to sipping my iced tea and turn the page in my book. I've been flipping through it without really seeing what's on each page. Blue, red, brown—they're all just birds.

He shifts on his feet and adjusts his hat. "Till."

"Hang on." I flip another page.

He clears his throat. "Book's upside down."

I study the words my eyes have been skimming and see he's...right.

When I look up at him, he's still wearing his favorite cowboy hat, which is both practical in blocking the sun and easily making him the sexiest person alive. It's doing its job since his eyes are in full shadow, and I can barely see them. Good thing he's always been obvious with his body language. A thrill flits through me as I think about just how good.

Slapping my book shut, I swing my legs to the side and stand. No more upside-down books, thoughts of bodies, or broody, half-naked men. "I think I've had enough sunbathing for the day."

"Are you sure?"

I'm strangling the neck of the iced tea in my hand. "Positive."

I may not be able to see his eyes, but I can see his mouth, and there's an annoying smirk there I want to rub off with my lips.

"I'm almost done here, and then I'll move on to the other cabins," he says, strangely unaffected. Maybe he isn't.

I can't tell what he's thinking. His voice is even, and he doesn't seem frustrated like he was earlier. He's not acting like some tormented soul by a woman in a gold bikini, either. I don't know how to feel about that.

"Well, I'm going inside now."

He nods once. "Sounds good."

I stand taller on my wedge heels. "Will you be at dinner tonight?"

"Not tonight. Told my folks I'd make dinner for us."

The way my gut quivers at the thought of Ronny in the kitchen making a home-cooked meal for his family bothers me. I wish I didn't like it so much. "Fine," I reply gruffly to counteract the way my heart beats erratically in my chest. "Bye."

"I'll see you later."

I walk past him. "Or you won't."

"Or I won't," he repeats.

I whirl around just as he darts his gaze upward. "And don't look at my ass."

He raises his chin and crosses his arms, highlighting those perfect pectorals, which does nothing to cool me off. "No promises."

I jab a finger in his direction and walk backward. "I'm serious."

"So am I."

I stop walking backward when I get to the porch. I'll have to turn around if I don't want to fall on my face. Looks like he's going to enjoy the view after all. Might as well make a show of it.

I don't bother tugging the edges of my suit down even if my ass cheeks are hanging out. There really isn't a version with this bathing suit where they aren't. So, I own it. Turning around slowly, I walk up the steps one at a time and look back at him only when I get to the top.

He's still staring and not trying to hide it even a little bit.

"Let me know if you need anything," he says gruffly.

Before he turns around, I yell back, "I won't."

He shakes his head. "Bye, Till."

As he walks away, I'm not sure if I'm more upset that he checked out my ass or called me *Till* one too many times. Both feel far too intimate.

Twenty-Three

Ronny

"I move with the time. Whatever's happening in time, I'm in."
—Snoop Dogg

I could have throttled her for getting in the way while I was mowing and screwed her against the side of the house all in the same breath.

Tilly is clearly trying to make a point. I just don't know what that is yet. But I do know the snake prank is back on.

At first, I thought that was a clear indication she didn't want anything to happen again. But then, she walked outside in that tiny gold bikini like she was going to sunbathe at some five-star resort hotel and not the backyard. It said *hot* among other words I can't let myself think about right now.

The handle on the plastic scrubber I'm using to scour the outdoor tub snaps, and so do my thoughts. "Damn it." I hold up the broken handle but determine the rest of the brush still works and keep at it.

I decided to clean out the tub when Tilly offhandedly mentioned the other day she'd never used it before. After I finished mowing, I started scrubbing. Not only because I want her to enjoy the tub, but I also thought of how I'll get her with the snake. I just have to figure out the timing. Hopefully, she won't kill me.

"What are you doing?" Avery looms over the tub.

I'm up to my elbows in soap. I thought it was obvious. "Cleaning the tub."

"Why?" she asks.

"Tilly said she wanted to use it." I scrub the opposite wall.

"Oh," she says. "That's nice of you."

I squint up at her but say nothing. The chances of Tilly having told Avery what happened (or didn't) last night are high. I'm sure she has even more details than I do.

She tugs at the hem of her Thirst Trapp Farms T-shirt with Beethoven in red, heart-shaped sunglasses on it. I don't get it, but people are really into them. Sold out within a few hours. "I was actually looking for Tilly. Do you know where she is?" she asks.

I keep scrubbing. "Doing goat yoga with Stace and Deb."

"Oh no," she says under her breath.

I stop and rest my forearms on the edge. "What?"

"The goats aren't ready. Tilly, she isn't…"

"Ready?" I supply.

"Yeah." She stares at the ground in a daze. "Tilly will probably end up killing ScapeGoat and roast him for dinner tonight."

I don't hide my laugh. "You think Tilly knows how to cook a goat?"

"Well, no. But I wouldn't put it past her to try."

My forehead drips with sweat after all the work I've been doing here today. All of these chores weren't my original plan, but all my damn secrets got me roped into them.

"Will you go check on them?" Avery asks, hands clasped in front of her.

The scrubber is heavy in my hand, so I drop it and stand, wiping my brow as I do. "And why do you want *me* to check on them? Why don't you?"

She brackets her waist with her hands and juts out a sassy hip. "Because I have to go to town with Granny for more pie ingredients."

I mirror her stance. "Seems like you could swing by their pen and check things out before you go."

She glares. "What if ScapeGoat needs rescuing? Or Tilly? Please, Ronny! I don't think you understand. I gave her strict orders not to go into their pen without me."

"Deb and Stace are there," I retort.

"They don't possess the skill to get her to stop mid-murder!" Avery professes in a passionate tone with flailing arms I'm afraid will whack me in the face.

I sigh. "And you think I do?"

"Yes, I do. She'll listen to you."

That's funny. "We're talking about Tilly here! I'm probably the last person she'll listen to."

She shakes her head and lowers her voice. "You're wrong. I think you know it, too."

My throat bobs, and the sincere expression on Avery's face, paired with what she just alluded to, have me feeling hopeful. For what, I don't know exactly. There's a shift happening, and apparently, I'm not the only one who feels it. No matter how much Tilly wants to fight me on it, we're going to have to talk about things soon. I feel it coming.

"Okay. I'll do it. I'll go check on her and save one of them from each other."

She nods and starts walking backward. "Thank you."

The tub is clean, so I finish by rinsing it out with the hose and make my way toward the barn where I helped Wyatt build the goat pen off the side. Sure enough, Tilly, Stace, and Deb are all bending forward over their mats to touch their toes. Tilly is the only one with straight legs with her forehead to her shins, and the sight makes all the blood in my body rush south.

She retired the gold bikini and went straight for tight black yoga pants and a matching cropped sports bra. I'm not sure which is more distressing for my blood pressure.

I fist my hands at my sides to keep from thinking about it and stalk toward the pen. Standing upright, hands raised to the sky, Tilly catches me out of the corner of her eye.

"What are you doing?" I ask, brows drawn.

"Hi, Ronny," Stace says, and Deb repeats, blowing hair from her eyes.

I tip my hat, thankful I put my shirt back on earlier.

"We're doing goat yoga," Tilly says. "What does it look like?"

The two goats are happily standing on top of a wooden spool we put in their pen. I look back at her. "Is everyone...safe?"

Tilly points at Stace and Deb's mats. "Go ahead and do a few cat and cow stretches." She slips on her platform sandals and shuffles toward the gate. She has to dodge a few piles, then grabs a to-go mug on the fence post.

My eyes hone in on it like a beacon. "What the hell is on your mug?"

She takes a sip and then checks out what she just drank from. "Different types of tits."

I scowl in confusion.

"Women have different kinds of tits, Ronny."

I have the cojones to smirk and say, "I know."

She holds up a hand. "Do not think of saying anything more."

"You're the one with the mug," I mumble.

She sets it down on the post again. "Are you checking to see if all the goats are still alive?"

"Maybe." I cross my arms.

Her eyes drop to my pecs, but only for a second. "Did Avery send you over?"

"She's worried you're going to roast the goats."

"She thinks I know how to roast an animal?"

"That's what I said."

She stabs a finger at me. "Hey, watch it."

I'm stepping backward in case she decides to figure out how to roast me.

She looks over her shoulder. "They haven't been as annoying this time around. Maybe that means they're getting used to it."

Goat yoga was never on my radar until Avery brought it up at a monthly staff meeting, which is really just family dinners on Sundays. Even with their wedding in a few days, farm life never stops, and they're trying to train the goats for when guests come to stay on the farm in two weeks. Tilly practices yoga regularly, so naturally, Avery asked her to get the goats used to it. I'm not sure it's working, though, considering how close to death these assholes have come.

"Looks like it," I say and then change the subject. "By the way, I cleaned the tub out for you. Now you can take that bath whenever you want. Just ask Avery how to fill it."

"There are instructions in the cabin now," she says. "And you did what?"

"I cleaned out the tub."

"For me?" She points at her chest.

Yes, for her. "For...people."

"Ronny, are you being *nice*?"

I scrunch up my nose. "Nice? Me?" My lips and mouth make noises that sound a lot like a stuttering tea kettle.

"Thanks for that." Her voice is soft like she might actually be thankful and not just giving me some sarcasm.

A smile creeps onto my face, and I have to purse my lips to hide it. "Great. Well, if everything's good here, I'm going to head out."

"You're leaving?"

"Yeah. Unless you need anything?" *Need something. Give me a reason to stay.*

"No, I'm good," she says with a few shakes of her head. "I guess I'll see you tomorrow for the bachelor and bachelorette parties."

Avery and Wyatt decided on a joint celebration since the wedding party is only Tilly, me, Stace, and her husband, Bryan. Dinner at the Grand Hotel in downtown Big Timber, followed by a pub crawl, was their idea of a good time. Don't get me wrong, it sounds great to me, too. But it also reminds me too much of the first night I met Tilly. It started at the Thirsty Hippo and ended in her cabin.

"I'll be there. I'm driving Wyatt's truck."

"Why not yours?"

I hook a thumb toward Wyatt's truck parked outside the farmhouse. "His has more space in the cab for the four of us."

Her brows dive together. "What about Stace and Bryan?"

Stace pipes up from behind her. "We're driving our car. We won't be out as late as you guys," she says and then goes back to her flow.

"Okay. Tomorrow then," Tilly says to me with a nod.

I grin because I'm past being able to help it. "Tomorrow."

Twenty-Four

Ronny

"There's no such thing as losing touch." —Snoop Dogg

Wyatt, this is Camila."

We both watched her pull up the long drive of Adler Farms in her silver Honda. I'd be lying if I said my neck didn't hurt from rubbing it raw. I haven't introduced anyone to Camila and Gia yet. I've lived with one foot in two different worlds, but today, they merge.

Hell if that doesn't put me a scratch away from hives.

Wyatt nods at Camila, who is wearing her curly black hair in a low ponytail today and still in her apron from the hardware store she works at in Livingston. "Nice to meet you, Camila."

"Thanks for agreeing to meet me. Ronny told me about the wedding, but," she braces her hands on Gia's slight shoulders, "I'm protective and haven't wanted to introduce too many people. But I think it's time."

Camila looks at me, the full weight of her trust in the words she just spoke. For two years I've waited to share Gia with Wyatt's family. My parents have known, encouraging me to tell them, but Camila wasn't convinced that our one-night stand that produced Gia would make me an involved father.

I needed to demonstrate to her, and myself, that I could do this.

Weekly visits lasting a handful of hours for two years finally showed her I was serious. I'm not about to shirk off my responsibilities like my birth parents did. Especially when it's a child—it's Gia.

We met when she was two, and her big brown eyes looked up like they'd been staring at me in the mirror my entire life. Her eyes might match mine, but her hair and confidence are all Camila. It was hard to find out I was a father, hard to feel like my time with her wasn't enough when Camila waited so long to tell me. It still grates on me at times. I would have been there for her every step, moment, and smile if she let me. It's hard to know she doubted me at all. But I've done a hell of a job showing up, and I'm here now no matter what.

I rock back on my heels, giving Camila steady eye contact that says I'm Grateful with a capital "G." I'm fucking terrified to share my daughter with everyone at Wyatt and Avery's wedding. Everyone in this city, family friends, coworkers...they're all going to pry and ask what they want. In their mind, boundaries are meant for livestock, not people.

"I was surprised to hear Ronny had a...Gia," he says with raised brows and then looks back at me. "Well, maybe not that surprised."

"Not helping." I shake my head.

"Ronny has been more involved than I ever thought he'd be," she says to Wyatt. "The cowboy thing and picking up random women in bars concerned me."

I scratch my jaw. "I'm right here, you know."

"Right." Camila clears her throat and bends down to eye level with Gia. "Sweetie, this is Wyatt. He's daddy's friend."

Daddy.

God, I never get tired of hearing that name.

Wyatt squats low and gives my daughter his widest smile. "Hi, Gia. It's so nice to meet you."

Gia's curly black hair sways around her shoulders as she twists. "Do you have horses, too?"

Wyatt nods. "I do. Not as many as your dad, but mine are prettier."

"Really?" Gia's eyes light up as she looks at me in question.

I cross my arms and beam sparkles and rainbows at my favorite girl. "He's lying. Don't listen to him, sweetheart."

Camila stands. "So you'll bring her home in a couple hours?"

I nod once. "I've got the spare car seat in the barn. I'll make sure she's home by seven." That gives us two hours to do whatever she wants since Camila's two-bedroom apartment is only thirty minutes away. Gia's favorite activities mostly involve being around the horses, baking cookies with Mama, or airplane rides with Pop where he balances her on her stomach, arms splayed wide as he raises her up and down. I've never seen him act so spry.

Seeing my parents become grandparents overnight was nothing short of amazing. They barely blinked before scooping Gia and Camila into their arms. It gives me an idea of how they were when they found out they'd be bringing me home. Gia is blood, and I wasn't. But my DNA never mattered. Mama likes to say I was the child born from her heart instead of her womb. As a father, I get that in many ways since I never had to go through the pregnancy and birth part. I still love Gia all the same.

"Thanks, Ronny. I'll be back home by then. Just going out with friends," Camila says. "Tell Merv and Esther I said hello."

"Will do."

We haven't done any overnights yet since Camila has been insanely protective as someone who's been a single mother for so long, but I don't exactly have the space for Gia right now, either. My apartment loft is maxed out when it comes to furniture, which is why I've been stashing my earnings from working at Thirst Trapp Farms so I can build a two-bedroom cabin down the way from my folks. I've finally saved enough to afford pouring the foundation and building materials to get started. We break ground next spring.

Anything for my baby girl.

Camila kisses the top of Gia's head. "Have fun with Daddy, lovebug. I'll see you soon."

Gia hugs Camila's legs, then runs over to grab my hand. Her small palm fits perfectly in mine, and nothing gives me greater joy than to hold it. We stay in the drive until Camila gets in her car and waves goodbye.

Then Wyatt turns to face us. His eyes track from Camila to me. "What do you say we play a game, Gia?"

"Okay!" She nods, bouncing on the balls of her feet.

"We're going to need a judge." Wyatt glances at me then back to Gia. "Would you like that job?"

"Yes!" Gia shouts, pumping her other fist in the air. "What's a judge?"

"I'll tell you." Wyatt claps his hands. "Judge Gia can sit right there on the porch steps." He gestures to the farmhouse stairs. "And I'm going to race your dad from here," he points at the ground in front of him, "to the end of the drive just like we used to as kids. You get to tell us who wins. But a judge has to be fair and honest. Can you do that?"

She gives a few exaggerated nods. "Daddy is really fast."

Wyatt straightens, and he speaks to me. "We'll see about that."

I shake my head and roll my eyes. "Do you think that beard will slow you down?"

"How do you figure?"

I shrug. "Wind resistance?"

He glares. "I remember beating you when I was hungover—"

"Hey," I cut him off. "Small ears."

"Oh, right. Sorry." Wyatt shrugs. "Gotta get used to that."

I flick off my hat and plop it on Gia's head. "This won't take long, sweetheart. We'll be making cookies in thirty seconds."

Gia claps her hands.

Wyatt raises his brows and toes a line in the gravel for us to start from. "Confident, are we?"

"Always."

"On the count of three," Wyatt says, then hooks a thumb at Gia and lowers his voice. "Does she know how to count to three?"

I can't help laughing as I line up the top of my boot on the line by Wyatt. "She does." I shouldn't be surprised he'd ask. Not long ago, neither of us had been around many kids since Jack and Annie are so grown.

Now, I have one.

A pretty damn great one.

"Ready, Gia? We'll start at one." Wyatt holds up a finger, counting down with Gia's help. "One...two..."

"Hey, thank you," I interject.

"For what?"

I lower my voice so Gia can't hear us talking. "For treating Gia and Camila like they belong. Like she wasn't a mistake and even though it didn't happen the way I thought it would, that she's still part of me—a part of our family."

Wyatt straightens slightly. "Of course, man. Honestly, I was expecting you to tell me you got a puppy, but a daughter is way better."

I can't help but laugh and peer back at Gia who is busy stacking small rocks, retiring her role as judge.

I look back at my friend—the best of them. "Wyatt?"

"Hm?" he murmurs.

I smile and say, "Three," before taking off down the drive, pumping my arms like I mean to win.

But really, I already have.

Twenty-Five

Tilly

"I tell the truth. And I know what I'm talking about. That's why I'm a threat." —Snoop Dogg

This is exactly what I needed: a bath under the stars.

At least, I think they're stars and not satellites.

Avery hasn't shut up about this outdoor tub since Wyatt built it. But there was no way I was going to use it after guessing the kinds of things they did in it. I'd planned to clean it myself, but Ronny beat me to it.

I've tried not to think of the clean tub as a marriage proposal, but it's hard when he's not actively trying to annoy me like he was before. After making out and sleeping in the same bed, I figured the whole snake ordeal would help us get back to the normal kind of hate we wielded like arrows before. Now he's just acting *nice*.

Ronny isn't your typical nice guy, offering sweet gestures like adding a few delicious-smelling candles and my favorite chocolate near the tub for me to find and read into. He can't win me over like that. I thought thirst-trapping me was playing dirty, but then he went and got caramel-filled dark chocolate. This is *war*.

Sinking below the water, I'm pretty sure I let out a moan that can be heard across state lines. I can't keep it in. Not when my body is still tight from doing more yoga this afternoon and getting stabbed in the stomach by ScapeGoat's hooves during the ab circuit. Ronny had already left and couldn't save him from the handful of dirt I threw his way. Lucky for him, I missed, and Avery still has two goats.

I still say they'd be cuter mounted on a wall.

The steam lifting off the water is a thick plume of moisture in my nose and mouth as I breathe in and breathe out. This week has already shaped up to be stressful since I'm so focused on keeping my heart intact and not wringing Ronny's neck while finishing last-minute wedding prep. Avery finalized the guest list with the caterer while I helped her pack by removing all of her clothing. What else do you need on a honeymoon anyway?

Not allowing Ronny's charm to get to me has been more challenging than I thought it would be and easier than I want. It scares me just how simple it was to fall back into our old patterns.

But this is one unhurried moment where Ronny is safely back on his farm, and I don't have to worry or think about any of that. I can float and let the weightless feeling water gives me help me pretend I'm not carrying burdens I don't know how to lift or set down. The chickens are quiet after being tucked into their little house for the night, and other than an intermittent bellowing noise, the cows are quiet, too.

It's not as bad as I thought, living on a farm. It's only been six days, but by the end of the week, it will be the longest I've ever spent here since Avery moved. She tells me often enough how magical this place is. I guess right now, with my arms resting on the edges of the metal tub, my eyes closed while the bubbles dance across my chest, and the moon acting as mood lighting, I can see why.

It's relaxing in a completely different way. Quiet that doesn't scream in your ear but might whisper that you need that individual waffle maker you found on a lightning deal online. Good thing I left my phone inside.

A soft plunking sound in the water grabs my attention, and I fling my eyes open. *What was that?* I look around and see nothing, but my view is partially blocked in the direction of the farmhouse since there's a trifold privacy screen made of wood with hooks and hanging towels.

I don't see anything, but is that—

I scream and pull my legs in, scrambling to one side of the tub.

It was on my leg! Something touched me. It was light but dense and definitely not there before. It fell from the sky. I heard it fall into the water. Is it an...animal? The thought has me clutching me knees closer to my chest.

My breathing is erratic as I try to calm down and think rationally. I need to either streak back inside and risk giving Wyatt's family and/or the animals a show or find out what's beneath the water's surface before it finds me. But I don't want to get out. This is my *treat yo self* moment. And I was here first anyway.

It's likely just a stick. *No, too light.*

Or maybe a candle fell in that I didn't notice. *No, too heavy.*

What if it was a black-headed grosbeak bird? *No, too...feathery.*

What I felt was too slimy.

Wait. *Slimy?*

I look around the area again, scanning every tree in the forest, cabins, and expanse of grass that Ronny mowed today. There's nothing. Well, there are lots of somethings; I just can't see them through the pitch-black darkness.

I steady my breathing, then reach a curious toe to the end of the tub. Feeling around, I try to find the offender ruining my bath. My toe touches the slimy artifact, and I pull back with a yelp. But further rational thought proves that I know what that is. I've touched it, held it in my hands, stuffed it in Ronny's boot, and hung it from his visor.

I lean forward and feel around with my hand until I touch it. Grabbing it, I hoist it above the water's surface like a fish I caught with my bare hand just as someone starts laughing. But not just any *someone*. It's Ronny, bent at the waist as he comes around the privacy screen to the rock-tiled platform the tub sits on.

My jaw locks tight, and I narrow my eyes at him while covering my tits with one arm. Then I chuck the rubber snake in his direction, but he's too busy laughing and doesn't catch it. I'm too busy sinking further under the water. Bubbles can only hide so much.

"You need to leave." I'm so stern. He should be afraid.

He wipes under his eyes and stands straighter as his laughter dissipates. "Why?"

"Because I'm having a bath, and *you* interrupted it." And I'm very naked under these bubbles.

"I'm well aware of that fact," he says in a gravelly tone. God, it's like those same butterflies have hatched inside my stomach, making it flutter. "I was the one who cleaned out the tub for you earlier, remember?"

My shoulders rise above the bubble line. "You're telling me you did that just so you could get me back with that damn snake?"

"Yup."

The cocky way he says this makes me want to strangle him with said snake. Here I thought he was doing something kind for me. More proof I can't trust him.

So much for being a *nice* guy.

I look straight ahead and grind my teeth. "Leave."

"Why?"

"We've already been over this," I spit back. "And I'm not clothed."

"I noticed." He stuffs his hands in his pockets.

I snap my gaze to meet his, narrowing my eyes in hopes that I somehow possess powers to turn him to ash. It's not working. If I didn't need these bubbles for protection, I would fling them at him. "Just because you've seen me naked in the past doesn't mean you're going to in the future."

He strides over the paver stones, closer to the tub, pulling his hands from his jeans to rest them along the edge of the tub. "And what about the present?"

Sounds like Flirty Ronny came to play.

All I'd have to do is tilt my head to look up at him, and our mouths would collide in that familiar, inebriating way. But I won't do it. I won't look at him and get distracted by those rich, dark eyes of his and fall prey to their tactics. Instead, I risk a little boob flash and fling water on him.

He jumps back and uses the sleeve of his flannel to wipe his face, but his shirt is well and soaked. *Good.*

His laugh is low and strained. "You know you could just invite me in there instead of getting me all wet."

"Not as fun," I manage to say with a straight face.

"Are you sure about that?"

The way my body thrums and pulses hearing him say this is not good. I'm starting to think maybe he'll always have this effect on me. I should just learn to live with it, like a monthly period or the birthmark on my lower back shaped like Iceland.

I clear my throat and sink a little lower. "Positive." He picks up the rubber snake, and I stab one finger at him. "Don't you dare think of taking that. It's my turn."

He holds up his hand with the snake and slowly reaches behind him to hang the coiled rubber on the small hooks used for towels and personal items. "I know," he whispers, then turns back to me. "I might play dirty, but I'm fair. You'll get your turn."

Why does it sound like we aren't talking about the rubber snake anymore?

The way my heart starts to race and a stronger heartbeat starts pounding between my legs is not okay. I'm angry at him, yes, but I'm more upset that he can make me feel like this with a few well-placed words. I've practically been pitching him softballs this whole time.

He walks closer to the tub again, and my body tightens against the swelling ache. This time, he leans in behind my shoulder—the same one he used to trace shapes on as he held me—running his hands along either side of the tub to box me in. His lips are close to my ear when he whispers, "I'll see you tomorrow…Till."

My lips part, and I'm pretty sure a gust of air passes through them. If I haven't orgasmed, I will tonight at the reminder of him using that nickname, the tingles of breath on my skin.

He brushes the slick strands of hair from my neck that wouldn't stay in my claw clip. "Are you sure you don't want me to wash your hair again?"

I close my eyes against the memory. I've lost all control, which is what he wants. I can't let him do that. I need to be stronger.

Opening my eyes, I decide to throw him a curveball. I don't even watch baseball, but this feels right. I curl a hand around the back of his neck and pull him closer, his rough cheek skimming mine. I love the gritty texture of this man, but I won't give in.

I turn my head so my nose trails against his cheek and then down his neck. I'm barely keeping myself together as my lips hover at the edge of his five o'clock shadow, the brush so soft and gentle, teasing him like he's teasing me.

One of his hands moves to graze the opposite side of my neck, tracing the outline of my collarbone when I open my mouth and feel his neck bob against my lips as he swallows. Right when he thinks this is going in a different direction, I sink my teeth into the flesh of his neck. *Hard.*

He curses and jumps back, cradling the mark I know I left.

I try to keep my smile under control, but I can't help but feel pleased with myself. "Oh, I'm sorry. Was that too hard?"

His face is shadowed by the faint lights and flickering candle flames, but I can see enough of his expression to know he isn't sure how to feel. Turned on, confused, shocked. They all war for time on his face, but eventually, he goes with smug—the look he wears most of the time.

He rubs his neck. There's no way that didn't hurt him. "Thank you for the good night kiss," he says, then backs away, stepping over the edge of the pavers and to the other side of the privacy screen. "See you tomorrow, Till."

"Maybe you won't," I yell after him too many seconds later, but he doesn't respond. He's already gone.

Finally, I'm alone again, and I don't have to worry about rubber snakes being thrown into my bathtub or annoying cowboys appearing out of nowhere.

But I do have to deal with the feelings clog-dancing on top of my chest.

Those might be the most terrifying of all.

Twenty-Six

Ronny

"Growing up, I didn't dream of being nothing, of living in the ghetto my whole life. I wanted to get out." —Snoop Dogg

W here've you been?" Mama asks, working her crochet hook in a rhythmic pattern. "Looks like you've been through hell and back."

Or near Tilly's tub and back. Same thing.

I wasn't exactly expecting to be invited to stay, but the prospect was enticing when Tilly pulled me close like she meant to kiss me. Too bad the bite didn't even dissuade me. I would've stripped down right there if she asked me to.

This is my problem.

I have so much I need to tell her, but I get too sucked in anytime I'm around her. I forget the things I need to say, and instead get lost in her.

"I'm good, Mama." I slowly drag myself up the few steps onto the porch where she's sitting in her wooden rocker. When I parked and saw her sitting out here alone, I decided to swing by before going to my apartment. "Pop already asleep?"

"You know he isn't."

I scrub a hand down my face and look out at the fields, though I'm not sure why. It's pitch black. I guess a part of me just expects Pop to be out there with his headlamp working like I've seen so many times before. Whether it's a birthing animal, or he's patrolling for a predator with his shotgun at the ready, this work doesn't end with a clock.

I take the rocking chair next to hers. "How'd the branding go?"

182

"All good from what I heard." Mama's wrist twists with every pull and tug of her yarn. I grew up seeing this so many times, I'm as good as a second-hand crocheter. "He's organizing something in the barn. Haven't seen him around since after dinner."

Not surprising. "What are you making?"

"A baby blanket."

The porch light is bright enough to see the lavender colored yarn. "For who?"

"Wyatt and Avery."

My mouth gapes. "They aren't even married, Mama. Why are you making them one?"

I'm sure there isn't some secret love child Wyatt forgot to mention after I told him about mine.

She pulls more yarn from the roll in a bag at her feet, finally looking at me with a smirk. "I'm only kidding." Her chin falls to the work in her hands again as she chuckles. "This is for Gia."

The color makes sense now. Gia loves purple. "Didn't you already make her one?" Camila told me she sleeps with it every night.

"I did. But this one is for her doll. Said she needed a matching one the other day, so I got started."

It's not unlike Mama to do this; I just appreciate her more every time she does. The way she loves my daughter even if I did things out of order from how her and Pop did.

The knot that's been forming inside me tightens a little more like the ones Mama is purposefully creating in the blanket. But this isn't some overhand loop; it's like a Palomar knot—seemingly basic but the strongest kind. Every day that has gone by keeping Camila and Gia a secret, it pulls tighter. It's so tight now that the only way to release some tension when I feel the active pulling is to release a long, slow breath.

Mama peers over from her work. "Did you tell her?"

How she always seems to know what I'm thinking is a mystery. "No."

She nods and keeps working. By now Mama and Pop know the timing is up to me. Camila has become more and more comfortable as time has worn on, but I think I've been keeping Gia a secret because of what's on the other side of it. People will say what they want, but it's the opinions from the ones who matter which make me hesitant.

Telling Wyatt was a relief. He treated me like Mama and Pop did—accepting without question. But Tilly is another story.

"Once I say something, she might never talk to me again. It'll be like my birth parents all over but worse since Avery's her best friend, and she'll be around." I say this because, apparently, I take sadistic pleasure from making jabs at what I lack, but Mama sinks her teeth into it.

"Since when do you speak ill of your birth parents in my house?"

"We're on the porch, Ma."

"Same difference."

The rocking chair starts squeaking like a Chipmunk with my movement. "It's true, though. They all but drove to the hospital and gave me up. I did the same thing to Tilly."

"Chose, you mean."

"What?"

She sets her hands on her lap. "They chose adoption, son."

"Same difference," I state.

She gives me a side-long look. "There's dignity in a choice and a whole lot of shame without."

"So just because they chose to put me up for adoption means I should think better of them?"

"I'm saying it'll serve you well to remember what they chose for you. They were young; you know that. Money was tight, jobs were few…from what I understand, they were still trying to finish high school. So they chose a life for you they wouldn't have been able to provide otherwise. That, boy, is a kind of love we'll never know intimately, but we both benefitted nonetheless."

Mama's words hit. "Hadn't thought of it like that."

"You chose to end things with Tilly for Gia. There's dignity in the choice you made because Gia is your daughter and Camila needed help. But there were some casualties along the way. Now you're trying to fix things. But don't forget to consider what you want, too."

What I want feels so far off, I can't even see it with binoculars. I've been so focused on Gia, my family, this farm, that I haven't allowed myself to think about what's best for me—*who* I want.

"Mama?"

She hums a "Yes?"

"I don't know if I can tell her." I know how cowardly I sound, especially when I can't seem to keep my hands off Tilly anytime I'm around her. The excuse to be close to her indicates she's more than my enemy or friend. "It's been too long."

"It has," she agrees, curling her hook through the new loops she's made. "But regardless of where things go, you have to be honest."

I run a hand down the front of my shirt—*wet* shirt. The memory reminds me of how much that woman has me feeling.

"What if she still hates me?"

"What if she doesn't?"

Another slow breath whistles out of me as I rub my palms along the tops of my thighs. "I doubt that will be the case. It's been two years, Mama."

"Oh, I know," she says. "I thought she should've known a long time ago, but bringing up the past now isn't going to do us any good." She stops stitching, and drops her hands to her lap before looking at me. "Anything worth doing is bound to scare you a little, too. There's been plenty of times over the years where I thought we wouldn't make it. Not just the farm, but me and your father."

I haven't heard her talk about their relationship like this before.

"I'm convinced it was our honesty that's pulled us through everything. Not the filtered kind of honest. The kind where it feels like you're risking, like you're standing on stage in front of the whole town...naked."

"Mama, really?"

"Yes, really," she says with a stuttered laugh then she sobers, volume dropping low. "It's the kind of honesty that hurts as it comes out because it lives under the rocks in your soul. Give it some light and see what happens. That's what you're facing right now in sharing Gia with the world, but that little girl—Tilly—deserves this kind of risk."

"But I've already hurt Tilly," I protest. "I don't think I've got it in me to do it again."

She lowers the narrow reading glasses perched on the brim of her nose and levels me with a stare that makes me feel like a young boy stealing cut strawberries set aside for pie making. "You're hurting her by saying nothing."

I blow out another breath and slowly rock in the chair, looking up at the stars. I've always lived like my business is mine to deal with, but with Tilly, I want her to know me like this. I don't know if that says she's it for me or what, but leave it to Mama to ease the knot a little. Not because I've even done anything about it yet, but because being seen and heard—known in those deepest places—makes it feel possible.

And possible is all I need.

Twenty-Seven

Ronny

"Drop it like it's hot." —Snoop Dogg

I'm not sure what's sexier. Tilly naked under a pile of bubbles or Tilly naked under a light blue flowy, two-piece summer dress.

We're seated across from each other after just finishing dinner at the Grand Hotel for the bachelor and bachelorette parties. It's dark in here, with dim mood lighting and small candles on every table. Bison, moose, and elk heads are hung at close intervals along the walls, but the plush fabric-wrapped chairs make this a fine dining experience in our town.

The ruffle along Tilly's curved bodice has been like a siren calling to me all throughout dinner while Stace has been chatting with her about perimenopause. I tuned out after things got graphic. The thin straps are no more than dental floss, and it hugs her ribs, revealing a sliver of tanned skin before the matching skirt flows out from her waist and tangles around her smooth legs.

I know I've been staring, and I know she's noticed. But caring is another thing entirely. My mind has started lying to me. Seeing Tilly again, spending time with her, and feeling how good we are together has me thinking maybe Mama's right—maybe she won't hate me. Giving these feelings a name and a comfortable spot to sit down in my brain just sounds flat reckless.

The two whiskeys I've had probably aren't helping, either.

"Ronny...hello?"

My glass is empty, so I slam it down a little too hard when I realize Wyatt, who is sitting right next to me at the head of the table, is talking to me. "Did you say something?"

"Yeah, trying to. What's up with you tonight? You've been...distracted." He leans over the corner edge.

I shake my head. "Just a lot on my mind."

"Like what?"

"Farm stuff." I roll my eyes. "Now, what did you want?"

"You ready to go to the Thirsty Hippo?"

Adjusting the Stetson on my head, I look up at Tilly across the table. She sees me staring again but looks away quickly, laughing at something Avery says. "Yeah, let's go." I tear my gaze away and look back at Wyatt. He's wearing a bedazzled black T-shirt that says *GROOM* in all caps across his chest. "I can't take you seriously in that."

He looks down, running his hand along the shiny gemstones. "Avery insisted on making me one to match hers. Don't laugh because one day this'll be you."

"I doubt it," I say to Wyatt without looking back at him. I don't sound very convincing, but thinking like this before I talk to Tilly won't do me any good.

Tilly's short hair dances around the top of her delicate shoulder blades, leaving my mouth dry as fuck. Have I even told her how much I like it? She added a few curls tonight, giving it texture and volume to highlight her angular jaw and columned neck. I know she's been covering up the hickey I gave her, and I don't like it.

Everything about us has always felt hidden or undefined in a way. We never even slapped labels on each other like *boyfriend* and *girlfriend* because we just were. I wasn't hanging out or seeing anyone else and neither was she. We were exclusive in that regard, but official? Not really. Not how I want.

The bite mark she gave me is still on my neck. She might have a harder time hiding one of those. Thoughts of sinking my teeth into her skin has me licking my lips. I hastily stand, grabbing my jean jacket off the back of the chair and shoving my arms through. This restaurant is getting stuffier by the minute, and I need to get out. Pulling at my collared shirt, I undo a few of the top buttons. Everyone else stands, too, and we walk toward the entrance but they stay back to use the restrooms while I push through the front door to inhale as much air as possible.

The streets are quieter than my thoughts with blaring music filtering onto the street, and people hollering about God knows what. Welcome to Friday night on Main Street. Living in a small town means the amount of action these establishments see is far more than I've had in the last few years.

"Feeling alright there, *pal*?" A hand slaps my back as I whip around to face her. The nickname Tilly uses sounds more like a slight. "The night is just getting started."

I set my jaw. "All good."

"How's the bite mark?" She points at my neck. "It's looking a little red."

"How's the hickey?"

There's enough light filtering from the hotel to see her swallow. "Covered."

I lower my gaze to the spot I left it. There isn't even a hint of a reddish mark on her skin to show I'd been there, that it really happened—we'd kissed. I can't keep pretending it didn't happen. Going back to our games without being able to get close to her again has been torture. I'm sick of acting.

Licking my thumb, I swipe along the base of her neck where I kissed her. It shocks her enough that she gasps, her lips falling open. When I remove my thumb, I can see it—barely—but it's there.

"Now it's not."

The intrusive thought to drop my hand and slip a finger in the waistband of her skirt and tug her closer is loud between my ears. I shove my hands in my pockets instead, taking a step back. It's not that I don't want to do it. It's how unfair it would be to keep doing this to her if I did. I can't keep going back and forth on things and screwing around.

Tilly deserves better.

Maybe I don't deserve her. But damn if I don't want to. She'll get to decide that.

"Ready to go?" Avery skips out of the restaurant while tugging Wyatt by the hand.

"Ready," Tilly says, desire still thick in her throat.

It isn't long before Stace and Bryan join us on the sidewalk. The fresh air helps shake loose the whiskey's hold on me, and my breathing evens out after feeling like I'd been holding it the entire meal.

Stace loops an arm through Tilly's and tugs her along the jagged walk. Cars and trucks of all sizes are parked at an angle along the curb, and the glow of the neon signs belonging to a few businesses light the way. I follow at a distance behind the group. I just need to make it through tonight without doing anything I'll regret in the morning.

Avery jumps on Wyatt's back and shoots an arm in the air. "WE'RE GETTING MARRIED IN TWO DAYS!"

Wyatt trots like he's a horse carrying his rider, and Avery giggles uncontrollably. A few stragglers hanging outside one of the bars, or others on their way inside one, hoot and howl right back. I'm sure we'll see most of these people Sunday for the wedding, and I'd be surprised if we didn't get a repeat performance.

By the time we reach the four-way stop, Stace and Bryan are saying goodbye and heading to their vehicle. I wave at them and continue across the street with Wyatt, Tilly, and Avery until we reach the glass door with the flickering *open* sign above it. Walking in, the familiar scent of fried food and strong beer greets me like an old friend I saw last week. Probably because I did. Living in a small town means there are few things to do outside of working and visiting the local bars, and the Thirsty Hippo is top tier.

The hanging blowfish light, taxidermied animals, and tiki-themed paraphernalia might send a tourist into an existential crisis. But to me, it's as much of a home as the land I grew up exploring. Wyatt and I knew our way around every burger on the menu at one point and, eventually, the different local beers. Betty hasn't changed the menu all that much. The one thing you can bank on in this town is when the things you count on staying the same end up changing—there are riots involved, decades-long friendships broken, and brawls to be had between people over the simple things.

The Thirsty Hippo is the spot to go when you're looking to watch a game, catch up on any worthwhile drama, or find a hookup. Might be because of all the good music Betty offers here along with an open dance floor at the center of the room. There are few people who use it, but that doesn't stop Betty from hosting line-dances with the disco ball lighting the way or a free dessert to the person who can do the best Macarena. That was me, but I'll deny it if asked. Wouldn't even let Betty take my picture to hang on the wall with all the other losers who compete in her fun.

There was a time when Tilly and I danced for hours out on the raised wood parquet floor that has duct tape holding down all four sides. Betty likes to change the color every time it starts to peel up and right now, it's a black and white checked pattern. When Tilly and I were here together two years ago, it was hot pink. It was one of the best nights I can remember. Not many people like to dance. But Tilly does. She loves it almost as much as I do, and maybe that's where the nostalgia comes from, washing over me with tidal force to pull me under as Tilly leans over the bar to order.

I'm about to fake an illness just to get the hell out of here and avoid the memories. I've got enough work to keep me busy and plenty of thoughts to sort like tools in a messy shed.

I walk up to the bar near Wyatt and slap him on the shoulder. "What are you getting?"

"Old Fashioned."

"And what about you?" a familiar voice behind the bar asks.

I flash a cocky grin at Betty, whose gray-black hair is tangled up in a ponytail. "Do you even have to ask?"

She lets out a clipped laugh as she fills a glass from the tap. "Depends on what part of the night you're on. If I'm your first stop, I'll get you a whiskey," she says, mopping up some spilled beer. "Otherwise, I'll get you a beer."

Pulling off my jacket and draping it over the barstool, I rest my forearm on the bar top. "Beer, please."

She nods, and we both share a knowing look. Betty has been the one working here all these years, hiring a few people here and there to pick up the slack and give her a break, like when her grandkids were born.

There was never pulling anything over on her when we came in as nineteen-year-old kids. She knew our parents, and worse, she knew their numbers. This town is notorious for making sure any move you make is retold in freaky, accurate detail. They would've had all the evidence they needed if we flashed a fake ID or screwed around too much.

I can barely go to the liquor store and buy myself some whiskey without someone calling my mama and letting her know. It's not like she's surprised I'm buying it, but she does like me to know she's aware. With a smile on her face, of course.

But Betty has also been our greatest ally. I got shitface drunk on my twenty-one run, and she cut me off and drove me home to make sure I got there. Not sure I ever thanked her properly for that.

Betty slides an ice-cold glass across the glossy wood bar top, and I immediately lift it to my lips. It'll be my last drink of the night since I'm driving, so I savor that first sip, letting the crisp liquid slide down my throat while the foam hides my top lip.

Tilly and Avery are already nursing their drinks, both festive-style beverages served in tiki glasses with fruit bobbing on the top and an umbrella hanging off the side. If you ask me, fruit shouldn't bob.

I shake my head and raise my glass. "To Wyatt and Avery."

Everyone raises their glass.

"Aw, Ronny! You know I love a good toast." Avery winks at me.

I'm not one for speeches, but here, with limited eyes on me and music that's already on the verge of ear-splitting, I don't mind so much. "That you both have the best day to start the rest of your lives."

Avery clutches her heart while Wyatt smiles wide, his damn *GROOM* shirt matching how happy he looks next to his woman—stupidly in love. Tilly just stares at me through a squint as though she's trying to decipher every single word that came out of my mouth.

We all clink our glasses and take another sip before Avery asks me to recite a poem or some shit. I bounce my gaze and clock all the regulars I know. The mix of people you'll get in here ranges. Old, young, those passing through, and the die-hards at the pool table playing for pride. There are two men I've seen at the hardware store on the slot machines, two middle-aged couples two-steppin' on the dance floor, and a few younger guys seated on the corner of the bar. I've never seen them before. Must be passing through or working in the area.

They don't seem to be interested in anything other than Tilly and Avery.

Wyatt doesn't notice yet, but his back is to them, and he's pulling Avery against his chest. He can't keep his hands off her. That's how it's always been. Since the moment the word *boss* turned into mince meat, they've been inseparable.

It's been so long since I've been in a relationship; I wonder what that's like. To touch someone you love so freely. It's comforting to know that at the end of a night like this and every other one, they're coming home with you. I shake my head and go back to watching the guys I don't recognize.

Tilly isn't looking at either of them, but I'm not sure that matters since one of the guys with a cowboy hat and a clean hooded sweatshirt hops down and comes strolling around the bar. Toward us—*her*. I'm feet away from her, so it doesn't look like we're together. I look like them: a man with his eyes on a beautiful woman. Warning bells go off inside me as he waltzes past Wyatt and Avery, going straight for Tilly. She whirls around and puts her elbows on the bar behind her when he approaches.

My grip tightens around my glass. This douche is really just going to come up to her. What if she were mine? He'd be taking his life into his hands if she were. But we haven't even touched since walking in here. If she were mine, I wouldn't hesitate putting a hand on the small of her back, lacing our fingers, or circling my arms around her the whole damn time so every other douche in this place would know she's with me.

But she isn't.

She isn't with me because I pushed her away.

But that's not what I want.

What I want is to break this fucker's nose for getting this close.

The guy is saying words I can't hear and shouldn't care this much about. But I do because I'm in this too deep now. I was that first day two years ago when Tilly arrived in cowgirl boots. I was when I hastily kissed her last summer. When I told her we couldn't keep seeing each other. And I am right now.

The hickey *I* put on her neck is slightly visible at this angle, and I want to kiss her there again until it's fucking evident to this guy not to mess with her.

Wyatt takes a gander over Avery's shoulder and gives me some kind of look, indicating maybe I should step in and do something. Would Tilly want that? Or does she want...him?

He's the definition of *all hat and no cattle*. His jeans are too clean and worn in all the wrong places. If you're sitting on a horse all day, driving a head of cattle, and getting shit done, the insides of your thighs and upper calves are where your jeans show it. But his are worn down on his quads. It's all wrong.

I should rip that cowboy hat right off his head and shove it up his ass for claiming to be something he's not.

The guy is crowding her space, leaning closer to whisper something in her ear while curling talon-like fingers around her bicep. I grit my teeth and focus on anything in front of me so I don't yank his hand off her with the force of a thousand tornados. The bottles of liquor across from the bar are all lined perfectly with half-empty ones on the bottom shelves and fuller ones on the top. The neon sign Betty got on a craft site a few years ago glows white and could blind me if I keep staring.

Nothing is working.

Tilly's laugh is tuned to the right frequency in my ears to hear every inflection. It isn't one of her belly laughs where she starts and can't stop. But it isn't an annoyed laugh, either. What does it mean? God, I'm pathetic. Analyzing her laughs to see if she's really into this guy.

I could just turn around, toss the rest of my beer in his face, and punch him square in the jaw for talking to her. Or I could pull her aside and ask. Instead, the perfect excuse to insert myself starts playing through the speakers from Betty's ancient iPod.

Drop it Like it's Hot.

I drain my beer faster than I wanted to and set it on the coaster before repositioning my hat on my head. I'm pushing off the bar and stepping around a stool before I can think better of it.

"Excuse me," I say to the guy without looking at him. My eyes are locked on Tilly's. It takes her a minute to register what I'm doing. Hell, I'm still not sure, but I offer her my hand. "Want to dance?"

Maybe it's just me, but it seems like her lips curl into a wider smile, as she looks between him and me before grabbing my hand. She shrugs and mouths *sorry* to the guy while letting me tug her toward the dance floor.

I walk backward until my heel hits the parquet and then whirl her around toward the middle before flattening her against my chest. She feels so good here. Curves fitting in all the right places and her lithe body in the palms of my hands. It's heady and overtakes any rationale I might have had ten minutes ago. But I don't think I even had it then.

She tilts her chin up to look at me, lacing her fingers around the back of my neck, whispering, "Took you long enough."

Twenty-Eight

Tilly

"The fact is, the truth will come out. The truth will come out when it's time." —Snoop Dogg

I can't remember how many songs we've danced to so far. All I know is it will never feel like enough, even in heels.

He twirls me around like I'm nothing more than a ballerina in a jewelry box, never taking a break until the music stops. My skin is slick with my effort, my body hungry for each time Ronny rolls his hips against mine.

It's like we're back in his room, making out on his bed and touching like we mean more. But this time, all of our clothes are on, and we have an audience. There are still a couple people dancing, but Ronny's made sure to eat up enough of the dance floor that there isn't a lot of room. He takes up space anywhere he goes, but especially when there's a good beat.

He spins me around so my back faces him, gripping my hip so I stay close. I swivel my hips and play with my hair as his hand slides to my stomach and the narrow split between my top and skirt. His thumb hooks onto my skirt, teasing my body with that one finger.

I prod him with my ass. "Don't be putting your hands where they don't belong."

His hands are spinning me around to face him, crushing our chests together. "Who says they don't belong there?"

I peer up at him, the warmth of him seeping into the chilled areas of me. "I—"

I'm so thirsty. Again.

I threw back my tiki drink after the first couple of songs, almost choking on a chunk of pineapple. Then I moved to chugging water, or else I would be having my own Coyote Ugly moment on the bar top.

We're crossing whatever lines existed before this dance, and I don't know how to stop it. I don't know that I want to. Finishing my sentence is impossible, leaving him on read to guess what was about to come out of my mouth.

I don't even know.

One hand slides down my hip, cradling the side of my ass like it's been here before. At least enough times to be familiar with the layout. Welcome to my ass cheek, the birthmark shaped like Iceland is north of here, but there's a freckle due east.

Like he doesn't already know his way around.

Crushed against him, I feel everything. The bits—that aren't so bitty—and pieces that are all him. His body hasn't stopped moving this whole time, he stares down at me through hooded lids. He's saying more by *not* saying anything. I try to keep with the rhythm, but my mouth. It's the Sahara desert with a box fan set on high—or drier than the chicken I made the other night.

Leaving to go get water now would mean leaving the circle of Ronny's arms. But I can't go another second without water.

"I'm thirsty," I blurt out quickly, pulling away from him enough so my brain can boot up again. The constant dial-up tone was starting to grate on me.

He nods and then grabs me by the hand to walk off the floor we've occupied for most of the night after that guy tried to hit on me. A swirl settles low in my abdomen every time I think about how Ronny stepped in. *Want to dance?* I could have kissed him right there.

Avery and Wyatt are still at the bar, but we pass right by them. Ronny tugs me down the hallway leading to the bathrooms where the walls are painted a dark brown and the lighting is even darker. One of them flickers, threatening to quit work early.

Water isn't back here; it's up at the bar. But there's barely any time to think before Ronny twirls me around and flattens me against the wall, pressing his hips into mine and pinning me in place. His wide-brimmed hat is askew on his head, and something about that small shift makes me close to feral.

I can feel enough of him through his jeans and my flimsy skirt that I bite my lower lip to hold back my sharply drawn breath.

I rest my head on the wall behind me, allowing him to keep me there like a tack in corkboard. Avery would be appalled that I'm touching the wall. Even though she's come to love this place as much as Wyatt and Ronny, she still brings a few disinfecting wipes in case.

But I couldn't care less about germs or weird, unknown substances on the wall when Ronny's hips are on mine and his lips lower to graze the fine hairs on my neck.

"You smell good," he says, nuzzling me while I try to breathe.

Something happened between dancing and *I need water*.

A lot of *somethings*.

Probably enough that could fit into this entire week.

This isn't an isolated incident. This is the kind of danger that only comes from spending too much time in Ronny's presence.

His fingers grip handfuls of my skirt, and I instinctively curl my arms around his waist, wrapping a finger around his belt loops to pull him closer. Dancing and *this* aren't that different. They both involve close proximity, grinding, and sweat.

But only one of them is better suited for a dark hallway with loud music to muffle any sound. The possibility of someone coming back here isn't enough to stop. To say we're the first couple to do this would be shocking.

Maybe Avery was right.

Wait.

Couple?

We aren't a couple. We're...

Shit. What are we?

He kisses up my neck and jaw until he reaches my lips. He hovers over my mouth for only a second, knocking his nose with mine before crushing our lips together. His tongue is pushing into my mouth before I can think better of it. I let him in, opening wide and inviting him to stay awhile. I want his best and his worst. The rough, demanding kind of kisses I know he's capable of.

This is what we are.

His hips rock into mine while I moan into his mouth. He pulls back enough to say, "See what you do to me? It's all you. Every time. Every second I'm with you."

Those words tickle my lips and shoot straight between my legs.

I reach a hand up behind his neck and kiss him harder, licking my way into his mouth and begging him for more. That has always been the problem with us. More is never enough. But the way Ronny stepped in when that guy started talking to me wasn't *nothing*. What he shared in his apartment about being adopted was *something*. Why now? What is happening between us?

He grabs my thigh and lifts one leg, nestling himself further between them and using his newfound space to roll his hardened length into me, reminding me what he can do, what he's capable of doing for me. My mind is scrambled eggs, and I can't think straight.

This isn't nothing.

"Ronny," I say through panting breaths. A plea, a question—always a question—I don't know.

His hand squeezes my thigh tighter while the other holds me against the wall at my waist. Those strong, calloused fingers of his dip under my cropped tank, inching as high as my outfit will allow him, which isn't much. He grunts his displeasure at not being able to have more of me in his hands but settles on gripping my ass over my skirt instead.

"I have to have you," he says, placing hot kisses along my ear.

I rock my hips forward, forgetting the questions flying through my head at the feel of him. "Have me."

"Not here."

I bite his lower lip and tug, letting it ricochet back as he groans. "Where are we going to go then?"

"Your place," he murmurs, moving to kiss the edge of my bodice.

"Can't," I say, tilting my chin toward the ceiling. "Too risky."

He growls and pulls his lips from my pulse point. "Who cares?"

Eyes wide and searching, his expression has never looked so serious. Not stern like he would if he were annoyed or demanding, as if he were tossing me on a bed. It's more like he's desperate for me to believe him.

I close my lips, my thigh still held firmly between his forearm and hip. "I don't know," I whisper, "who cares?"

His jaw works under his shadowed cheek, breathing through his nose. "Not me. I don't care what anyone else thinks. I was wrong. I don't care what I said before—"

The air rushes out of me, deflating like a balloon and going limp against this grimy wall in the back of this dive bar. I'm going to have a questionable stain on my ass, but I don't care. That's what spot treatment is for.

My skirt is hiked up and askew on my waist while one of the thin straps of my crop top fell down my bicep, my hair already a mussed disaster.

"What do you mean?" I ask. "What are you saying?"

He drops his gaze to where our bodies are still connected and then slowly lowers my leg; the click of my heel on laminate sounds even louder than the dull thump of music feet away. He adjusts my skirt and lifts the strap of my top before running his thumb along my lips. But it isn't sensual like it was before. It's gentle and caring since he's wiping the red lipstick he just smeared.

I already feel the loss of him. The pulling away, the goodbyes that seem eternal.

He bends to pick up his hat and settle it back on his head but doesn't leave. The fronts of his boots are nearly touching the toes in my wedges. Not knowing what to do with my hands, I tuck them behind me at my lower back and wait for him to explain more or leave. I expect him to walk away. Just like my parents, like every other man, like *him*.

Looking down and back up again, he finally says, "Go on a ride with me tomorrow."

"Why?" I raise my chin higher, building those walls his lips tried to take down before he can hurt me.

He sighs heavily and scratches his jaw. "Because I want to take you out."

"On a date?"

"On a ride."

He's not offering me much more than what he's saying. We're as good as fuck buddies sometimes and enemies others. Going on a horseback ride isn't exactly what I want from him right now, but determining what I want would mean I'd have to think about it. I'd have to lower the walls to let myself in.

I slowly shake my head. "That isn't a good idea."

"Why?" His brows pull together, and he shoves his hands in his front pockets.

I peer back down the hallway toward the rest of the bar. "Because."

He hooks a finger under my chin and pulls my attention back. "Because why?"

"Now who's the one asking questions?"

"Tell me why, Tilly."

I point between us. "Because this is all we are, Ronny. Stolen kisses in quiet hallways, sex in the middle of the night so no one knows, and lives that will always intersect but never collide."

His nostrils flare, and he shakes his head.

"You know it's true," I whisper.

He told me as much. Now, I need to remind him of this because as much as I like him, I don't want him offering more just so he can sleep with me. That's what this is. The heat of the moment where desires are high and unruly, and he wants to satisfy an itch.

I open my mouth to say more at the same time Avery walks down the hallway. "There you are."

My smile is as weak as my knees when I look her way, "We were just about to come back out."

"Okay, well, we were going to head back across the street," she says, pulling her blonde hair over her shoulder and looking between the two of us. "Wyatt heard there was a cover band playing at the bar closer to Main Street. Do you both want to join?"

"Yes—" I say at the same time Ronny says, "—No."

I look back at him, and the intensity in his gaze makes me wonder if his eyes have been on me this whole time, not even bothering to glance at Avery.

"I'll join." I match his heated gaze. He doesn't have much of a choice since he's the driver tonight, but I know he isn't happy about leaving this moment for the next one.

He finally looks away from me to Avery. "Me too."

Avery nods. "Great." She hooks a thumb over her shoulder. "I'll meet you guys at the front then. Wyatt's just paying the tab now." She turns and starts walking away, then whirls around. "And Tilly?"

"Yeah?"

She scrunches her nose in disgust. "You shouldn't stand against that wall. There's probably used gum or boogers on there."

Always a friend.

I side-step out of the sandwich Ronny created with me and the wall, Avery turning to leave. I go to follow her, but Ronny grabs my wrist. "Wait," he says.

I pause and let him pull me back by my wrist until we're face-to-face again. He's so close I can smell the spiced scent of his body wash. He doesn't wear cologne, but I've never missed smelling it on him. The musky scent of his skin after a hard day of work is one of my favorites. But freshly showered Ronny has that classic Old Spice flavor working for him.

"One more dance," he says, tucking my hair behind my ear.

Usher is belting the same word repeatedly in the background, and the beat is already enticing me to move my hips. Ronny's expression is earnest, waiting for me to say *yeah*.

In the short time I removed a few bricks and let him slip in, I realized something. I think he'll always have a way of making it hard to say no, to fully shut him out, because he was the easiest *yes* I've ever said.

I hold up a finger. "One more."

Twenty-Nine

Tilly

"It's an unexplainable feeling, an expression. It's a touch, it's a feel. Once you feel it, it's like no other thing in the world." —Snoop Dogg

One more song turned into three more songs at the next bar, ending with him hauling me out to the side of the building.

"These legs," he mumbles against my neck, sliding a hand down the side of my hip all the way to my knee. His fingers inch along my bare thigh as he lifts his hand higher. "What are you doing to me?"

Nothing he isn't currently doing to me.

I lift his face, cornering his mouth until my lips are on his. My lipstick said goodbye for good after the second time Ronny took it off with his mouth, and I'm worried I'll get a rip in my skirt, thanks to his greedy hands. But the way his tongue teases and tastes leaves me breathless and ready to rip my own skirt. How his body rolls against mine, using the pressure of the wall behind me to every advantage.

Hiking my leg up like he did in the hallway, he slides his hand all the way up until he's cupping my ass again. "No underwear tonight then?"

I speak through his rough kisses. "Thong."

"Damn it."

I pull back. "What? I thought you liked—"

"I love them," he deadpans then moves his hand from my ass to the inside of my thigh and higher.

"You weren't kidding." I'm breathless as he strokes a light hand over the front of my underwear. He kisses his way up my neck, and I whimper.

"I told you I don't joke."

"We need to go somewhere." Holding his head to my neck, he licks, kisses, and sucks. If he gives me another hickey, I won't complain. "We can't stay here."

He removes his hand from the coil of nerves all collectively screaming *yes please*. Bracing a hand on the wall beside my head, he drops my leg and stares at me. "I can't leave Wyatt and Avery."

This isn't a time for loyalty. "Isn't there someone in town who could take them home?"

"Yeah," he says, "me."

I let my hands drag down his pecs until they're at the waistband of his jeans. I have three days left before driving home. I'm not going to waste it. Dipping a finger inside just enough for him to get why I'm asking.

"I can't," he says, almost begging.

He has a different belt on, but it's easy enough to undo. A clanking sound fills my ears as I do just that. "Are you sure?"

He sucks in a breath, his other hand fisting my skirt. "I'm sure."

The slow slide of a zipper rips through the night air. It's enough to make my legs weak and ask him for a quickie. No one has passed by the whole five minutes we've been outside anyway.

For once, we both agree.

We can be adults about this and fuck first and think later.

My knuckle grazes the front of his underwear as I drag the zipper all the way down. He hisses at the contact, which makes sense since with only one graze I can tell he's hard and uncomfortable.

"Let me help you with this," I say into his ear.

"Not here."

I start to pull my hand away, but he grabs my wrist. "Then where? Wyatt's truck?" I ask.

He looks back toward Main Street from our place hidden in the shadows. "It's parked in the middle of everything. That won't work. Damn it. There's no privacy in this town. Someone probably already knows about this."

"Wait. Really?"

He shrugs, still boxing me in. "Probably."

He stands straighter, dropping his hand from the wall and bringing it to rest on my opposite hip. The way he's bunching handfuls of the fabric of my skirt in his palms and hasn't let go has me thinking that he's considering all of the options he hasn't agreed to yet.

"We've done this standing before; it's not impossible."

His gaze snaps to mine. "It is considering all of the things I want to do with you."

I swallow hard. "And what are those things?"

He smirks and kisses me. "You and your damn questions."

"I need to know," I mumble against his lips.

"You already know."

There's a beat between my thighs at his words. "Then let's get the lovebirds and go back to my place. We can say your truck died again when you were trying to leave the farmhouse."

He tilts his head. "I don't know if they'll buy it. Gertie isn't that unreliable."

I grab the sides of his shoulders. "We are doing this *tonight*, Ronny. I don't care if it's on the side of this building, in a bed, or a swing. We're doing this."

He studies my face. I know what he won't find there is hesitation. I made up my mind after leaving the Thirsty Hippo. We may not be cut out for a relationship like Wyatt and Avery, but doing this is far more enjoyable. After a few more dances, he seemed convinced, too.

I've apparently moved onto the fifth stage of grief: acceptance.

"Let's go get them," I say, tugging his shirt.

"Hold up," he says, holding his ground. His eyes meet mine as he zips his pants and does the belt, undoing all of my hard work. Then, he laces his fingers with mine. "Ready."

Or not.

***

THIS MIGHT BE the most awkward drive I've ever experienced.

Ronny clears his throat. "You doing alright there, Wyatt?"

Wyatt groans, his head pressed to the window. "I'm fine."

Avery leans closer to me, but the cab is only so big, and I know Ronny can hear. "He's not fine."

"Looks like we found you just in time." Avery pats Wyatt's shoulder. "He's never done well with tiki drinks. He's allergic to pineapple. I tried to remind him, but he said that it was a long time ago."

"My stomach is going to revolt," Wyatt whimpers.

"Better your truck than mine," Ronny mumbles.

But mumbling when we're sitting shoulder to shoulder might as well be full volume.

Avery leans over Wyatt. "Maybe we should open a window."

"No!" he protests. "It's my pillow."

Avery looks back at me and rolls her eyes, and I laugh. "Just a little bit," she assures him.

The cold blast of air that enters the truck bites my bare skin, putting all of my hairs on high-alert. I rub my arm like it will do something, but it doesn't help. Ronny places a heavy hand on my leg, warming my internal body temperature as I trace the breadth of his hand with each passing headlight.

The truck is silent, but I can feel Avery's eyes on me like she's trying to communicate via telepathy. I look at her and mouth *what*, but the cab is barely light enough to read lips. I knew we should've learned Morse code.

Her eyes drop to Ronny's hand, and I rub my arms, showing her he's just doing this because I'm cold.

He's not.

I know that now, after he had his mouth all over my neck and his hand up my skirt. But admitting what we're about to do, even to my best friend, doesn't feel right yet. It'll probably jinx it. And how am I supposed to explain this is just a fling? Nothing to see here.

But knowing Avery, she'll make it something to see. She'll ask me if I've changed my mind about liking Ronny—I haven't—or where I see us being in five years—I don't.

This is just fucking.

I slowly shake my head, trying to fend her off. So I start a different conversation. One outside of the group chat that is our eyeballs. "Avery, what time do we need to be ready for the rehearsal tomorrow?"

She clears her throat. "I don't know, Tilly. Are you thinking you like rehearsals now?"

Here we go.

She isn't talking about the rehearsal.

"I like certain things about rehearsals more than others, but I'm still going," I say, confirming with a wide-eyed look that I will be screwing Ronny tonight, and I don't need a relationship to do it.

"I know how much you *love* the dinner afterward, but there's a lot of things that need to come first, like preparing to walk down the aisle without falling or declaring your love in front of everyone."

Okay, wow. Could she be more obvious?

"Are we talking about the rehearsal dinner tomorrow?" Ronny asks.

Avery leans forward as Wyatt groans beside her. "Yes, Ronny. *We* are most definitely talking about the rehearsal." He loosens his fingers on the wheel and holds them up as his white flag.

It's my turn to clear my throat just as Ronny pulls down the drive toward the farmhouse. It's bumpier as we traverse the gravel, and I have to cling to his hand still staunchly taking up space on my thigh. "The dinner is going to happen whether we practice or not," I say to Avery.

Wyatt isn't being quiet about his dislike for the bumpy ride.

"Wyatt! Sh!" she scolds then looks at me. "Practice is important, too, though,"

"Sometimes," I retort. "Sometimes the dinner is better."

She talks through her teeth. "Sometimes it's not."

By the time Ronny rounds the circle drive to park in front of the farmhouse, Wyatt is shoving open the door and puking on the gravel.

Avery holds up a hand like she's directing traffic. "We'll talk about this later."

"Make sure you sign your name at the end of the diary entry," I say as she slides out to help Wyatt.

Ronny kills the engine, and we both sit there for a beat, listening to Wyatt get sick right outside the truck.

"Maybe I should drive home tonight."

I'm still gripping his hand on my thigh, so I squeeze harder and look directly into those watercolor-brown eyes of his. "No."

"No?" he questions.

Wyatt groans again before releasing the steak from the clutches of his stomach and using his *GROOM* shirt to wipe his mouth.

I shake my head. "Just stay, Ronny, and stop acting like you're not going to."

It's like two cherubs are lifting the corners of his mouth in a grand opening that features his smile. I love that smile. But even with Wyatt retching outside, and Avery's obvious warnings, I'm positive of one thing:

I want to bury that smile between my legs.

Thirty

Ronny

"I'm just doing what I do best and that's what makes good music, and that's how you can relate to people." —Snoop Dogg

Need anything else before we go?" I ask Avery after getting Wyatt upstairs and tucked into bed.

We all stare down at Wyatt who has his mouth open, arms circled around a pillow, and is halfway asleep with a bowl beside him on the floor. I'm going to give him so much shit for this. But not tonight.

Tonight, I have other plans.

"Hopefully he sleeps it off," Avery says. "He said it's just his stomach that feels off, and his tongue is swollen. I'm sure he'll be fine." She pauses. "He better be fine."

Tilly hides her upturned mouth with her hand.

I clear my throat. "He'll be ready for the rehearsal dinner."

Avery gasps and whips around to face Tilly. "The rehearsal dinner!"

Tilly looks between us, but I keep my mouth shut. Something tells me *rehearsal dinner* is code for something else. I'm not about to get in the middle of anything. Especially if Avery is trying to talk Tilly out of it. Hell, maybe she should. Maybe Avery would be doing me a favor not to head straight into disaster with my eyes wide open because I sure as fuck won't be able to say no again. I've done it enough times this week to know I don't like it.

Tilly asked—begged—for us to keep things casual.

I can do casual. Too well.

And even though it isn't what I want, maybe telling Tilly about Gia after we sleep together will be better. All hyped up on oxytocin sounds like a decent plan. I'm not ready to let Tilly leave in a couple of days without at least showing her she means more to me than the fling we started with.

Wyatt promised he'd keep Gia a secret a little longer until I can tell Tilly, but time is running out. The wedding is in two days and Gia will be there with my folks. Camila and I have been planning this for a while now. I figured a wedding might soften the blow when I started telling people. Here's to hoping I was right.

Tilly places a hand on Avery's arm. "The rehearsal dinner might not happen."

Avery's eyes widen. "Are we talking about the actual rehearsal dinner?" She leans in and whispers, though I can still hear her. "Or sex with..." She tips her head toward me.

Tilly looks at me, and I shrug. Not getting involved.

She sighs. "Avery, I'm going to leave now. With Ronny," she adds. "I'll divulge every detail of what does or does not happen tomorrow."

"Okay, fine," Avery huffs.

That was easy.

"You know I'm trying to sleep," Wyatt says with his eyes still closed.

Avery ruffles his hair. "I'm going to shower."

"Can I come?" Wyatt shoots his shot despite looking like a ghost.

"Not tonight, babe."

He groans before Avery hugs Tilly, and we descend the stairs, slip on our shoes, and head outside again.

Tilly audibly inhales through her nose. "I'm kind of getting used to walking outside and smelling shit."

I smile. "It grows on you."

She looks at me after I shut the door behind us. Our feet are planted on the porch, and one of two options are in front of us. First, we can either go our separate ways—her to the cabin and me getting back in my truck to drive home like a good boy would do. Or, second, we can go somewhere together—my place or hers. I'm not picky.

There's a flicker in her eye, and I note the moment she's decided what to do. She bolts off the porch steps and yells behind her, "Race you to the cabin."

"What the—" Words are stolen right out of my mouth.

I might have my cowboy boots and hat on, but she's in heels, or wedges—whatever she calls them—and there's never been a race I haven't tried to win.

I take off after her, gravel crunching beneath my boots, holding my hat to my head, and eyes focused on Tilly's back as she pumps her arms and legs. I don't know how she's managing to run in heels and a skirt, but she had a good head start to figure it out. I'm right behind her as she bounds up the steps and opens the front door. I jump all three steps at a time, then walk through the open door, shutting it behind me while I catch my breath.

Tilly is standing in the center of the living room, shoes tossed on the rug and chest heaving. "I win."

I toe off my boots, keeping my eyes on her the entire time. "You did," I say quietly. "I'm okay with that."

She rests her hands on her hips, still breathing hard. "You are?"

I hang up my jean jacket but leave my hat on and stalk toward her, sweeping behind her legs to pick her up and cradle her against my chest. "Yeah, because I still win."

Her arms wrap around my neck and time holds up a stop sign. The eyes I've stared into more times than I could count, her hair that's perfectly windblown, and the feel of her rapid heartbeat audible between us are enough to confess everything. To lay it all on the line regardless of what she says or doesn't. Mountains are crumbling all around me, skies are falling, the earth is rattling like its very existence will cease and still. I don't think I've ever been so sure about *her*.

I kiss the side of her neck and amble toward her bedroom down the short hall. She tilts her head to give me more of her neck, her heart rate now apparent as I kiss the pulse beneath her chin.

The room is as I remember. Darker than usual, but still light enough with the moon shining in to see where I'm going. Tossing her back on the bed, I drag a rough hand up her thigh until I'm hovering over her. She grabs behind my neck and tries to nip at my lips. "Hold on."

She pushes up to her elbows. "Why? I don't want to play games. I just—"

"Trust me." I hold up one finger then grab the hat off my head and set it on hers.

She yelps and holds onto the hat as I pull her to sit. Her eyes rake up my body until those endless dark eyes flick to mine. The moon is highlighting the parts of her I could draw by memory even though I've never picked up a charcoal pencil in my life.

I smooth my thumb across her cheek, and she captures my hand. "Are we really doing this?"

My voice is low. "You mean, are we really going to have the rehearsal dinner?"

She laughs. "I'm serious."

"So am I, Till."

The light in her eyes dims. "You used to call me that all the time."

My mouth turns down. "Do you want me to stop?"

"No." Our gazes link together for a countless chain of seconds before she pushes my chest, stands from the edge of the bed, and presses her body against me. My hands find her waist while hers curl around the back of my neck, and she whispers, "I don't want you to call me anything else for the whole night."

I drag my lips across hers, feeling how soft and pliant they are for me. Only me. For tonight at least. "You underestimate me."

Her breath tickles my face. "How so?"

"You think the whole night is going to be long enough for all the things I want to do."

"I only have three more days."

Our lips hover a breath away from each other, and I feel how the corners of hers tip upward as I say, "Start the clock."

She pushes to her toes and kisses me hard, lifting her leg for me to hold. We're everywhere all at once. Hands sliding and gripping, hips flexing, mouths open and tongues thorough, sweeping into their second home.

I step forward and lay her back on the bed, my hat falling off her as my hand slides up her thigh and under her skirt. She moans softly against my mouth and locks her ankles around my lower back. The skirt is tight around her hips and waist, making it impossible to touch her the way I want.

"Where's the zipper on this?"

"The back." She drops her legs and rolls to her stomach.

I inhale a strangled breath at the view of her. Having had my hands up her skirt plenty tonight, I know what she's wearing underneath, and her thong has been driving me wild; a flimsy piece of fabric means nothing to me. I cup a hand over my mouth and rub my jaw.

She props her chin in her hand and looks back at me. "Aren't you going to unzip it?"

"I'm taking my time," I say with a strained voice.

She laughs. "I'll put it on again later so you can take it off."

"Okay." I quickly go for her zipper, pulling it down and revealing a cream-colored lace thong. It's just as I pictured it and nothing like I thought. "Hot damn."

She reaches around and hooks a thumb under the skinny elastic, hiking it higher up her hip bone. The curve of her ass is just barely visible, so I grip the sides of the fabric and tug lightly to pull it down. All of her—every part—makes my mouth water, and my dick hard.

She lays her head on folded hands. "Like what you see?"

"You have no idea." I pull her skirt all the way off and lean forward, pressing my hardened length between her ass, flexing my hips to feel the luscious curves of her.

I tug both of her hands above her head and flatten my palms over hers, rolling against her again and again until I'm breathing harder than when I ran. Slowing this down is the only way I'll make it through. I've waited for this—for her.

I push off the bed and roll her over to her back. Her thong is already askew, revealing the slick flesh between her legs. Her eyes study me as her hands rest on her stomach.

She's so beautiful like this. "Till."

"What?" she all but whispers.

"I have to tell you something. We need to talk."

"Not tonight." Her hands skate up between her breasts. "Tonight, we're not going to talk about *before*. We're not going to talk about tomorrow, either. We're going to be here. Right now. Just the two of us."

"The two of us," I repeat. It sounds so good that I want to eat those words at every meal.

I hate there is still so much unsaid between us, but she doesn't want me to tell her how I feel. She wants me to show her.

I point at her top. "Take that off."

She pushes up to sit, her mouth dangerously close to my imprisoned cock in my jeans. "Say, please."

"I don't say please in the bedroom."

She gapes and grabs the buckle of my jeans to undo it. "There's a first for everything then."

Her hair is wild, and the lipstick she started the night wearing is all but gone except for the hint of red outlining those perfect lips. Damn, I want her. Worse than I've ever wanted anyone. It's terrifying just how much. I tug at the barely-there strap over her shoulder, but she swats my hand away and yanks me closer.

"Ah-ah. Say please first." She looks up at me through her lashes, then lifts the hem of my shirt and places a feather-soft kiss right above the button on my jeans.

I suck in a breath as she pulls away. I'm begging her in my mind not to stop. To *please* keep kissing me there. To *please* take off her top so I can cup her breasts while ravaging her. But this woman won't be satisfied until I say it out loud.

My eyes track to the ceiling, rolling behind my lids. "*Please.*"

She slaps my ass and starts unbuttoning my jeans. "Good boy."

Thirty-One

Tilly

"Nobody needs a movie to give them an idea." —Snoop Dogg

I never noticed the popcorn ceiling in the cabin before tonight. But staring up at it through a haze of desire and lust, I'll never forget.

I'll never forget how Ronny's tongue thrusts in and out of me in between his relentless focus on my clit.

I'll never forget how he holds one of my breasts in his warm palm, rolling my taut nipple between his fingers while kissing between my thighs.

I'll never forget how he mumbles things he doesn't think I can hear. *Yes. You taste so good* and my personal new favorite, *please.*

And I'll never forget how I shattered, seeing the millions of stars in the sky like the ceiling didn't even exist.

His tongue flattens on my clit as I shudder, and my thighs clench the sides of his head tighter. He doesn't seem to care that he's trapped there, face buried in the most intimate of ways. He runs his hands along the outsides of my thighs, letting me know he isn't struggling for air while every tense muscle starts to release one by one. My head softens into the mattress, and my shoulders, abs, and spine become boneless before my quads release their hold on his head.

He says nothing as he stands and kicks off his jeans, the clank of his belt on the floor my only indication he's still in front of me. Then the tip of his cock is swiping across my entrance.

I lift my head to watch him.

"Letting nothing go to waste," he says.

Using the evidence of my orgasm, he pumps his cock a few times until it's slick and glistening from *my* come. Holy fuck. I've never seen anyone do this, but the pulse that beats between my legs at the sight reminds me I'm not dealing with just anyone.

This man is going to destroy me.

He always has.

He always will.

And I *want* him to.

I want him rugged and crazed. I want him in and out—on and beneath.

I push up to my elbows as he closes his eyes, still manhandling his own cock. I sit up further and slap his wrist. "Let go."

He opens his eyes and smirks. "Say, please."

I scoot forward and wrap my hand around his at the base of his swollen cock, then put the first inch of him in my mouth while mumbling, "Please."

"Damn," he says on an exhale, loosening his grip and letting me take him all the way. "I'm not going like this, Till. It's either inside of you or nothing." I swirl my tongue around his tip, pulling my mouth from him. "So picky."

"You have no idea," he says again for the second time tonight.

But I think I do know. I know what it's been like to live without this heady feeling. I've been doing it for two years. Maybe it's because neither of us found someone else we wanted to be with. Or maybe it's because we wanted *this*, right here, together. Holding out and torturing ourselves until we couldn't do it anymore.

I kiss along the sides of his cock, still slick from my orgasm and mouth, but he was serious. He isn't letting me have him like this. Not tonight, at least.

He steps back and grabs my face between his hands, leaning to kiss me with all of the unbridled passion he's carried like heavy dumbbells. I stand and meet his intensity, pushing my naked body flush to his. He turns us around, keeping our bodies pressed together until he's lying back on the bed with me on top of him. I pull my legs up and straddle him, rotating my hips on his lap.

"Till," he orders between kisses. I keep moving my hips, and he grabs my breasts, squeezing tightly.

I rear back from how hard he's handling me. "What the hell?"

"I need you to stop moving," he says in a strained voice.

"Why?" I ask.

"Too many questions," he murmurs with a smile while breathing hard.

I smile, too, then reach over him to grab his cowboy hat on the bed. "One more question."

I sit back on his dick, one hand holding the hat in place and the other resting on his hard stomach.

"God, you're beautiful," he says reverently. "One more question, and then you're mine."

"Is it difficult to ride a cowboy?"

He laughs out loud and grips my hips, lifting me slightly. "No. I know you'll be good at it."

"How do you know?"

He rotates his hips upward, but I'm standing on my knees and he can't quite reach. "You've done it before."

"I have," I agree. "But it's been awhile." His face turns ashen, but I don't want the mood to shift, so I grab his cock and line him up between my folds. "So teach me how."

I sink down an inch, and he hisses. "Wait." His voice is strangled. "Are you on birth control?"

I hold him steady—so close but not quite. My legs quake as my expression falls. Is this where it ends? "No," I admit.

"Damn it," he grinds out between his teeth. He looks pained.

I feel how hard he is, how desperate he is to say *fuck it* and sink into me bare. But he's right. We can't do that. It wouldn't be smart, considering the pull-out method is a sure way to get ourselves in a tangle.

"Hold on." I roll off him and rummage through my bedside table. "Will this work?"

He lifts his head then drops it back. "Fuck yes."

I rip open the condom wrapper and crawl back on my hands and knees to put it on him.

"I got checked awhile ago, but I haven't been with anyone else," he states plainly, staring up at me from his back. He smooths a hand over my stomach and under my chest, tracing me like I'm his muse.

I pause everything I'm doing. I can't help it. He just admitted he hasn't been with *anyone*. "No one else?" I hold the condom wrapper up. "Like this? What about—"

He shakes his head. "Like everything."

Well, shit. I wasn't expecting that. I thought when I admitted this to him the other night, I was being too honest and should have played that one cooler rather than admitting it. But here he is, offering me yet another moment that feels like more.

The thought clenches my heart in a death grip. *Wait a minute.* So this cock was inside me last? No one else? It's been mine since the last time he was buried deep inside me. The thought is sobering. As much as Ronny has told me we won't work, we can't be together, we don't fit, he's been lying. At least a little.

But this is just sex.

We agreed to that earlier tonight. Didn't we?

I want to ask more questions and figure out if this is really true, to maybe set some terms, but instead, he grabs my leg, swinging it over him and seating me on his lap once more. He thrusts against my opening and my questions are sticky notes on the wall to be looked at later.

I lift enough to grab his cock and position him inside me one slow push at a time until I'm completely full of him. He rocks up again to make sure of that.

I feel so much of him, so much of what we were coming back into focus. Tears rise unbidden, and maybe it's because this feels too right, or he admitted in as many words it's *always* been me.

His fingers dig into the soft flesh of my hips as he instructs, "Keep your spine straight and your hips loose." I do as he says, letting my lower half become pliant in his hands as he rolls his pelvis up and down rhythmically. "Hands on my chest."

I follow his instructions, placing both hands over his pecs like my reins, changing the angle he's positioned inside me, earning another sharp breath from him. He lifts up and licks between my breasts, abs straining as he holds himself up to kiss his way around my nipple.

"Yes," I whimper, pushing closer for more of his mouth, more of his scorching touch.

It's not nearly long enough before he lays back and starts slowly rolling upward.

"I want to go faster," I say. "Feel the wind in my hair."

"Move with me," he says, pounding into me harder and faster. The hat falls off my head, but I don't reach for it. "Keep your pelvis loose, like you're in the saddle, spine straight, and move."

He hammers into me, and I roll down in a rhythmic motion that hits my clit at just the right place. It's so intense, the feeling steals my next breath. But I keep going—keep moving.

He starts off slow, and I savor the feel of him sliding in and out enough to create friction and heat, tingles, and a sharp build in my core. Then he's moving faster, thrusting so high, so hard until his cock is buried to the hilt and he's rolling halfway out again.

I follow his movements like waves rolling over the surface of the ocean. "You're going to come with me, Till."

My head lolls back, sweat beading on my brow. "Am I?"

"You are." He states this like it's fact. Maybe it is. Maybe I want it to be. "Tell me when you're close."

"I'm close," I say without pause.

"Me, too."

He thrashes into me harder and grunts when I grab my own breast. I moan when his thumb reaches down to circle my clit. But as the orgasm builds inside and outside—all over me—he rolls me to my back. I gasp since he slips out of me, but he's quick to guide himself back in. I wrap my legs around his hips to lock him in place for now and forever. I don't want that happening again. I want to make it to the finish line, wind rushing past my ears, his hips moving in time with racing hooves on the ground.

But the frenzied pace slows some, and the achingly slow drag of his cock in and out, rubbing against my walls, is too much. I feel the build coming again without being able to stop it, without wanting to.

"Now," I manage to say. "I'm going to come now—"

I'm cut off by my own shuddering gasp that Ronny swallows with his mouth, kissing me as his rhythm becomes messy and inconsistent. His hips slow, and the tender shift happening is both unfamiliar and second nature.

I cry out with a voice I'm not used to hearing, a woman I haven't been in awhile. But I've never felt more alive, more like me.

Clenching around him after my orgasm, he's right behind me, shuddering with his own.

The way he stays pulsing inside of me until the very last wave rushes across the sand. How he kisses my neck and pushes my hair out of my face to stare so deeply into my eyes. How I grip the back of his head and hold his face inches from mine, so he can't leave. And how he pushes the very last inch of himself inside me, not wasting a second of our waning orgasms. Pretty sure I just let every single one of my walls down.

All of it is like a dream I've had for two years and never woke up from. I swear to myself I won't forget this. I never did. I never could.

He gives me a tender peck, so much softer than any others tonight, and whispers, "Till," one more time.

I can't help but feel this wasn't just sex.

***

HE SEARCHES MY face from beside me where we lay facing each other. "I'm going to take you on a ride tomorrow."

I wiggle my brows. "I like rides."

He traces the curve of my shoulder with his thumb. "I know you do."

"So, is this like a picnic?" I ask, curling closer to his bare chest, though it's anything but bare with his dark chest hair.

"I can bring food if you want." He rubs my back in slow, methodical patterns that just might put me to sleep.

The same raw earnestness is still in his gaze as it has been all night. There isn't a fraction of reluctance in his expression. His jaw is set, but his lips have taken on a slight, permanent curve I can't help admiring.

I desperately want to lean in and kiss him again. Taste and discover until he tells me everything that's going on in his head. Why he wants to go on a ride, if he feels any different. Did he think that was just sex? Did he feel more?

I settle on a statement instead of asking more questions that probably don't even have answers. Or at least none that I want to hear. "We just have to be back by five for the rehearsal dinner."

His fingers trail lower underneath the sheet before rubbing circles into my hip. "Which one?"

My smile is broad and obvious. "Both."

"I'll make sure of it."

"Good," I say.

"Good." He kisses down my neck and arm, then pulls the sheet over his head.

I can't help but laugh as he continues kissing down my breasts and over my stomach.

But when he reaches my hip bone, I'm not laughing anymore.

I'm begging.

Thirty-Two

Ronny

"I think people understand me, me as a person and what I went through because I kept it on the plate. I never hid nothing." —Snoop Dogg

I'm waiting outside Tilly's cabin, having already knocked once with no answer.

I left her early this morning so I could go do some chores and pack some snacks. The memory of her legs sprawled out under the sheets with her two perfect nipples visible above it was enough to make my dick hard and ask for her. But I had work to do, which included figuring out what I'm going to say now.

I knock again, this time a little harder. I could walk in, but just because I was in her bed last night doesn't mean I'm going to assume I'll be welcome today.

After all of my pounding, Tilly finally opens the door. I expect to see her in pajamas still, maybe nothing at all. But she has on a tight pair of jeans with boots, a black tank, and a blue-colored flannel wrapped around her waist—*my* flannel.

This is Farm Tilly 2.0, and there's nothing I'm thinking about more at this moment than taking her to the barn, tossing her in a pile of hay, and having at it.

"Good morning," she says with a lazy smile.

I'm reading way too much into those two words because I'm convinced she might as well have said *you're mine.*

I reluctantly drag my eyes back up her body and coach my thoughts down. "Morning." It's nearing ten, but I've been up for hours already. Might as well be afternoon. I clear my throat. "Ready?"

"Yeah, I think so. You promise you brought food? I get hangry and will probably bite your head clean off if you didn't bring enough. And you already know how sharp my teeth are."

I could laugh if I didn't know how serious she was. "Oh, I know. I brought plenty of food and all of your favorites, too."

I turn and walk down the steps back to June ready to do what I need to. Mama's words from the other night replay in my head. *You have to be honest.* There's no turning back, no second-guessing. It's time to be honest.

"Peanut butter and jelly with chips in the middle?" she asks, trailing me.

"Yup." I stroke a hand down June's speckled white neck. "With cream soda and those sour gummy straws you like."

She stops in front of June and pets between her eyes. "I can see why Avery calls me a teenage boy now. When did you get all of this?"

I wave her closer. "This morning."

She walks hesitantly toward me, looking between me and June. "Really? You had time to go to the store and get all of that? After being up late doing...you know. I just woke up thirty minutes ago."

When she's close enough, I grab her by the waist, pointing at the stirrup and tapping her left leg. "The store is open early. It's not that crazy. I needed something to bargain with in case you changed your mind."

And I made sure they were all soft in case she decides to lob them at my head.

Even the cream soda is in a can and not a glass for this reason.

Her foot is in the stirrup, one hand on the pommel and the other on the rear of the saddle, but she pauses and turns to look at me over her shoulder. "You thought I'd change my mind?"

Her face is so close I could lean a few inches and be at her lips. I could kiss off that surprised look she has, thinking I wouldn't do something as simple as getting her favorite foods and showing up. No matter what happens today, I'm going to show up for this woman. But I keep my lips to myself and say, "Is it really that crazy to think you'd cancel on me? We don't exactly have the kind of track record that proves otherwise."

Yet.

"Fair," she says, facing June again. She bounces her supporting foot on the ground and hoists herself up with a low grunt.

She's been on a horse enough times now to know how to mount and dismount, but it doesn't stop me from cradling both sides of her waist for support until I'm positive she's steady. I hand her the reins once she's settled.

"Are you going to walk? Such a gentleman."

I squint up as the sun relentlessly tries to blind me. "Nope. I'm riding with you."

"With me—"

Her words are cut off as I slip her foot from the stirrup and use it to lift myself up, bracketing the back of the saddle behind her. "You can put your feet back in the stirrups now."

She looks over her shoulder and gapes. "You're just going to ride back there and hope you don't fall off?"

"I won't fall off." I slip an arm around her waist, gripping her opposite hip with my hand. "You're going to make sure I stay on."

"I'm still holding the reins," she says, facing forward as June walks toward her usual route.

"I wouldn't expect anything different."

"Where are we even going?"

I smile despite myself and bend closer to her ear. "Now that's a surprise."

One I'm hoping she'll like more than the one I'm about to tell her.

She shakes her head. "Did you let June in on your little secret? She seems to know where we're headed."

I laugh. "June always knows where she's going. Don't worry."

June couldn't care less what I have planned, but she's been back and forth enough times, she's confident in the steps to get us back to Adler Farms. Since that's where I plan to take Tilly, I don't have to worry about steering her. We can enjoy the ride.

There's a trail that veers off along the way, heading toward the hills overlooking our ranch. I didn't have any idea where I'd planned to take her when I asked her to come for this joy ride with me last night. But I knew we needed to talk. What better place to do that than in the spot that holds everything I am—our land.

I know these mountains as well as I know every sound my coffee maker makes, having explored them plenty as a kid. It's the talking I'm not exactly keen on. After waking up at seven this morning, I should have thought to write down what I wanted to say. It would have given me a head start. Now, I'm just hoping I don't make a fool of myself.

Just be honest.

She swivels slightly in the saddle. "You good back there?"

"Never better," I reply, and it's the truth.

The short wisps of her hair move with the wind, carrying all of her subtle smells of new beginnings. Maybe I'm just hoping for that. Falling into bed together wasn't hard. It never has been. But figuring out where we go from here has been the problem. It's never been the right time. But I know Tilly enough to know she felt the difference last night.

We weren't fucking.

We were making love.

There's a lot I know about Tilly. Some of the things that everyone knows, like how she can't cook to save her life. She loves adventure, but only if she can wear some kind of heel while doing it. And where she is every Monday night at seven. The Bachelor has always been her favorite show.

But there are also things about her I like to think I'm the only one who knows. I know what she sounds like when she's turned on. I know she likes to feel untethered and free but wants nothing more than to feel protected and secure. And I know she's just as scared of commitment as I am, maybe even more.

My parents didn't divorce like hers did, but my hang-ups are there. I don't want to start something that won't last. Maybe that's why hookups without strings were always easier. I didn't have to make any promises, change my life, or ask someone to change theirs.

Yet here I am, willing to risk all of that.

"You're quiet," Tilly says. "Tell me what you're thinking about."

Grabbing around her for the reins, I steer June closer to the edge of the trail so I can lean over and grab a few huckleberries. It finally looks like a few might be ready. "Thinking about the cover band from last night."

"Liar."

She's not wrong. "You didn't let me finish." I pluck as many juicy dark blue berries as I can. It's still early in the season, but the early summer weather this year has helped. "I was thinking about how horrible they sounded."

She scoffs and puts her hand out. "Whatever. It takes guts to get up on stage and sing your heart out. I didn't see you getting up there to sing with them."

I put a couple of nearly ripe ones in her hand. "They never offered."

June walks back to the center of the grooved trail, abandoning the huckleberry bushes for the promise of water and alfalfa back at the barn. I'm hoping she'll forgive me for the detour we're making first.

"And what are you thinking about?" I ask.

Without skipping a beat, she says, "I'm thinking about whether you're going to use that tiny shovel attached to your pack to dig a hole and bury me alive."

A hearty laugh bursts out of me. "Do you have to be so morbid?"

She rests her head back against my shoulder. "I lived with Avery for years. It's basically ingrained in me now."

Avery is better but tends to think life is more of a horror movie than a box of chocolates.

The smell of dried pine baking in the sun and the huffs June makes through her nostrils keep my mind calm while my heart hammers inside my chest. We're coming up to the fork in the trail. One way is a shortcut that leads directly to the barn and main house, while the other takes the longer, scenic route over a ridge and, quite literally, through the woods. But there's an overlook at the top I want to take her. Not because we'll finally be well and truly alone but because of what that place means to me and the other secrets it holds a couple feet below the gritty fibers of the earth.

Steering June to the right, Tilly doesn't miss a beat. "So we're going to your apartment then? Need to make sure we christen your place, too?"

"We'll do that later. First, I've got something to show you."

"As long as it has nothing to do with that shovel," she murmurs, but I'm close enough to hear and feel every breath she does and doesn't take.

"It does," I confirm through a smile she can't see.

The trail starts to climb at the same time it widens to accommodate a vehicle like an ATV. It's usually how I've gotten up here in the past, but it's been a while since I've been back. I'm not even sure if I'll find what I hid there all those years ago, but I'm still going to try.

I'm so stuck in my head, I almost miss the lookout point on top of the ridge, but Tilly gasps. At first, I assume the worst and reach for the bear spray hooked onto my pack slung over June's shoulders before realizing what she's really seeing.

I follow her gaze to the mid-morning view of the valley. The sky is as blue as if Bob Ross painted it himself. Plumes of clouds float above us with a hello and goodbye as the wind carries them over the land like it's been doing for generations. Nature doesn't stop living just because we do. It has its own trauma and hardships, but through the generations, it's still here. It exists and does a damn good job at it, too.

"This...is beautiful," Tilly says under her breath.

"It is," I agree. It's the simple kind of beauty that doesn't take a human lifting their hand to manufacture. It just *is,* and that might be exactly why this untainted view is my favorite.

I slide off June and help Tilly down as well, loosely tying June up to a low-hanging tree limb where she can reach some leaves to snack on. There's plenty of space in this clearing, with a few scattered trees dotting the rocky terrain at the back and an unobstructed view of Adler Farms. The barn I live and work in, the house I grew up in, the fields I toiled in on the hottest of days. The fences I've mended that stretch for miles and feet, corralling our livelihood in the form of black, white, and mud because, let's face it, mud is it's own color when it comes to raising cows.

Tilly's arms stretch wide as she approaches the edge where dirt and rocks dive down the hill, but not quite wide enough when she asks, "Is this all your family's?"

I sidle up behind her and reach to grab her wrists from behind, widening them until her shoulder blades are kissing. "This is my family's farm."

My joy and my heartache all in one.

The easy days are seeing the farm from this vantage point. The hard days are seeing it up close when blood, sweat, and tears are all real, not just a nice story. I've got visible scars to show for those hard days, and for all the ones you can't see, I carry those, too.

"Welcome to June in Montana," I say into her ear, keeping my hands on her arms as she drops them to her side.

The breeze is relentless up here, and Tilly's hair whips me in the face, sticking to my lips and dragging across the scruff along my cheeks and neck I've ignored for two days. I savor every close second, letting the feelings I have in this moment be what lights a fire under my ass to share the others. If I could just touch her, kiss her, or hold her for a little bit longer like I did last night, maybe I'd find the same courage I seemed to have then.

Maybe we *should* have gone to my apartment first.

"Everything is so green from up here," she says.

"We had a lot of rain this spring, so everything has stayed green longer than usual."

I step away from her, heading straight for the rolled blanket in my pack before I get lost and forget my way back. Snatching the main attraction from my saddlebag and whirling around, I say to Tilly, "Think fast."

She holds her hands out in time to catch the sandwich I promised her. Better she have a full stomach before we do this.

She opens the wrapper and takes a bite. I swear I can hear the crunch even from a few paces away. "You *did* add chips."

"You thought I was lying?"

"I'm still surprised you remembered." She doesn't bother lowering her voice so I can't hear her. She wants me to. "There's a lot you've remembered."

"I don't easily forget."

"And why is that?" she questions.

I nod toward her sandwich while I lay the blanket out on the ground where the rocks don't look like they want to stab you. "Eat first."

She rolls her eyes. "Yes, *Mom*."

I smile as I set up the small picnic area, complete with all of the other favorites she mentioned earlier. She's halfway through her sandwich as I pull the shovel off my pack. It's a portable folding shovel and nothing compared to a full-size one, but still good for small jobs like this one.

She starts nodding while sitting down cross-legged on the blanket. "So you *are* going to bury me alive."

"Not today." I kick at a few rocks on the ground until I find the biggest one. It doesn't move an inch when I toe it. Another reason I love the consistency of nature: it stays exactly where you put it.

"Are you digging for gold then?" she asks.

"I'm sure all those who came here for the gold rush found what needed to be found a long time ago."

She leans her elbows on her knees. "And what if they didn't? What if there's gold buried up here or somewhere else on your land? Wouldn't you want to know?"

I move the large rock out of the way and squat down. Tilly's face is but a couple feet from mine on the blanket that might as well be an island, but I don't think I'll ever get used to having her this close. It does a man in.

"Then it belongs to the land." I shrug. "A thank you gift for giving our cattle a fighting chance when so many farms struggle."

She nods approvingly.

I tip my hat back so I can see more of her without an obstructed view. "Any more questions?"

She twists her lips to the side like she's thinking. "Just one."

I wave at her. "Go ahead then."

"Can I wear your hat?"

A smile peels across my face, and I lift it off my head. "Always."

Thirty-Three

Tilly

"I'm destined to live and say things." —Snoop Dogg

I bounce my foot over my crossed ankles. He's been digging for the better part of fifteen minutes, but it's starting to get warm, and the shade from the trees will abandon us soon. I've already drained my cream soda well before I opened the pack of sour gummy straws—wrong choice. My face has been in a perpetual pucker since.

He wipes the beads of sweat on his brow with the hem of his shirt. "Almost done."

How does he know? What the hell is he digging for? This whole morning trip has been a complete surprise. I don't hate it since I love surprises, but I don't have a clue what this is all about.

I've never had a man I slept with and kind of hated just yesterday take me on horseback to his family's farm to dig me a hole. My mind can't help but go to every horrible thought my imagination can think up. Is he digging up a body? A dead animal? Money? Maybe this is where all cowboys store their cash.

I'm surprised he hasn't reached China, considering how hard he's been working, but the hole is only about two feet deep at this point. He methodically scoops a load of dirt and hucks it to the same side, earning him a pile of earth, twigs, rock, and nothing more.

Until finally, his shovel makes it to London, or close.

"You found something!" I yell, my spine straightening.

He brushes some of the dirt aside, and a piece of ripped, red fabric becomes visible. Ronny looks up at me, taking short, heavy breaths.

Then, he keeps digging, and still, I continue to watch like this is the most fascinating show I've ever seen. Truly, I could watch this man knit potholders for all of eternity if I had to. Even if I didn't.

More digging.

More dirt flying.

More wondering.

I rock forward onto my hands and knees and peer into the hole to get a better look. There's a small plastic part now visible. "It looks like a buckle."

Ronny touches it, rubbing his thumb to swipe some of the dirt away. "It is." He tugs at it, dirt flinging with the motion. "It's attached to a paracord."

"Keep digging," I tell him firmly, wanting more than ever to know what this buried treasure is.

He digs out a cavern around the edges of what now looks like a backpack. The paracord on the front crisscrosses in a zig-zag pattern, so Ronny grabs it and tugs. The pack is heavy and still held under by the corners of the earth, making it difficult to pull free.

"What the hell is in there?" I know I've asked a lot of questions, but I will likely ask fifty more. Especially when there's a hole and shovel involved.

Ronny grunts as he pulls the pack even harder until, eventually, the ground releases its hold. He sits back on his heels at the edge of the hole with the backpack bracketed between his dirty palms. He twists it around in his lap and stares at it with a great, big smile. A smile you don't give just anyone or, apparently, any*thing*.

I sit back on my heels, too. "Do you want me to give you two a moment?"

His gaze stutters between me and the pack. "No, no. Just...this holds a lot of memories."

"Right," I say. "Is this where you store all of your backpacks?"

He shakes his head and starts undoing the buckle. "Only the important ones."

Color me confused.

After the buckle, he undoes the cord next.

Ronny meets my gaze and stares without blinking like he's trying to guess what I'm thinking. I don't know what I'm thinking. Up until this moment, I thought there wasn't anything else Ronny could do that would force an open-mouth response. Sleeping with me? Total shocker. Being nice instead of cold? Constant state of bewilderment. But this? I might need to phone a friend once I start blinking again.

He swallows and then looks at me. "I'm going to open it."

"Good," I whisper. "I think you should."

If it's money, gold, or human remains, I'm invested and need to know how this story ends.

He rolls the backpack off his lap to the ground, and I stay balanced on my heels.

Unclipping the buckle, he pulls the flap back, then has to pull the neckline of his T-shirt over his nose to wipe away the dirt evidence of his effort. He tugs at the drawstring to open the top before precariously peeking inside. He looks at me and then back at whatever is in there with wide eyes.

"What is it? What's in that bag?" I ask in a rush, still keeping my distance.

The way he reaches his arm inside up to his elbow has me cringing. Whatever's in there has been for some time, and he's touching it. The red on the pack is faded, the gray is stained with dirt, so I assume there has to be something just as old and gross inside.

When he pulls his arm out, he's holding a small tin can. The kind you'd find small tea cookies sold in forty or fifty years ago. In fact, I'm positive my mom kept her meager sewing supplies in one of them.

I doubt Ronny is about to open a tin of cookies, though. He's not exactly a tea party kind of guy.

He sets the backpack down and cradles the tin before brushing the dirt, debris, and age from the top. The way he holds it is reverent. Like whatever's in there means something to him.

"This is mine," he starts. "I buried this stuff in an old backpack when I was thirteen."

"Over fifteen years ago?"

He nods. "I guess it was supposed to be a time capsule of sorts."

Deeming it safe, I crawl closer and sit on the edge of the blanket closer to him.

"I promised myself I wouldn't dig it up until I turned thirty," he says, staring at the tin but not making a move to open it.

"But you're not thirty."

"No," he says, shaking his head, "I'm not. But it's time."

"Why now?"

I know how he feels about all of my questions, but I can't help it. This is the first time I've seen Ronny like this. He isn't hard or soft, tinkering with something or hiding snakes in my bathtub. He's...in his feels.

He looks over at me, then at the tin. His fingers curl around the edge of the lid, and he works to yank it off. After years of being unused, buried beneath the earth, it doesn't budge. Swiveling it around and trying a different side, he continues to work at it, muscles straining, mouth closed, until it loosens and pops up. Rust stains the rim, and some parts are warped with age.

One deep inhale, then he pulls the lid fully off, setting it to the side.

Folded and discolored papers, bent edges around a photo, and knick-knacks fill the tin. He quickly rifles through everything before I can decipher what they are. An exhale leaves his body in a rush. "It's all still here." He lifts a plastic bracelet that looks like something you'd wear around your wrist at a hospital. It was once white and looks like it had been clipped off. "My hospital bracelet I had as a baby."

He hands it to me, and I take it. The writing on the widest parts reads *BB Adler*. "What does *BB* stand for?"

"Baby Boy," he says, looking at the bracelet in my hand. "That's what they call all of the newborn babies who are going to be adopted. I didn't have a name yet."

Everything comes into focus with that one word.

Adopted.

He lifts up a Polaroid with a ripped edge and age spots in the darkest parts and stares for the longest time. I can't keep my eyes off him knowing what the contents of this tin mean to him, but why he's digging it up *now*—why he's showing me—has me coming up with my own ideas, which is always an unhinged place in my mind. Is he pregnant? Am I? No, no. He's going to tell me he has a week left to live. My heart pangs wildly, and I start to panic.

Eventually, he passes me the photo. "My birth parents."

"This is them?" I ask, dumbfounded. "Or was."

The two individuals in the photo are smiling, but nothing about their expressions says *happy*. The young girl with dark hair and olive skin, sitting in the hospital bed with a gown of geometric shapes and pastel colors, is cradling her stomach with both hands—almost clinging.

The young boy beside her has darker skin, just like Ronny, with a hand on her shoulder that says *what the fuck are we doing*. They aren't happy or sad—they're frightened.

I look up at Ronny and down at the photo, finding every similar attribute I can. He's busy reading a piece of paper with crease lines intersecting from being folded.

"You look just like them." The words are out of my mouth before I can determine if they're insensitive. I don't know if this is a compliment since I just found out a few days ago Ronny was adopted. He's had years to live with this and develop feelings one way or another.

But before I can take my words back, he says, "I always thought so. But other than looks, I know nothing. I don't know where they are now, if they're together or not. If they had more kids." He shakes his head as I hand the photo back to him. "That's why I buried everything I had of them. I was preserving it forever, yes, but also because it wasn't enough to cling to. I mean, this is all I've ever had of them. Part of me didn't want to let these small things take up too much space in my life. It's not like I took up any space in theirs."

He covers his mouth with his hand. Dirt streaks trail along his knuckles and wrists, showing all it took to unearth these mementos—these small pieces too big to ever really be contained.

"It didn't help, though. No matter what, I couldn't forget my past—*them*. I was always going to know I was adopted. I would always wonder and question," he says quietly.

Scooting closer, I rub the back of his shoulder. The soft woven strands of his T-shirt are smooth beneath my palm. Back and forth for as long as he'll stand it.

"I guess I decided to dig it up because it's time," he says, dropping his hand. "They aren't part of my life—my story—now. But that doesn't mean they never were."

My heart aches in too many places to count, and all I want to do is curl around him and cover him with my whole body. I'd lay on top of him and protect these tender places from being hurt by the roof caving in on this metaphorical house I've envisioned that's starting to collapse. I don't want anything to hurt him.

"Maybe I thought burying this would take away the reality that I'm not Merv and Esther's biological kid. I'd legitimize myself more if I forgot. But I don't think I did. I don't want to forget anymore." He looks at me. "I don't want to forget us, either."

"Is this why you dug this up? Why you brought me here?"

"No."

"Then why?" I move even closer until my bent knees are pressing into the side of his folded legs, and I comb my fingers through the short hairs I trimmed at the back of his neck. I lower my voice to a whisper meant for two people. "Why are you showing me this?"

He stares at his hands for a long time. So long, I don't think he'll answer. I worry that I've asked one too many questions. That he's shutting me out at the first sign of being let in even a little bit.

"Because being adopted taught me something," he starts. "I'll be there for my daughter no matter what. I'm going to do it differently. I'm gonna figure my shit out. I'm gonna give her the kind of life I had with my folks because my birth parents chose that for me. It'll be better."

He isn't making sense. *Daughter?*

He swallows and looks at me. "I have a daughter, Tilly. Her name is Gianna—Gia. She's four."

Four?! I cover my mouth, and my next breath gets strangled in my throat.

"I'm telling you this because you deserve to know the truth and because..." He puffs out a breath then inhales through his nose and looks me dead in the eyes. "Because I think I love you, Till."

Thirty-Four

Tilly

"There'll be ups and downs, smiles and frowns." —Snoop Dogg

The earrings I'm wearing for the rehearsal dinner are almost as heavy as my thoughts. Round and gold with a crimped effect that reflect light with every turn of my head. They dance with the few pieces of curled hair I let hang around my face and the back of my neck.

I have a daughter.

Gianna.

I think I love you, Till.

I'm underwater.

Preferably in a pool with a diving board and cabana rather than the scary ocean, but obviously submerged to the point it's still hard to believe I heard him right.

He loves me.

I step in front of the full-length mirror and stare at myself, trying to rectify the Tilly of now with the Tilly of three hours ago.

I think I love you, Till.

I think...

I love you...

Till.

The words reverberate off my skull as if he's saying it over and over again. But he isn't because he isn't here and didn't mean those words. Not Ronny, the man who told me he could never love me. Not the man who didn't tell me he has a daughter. I spent enough time convincing myself we wouldn't happen. We aren't cut out for love. The kind that lasts, anyway.

He loves me not.

It was the sex.

It had to be the sex.

It's *always* the sex.

Say something, Till. Please, he begged. But all I could do was ask him to take me home. No one was pregnant. He already has a *daughter*. He couldn't even get another word out to explain everything other than a few jumbled sentences. One of which he said she'd be at the wedding—*Gia*.

She's four and has Ronny's DNA, but I know nothing else apart from that. I don't know who her mom is, where they live, or if Gia has his wide grin. I don't know what he's like as a father. If he held her in the middle of the night, carried her around on his shoulders, or rolled on the ground, tickling her until she laughed so hard she couldn't breathe.

I don't know any of that because *I wasn't there.*

He never told me.

Ronny has always kept things private, but this is on another level. But then he opened up about his life, his birth parents, the deepest places of his heart that he was all but welcoming me into while up on that hillside.

He loves me.

But we only broke things off two years ago. How could he hide something like this? Avery said she didn't know, but how? How could you hide something like a child? Did he not tell anyone? His parents? Wyatt?

He loves me not.

The thought niggles at my mind as I twist back and forth, my rust-colored chiffon dress swishing around my legs to where it hits mid-calf. I chose it for the top that looks more like a corset with the boning to add more structure to the flouncy fabric and thin straps. I never thought I'd be wearing it to the rehearsal dinner where I'll have to stare at Ronny, remembering everything he told me. How his mouth tastes and his body feels in my hands, the sensation of him moving inside me. How his heart feels when pressed against mine.

He loves me.

I shake my head and bend to grab a few of the heel options I brought. Deciding on the ones with clear straps and a thick see-through sole, I slip them on and step back in front of the mirror.

He can't say he loves me after he told me he never could. After he lied.

He loves me not.

I tuck a strand of hair behind my ear and then quickly pull it back out. My whole look is the only thing I'm settled on, even if I can't decide how I should feel about everything else while wearing it. Leaning closer to the mirror, I go to touch up my makeup, but there's nothing to fix. So I smooth my dress over my hips again and check my teeth for a sprig of spinach I never ate today.

All that's left to do is go to dinner—the rehearsal dinner I've been *dreading*.

I spent the rest of the day after our fifty-shades-of-truth-ride helping Avery set up the outdoor dining area beneath the large tree. We strung lights, swept off the rock tiles beneath the table and chairs, and decorated the large oak table on top of them. Afterward, we confirmed the caterer would be there at the scheduled time before rushing to meet others for the rehearsal near the barn.

Avery made me my very own bedazzled MAID OF HONOR shirt. I cried when she handed it to me right before I had to walk down the aisle with a very-concerned Ronny. She pulled me in for a hug, and I wet her BRIDE shirt with my big feelings. It was more than the situation called for, but I couldn't seem to stop once I got started.

My heart was breaking all over again. I told myself I didn't care. *It was just sex.*

But it wasn't.

I knew that when walking beside him between the white folding chairs lined just so on the grass—thanks to Stace's neurotic perfection—and splitting like hairs at the arbor to take our respective spots beside our friends. I could barely look at him. But I felt him. I knew. He knew.

And yet, we said nothing more.

I was glad because I didn't have *more* to give.

Then I spent the last couple hours showering, getting ready, and forgetting everything Ronny said and doing an awful job at it.

Dinner is going to be an intimate affair with Wyatt's family and Avery's parents, plus Ronny and me. I'm hoping it won't be awkward, but how am I supposed to sit across from him now that I know *he loves me*? That he's a *dad*?

I sigh heavily, then grab the black shawl I brought for when the cold evening air rolls in. All it takes is a setting sun for the skies to forget the panty-dropping kind of heat from the daytime. Walking out the front door of the cabin, I shut it behind me, not even bothering to lock it, and stride carefully across the gravel drive toward the farmhouse. I don't go inside since everyone will likely already be out back where the dinner is being hosted, so I round the corner of the house and see everyone there, chatting loudly and laughing even louder.

But something is seriously wrong.

Avery is in her knee-length white dress that hangs off one shoulder and is cut slim. Wyatt is beside her in khakis and a breezy linen button-up, talking to her parents, Dale and Elaine. Stace and Bryan are helping their kids, Annie and Jack, pour a glass of lemonade while Granny stealthily adds more wine to her mug. Ronny is nowhere to be seen, but it's who Deb and Carl are talking to I hone in on.

A twinge grips every vertebra in my spine, seeing the familiar bobbed haircut from the back. It's dark like mine but shorter. I'm familiar enough with it since I cut that hair once. Not anymore. I rarely see her, but she's had the same style since I was twelve.

My *mom* is here.

And she isn't alone.

There's a man standing next to her, hand on her lower back, fully engaged in whatever is being said.

He isn't my dad.

In fact, I've never seen this man before, and he's touching her like he's known her for a while. Like he's touched her this way for months in all sorts of settings—the grocery store, in the airport, standing in lines, and now here, at Avery and Wyatt's rehearsal dinner.

A feather-light caress skates down my arm, and I startle, snapping my head to the side only to find Ronny.

He gives me a small smile. "You look beautiful."

My heart immediately shouts *he loves me*.

I clamp a lid on the thought—*he loves me not*.

He looks the same except for the button-up shirt he's wearing with the sleeves rolled to the elbows. I guess confessing he's a dad didn't change his outward appearance all that much. But I can't get myself to turn my frown upside down or say anything really. I'm too focused staring back at the man I've never met.

The man holding my mother's hand.

Ronny tucks his hands in his pockets, but I can feel the heat of his skin against my arm since he's standing so close. "Are you mad? You have every right—"

"I—"

My words are stuck like dry bread in my throat. Seconds pass, and neither of us says anything. Either because there's too much to say, and it never feels like the right time. Or because I'm trying to figure out what to do about the fact my mom is *here*. Now. She isn't supposed to be. She told me she couldn't come. In fact, she said she wouldn't even be in the country.

So why is she here?

And why is *he* here?

Who is *he*?

Is this some rando she met in the airport on her flight here? Did they agree to fake date and come to Avery's wedding? That has to be it. Why else wouldn't she have told me?

"Are you okay?" Ronny asks from beside me when I don't answer him. "I know I should've—"

"I'm fine. Let's go eat." I can feel his gaze on me, but I don't turn to look. Anger is already heating up my veins.

I start walking and leave him behind. I can only deal with one thing tonight, and my long-lost mother and her fake boyfriend are the sum of two.

My pace picks up the closer I get until I'm standing behind her and *him*. "Mom?"

She turns her head first before the rest of her body follows. Recognition washes over her features, softening them like she's actually excited to see me. "Matilda."

"Tilly," I correct. I'm not playing this game with her tonight. "What are you doing here?"

Mom looks around like she's worried we're making a scene. She's not, but I am. The man beside her, who's been quietly smiling at me with his wicked nice teeth, determines it's the right time to introduce himself.

"Hi, I'm Ricardo." He extends a hand toward me.

I stare down at it. The man has a ring for nearly every finger. His cuticles are neatly trimmed and clean, which I wouldn't have noticed if I hadn't spent a considerable amount of time cleaning the dirt from mine this last week. The outfit he's wearing isn't entirely out of place with his short-sleeve polyester shirt and Bermuda-style pants. But the large Hawaiian flowers around his neck are a dead giveaway that he wasn't planning to wear this here, on a farm, meeting the daughter of a woman he could have met on a snorkeling adventure.

I shake his hand anyway, this man who has no idea what he just walked into. But he's here now, and there's no turning back. Crossing my arms,

I look between both of them and then ask the question making my eye twitch in time with my heartbeat, "Where did you two meet?"

The whole dinner party is quiet, waiting to hear what they'll say. There isn't even any livestock mating calls happening to drown out the silence before he answers. I'm clearly not the only one who's curious. Mom has had dates and boyfriends before, but I knew about them. She's never talked about *Ricardo* before.

Ricardo smiles down at my mother. "We met surfing."

"Surfing?" I repeat. It's not snorkeling but close.

My mom glares at me. "Yes, surfing. I've been known to get on a board every once in a while. At least when the waves are good."

If my mouth isn't open, it should be, but I can't tell since my entire body is numb. I'm a mannequin stuck in a display window wearing an ugly ass outfit that I can't say anything about. I can't figure out when I've ever seen or heard of my mother *surfing*. There's no way she's dropped that in casual conversation before. My mom, the tidy, do-everything-right, and always-fold-the-hand-towels-in-the-bathroom-the-right-way human, is not out there surfing waves and hanging with the bros.

Avery steps around us and slinks an arm around my waist. "We should get dinner started."

My eyes are boring a hole into my mother's, but she hasn't looked away. Poor *Ricardo* is stammering while trying to encourage her to sit down. I stand my ground and wait for her to sit first. Once her back is to me, I exhale slightly and peer at Avery, mouthing, *oh my God*!

She squeezes my waist and leans in to whisper, "Just try to ignore her."

"And him! It's her *and* him. Who is this him?" I whisper-shout at her.

"I know, I know. It's a surprise. I'll sit them next to my parents, and maybe they can be annoying together," Avery says with a sure nod. I'm nodding, too, but mine are anything but sure. "You're sitting by me and will be far enough away that she shouldn't bother you. I just really want this dinner to go well. It's the first time my parents are meeting Wyatt's in person."

"You're right." I blink rapidly, coming awake from this nightmare. "I know how important this is to you. I promise I'll keep everything low-key."

I turn on my heel to follow her to our seats, careful not to trip on any of the tiles, and stalk toward the end of the table where Wyatt and Ronny are already seated. Unfortunately, mother-dearest isn't far enough away, since she's still in Montana.

I sit down beside Avery, who is next to Wyatt at the head of the table, while Ronny sits across from me, twisting his wine glass in a circle and studying me like I might actually combust.

To be determined.

He wisely chooses not to say anything to me right now. Mom and *Ricardo* sit closer to the other end of the table across from Avery's parents, with Wyatt's family nestled awkwardly in between. I have a direct line of sight to Mom, who is peering down the table at me over food containers of meat and vegetables of some kind. Avery told me what we were eating, but I can't remember. We could be eating cow brain with chicken feet garnish for all I care.

Okay, maybe I do care about that.

But all of my thoughts are eaten up by my mother materializing out of nowhere to a wedding she already told me she wouldn't be at, and with *him*.

HIM!

The *him* I didn't know about until five minutes ago.

How could she keep *him* from me?

There's a light tap on my shin that makes me jump in my seat. Ronny is waiting to catch my gaze. His expression is soft, eyes lowered and focused on me while his lips press lightly together. He isn't smiling, but he isn't frowning either.

No words pass from his lips, but his eyes hold me steady while the rest of my world is caught on some cosmic wave about to crash over me. And unlike Mom, I've never been surfing before.

Thirty-Five

Tilly

"You might not have a car or a big gold chain, stay true to yourself and things will change." —Snoop Dogg

I'm stabbing my piece of meat so hard, the fork scratches the plate, creating the most offensive sound.

Everyone at the table thinks so, too, since they turn and stare.

I don't apologize. I don't speak. I don't do anything except glare at my mom.

Who does she think she is? Bringing a complete stranger to a small family gathering—my best friend's wedding—without telling me. This isn't some event with over three hundred people where she and her new boy toy can get lost in the crowd. Did Avery even okay my mother bringing a guest? This was supposed to be a wedding for family and close friends. There was an RSVP for a reason. Sure, *close friends* constitutes the whole town of Big Timber, but it's still a relatively small group.

I lean into Avery beside me, keeping my eyes on the woman down the table runner with an enviable smokey eye and defined lip. "Did she ask to bring a plus one?"

"I'm guessing you're talking about your mom?" she asks in a quieter tone than what I've been using to ask random questions all night.

"Yes, I'm talking about the woman who could have a palm tree tattooed on her ass for all I know," I spit back.

Avery waves a dismissive hand. "She didn't ask, but they aren't staying on the farm. They got a hotel room in town, so it's not a big deal."

I fling my gaze to meet hers. "Of course it's a big deal. It's the biggest deal."

"I didn't mean it like that. I just meant that it's fine by me that she's here, and who am I to say she can't bring her boyfriend? Everyone had a plus one."

Avery's right, of course. And I hate it.

I glance across the table at Ronny, letting Avery get back to chatting with her soon-to-be-husband. He's pensively cutting his own slab of steak, dipping it into the special horseradish sauce, and chewing thoroughly, his rough-hewn jaw working hard with the motion. It's the first time I've really looked at him tonight. He isn't wearing his hat—my second favorite look of his, the first being with a hat. A few of the buttons are undone near his neck, revealing a smattering of chest hair I've become very well acquainted with.

He's so attractive I feel a physical ache in my gut.

He loves me.

He loves me not.

I have no idea which is true. The *love* he said he feels could just be the attraction we've always had for each other. But he's never opened up to me the way he did earlier today. It wasn't just a piece, but a whole slab of his heart laid on a platter for me with a butcher knife stuck in the middle.

Yet he's a *father*. A title he's lied to me about the entire time I've known him.

And I'm still me.

I'm still the woman who struggles with love, having watched most of the people around me fall out of it. How do I know all of these feelings I'm experiencing are even real?

Dropping my chin to my chest, I stare at my own steak, ignoring the rising emotions that come when thinking about this whole mess. How did things change so much in the span of a day?

Pretending to eat this food *here*, of all places, is just weird. This could be the brother or sister to one of the cows out in the pasture right now. I look up at everyone else. Am I the only one who thinks this is odd? Deb and Carl seem to be enjoying it, and while Stace is busy chatting with

Bryan and cutting up Annie's meat, half of her's is already gone. Even Granny is chomping away at the beef cut into nice cubes on her plate.

Mom is too busy chatting and swapping luau stories with *Ricardo*, Elaine, and Dale to finish her meal. It sits forgotten as she yammers away. Based on the smile she's sporting, I'm guessing they're enjoying the conversation. I've never seen my mom so giddy.

"I'm going to do something rash, I just know it." My words were meant for Avery, but I suppose I said them too loud.

"You have a rash?" Granny's brows draw tight.

"No, I—"

"Just put some coconut oil on it," Stace leans over Bryan to say. "I learned that one from Avery. You can put that stuff on everything."

I know, I think to myself. I'm the one who told Avery.

It's when I try to explain coconut oil is the best thing since sliced bread, and I don't have a rash, that Mom puts her hand on *Ricardo's* shoulder. My fork drops with a loud clanging sound. No, wait, that wasn't just my fork. It was my water glass I must have been holding. Water pools on my plate along with broken glass and rushes off the tablecloth and onto my lap as I let out a gasp.

Stace startles, too, dropping her fork.

"Is it the rash?" Granny clutches one hand to her chest, her utensil held high in one hand like a pitchfork.

"Tilly, are you okay?" Stace's voice is even. "If you need to borrow some coconut oil, I have some in my purse."

"I don't need coconut oil!" I scream, brushing water off me and stray bits of glass. "There's no rash." Although, the heat climbing my exposed neck would say otherwise. I slowly shake my head. My eyes are locked and loaded on the giant diamond sitting pretty on Mom's left ring finger, glinting in the overhanging lights. "What. Is. That?" I ask through a clenched jaw, looking at Mom with wide eyes.

There are so many surprises, untold secrets being shot out of canons as confessions.

All aimed at me.

Her mouth starts to fall, and she scratches the back of her neck. "I was going to tell you—"

"You're *married*?" I ask on an exhale, leaning further into the table.

The way all of the blood rises to my face leaves me feeling too hot to function and definitely too angry to talk about this, but I still try.

My chair scrapes loudly on the rock tiles as I shove away from the table, forcing an echo that bounces off every barn, fence, tree, and animal on this damn farm. I stand and ball my hands into fists at my side. Looking at her makes me boil with rage.

"You're married?" I repeat. I need her to confirm that the ring on her finger isn't from a twenty-five-cent machine at the mall. That *he* put a ring on it.

She has the nerve to sit straighter as she simply says, "Engaged."

"Well, that was unexpected," Avery murmurs quietly.

"Are you fucking serious?" My question is one pitch above irate.

"Language!" Stace barks, covering Annie's ears an eff word too late.

"I think this one's warranted." Granny raises her brows at Stace.

I can't even apologize like I normally would for swearing around Wyatt's family.

"Matilda—"

"It's Tilly!" I scream, throwing my napkin down on the plate. I'm so angry.

No, pissed.

No, *enraged.* I'm enraged.

She lowers her voice while staring around the table at all of the stunned faces.

Mom clears her throat. "*Tilly*, I was planning to tell you. That's why we decided to come to the wedding this weekend, so I could see you and share the exciting news."

Exciting news? I scoff. "So, you came here to crash Avery and Wyatt's wedding with *your* engagement?"

My mouth drops. I'd completely forgotten where we were and what this entire dinner was about until this very second. *Shit*. I turn to Avery with an apologetic stare. "Avery. I'm so—"

She holds up a hand, trying to keep it together, but I can tell I've upset her. "Just...don't."

I turn back to the rest of the table and my mom, who is now standing alongside *Ricardo*. They're holding hands, and even though he has a nervous smile on his face, he seems sincere in his saddened expression. If I weren't so caught up in the shock of seeing my mother with another man only to find out she locked him down without telling me, maybe I would feel sorry for him.

But I don't.

I don't feel sorry for myself, either. I fucked everything up, ruining this whole dinner.

"I think we should get going," Mom finally says. "Elaine, Dale, it was so wonderful to see you again. It's been too long."

They offer her similar pleasantries, and then I watch them leave. I don't bother running after them, demanding an explanation. I feel completely deflated now that steam isn't coming out of all my pores. I don't have energy to face her and talk about her nuptials.

Does Dad know about this? God, he's going to be just as shocked. He hasn't even so much as dated since Mom left. Of course, Mom would expect me to tell him. That's just how she operates, always expecting me to just handle things.

I peer over at Avery, who has at some point stood up and is already facing me. "I'm so sorry, Avery—"

"I said *don't*," she says, cutting me off. "We can talk about this later."

"Till," Ronny chances across from me.

I snap my gaze to him. "It's Tilly! And don't even get me started on you!"

Tears are already rising to the surface the harder I try to act like seeing my mom *engaged* doesn't bother me, hurting my best friend won't break me, or hearing Ronny say my name like he cares doesn't twist a knife in south of my ribcage, straight to the gut.

I sniff and look back at Avery. "I'm gonna go. I just..." I lose my voice to the rising emotion.

Avery nods slowly but keeps her eyes on her plate. "I think that's a good idea."

Before I can completely lose it, Ronny's chair is scratching the tiles as he stands. "I'll walk you back."

I'm too caught in my own embarrassment now that the anger has dissipated that I don't protest. I round my chair and start walking toward the cabin, telling myself I won't cry until I get there. Only a few hundred yards, and then I'll be alone. I can cry and scream or laugh and journal my rage. Whatever emotions come, the cabin walls will box me in and protect me.

I'd forgotten Ronny was trailing behind me until he catches up as I reach the front corner of the cabin, and he places a steadying hand on my lower back like he did earlier. There aren't any ulterior motives to this touch. It's comforting, which is why the tears that were building inside me hit an all-time high and leak from my eyes. A gasp escapes next, and then I can't see through the blur, so I stop.

"Let me hold you," he says quietly.

The noise of the dinner party has started up again, drowning out any of the tears I could cry. The loud ones, the quiet ones, the ones that will sound like I'm being ripped in half. Ronny's chest would hide all of them.

Turning, I slam into him and let the walls of my pain crumble down around me. He's true to his word and holds me upright even when it feels like all of my weight is resting on him. He's somehow able to hold me.

He loves me.
He loves me not.
I think I love him.

Thirty-Six

Ronny

"Love goes unappreciated a lot of times, but you still gotta keep giving it." —Snoop Dogg

Tilly hasn't come out of her room since we got to her cabin last night.

I know this because I didn't feel right leaving, knowing how upset she was. So, I stayed on the couch. And when my eyes got too heavy, I conked out like a corpse. Now I'm staring up at the ceiling and listening carefully for any potential movement.

Nothing.

It's dead quiet, which means it's probably late...or early. I rub my eyes with the balls of my hands and then reach inside my pocket to locate my phone. Yup. Just like I thought. Five in the morning. I've lived on a farm my entire life, waking up at five for most of that time. I shouldn't be surprised that even sleeping in a different place, my internal clock would still wake me up.

Today is the wedding, but plenty of things have to happen before then. Cows need to be put out to pasture, horses need to be rubbed down, and stalls need to be cleaned. It's a Sunday, meaning it's just me and Pop to do it all before the wedding. Camila said she'd bring Gia over around two, and she'll hang with Mama, who will bring her to the ceremony at three. But I can't even think of all that right now until I know Tilly is alright.

Swinging my legs over, I set my feet lightly on the ground. I had enough good sense to take off my boots last night, but sleeping in jeans and a button-up shirt was akin to being in a straight jacket with weights tied to my feet and thrown into the ocean. Hopefully, Tilly got enough sleep for the both of us. She didn't eat any dinner last night and just pushed it around her plate even before she broke her glass.

As if I summoned her, footsteps pad across the creaky laminate floors like they're not concerned about waking anyone. And why would they be? It's not like she knows I'm here still.

Shit.

She doesn't know I'm here.

I blink against the darkness and try to stand and search for a light or lamp, whatever I can find as her door swings open with a creak. The coffee table decides to jump out and attack my leg, forcing me to grab it and grumble loudly.

"Till…" I try to say, but the pain radiating through my leg makes it sound garbled.

The footsteps have stopped as I'm hunched over, partially pivoting around the table. I swear the lamp was right—

A hard object connects straight to the middle of my back. I yell, arch, and crumple sideways into what I'm assuming is a chair and grab for the now aching spot. "Tilly…it's…me."

She doesn't answer.

"Ronny," I add.

"Ronny?" The lights flick on, and the living room is now flooded in color and clarity. She rushes over just as I sit on the edge of the floral-patterned chair. "Are you alright? What are you doing here? I thought you were an intruder, and all I had was a hairdryer on the bathroom counter."

A hairdryer? Is that what hit me? I'm going to have the imprint of it on my back. "Not an intruder," I confirm for the both of us. "I stayed over."

"Why?" She tugs my flannel tighter around herself. It's perfect on her, distracting me from answering her question. That and how her face is completely clear of any makeup. Her feet are bare, hair looking almost as disoriented as I feel.

I rub my shin and knee where the coffee table elbowed me with its sharp corner. "You were upset."

It's not really a complete answer, but it's all I've got. We haven't had a chance to talk about everything that went on yesterday and the fact I told her I love her—present tense—and have a daughter. There's been so much happening this week already, and adding these extra layers has only made this process more emotionally exhausting. I can see it in the darker colors of her skin, blanketing her underlashes. And I can feel it in my back.

That was a hard-ass hairdryer.

"So, you stayed the night? Where?" She looks around for evidence of where I slept, zeroing in on the couch across from her. "You slept on the couch?"

I nod once.

"That thing is hard as a rock," she says. "I can't believe you slept there."

I push to standing, grunting a little as I go. "I didn't say I slept good. You're right; the couch is on the firm side."

A corner of her mouth pulls up as she walks closer, standing behind the other armchair. It's the only thing creating space between us, and it already feels like too much.

She hugs her arms tighter around herself. "So, you stayed because I was upset..."

It doesn't sound like a question. More like confirming what I already told her and stacking it against her own mental reasonings. I can tell she's surprised I stayed even without the hairdryer to the back.

"How are you feeling?" I ask her.

She peers up at me. "As good as I can knowing my mom didn't tell me she got engaged, or that she had a boyfriend before that, or if my dad knows. I still feel like I'm learning so many new secrets, and now I'm going to have to see her today..." Her words trail off as she rounds the armchair and plops down. "I'll have to see *them* today."

Knowing I contributed to all this is enough to make me inwardly grimace, but it doesn't stop me from wanting to reach out and touch her. A little closer and our knees would knock together. But she keeps her distance, and for now, I keep mine. "Are you going to talk to her?"

She slowly shakes her head. "It's Avery and Wyatt's day. There's no way I'm going to make another scene like I did last night. One was enough." She stares straight ahead, looking deep in thought. "Which means I don't think I should talk to her at all. It's not like I can ask her how her cruise was or how she's been when *Ricardo* is standing right next to her, smiling like he really loves her and shit."

Maybe he does? I think to myself but don't dare say out loud. Family dynamics are hard enough as it is; I don't need to add to it.

She grabs a stray decorative pillow sandwiched between her hip and the chair and hugs it to her chest, propping her chin on the top. "When I first saw her, I thought she was here because of me. That she wanted to see me and left her vacation to do that." She blinks several times. "Instead she just wanted to show off her new fiancé."

Damn if I understand things with Tilly and her mom, but I still try to. "She shouldn't have bombarded you like that."

She looks up at me. "You're right, but she did."

Her volume dips, and an ache inside my chest starts pulsing harder. Seeing her so dejected physically pains me.

The sudden, overwhelming urge to apologize overtakes my body. "Till, I'm sorry."

She tilts her head in question and whispers, "For what part?"

"I guess there were a few." We haven't talked about *that* moment. The one where I pushed her away and told her every hang-up I could possibly think of for why we shouldn't be together. The moment I chose not to tell her about Gia. It's the only unsaid thing left standing between us, and I'm tired of it. "I'm sorry for pushing you away like I did. For not telling you why..."

Her lips part, and she raises her brows in unison. The shock written on her face is more defined. "What do you mean?"

I breathe deeply. "I've been thinking a lot about this, and I may not have all the right words yet, but I want to try to get it all out. Just bear with me, okay?"

She nods and angles herself in the chair, resting her elbow on the arm and leaning into her hand while staring straight at me, a direct line to my soul.

I slowly exhale and lean forward, resting my forearms on my knees. "I said a lot of stupid shit that day." I don't think I'll have to clarify what day I'm talking about. We wouldn't have started this week hating each other like we did otherwise. "I told you I didn't think we were right for each other."

Her chin twitches slightly, a subtle movement almost swallowed up by the faint light inside and the pitch black coming through the windows outside. But I saw it.

"I also said you were too wrapped up in yourself and that you wouldn't be a good wife." I can't even look at her while saying these things. The lies I told both of us.

"I remember," she says flatly.

I close my eyes, hearing the pain etched into those two words. I hurt her. Not her mom, a friend, a stranger, but *me*. I hate myself for it.

"I was lying." I venture to meet her eyes.

Her brows pull together.

I continue: "I lied and told you all of those things because I was scared. I just found out about Gia that morning. I had no idea she existed before that, and since her mother, Camila, was still figuring out if she could trust me, I thought it would be easier to pause everything, to stop seeing you. I didn't know what to expect. I was hurting and scared—so fucking scared. I didn't want to mess up my kid after everything I'd been through." I straighten and press flat palms into my thighs. "She was still so young—only two—and I knew the second I found out about her, she needed to be my focus. I was falling for you and knew if we kept on as we were, I would be in too deep. I wouldn't be able to walk away, and if you left me knowing I had Gia, I couldn't—"

She holds up a hand to stop me. "The fact you thought I would just walk away after finding out you were a *father* hurts even more. That isn't me, Ronny. I wouldn't have done that. I loved you! We talked about marriage and kids and futures. I would've been there for you if you let me, but you didn't."

"You loved me." The words are lifeless and bitter on my tongue, but only because they're past tense.

"You lied to me. You have a *child*. It's not like I'm finding out you stole a candy bar when you were twelve or have a new puppy."

"That's what Wyatt said, too." I lean my forearms on my thighs. "The puppy, I mean."

"Wyatt knows?" she asks in a forlorn way. "Who else knows besides me?"

"My parents are the only other ones, and I just told Wyatt the other day."

"So you've been lying to all of us for *two fucking years*?" She draws out her words. "You made me think something was wrong with me. That I wasn't worth loving. That you could just blink and be done with us." Her words ride the backs of her tears.

I'm a coward, but I can't stand looking at the saltwater streaking down her face, knowing I all but created them.

"I know." I drop my head. "I know, and I hate that I did. But it was messy."

She sniffles. "Are you and Camila together then?"

"No!" I snap, jolting forward to take a knee in front of her. "She was seeing a guy—still is. I swear there have never been any lingering feelings between us. The one night we fucked, that's all it was—*fucking*."

I emphasize the word because we both know this wasn't what we felt the other night. Tilly has been and always will be different to me.

I try to take her hand in mine, but she yanks it away. "You knew how much I cared for you." Fresh tears fill her eyes, but this time, I can't look away. Each one that falls is like a punch to the heart. I'd wipe them away if she let me. "God, I just feel like the burden to be loved is greater than the reward of receiving it."

I shake my head, wanting to clear it all away. I thought I was saving Gia by making her my sole focus. But instead, I made Tilly feel like what we had wasn't worth it. She hates me, just like I feared.

"Till." My words are a plea as tears fill my eyes. "I love you. I've always loved you—so fucking much. *Please.*"

She shakes her head and blinks a few times to prevent more tears from falling. "We have a complicated relationship, Ronny. Always have. But the last thing I need is you feeling sorry for me and needing to explain away everything you said before. You were right."

You. Were. Right.

Those words feel like daggers straight through my core. Tilly has never said anything close to *you were right,* and now she's saying it about the words I regret the most.

"But I wasn't—"

She laughs, but there's no humor in it. "I know you're trying to make me feel better by telling me all of this after the...situation last night with my mom, but you don't need to continue. In fact, I don't want you to."

Heat licks up my spine. "I told you I love you before your mom even showed up here. I want you to meet Gia. I want to be with you. I'm not bullshitting you, Till."

She hucks the throw pillow onto the couch and stands, looking down at me. "Yes. You are." Her gaze is fixed and unrelenting. "You told me all of those things a couple years ago—and yes, I remembered *every-thing*—because they were true. This," she waves a hand between us, "you and me have always just been a flame and nothing more. We burn hot but fast and then fizzle out. You don't love me. You're attracted to me. You like sleeping with me. You like fighting with me."

I stand, too, unable to take any more of this on my knee. "That's not true."

She takes one step back and speaks through a locked jaw. "Yes, it is."

I know exactly how I feel; she's just set on not believing me.

"We need to get ready for the wedding," she finally says through a shaky voice, breaking the silence and taking another step back. She's too far away in more ways than one. I can't reach out to her like I want to.

Every detail on her face tells me what I don't want to believe. The prominent cheekbones and strong jaw, the way her eyes glisten with moisture that she's forcibly trying to restrain. And the way her lips curve around one another, pressed tightly together but still soft despite her anger.

I hurt her. *Me.*

I know how I feel, but that small voice in my head can't help but think I ruined everything. I lied to her about my daughter. She's right: it's a big fucking deal. There were so many times I could have said something, but I told myself she'd be better off. I didn't want to box her into taking on a two-year-old like I was trying to do. And I couldn't watch her leave me, either, so I left first. I'd do it again if I knew Tilly would have the world.

Resignation fills the cracks inside me. "I'll leave then."

Silence stretches, and then she nods once.

I round the coffee table to slip my boots on, sensing her eyes on me but not feeling brave enough to look at her again. Then I walk out the front door of the cabin and stride to my truck just as the morning light starts to peek over the horizon.

I inhale the scent of farm living. It's familiar but only a little comforting. I've lived here my entire life, putting everything I had into making myself worthy of this legacy even if I wasn't born into it. I told myself Gia would always know she's loved—wanted. So I sacrificed what I wanted for her. And now, the moment I finally choose to stare love in the fucking face, I'm glaring down the reality that there's no coming back from here.

Tilly deserves better.

Thirty-Seven

Tilly

"I want to be loved while I'm here, and the only way to get love is to give love." —Snoop Dogg

Everyone smile," Millie says, the photographer and family friend Wyatt hired.

I fake a smile, feeling nowhere close to a real one.

I'm sure I probably look like I'm smiling at my dentist instead of a camera since Avery elbows me. I drop my arms, smoothing them over my dark green silk number. My nerves are all over the place after my talk with Ronny this morning, and the expectation of seeing Mom and *Ricardo* in a little bit has me feeling more than frayed. It would take one pull of a stray string for me to unravel.

The porch swing creaks to the rhythm of the breeze that rolls through while Jack and Annie take turns chasing each other around the front yard. Stace runs behind, yelling for them to keep their nice clothes clean, but they ignore her, having too much fun to stop. Wyatt and Ronny stand off to the side of the farmhouse porch chatting as Avery and I take a few photos together. The kind that remind us how close we've been over the years and also how I stomped all over her big day.

Deb and Carl went to pick up Granny, and Avery's parents, Elaine and Dale, snap a few of their own photos off to the side. They look almost...happy. Like just for today the weight of their past isn't sitting heavy on their minds. I wish I could say the same about the thoughts plaguing my conscience.

"You aren't smiling, and it's weird," Avery whispers.

"I'm so sorry," I whisper back.

After dropping to my knees in a show of my undying forgiveness earlier today, Avery merely lifted me by my shoulders, hugged me, and then she apologized. It made no sense why she'd do that since I'm the one who fucked up, but that's Avery.

I cried nearly the entire time I did her hair and only half of the time it took me to do Stace's. But I still feel like I owe her more.

"For not smiling?" she asks. "It's fine. Just do it."

I shake my head and pivot toward her. "No, I'm sorry for ruining last night."

Avery holds up a finger to Millie. "Give us a sec?" Millie nods as Avery turns to face me, grabbing my hands with the strength of a woman who knows she's wearing a fabulous dress. "We've been over this. You didn't ruin everything."

"But I did," I push back. "It was your big night, and I made it all about me. I know I've been doing that a lot lately, and I can't seem to help it. So much is happening, and after yesterday, I was completely on edge."

Finding out the man you apparently love has a love-child with someone else, didn't trust you enough to tell you, and he was willing to break things off, does a number on the self-esteem. I'd been spiraling all week until I finally hit the bottom.

It's dark down here, and I don't like it.

"Sure, it was a little awkward before, during, and after, but you were surprised," she says. "I realized that the moment I woke up feeling guilty for shutting you out."

I stare down at our joined hands. The very same ones that belong to the woman who owns all of my secrets. She's the one who was honest enough to tell me she didn't like when I rode motorized scooters around town and then bought me a helmet. There hasn't been a moment since we met I haven't wanted her by my side.

Tears are threatening to bombard my eyeballs again. "I should have been a better human diary."

"Tilly." She catches my gaze. "I'm sorry this week has been so rough. I'm sorry your mom showed up last minute. I'm sorry Pretty Boy over there lied to you. But can I ask you something?" I meet her eyes, and she continues, "I haven't made a diary entry all week, and I'm dying to get things off my mind."

A smile lifts the corner of my mouth, and I sniffle. "Spill."

She shifts on her feet. "So, there's this guy that really loves my best friend, like so much."

I tilt my head to the side and lift my brows, letting my exasperation show. "Really?"

"Sh. This is my entry."

I jut out my hip but humor her by listening. "She loves him, too," she adds, and I can't find words to protest. Mainly because I don't know what I feel. "He has a secret child, yes, but now that he's in a better place and able to see through the shock of finding out he's a dad, he wants to give them a shot."

"And what am I supposed to say?" I ask. Am I just supposed to forgive and forget?

She squeezes my hands. "What advice would you give her?"

The deep blue eyes of my friend don't give me an answer I hoped to find somewhere in their depths—through the years of knowing each other, the shared and solo experiences, the fear, and love, and everything else we've been through together. But there isn't one.

Looking past her shoulder, Ronny's already staring at me like he always has. You could change the setting—the Thirsty Hippo, the farmhouse, the barn, my cabin, his apartment—and he'd still be looking at me with that same smolder. Even though my entire world changed when he told me about his daughter and knowing he loves me, that look hasn't changed.

Brows still lowered, lips still in a perpetual smirk, eyes still searching for me whether there's one person around or many. My heartbeat sprints around my body, soaring up my spine, rocketing between my rib cage, and bouncing around my gut. If this is truly what love feels like, then can it really be turned off like a hose spigot? Does love—the kind that sticks—just end?

"Think about it," Avery says in a low voice, then winks like she does this all the time—she doesn't. "I think you'd find you and her have a lot in common."

I nod slowly and mouth *thank you* because saying *I love you* would force the tears out.

She pulls me in for another hug, then I hold her at arm's length. Her long blonde hair is folded into a braid, just as impressive as the picture she showed me in one of those wedding magazines she loves. It trails her open back with small beaded pearls woven throughout. She's always stunning, but right now, the natural makeup and simple silver chain dangling from her neck that Wyatt gave her as a wedding gift all conspire to steal my breath.

"You're beautiful," I say, kissing her cheek.

She clasps my forearm. "Thank you for being here."

"Let's get married!" I squeal.

Wyatt walks up the steps with Ronny on his heels. "She's *my* wife, Tilly."

"I had her first." I swat his chest and then straighten his pocket square. "You're stuck with me whether you like it or not."

His smile is genuine. "Without you, we may not be here. You know I'll always love you for that."

Warmth floods me just remembering how I practically shoved Avery out of our home, telling her she'd always regret not giving the spa gig at a farm a try. I didn't know she'd find someone to eventually share all of her forevers with, but I knew she needed the risk. Not for anyone other than her.

I grip my best friend's hand. "Smile."

Her mouth curves up before staring straight ahead at the camera again with Wyatt and Ronny on the other side.

I shift my weight to one leg, bending my knee so the slit in my dress is visible. The family-friendly version that is.

"Tilly!"

I snap my gaze to Granny as she gets out of Deb and Carl's car in the drive. "What?"

Her finger is wildly pointing at my leg. "Your dress is ripped. Let me get my sewing kit."

My mouth gapes, and I start laughing. "Granny, this is how it's supposed to be."

"You bought it like that?"

"Well, yeah. It's called a slit. Remember?"

She gingerly walks over the gravel toward the farmhouse porch. "More like a rip."

Ronny clears his throat from beside Wyatt, and I steal a look at his smug expression. He looks better than I've ever seen him. But that's how it is with Ronny, his attractive qualities grow faster than a chia pet. Today, he's wearing a black suit jacket and white collared shirt with his Wrangler jeans and boots. It doesn't matter what he puts on; he's still *him*. Still devilishly attractive, still the Pretty Boy of Thirst Trapp Farms.

When he catches me staring, I look back to where Granny climbs the steps, and I hold a hand out for her to grab.

"Let's take these pictures before I start sweatin'." She stands beside me. "I still have a ceremony to perform."

Granny got licensed online just for the occasion, and she's damn proud of that fact. Even had business cards made with her face on them that she hands out frequently.

We take a few more photos in front of the farmhouse and then walk over to the barn where we take even more. Every time my gaze slips to Ronny, I find him looking at me. It forces my eyes elsewhere, but I can't help but replay what he said in my cabin earlier. If he's serious...

No. I can't think like that. I'm leaving tomorrow to head back to my life. Back to forgetting how much this man has found a long-stay hotel room inside me. The one who will always be as familiar as myself.

"Let's get some photos with the maid of honor and best man," Millie says.

"Excuse me?" I know I didn't hear her right.

"You and Ronny. I'll get a few pictures of you both together," she repeats.

Ronny steps beside me. "Where do you want us?"

Millie taps her chin while balancing her camera in the other hand. "How about near those barrels? We could do a couple with Tilly sitting on top."

"Done." He grabs my hand before I can protest.

I still do anyway. "Why do we need pictures? This is Wyatt and Avery's day."

He follows Millie, carefully navigating the grass and making sure I do, too. "Because we're a big part of it. We're the best friends."

I huff and let him pull me along, still unconvinced and even more rattled by how much I like touching him.

Millie points to the barrel. "Let me test out the light first. Just stand right in front...yeah, like that."

I stand in front of the barrel, but Ronny doesn't drop my hand.

The old whiskey barrels surrounding the dance floor hold poles that the string lights are attached to, making it possible to create a designated spot for everyone to dance late into the night. I'd been most excited for this since I can't say I've ever danced under the stars, but now, I'm just ready to get this day over with.

"Hey," he whispers as Millie snaps away.

I smile for the camera—for real this time—feeling Ronny's gaze locked on the side of my face. "Hm?"

I expect him to pick up our conversation from earlier. Instead, he simply says, "You have something on your dress." He slides his hand to my lower back, keeping his eyes on me.

"What is it?" I ask, a little breathless at the heat emanating from his hand.

"Something."

I scoff. "Something?"

"Yeah," he says, his hand pressed into the middle of my back. "Right here."

His fingers trail up the zipper on my back until his thumb curves around my shoulder blade. He toys with the spaghetti strap of my dress, dipping his thumb beneath it.

"Tilly, maybe close your mouth and look this way?" Millie suggests.

I manage to do what she asks even though Ronny's light touches have my blood turning into lava inside my veins.

He finally looks forward at the camera, too, but I don't miss how he steps closer. My body is a live wire, sparking and dancing under too much restrained electricity pulsing through.

"Why?" I ask, not entirely sure what I'm asking, just that I am.

Why are you doing this?

Why do you like touching me?

Why do you like me?

"Because," he states.

I glare at him, then back to Millie with a plastered smile, speaking through my teeth. "That's not even a real answer."

He drops his hand to my lower back as Millie says, "Okay, Tilly, are you able to sit on the barrel? I think we could get some good shots with you up there. Especially with that slit."

Before I can say anything, Ronny faces me, grips my waist, and lifts. My mouth runs dry as I hold the tops of his shoulders before he trails his hands down my ribs, hips, and thighs slowly. I don't think he's just admiring the silk of my dress.

His voice is low, only for me, when he says, "Because is a complete sentence when it comes to you, Till. You're my *because*. All my reasons."

I gulp as he turns to face the camera, resting his forearm on the barrel right by my thigh. Crossing my legs, I try to ignore the slick heat at my center—between my legs, in my gut, behind my ribs—at his words. The way my body wakes up like a bear from hibernation at his touch. How I miss him more than I want to admit when we're apart, or the way it feels to have all of his attention.

It's enough to make me want to be his *because*.

Thirty-Eight

Ronny

"The more information you have, the better you will be." —Snoop Dogg

Other than the fact Wyatt forgot to give me the rings and Bryan had to run back inside the farmhouse for them in the middle of the ceremony, or how ScapeGoat let out a shrill *meh* while Avery was saying her vows, the day has been unforgettable.

Gia is in the fifth row back with Mama and Pop and has waved to me every time I look her way, which is often. She's treating me like I'm a celebrity, and I don't know, maybe she makes me feel like one. The pale pink dress with embroidered flowers Camila picked out, and I paid for, is perfect on her. Gia was so proud to show me how it swishes and spins around her legs when she twists.

Tilly and I have stolen a few glances that aren't encrypted whatsoever. I'm being obvious as fuck, but she seems distracted by both her mom and Ricardo on the opposite side of the aisle. But then her gaze slides to Gia every so often, and it makes me wonder what she sees when she looks at her. Does she see me in my daughter? Does she see Camila, a woman she doesn't know? Does she see a family like I do?

If we weren't standing across from each other with a big ass arbor and our best friends between us, I might lean in and ask her. The wildflowers arching around the arbor—the ones Lettie, our postal worker, has been growing in her garden since she found out about the engagement—are making it impossible to see her fully the way I want. If we were closer, I'd brush the wisps of hair she left hanging beside her face away and take a hit of her scent.

Seeing how everything has come together is impressive. The shade tents I helped Wyatt set up are positioned off to the side since the sun is only at a forty-five-degree angle, and the barn does a fine job blocking some of the piercing light. It makes for an impressive backdrop in how it towers over us. The small stage at the end of the aisle Carl, Bryan, and Wyatt built just before the rehearsal dinner yesterday give everyone the view they were hoping for. Nothing is obstructed for the amount of photos guaranteed to be taken. Unflattering angles be damned. Even the chickens have optimal viewing.

I'm still scratching my head as to how everyone in the audience is keeping so quiet. Granny is mic'd up and everything, but this is the most hushed this town has ever been. Opinions normally flow as freely as the liquor in social situations such as this. It lends well to hearing every sniffle Tilly has made while Granny talks about the kind of love hoped for by many and experienced fully by few in her matching gold pantsuit.

I've never wanted to be part of the few so badly.

Ever since our fight this morning—which felt less like an all-out duel than usual—I've wanted to pull Tilly aside and talk to her. Or convince her, whichever she'll listen to. But I know her mental load is the size of ten hippos right now. I'm not above getting on my knees and groveling, but convincing someone you love with words can only go so far. I want to show her.

Keeping Gia a secret should have disqualified me from knowing what's going on in her head, but it doesn't stop me from wanting to know.

"I now pronounce you hitched!" Granny yells, thrusting the family Bible in the air.

The crowd filled with friends, family, bakery owners and grocery store employees, farmers and horse trainers, veterinarians and shop workers, all clap when Wyatt pulls Avery in for a kiss. It isn't chaste by any means, which only makes them more feral, shouting and hollering even more.

Everyone Wyatt and I have known from diapers to t-ball practice to first dates to now stands to their feet and claps as he proudly walks his bride back down the aisle thrown over his shoulder like a sack of grain.

Someone had the idea of filling vases with rocks—*so many vases*—and lining the aisle with them. But now I'm just worried Bob from the hardware store is going to jump too high for joy and knock one—or many—over. Looks like Mabel and Gabe have it under control when tethering him to the ground with their hands so he doesn't fly away.

I step forward and offer Tilly my arm. I'm surprised when she loops hers through mine, expecting her to deny me, or shove me away like she maybe should. But instead, her grip seems to tighten on my forearm and the small bouquet of—you guessed it—more wildflowers she's carrying in her other hand. Her eyes are locked and loaded straight ahead, not veering to the left or right. I just wish she'd look at me, so I'd know what's going through her head. She already knows what's going on in mine. I think.

Damn it. I hope she does.

I talk out of the side of my mouth while we slowly retrace our steps down the aisle. Everyone has their eyes on Wyatt's back and Avery's backside anyway. "Have I told you how beautiful you look today?"

"Only twice."

"That's not enough." I shake my head at this travesty.

She lowers her voice. "Probably not."

There's a distance in her words I want to blot with white-out, but if I want this to last, I can't rush this part. She needs to be angry at me for not telling her the truth. I just expected her to scream and get in my face more rather than this near silent treatment.

We pass Gia, and I wave at her. She's bouncing on her heels, dark curls springing with every movement like a slinky. Sometimes just looking at her makes my heart contract. I love her so much, the knot in my chest loosens when I see her.

"She looks just like you," Tilly says quietly. "Her smile, the particular dark brown shade of her eyes. It's all you."

She can't know how much those words mean to me. Until I dug up that picture of my birth parents, I'd forgotten I looked like them. I had told myself I didn't resemble anybody, but staring at the only photo I have of them in the hospital was enough to know there are at least three people in this world I look like—Gia included.

"Thank you," I whisper as we make it to the end of the aisle.

"You're welcome." Tilly pulls her arm from mine and nods once before walking away.

Again.

***

"WHO'S THIS?" GRANNY asks as we approach their table.

I beam with pride. "My daughter."

Stace and Deb desperately try not to share a look, but the side-eye they give each other is obvious and says enough. Someone's going to burst a blood vessel here soon.

Granny's eyes widen, too, and she inches her finger, beckoning me closer to her so Gia doesn't hear. "I know you didn't just say *daughter.*"

"I did," I whisper back and put a hand on Gia's small shoulder. "Granny, this is Gia."

"I'm four." Gia proudly pops up one finger at a time.

"I'm eighty-four." Granny starts putting up her fingers. "I ran out of fingers a long time ago, though."

Gia laughs as Stace props her hands on her knees and leans forward. "It's nice to meet you, Gia. Your daddy is pretty great."

"I know," Gia says with all of the confidence swirling around in her little body.

I don't miss how their gazes swing between Gia and me, cataloging the differences and similarities. There are enough of both to raise more questions, but they all keep their mouths shut. I'm not sure whether to be afraid or thankful.

Granny stands and puts her knuckles out for Gia, who eagerly bumps them. "You look like you enjoy cake, Gia. Am I right?"

"Only if it's chocolate!"

"Smart girl." Granny nods once. "Why don't you go with Esther—I mean…" Granny looks to me, asking with a shrug what Gia calls Mama.

My expression softens. "Gran."

Her brows relax some and hell if I don't see a smile on her lips. "Glad we'll get to share the privilege of the same name," Granny says. "Doesn't mean I'm sharing the secret ingredient in my pies, though. You best tell her that, Pretty Boy."

I laugh and bend down to point Gia in the direction of Mama near the buffet table, which is really just a giant charcuterie board. It's littered with every cheese, meat, dried fruit, and crackers you can think of. I've been by twice already with hopes for a third drive-by soon.

When I straighten, Granny's eyes are wide, and she wags a finger at me. "You mean to tell me you weren't just eating burgers down at the Thirsty Hippo all those times?"

"Mom!" Deb scolds, standing quietly to defend my honor—or what's left of it.

I shove my hands in my pockets. "I mean…sometimes I did. Just ask Betty."

"I mean to." Granny starts looking around for Betty. I saw her near the portable bathroom trailer Wyatt and Avery rented for the day, but I'm not about to tell Granny that.

Stace snickers and positions herself between the two women who know me better than most. "Oh, come on. Leave the poor boy alone. We all know he's too pretty for his own good." She curls an arm around her mom's shoulders and steers her in the direction of the cake Wyatt and Avery are currently preparing to cut into.

Granny stays rooted to her spot near the table, gold sparkles glittering like she's a human disco ball. I'm positive that was intentional.

"Well, surprise," I say jokingly with a wide grin.

She waves me off. "I knew something was different."

"What do you mean?"

She looks me up and down. "Do you take me for a fool, boy?"

"No, Ma'am." I shove my hands in my pockets and stand next to her, watching as Mama helps Gia with a plate.

Granny nods. "You don't live as long as me without learning how to read people."

"How long have you known?" I just assume she's known about Gia, maybe even longer than I have.

"Longer than you'll give me credit for," she retorts. "I didn't know about Gia, but I've seen the change in your posture. The way you worked to forget, and sometimes forget to work."

I guess she noticed or heard from Wyatt the few times I had to cancel my days at Thirst Trapp Farms to help watch Gia while Camila went to her job. Juggling a kid and work is something I've had to get used to.

I rub the back of my neck. "Yeah. I regret not saying anything sooner, though."

"She'll come around."

I look over at Granny who's too busy watching the crowd of people walk through the food line. "How'd you know I was talking about Tilly?"

She looks at me and smirks. "I didn't. But you just told me you were."

I laugh. "Smooth, Gran."

"Tilly can put away more pie than anyone I know," she says with a little pride in her tone. "But I learned something about her while sitting around the table with two forks and a round baking dish."

I scan the crowd for Tilly—a habit I don't know I'll be able to break. "And what's that?"

Granny lowers her voice, not in volume, but in pitch. She's serious now. "I learned she's quick to heat and steadier to hold a flame than even she knows."

The white curled hair on Granny's head should be enough to indicate her years of wisdom, but maybe it's just where she holds it all.

"She's like a gas stove—a reliable heat source that cooks evenly and fast—easy to burn things if you aren't watching it," she adds. "Why do you think the woman can't cook a damn thing without turning it black?"

A smile nearly splits my face in half, and a laugh bursts through, surprising me by how good it feels. But I'm sobered quickly by my next thought. "You think she'll forgive me?"

"I know it'll work out as it should."

"What makes you so sure?"

"I don't." She shakes her head. "But I know you're gonna forgive yourself, and at the end of the day, what else is there?"

I smile again, but this time, it's distant.

"Oh, and you better tell Wyatt what you're planning here soon before he decides to put you in a tutu instead of the cows to market Thirst Trapp Farms."

My mouth falls open. "How'd you…"

There's no way she could have known what I planned to talk to Wyatt about. How could she? I haven't shared it with a soul.

She starts slowly walking toward the food line. "I figured that one out by reading your horoscope in the newspaper."

I yell after her, "Horoscopes don't tell you that much."

"Yours did!" she bellows over her shoulder then raises a pointed finger in the air. "New things are on the horizon. Just you wait and see."

The woman may not be able to distinguish between a horoscope and a fortune cookie, but having known me all my life, I'm more certain than ever she knows me.

Thirty-Nine

Tilly

"It makes me feel the way I need to feel." —Snoop Dogg

D ad?"

"Hi, Sugar Plum," he says on the other end of the line. He seems so close despite the five hundred miles that separate us. "Aren't you supposed to be at a wedding right now?"

"I am." But I'm currently pacing the inside of the barn in my heels, making sure I don't step in any unknown substance. Thank God Wyatt keeps this place clean. "I'm just...taking a break."

After the ceremony where Granny really went whole hog on the lovey dovey stuff, seeing Gia, and watching my mom lean into *Ricardo's* shoulder like he was her safe haven in a Nicholas Sparks book, I needed a minute. Or twenty. But I couldn't slip away unnoticed until after the bouquet toss, which landed straight into the waiting arms of Mabel. All of the other women screamed to congratulate her while I ran in here to hide with Axel and the other horses.

It's much preferred.

"I'm sorry I couldn't be there. Had a bowling tournament earlier this morning."

"That's okay." It's what I always say even when it's not. There's a reason I'm Hail Mary calling him. I need him. "Did you win?"

"We lost terribly, but I love it all the same." The muted sounds outside the barn filter in as the silence stretches taut on the line before he quietly says, "I'm guessing you didn't call just to ask about the tournament. So what is it, Tilly?"

I take a deep inhale, peering around at the hooks lining the raw wood outside the stalls with bridles and rope, a broom and bucket. It smells of manure, but the soft rustling of hay only makes this place feel oddly calming.

A chill sneaks in through the shawl wrapped around my shoulders, and I shiver. "I have to tell you something."

Here it goes. The thing I've needed to say since I saw Mom and *Ricardo* yesterday.

"Of course, bug. What is it?" There isn't worry in his voice. He probably thinks my biggest problem is forgetting my gift for the wedding.

Well, shit. I forgot one of those, too.

I pause and look for a hay bale to park myself on, but there's nothing in this hall of sorts with stalls flanking the length of either side. "Mom's here."

"Is she?" he asks. "I thought she was still in Alaska."

"The Caribbean," I correct.

"That's right. Alaska was a few months ago."

I cross my arms and stare up at the peaked roof wood trusses. "She brought someone with her."

"Oh that's nice. Grandma Jewel?"

"Nope."

"Her sister?"

My aunt has never left North Dakota. "Not her either."

Damn it. Now I'm going to have to tell him. What will he think?

With rings, dark, broody eyes, and a low-key smolder, *Ricardo* is nothing like my dad who is blind as an extra blind bat without his glasses and reads the comic on his Far Side calendar every day—religiously. I'm still trying to stack these two men side-by-side, wondering what the hell my mom's type even is.

"She brought...a man."

"Ricardo?" he asks.

I blink rapidly and stutter. "Y-yeah, but how'd you know?"

He blows air through tight lips. "She mentioned something about him last week. Said they met a while ago in the Caribbean, I suppose. I swore it was Alaska."

"And you knew about him?"

He clears his throat. "Well, yeah, your mother mentioned it on the phone—"

"Wait." My brain is barely keeping up with this conversation. "You guys talk?"

He laughs. "Sometimes, yeah."

"And you're not upset?"

"No...should I be?" he asks in that sing-song way of his. "Did you think I would?"

I guess there's more I didn't know. "I just assumed you both hated each other and didn't talk."

Mom should have told me, but she didn't. She told Dad.

"We don't hate each other," he starts, "we just didn't work well as a couple. Your mother is a wonderful woman, but marriage didn't work for us."

I sniffle and stare at my feet again. The silver polish on my toes is forgiving enough not to highlight all of the places I colored outside the lines. It was a rushed job like the rest of today has been.

More questions roll through my mind as my childhood and adolescent years flicker like a highlight reel across my memory screen. Skipping by the time I had braces in fifth grade, wore sneakers to prom (sacrilege), and went on that family trip to Mount Rushmore, one sticks out: Dad telling me how he met Mom.

"How did you know you were in love with Mom?"

It's his turn to stutter. "Well, I...we met in college, as you know, and we spent a lot of time together."

"But how did you know she wasn't just a friend?" I've never been bold enough to ask this, but right now, minutes from having to give my maid of honor speech about the forever kind of love and commitment, I have no clue what I'll say.

He's quiet on the other end of the line before he says, "I knew I loved her when there wasn't anyone else I wanted to spend more time with than her. When we weren't together, I thought about her. When we were together, I thought about her. She consumed all of my thoughts."

I was afraid of that. There isn't another human on this planet that occupies more of my thoughts on a regular basis than Ronny. I thought that was my problem this whole time. When he broke things off, I was devastated but convinced myself I just needed to forget.

Two years later, I still haven't been able to.

The next question I ask makes my stomach flip on its side, but asking it feels pertinent somehow. I have to know. "Dad, what made you stop loving Mom?"

He sighs through the receiver. "Life had a way of knocking us around. You get busy, you forget to put in the work, you focus on your kid, which isn't necessarily a bad thing, but from there, things changed." He pauses. "I think there are low moments for individuals in a relationship where someone wants to call it quits and the other person doesn't. Well, your mother and I got to a point where we were both done at the same time. There was no one else to fight for the marriage."

The tears I've been swallowing since this morning—when I shoved a head-size cinnamon roll made by Helen and Mabel in my mouth, tears streaking down my cheeks with a curling wand in my other hand—rise to the surface and fill the corners of my eyes. I blink but there are so many. "That's what I'm scared of."

I didn't realize I'd said this out loud until Dad responds, "Princess, you can't let our relationship determine yours."

Tears roll slowly down the apples of my cheeks, and I hurry to swipe them away. "Why not?"

He sighs again. "Love is a finicky thing. Timing is everything. One minute you think you can control it, the next, you realize you can't. I don't have all the answers, but I do know there are some kinds of love that never fade. Like you. I will always love you, Tilly."

I cover my mouth with my hand as my shoulders shake. The emotion wants to burst right out of me like fireworks. I think about my parents and while stunted and weird at times, I know they love me deep down. Some days deeper than others. They suck at expressing it, and maybe I suck at receiving it, but right now, with my dad's words between us, I know they're true. I feel them in my core as small seeds sprout up through my chest and wrap around my heart. Flowers bloom, leaves angle themselves to receive the warmth of these words, and I realize something that makes me stand a little taller.

"I love you, too, Dad." The words flow right out of me. "Thank you for sharing all of this, but I have to go. I have a speech to make."

Forty

Tilly

"Nobody likes not having freedom."—Snoop Dogg

Hello. Welcome, everybody," I say into the microphone attached to Stace's Karaoke machine. Bryan is acting DJ and thought it was a smart idea to hand me the mic when water is the only thing flowing through my veins. "Thank you for being here today."

Strong start.

I figured I'd just get up here and the words would flow out of me like they usually do. This is my best friend, after all. But I suck at speaking in front of people. S.U.C.K. But here I am, standing in front of the bridal party table on the dance floor. I'm armed with a sticky note full of random tidbits I thought of in between styling Deb's hair and cutting Stace's champagne with sparkling water. She was ready to party and went a little heavy-handed too early.

All eyes are on me, and while I'm normally the life of the party, it only takes everyone's eyeballs on me and crickets chirping somewhere in the background to shut me up—these are actual crickets, mind you.

"Hello." I already said that. "Welcome." I said that, too. I clear my throat in the microphone and must have been standing too close so the feedback kicks in, effectively causing me to lose all hearing. "That was loud. How's everyone's ears?"

"What?" Granny screams from the table beside the center one.

I laugh and throw her an honorary thumbs-up, but she doesn't smile back. Okay, so maybe she really can't hear me. I'll talk louder. "Hel-looooo."

This is not going well.

Just move on.

"We are gathered here today—" I stop myself abruptly, not liking where that was going either. There's a cloying mix of strong-hold hairspray and whiskey in the air penetrating my senses. At least that's what I blame the next word out of my mouth on. "Shi—"

"Language!" Granny yells.

I tilt my head. "Now you hear me?"

Granny smirks and shrugs. "What?"

The crowd chuckles after hearing this exchange because I didn't move the mic away from my mouth. Maybe I can still pull this off as a comedy bit and not that I'm actually trembling in terror with sweat dripping down parts of me I'd rather not say.

I shake my head and clutch the mic tighter. "As I was saying...thank you for coming today. I'm Tilly, Avery's best friend, and Wyatt's other best friend." I wink at both of them and rock on my feet. "Obviously we're all here because they got married. It's a special time in everyone's life—well, not everyone's. Some people don't get married." I risk a glance at the other family table my mother and *Ricardo* scored a seat at. "And then apparently some people get engaged."

Not the time to be airing out my mommy issues.

I smooth the side of my dress and stare down at my sticky note, looking for answers. But it doesn't tell me much—*best friends, human diary, she loves Wyatt, he loves her, and something about getting more toothpaste.* My dad's words from earlier are all but forgotten. I should have written those down instead. Something to do with timing...not giving up...or was it knowing when to give up?

When I look back up, Ronny is standing from his seat and rounding the table. He adjusts his hat, even though it hasn't moved for hours, and comes to stand beside me.

He's so close, I swear I smell freshly cut wood on him. I lean closer and whisper, "Did you just chop a tree down or something?"

He smirks. "Good nose. Yeah, I chopped some wood for the bonfire earlier."

Oh, so he really did come in contact with trees.

There's a bonfire pit further away from guests (and any tablecloths) with Adirondack chairs and thick blankets surrounding it. But I realize he's not standing by me so I can smell him. "What are you doing up here?"

"Helping." He extends his hand for the mic, and I gratefully hand it over. Positioning it in front of his mouth, he lets it rest on his chin. "As Tilly said, thank you for joining us tonight to celebrate some of the two finest people in our town."

The guests whoop and cheer before clinking their mason jars with their silverware for the bride and groom to kiss. It's been a staple activity all night, and Avery and Wyatt are happy to oblige yet again and lean in for a sweet peck. They aren't all like that.

Ronny continues. "We've all been planning and looking forward to this day for months," he glances at me, "where two people make a public declaration of their love to their friends and family."

He says this like he's saying it to me. Maybe I shouldn't have given him the mic, but I would've handed it over to just about anyone—drunk third cousin twice removed included—to save me from this embarrassing moment. I knew I should have started with a goat joke.

"When these two met, there wasn't anything that could keep them apart." He looks at our friends, and I follow his gaze. Avery's cheeks are red and plump, denoting the hours she's spent smiling, and Wyatt's arm is looped around her shoulders, rubbing her bicep. "They wanted to be where the other person was. I started noticing Wyatt disappearing more throughout the day, but I didn't need to investigate. I knew he'd be with you, Avery."

She nods and shifts her attention to her husband. Those early days in their relationship were so sweet. They got the timing right and fell in love like they meant it.

Ronny's eyes are back on me. They're like two hands skating across every exposed part of me at once even if they never leave my face. "I watched my best friend find his person. And I've learned there isn't anything stronger than love."

My lips part and air rushes out.

"Fear, distance, time, and circumstances, don't hold anything to the strength of what love is capable of. It can build bridges out of nothing, it can heal, it can force you to wear bedazzled T-shirts." Wyatt barks out a laugh while rubbing his chest like he was wounded by Ronny's barb. "Love can teach you things about the world you never knew. It can apologize and forgive."

Ronny's gaze soaks in every twitch and breath I take, but I can't make eye contact for long. I'm too busy looking for exits that don't exist. I'm nervous for what will come out of his mouth next, what he'll make me feel and want.

So, in a rushed decision, I pluck the mic from his hand, keeping my eyes glued to his. I may have even taken a step closer, the click of my heel telling me so. "Love can make you laugh when you don't want to."

He steps closer and grips the bottom of the mic and leans in. "It can't cook but still tries."

The corner of my mouth lifts. "It can push you halfway to crazy."

"If it hasn't already pushed you all the way there." He purses his lips in a challenge.

The twinkling lights hanging around the dance floor are blocked by the brim of Ronny's hat, veiling us from any distractions. My chest is tight, and it feels like I won't be able to take another breath. But then I do. So, I take another and say, "Love can cost you a lot. Maybe more than what you have."

He shakes his head slowly, tugging the mic closer. "It's a solid investment."

"It can hurt."

"It can overcome."

I suck in a breath through my nose and pull the mic toward my mouth. "Love can get tired."

My voice cracks slightly on the last word as the tears I've been holding back push forward. They want out. They want to rip through me and make the small, but still audible voice that says *he loves me* and *I love him* louder. They want to put their defenses down for once.

Isn't this what happened to my parents? Their love got tired. I don't want that to happen to us. But maybe two years ago wasn't our time. Maybe now is. Maybe it's all the running that has me tired.

Ronny lifts his other hand and covers it where mine grips the mic within an inch of its life. "Love will fight," he grinds out in a gruff tone.

Instead of feedback, his voice reverberates through the speaker, bottoming out its baritone limit.

I blink quickly, breathing heavier as my chest rises and falls with each one of his. But he doesn't look away. Our toes touch, my high heels to his boots. I swear I can taste his aftershave, it's so strong—so overpowering.

He swallows, remembering where we're at when I can no longer form two words. Still holding the mic, he rotates his head and speaks directly to Wyatt and Avery. "Cheers for all that love can do."

Stace appears from beside Ronny, cradling two flutes half-full of champagne, and hands them to each of us. I take one even though my hands are shaking, and lift it toward our friends. I'm worried we've just made another scene, but when I look at Avery, she swipes a tear from under her lashes and smiles at me.

"To Wyatt and Avery," Ronny says, and I repeat after him along with the rest of the guests.

Ronny tips his flute back to drink, then clinks his glass with mine, focusing back on all his adoring fans after saving me. The high-pitched bell sound pulls me out of the moment. But this time, instead of feeling like I'm in a daze, confused by the competing voices in my head. I only hear one. It's so quiet, so small, he doesn't hear me. But I do. Because it's mine.

"I love you."

Forty-One

Ronny

"You got to be who you are when you are." —Snoop Dogg

Everyone is cheering and clapping around us, but I'm too distract-ed by whatever Tilly's mumbling under her breath when I look back at her. "Tilly?"

"You love me." She says this as the crowd quiets again and she holds the mic, which is very much on.

I gesture to it, but she doesn't seem to understand. "You told me you loved me yesterday, and I didn't say anything," she states loud and clear.

Pins are dropping all over the place, and I can hear every one of them.

This one way conversation she's having in her mind is being broad-cast in front of everyone. I peer at the questioning eyes on us. "Tilly."

"I just have to say this, Ronny. I have to get it out."

Not knowing exactly what she has to *get out*, I lean in and quickly whisper, "The mic is still on."

She gasps, fumbling with the mic and close to hucking it across the dance floor while she looks for the off switch. I reach for it and slide the button down on the side before smiling to everyone and leading Tilly over to our table.

"Oh no! I can't believe I just said all that. Do you think they heard me?" She nearly rams into me when I turn to face her at the edge of the table where the karaoke machine sits.

"There's no way they didn't."

Her hand flies to cover her mouth.

I reach for her wrist to pull her hand down. "It's okay. Everything you said was the truth."

"Not the whole truth." She shakes her head and sets her flute down on the table.

My eyes narrow as I do the same.

"Ronny, I think I love you, too." She bites her lip and does a slow blink. "I *know* I love you."

Hearing her say this doesn't feel like I thought it would. It's better. The inflection of her voice, the honest vulnerability, and almost desperate hope she has in her eyes make me want to put her at ease. Tell her I love her back and kiss her to seal in this moment where her heart reaches for mine. *Finally*.

Instead, I don't say anything for a long while. There's more we need to talk about now that we aren't the only two people in this relationship. But doing so right here doesn't feel like the right time. God, I'm so sick of waiting.

All I can do is rummage through my jacket pocket and pull out the rubber snake that somehow reminded us of the spark that never died. Hopefully, this says enough for now.

Her mouth gapes. "Why do you have this?"

I start coiling it around her bare arm. "You forgot it. After you took a bath, I hung it on the hook, and you forgot to grab it." She looks between my eyes and fuck if I can't wait any longer to tell her. "Till, I have to—"

"Hey!" a voice shouts.

We search the tables and see Jack standing behind Granny, pointing at Tilly's arm. "That's my snake!"

Tilly's wide eyes get wider until we both start laughing, bent at the waist, and holding each other up. No one says a thing as we struggle to breathe through our fit of laughter.

Tilly swipes beneath her eyes. "You didn't put it in my cabin."

"I told you!" I say, nearly crying myself.

"I swore you did."

"I didn't!"

Jack puts his hand out for the snake, and Tilly reluctantly unravels it from her arm and drops it in his hands. "You should really be careful where you leave your things, Jack," she winks at me, "you never know the kind of hands it'll fall into."

"Okayyy." Jack draws out the words and stuffs the snake in his pocket.

"Did you figure things out with Card Guy?" Granny asks Tilly, changing the subject entirely. She has a way of doing that. Seeing as she's in her eighties, she gets away with it.

"Card Guy?" I question.

Tilly waves a hand. "It's a long story."

"Not that long," Granny mumbles.

Tilly shoots her a glare that has Granny raising her hands in surrender.

I'm about to comment further when Mama and Pop are walking this way, Gia between them, holding their hands. This moment with Tilly is getting stretched to its brink. We need to talk about this but not here. Right now, I have someone I want her to meet that might be able to match her sass.

I quickly squat down and open my arms. Gia releases their hands when my folks get held up chatting with someone, and she comes rushing at me. I pretend like she's about to knock me backward, which earns me an earful of her high-pitched giggles.

Scooping her up, I stand and face Tilly again. Her mouth is open, arms loosely crossed, studying the two of us. She's smiling, which I take as a good sign.

"Tilly." I swing my gaze to Gia for the strength to keep going. She's smiling at me like there isn't anything I could do or say that could go wrong. "This is my daughter, Gia."

Gia sticks out her hand toward Tilly, and she grabs it. "Oh—hi, Gia. I'm Tilly."

Gia lets go of her hands and rests it on my chest. "I know."

I look back at my innocent four-year-old. "You've never met Tilly before, sweetheart."

"Not in person." She rolls her eyes. "Uncle Wyatt told me about her."

I keep my eyes on Tilly as she bites her bottom lip to keep from smiling. "Oh, he did now, huh?" Wyatt and Avery are just beyond Tilly, standing to take their first dance and oblivious to the arrows I'm currently throwing at him.

"Yup!" Gia says proudly. "He said you two were in love."

My mouth actually falls open, and I think I make a sound that draws Granny's attention. "You know what they say about trying to hide the truth," Granny chides.

"No, I don't," I manage to say. "What do *they* say?"

"Don't do it."

Tilly snickers beside us, and I'm speechless. I don't have words to confirm or deny what Wyatt told Gia. I'm going to at least give him a dead arm when I see him. I don't care that it's his wedding day.

I look at Gia, sitting like a queen in my arms. "What do you say we go dance right next to Uncle Wyatt?"

"Yay!" Gia shouts.

I set her down and lightly grip Tilly's bicep. "Barn. Five minutes." If I stand here any longer, the fresh tangy smell of her is going to yank me to the barn sooner. I loosen my hold on her arm and drag my knuckle down her ribcage.

"Okay." She nods, goosebumps rising across her skin. "She's perfect, Ronny."

I peer out at the dance floor after Gia who ran ahead and is already twirling next to Avery. I don't know how my heart has found room to love so much in this short span of time, but it has. It's overwhelming and uplifting, terrifying and a lifetime short of deserving. But, I don't know, maybe if they can love me, maybe that makes me worthy of their love. I'm okay with that.

I'm gone for these girls. *My* girls.

I smile down at Tilly. "She's at least ten percent less perfect when she's throwing a tantrum over which plate I gave her."

"Liar."

"You'll have to see for yourself," I whisper.

"Maybe I will." I really hope this is a threat. She smirks and steps out of my space but never my orbit. "Now, go dance. You promised me five minutes."

I keep facing her while walking backward toward the dance floor. There's a lot more than that I'm willing to promise.

Forty-Two

Tilly

"I just change with the times. I really don't have a say in what's going on. Music was here before me." —Snoop Dogg

Y ou're drooling," Granny says from the chair beside me.

I swipe at my mouth, sitting straighter and narrowing my gaze at her. "No, I'm not."

"Not yet anyway."

I rest my forearms back on the table, wishing I had some bird-watching binoculars to get a closer look at the dance floor. "They're so cute together."

Without having to mention who I'm talking about, Granny says, "They are."

Gia has been standing on the tops of Ronny's boots while he moves around like a robot. The song before this one, he held her in his arms, one hand poised to hold her small one as he spun and dipped her back. She giggled the whole time.

I can't keep my eyes off them.

"And you really didn't know?" I ask Granny.

"Found out today," she confirms. "Don't tell Ronny, but I'm not all that surprised."

"Really?" I look at her out of the corner of my eye.

She crosses her legs, leaning back in the chair. "There's a reason I gave him the nickname *Pretty Boy*."

"That was you?" My mouth slackens.

"Of course it was," she defends. "Wyatt just likes to take the credit."

I curl my lips in when all they want to do is lift and turn back to watch the two of them some more. Ronny's looking at me this time and hell if I don't feel it in every pore of my body. I've seen a lot of his smiles but none like this one. The kind he apparently wears when dancing with his daughter. It's wide, revealing all of his teeth behind his full lips. His eyes are crinkled at the sides, making me want to scream that I love him from here.

"She came at the right time, you know," Granny says.

He looks down when Gia tugs on his shirt.

I rest my chin in my propped hand. "How do you figure?"

There's a twinge inside me wishing again that he would've just told me. We wouldn't have had to live through this hell the last two years. Maybe we would've been together this whole time. Maybe it would have been the same, but he robbed us of ever knowing. I suppose *maybes* won't change anything, but my brain eats them up like candy.

"Ronny has always lived like he's got a hole in his heart," she starts.

"From being adopted?"

"Mhm. Glad he told you about that, too."

He didn't. I had to figure that out myself.

"Now, don't hear me wrong here. Esther and Merv love him more than anything. He's had a good life. But that doesn't mean the question of *where are they* goes away. He needed the love of a child—*his* child. The kind that loves you despite everything. Not sure he would've understood how to accept or give it otherwise."

Ronny lifts Gia and tosses her in the air before catching and bringing her close to his chest again. Her face is beaming with joy, and I wish I could bottle this moment because I'm starting to get what Granny is saying. Learning to allow space for love isn't easy, but with Gia, she pried his heart right open.

Ronny has been wondering about his birth parents his whole life, but Gia knows hers. He's giving her that. God, it makes my chest tighten with even more love for this man.

The song ends, and Wyatt high-fives Gia while Avery bends to say hello.

"How'd you get so wise, Granny?" I ask, looking over at her.

"It's a secret, but I'll tell ya if you promise not to say anything." Her legs are still crossed, and her hands rest easily in her lap.

"Alright," I agree. "Do you need me to sign something in blood? Maybe show my loyalty some other way?"

"You already have." She waves me off.

I turn more fully in my chair to study her, waiting for her to add her own diary entry.

"My late husband. He was the first one to teach me about love, and I never forgot it. Just ask Avery. Love doesn't wait for you to be less afraid, to have your life in order, or know all the answers. It reaches inside your chest and grabs your heart." She stares off toward the dance floor. "I miss him on days like this. Damn cancer."

I don't even bat an eye that she just swore. I only add, "Damn cancer."

Granny clears her throat. "Something he always used to say was love is a choice that sometimes chooses us before we can choose it."

My throat closes, and the strong desire to let the tears welling in my eyes out is tempting. In all the things she's ever said to me, this one hits different. Love chose me. Ronny chose me.

"Do you think she'd choose me?" I nod toward Gia. "You know, as the bonus mom in her life?"

"Did you get engaged to Card Guy without me knowing?"

A laugh spills out of me. "No, not even close. But, I don't know, I've never been with anyone who had a kid before. It feels...important."

"It is," Granny says. "But kids have a way of choosing the good ones, too."

She winks at me just as Ronny strides back with Gia, likely ready to haul me to the barn like he promised fifteen minutes ago. But then a light tap on my shoulder from behind grabs my attention. "Mom."

She twiddles her thumbs. She never twiddles.

"Can we talk?" Her hair is swept up in a neat low bun, but the dark circles under her eyes remind me she's still human.

I look back at Granny, and she waves me off like she didn't just do something to the chemistry of my soul. "Tell Ronny I'll be back in a bit."

She nods, and I stand to trail my mother away from the tables filled with chattering folks of all ages. We skirt to the back to where the string lights end before turning into pitch black night. Facing me, she crosses her arms to fend off a chill. Her light blue dress hugs the curves she has even in her fifties, but the sharp angled neckline gives her a sophisticated flair that's all her.

"I'm sorry," she says. "For showing up here like this."

My eyes twitch as I lower them, focusing harder on the words she's saying. "What was that?" I've rarely heard this woman apologize.

"I'm sorry, Tilly."

I might be more shocked she just used my *real* name than the apology.

She continues. "I should have told you I was coming even though it was last minute. I should have told you about Ricardo. I should have told you so many things. But I didn't." She huffs and drops her hands. "There's a lot I wish I would've done differently. And maybe in my way, I thought I was protecting you."

I stand so still, I wonder if I've blinked. I can't tell.

"Meeting Ricardo wasn't planned—neither was getting engaged. But getting to know him as the woman I am today was different than it was with your father. My heart was more open; I was ready." She drops her chin to her chest. "I'm probably not making sense. I practiced what I'd say through the whole ceremony, but I'm still bumbling it."

I snap my eyes to hers. "No," I say. "You're not. I'm just...surprised is all. I wasn't expecting to talk to you about any of this. I wasn't planning to see you here at all. I guess I'm still trying to wrap my head around everything." I take a breath. "We don't talk as much as we used to."

"I know," she whispers with tears moistening her eyes. "I know. I did that, Tilly. I cut you out when I was hurting after the divorce. I didn't mean to, but I did."

I nod slowly, seeing for the first time from her perspective. "You were trying to survive," I say matter-of-factly. "Letting people in when you're in that state probably wasn't easy."

She shakes her head. "It wasn't. But I should have done better. I could have been better."

Probably. I won't disagree. But seeing my mother with Ricardo tonight reminded me of what Granny said earlier. *Sometimes love chooses you.* In many ways, love chose my mom. I understand her on a different level than I ever have before. I didn't think I'd be someone to fall in love until...

"Ronny?"

He looks so handsome, I want to sign my name on his forehead. "Am I interrupting?"

Of course he is, but I think he already knows this. "No," I confirm and look at Mom. "We were just talking about...love."

She dabs beneath her eyes and looks between Ronny and me. "We can talk more later."

I nod, knowing the years it took to get here are years it will take to go somewhere else in our relationship. But before I walk off, I offer her my hand, which she eagerly takes, and squeezes. It says I see you, and I'm still here. I'm still your daughter, and you're still my mom. It says I love you even when I struggle to say it.

"Do you both have to leave right away tomorrow?" I ask, dropping her hand as Ronny takes mine.

"Not right away."

I look at Ronny. "Breakfast at the farmhouse tomorrow then? I can get on the road a little later. Plus, Ronny makes a decent omelet."

"And Tilly can...set the table," Ronny says as I bump my hip into his.

"We'd love that." She reaches to squeeze Ronny's shoulder before walking off.

Ronny turns to face me, watching my mom walk away from over my shoulder. He rubs both of my arms. "There were no raised voices, so I'm taking that as a good sign."

I smile up at him. "Not this time. She threatened me by wanting to be in my life more, though."

He gives a mock gasp. "How dare she."

I laugh and hear Avery shout from the dance floor, "Tilly!"

She's miming the Macarena despite it being the wrong song.

"Be right there!" I yell back. "I guess we're going to have to postpone our barn meet-up again."

He traces the cowl neck of my dress, draping across my chest. "We have time yet."

"You don't think people will notice we're gone? We are the second most important people here."

"Granny will have your head for that," he says in jest, but we both know it's true. "I was hoping we'd be forgettable. At least for a little bit."

I bite my bottom lip as he skims the back of his hand down my arm. All I want to do is curl into his chest and wrap my arms around him. I want to tell him how much I love him, how much I want to love Gia, how desperate I am to make this work. But he steals all of the words from my mouth.

"Dance with me."

I reach for his offered hand without hesitation. "Always."

Forty-Three

Tilly

"They say I'm greedy, but I still want more, cause my eyes want to journey." —Snoop Dogg

How the hell did you get it back?" Surprise rockets out of my mouth when he pulls back the lapel of his suit jacket to reveal the rubber snake in his breast pocket like he's part of a covert mission. "Did you steal it from Jack? Am I going to have to report you to the cops who busted that guest Wyatt had a couple years ago?"

"That was a trip. We never ended up finding that money, either. Heard that was stashed in a backpack, too." He lets go of his lapel and tugs me closer, one hand holds mine between our chests while the other spans from my lower back to where my dress dips down in the back. I swear he's been trying to get his hands on my bare spine all night.

"You Montanans and your backpacks," I tease. "It belongs to the land now, I guess."

"To answer your other question, I didn't steal it," he says. "But then while you were talking to your mom, I asked if I could pay him for it."

"Shut up!" I shove him slightly, but he barely budges—*damn muscles*—only pulling me in closer. "What did you pay him?"

He slowly spins us around while the soft ballad has us all under a spell out here on the dance floor. "Fifty bucks."

My mouth falls open, and I quit moving my feet. "*Fifty*? For a rubber snake? He probably only got it for a couple bucks."

"Five."

"Ten times as much?!" I can't help laughing as he starts swaying again. "He played you."

He shrugs and lifts my hand to the back of his neck. Both of my hands meet the base of his hairline. "It's worth it. That rubber snake is priceless," he says.

"Why?"

"Because it's *ours,* and if I ever need to remind you why you love me, I'll have it for backup."

The growing smile on my face is bigger than a crescent moon. "And what makes you so sure you'll have to remind me?"

"Because you ask a lot of questions. Like *that.*" He laughs and pulls me closer until the space between our bodies doesn't exist. The next song has a good beat, asking for more hips and arms, but he keeps me pressed to him, slowly moving like we have all the time in the world. "I know I love you. Till, like you love me. We don't need a snake, a letter, or words. I knew it before you even said it."

I stroke the back of his head. "How'd you know?"

He trails light fingers along my spine. "I can hear it in your laugh, see how you respond when I touch you, the way your gaze can't help looking for me." He leans close to my mouth, knocking our noses. "How I can taste you before I even kiss you. The way my smell is ingrained in your memory—it's a wave of nostalgia that hits just right every time."

I can't help but laugh, feeling it vibrate against his body. "I never said that, either. How do you know I like how you smell?"

"Because I like how you smell, taste, look, feel, sound, Till. I love all of you. Just like you love all of me."

I rest my forehead on his. "You've always known."

His hand flattens on my low back. "I've always felt it."

"Me too," I say. "I don't think I ever stopped feeling it. I was going to tell you the day you broke things off."

"What?" he all but whispers.

"I loved you, Ronny. I still do. I love you so damn much." The way his body is pressed tight against mine, I can feel all of him. The fast beat of his heart, the way each of our breaths mix. "I want *us,* Ronny. I want to know Gia. I want to talk like we used to. I want to kiss you whenever I want. To call you mine and tell you I love you. *You*. Only you. I know you don't need words—I don't need them, either—but I have to tell you."

He doesn't wait for me to finish before his worn hands cradle either side of my face. The pads of his thumbs stroke the apples of my cheeks. "I'm going to kiss you in front of all these people," he says. "I'm going to kiss you good morning and good night. I'm going to kiss you in the middle of the day. I'm going to kiss you when you're sad or happy, when you want to strangle me and when you're undressing me with your eyes."

"I don't—"

"If you even lie to me right now..." He shakes his head slowly.

I sigh and grab his wrists. "Just kiss me."

He leans closer, tilting his head just right and hovering his lips over mine. I can feel his smile on my mouth, he's so close. I chase his lips, but he pulls away just enough so I can't catch him. It feels like another one of our games. One of us chasing, the other running. Either way, we always end up caught.

"I need to tell you one more thing."

The life leaves my body on an exhale. "Please tell me it's a puppy this time. Or a Parakeet."

His fingers stretch wide over my jaw and toward my hairline. "It's not a puppy," he confirms. "Or a bird."

"Damn it," I mutter, looping my hands around his waist. Whatever it is, I'm not going anywhere. Not after I finally told him I love him. He's going to have to pry me off him with a crowbar. "Just tell me then."

He looks between my eyes. "I quit my job at Thirst Trapp Farms."

"What?" I'm pretty sure time just froze. Or everyone just stopped moving because I screamed. I wave them off. "Everything's fine." I turn back and glare at him. "Explain."

Ronny's hands slide down my arms, finding their home on my waist. "I swear you are the first person to know about this. Other than Wyatt."

I cringe. "How did he take it?"

Ronny has been there for Wyatt since day one of accepting guests. They built this together. Plus, they're friends *and* neighbors. As Avery said the other day, it's messy. Quitting isn't that easy.

"Well, I'm still an investor, so it's not like—"

I rear back. "Woah, woah, woah. You're what?"

"An investor. In the business." He exhales slowly but keeps me pressed close to him, giving me no chance to squirm away. "Sorry, there's a lot we need to catch up on now that we don't hate each other."

I raise my eyebrows.

He studies me. "We don't hate each other...right?"

I relax my shoulders. "No. But you're right; there's a lot to talk about."

"Wyatt was understanding, especially since I'll be staying on to help until he can find someone to replace me," he says. "I just need to be spending more time at our family farm right now. I have...plans. Things I want to do to grow and expand. It's time, and I think Wyatt knew it, too. God, it feels so good to get it off my chest."

I slink my arms up to his shoulders again. "So...you invested when your friend needed help saving his farm."

He shrugs. "We're neighbors."

"And friends."

"That too," he agrees. "I would do just about anything for the people I love."

His gaze holds me like his hands hold me—no second-guessing. I feel his words at the heart of my core. In the deepest recesses.

"So, we love each other, you've just quit working with your best friend, you have a four-year-old and a baby mama..."

He rests his forehead back on mine. "Go on."

"Now what?"

"This is a question I'll happily answer." His forehead crinkles as he smiles with his whole face.

I stroke his jaw, which was free of stubble earlier, but it's well past five o'clock now. "Where do we go from here?"

"I have plans," he says.

"As you said." I start rubbing his earlobe, hoping he'll cave. "Are you going to tell me these plans of yours?"

"Some of them."

"Really?" I protest.

"I'm a private man, Till." He drops his lips to my neck, breathing me in.

"What if we go to the barn? Will you tell me then?" A girl can try.

He shakes his head, lips teasing up my neck. "You were right. People will notice we're gone."

"What if I stay for another couple days?"

"If we're bartering," he whispers against my jaw, "I want more than a couple days."

I hum. "And what if I bring you back with me?"

"I'd come," he all but pinky promises.

"Would you tell me your plans then?" I ask.

"I'll show you them."

I push back on his shoulders and lower my eyes, trying to read whatever he isn't saying in his expression. His smirk is firmly in place, and I can tell he isn't going to spill. He'll just continue evading my questions until I get tired of asking them.

"I have my own secrets, you know." I slip one hand under his lapel, close to his heart where I want to curl up and live.

"Oh yeah?" he all but growls. "What secrets?"

"For one..." I draw out the pause between my words. "I know what I'm wearing under this dress, and you don't."

His hands squeeze my hips lightly before his fingers move by Braille across my hip bone. "I think I could guess."

"I don't think you could."

"Mhm," he mumbles. "I bet it's something brightly colored."

"I'm not saying." I hold strong. "Secret for a secret?"

One of his hands skates above my ass before sprawling on my low back. His gaze is molten, but I won't let him melt me.

"Fine," he caves. "Tell me before I throw you over my shoulder and take you to the barn to find out."

I push up on my toes, my heels lifting off the ground as my mouth drifts over his. "Nothing," I whisper. "I'm wearing *nothing*." Then I kiss his full, needy lips. He inhales my last breath since I'm pretty sure I stop taking in air. I'm so focused on telling him how desperate I am to love him well. I promise things I'm still not sure I have any business promising, or may not know how to, but I do since Ronny is my *because*, too.

He's my person, and I'm his.

Epilogue

"My mind on my money, my money on my mind." —Snoop Dogg

One Year Later
Ronny

No peeking," I say, standing behind Tilly while leading her closer across dug up dirt and rocks.

There are also spare nails, sawdust, chunks and planks of wood scattered around that are a complete hazard. Especially when Tilly showed up at Adler Farms in boots with the fur *and* a heel. I guess I should be more specific the next time I say *come over at ten and wear boots.*

Gia hasn't been here for a couple days, but I showed her plenty of progress photos when she stayed the night at my folk's place last weekend. She loves getting to sleep over since Mama is set on spoiling her with pancakes each morning and a ride in the side-by-side off roader to chase the stars at night.

"Is this your way of getting out of the surf vacation with Mom and Ricardo? If so, I'm not mad about it. Just make sure I break a leg so we don't have to board that plane tomorrow morning."

I position her so when I remove my hands from her eyes, she'll have the perfect view. "I thought you were watching a lot of surfing videos on YouTube?"

"Watching and doing are two different things, Ronny." She puts her hands on her hips, elbowing me in the stomach in the process. "Then I got on some weird tangent about shark attacks, and now I can't unsee any of that."

"I bought shark repellent. We'll be fine." That doesn't exist, but I'm desperate enough for a vacation that I'm willing to say just about anything to make sure we get on that plane tomorrow.

Not because her mom is expectantly waiting to show us around their new bungalow on the beach, but rather, I've been wiping my brow for three straight months with more to go. Whether it was measuring, wielding a hammer, sawing wood, or managing the job site, I've been putting in long hours to see this project through. I'm ready for a vacation and to take *Beach Bum* to a whole new level.

And living in a swimsuit alongside my woman isn't so bad either.

"You're lying to me, and I take offense that you think I'd believe something like *shark repellant* exists." She drops her hands to her side.

"It's called not going in the water."

She huffs, tipping her chin to the sky. "Okay, *mister*, are we going to stand here all day? It's been a week since I've seen you, and I'm ready to rip your clothes off, shove you in a shower—or not—and a lot of other naughty things."

I gently bite her neck. "Don't tempt me." Then removing my hands from her eyes slowly, I say, "Open."

I'm not looking at the house I've spent plenty of years thinking about and even longer to plan and build it; I'm watching all of Tilly's reactions. The way her bottom lip pulls away from her top and her eyes widen. "It's a...house."

"Two bedrooms—with the potential to expand—two baths, twelve hundred square feet with a pitched metal roof and a mixture of composite siding and metal detailing. A garage big enough for a couple rigs and wood-wrapped posts," I say proudly. "Oh, and rocks I found around the property for some added texture along the walkway."

"Are you Zillow or my fiancé?"

"Both," I say with a smirk on my face.

This has easily been the biggest project I've ever undertaken, but I found an architect in Bismarck who drew up the plans for the house I wanted to build on our land. It's only about a quarter mile away from Mama and Pop on the other side of the barn, skirting the dirt road in, nestled under a few large pine trees I couldn't part with. The wind-blocking and shade they'll provide will be worth it.

She turns to look at me. "It's the most perfect house I've ever seen, Ronny. It looks nothing like the drawings but only because it's a real *house* with walls and a roof. I can't believe you did this—" She gasps. "Is that a porch swing?"

I smile to myself. That addition was completed yesterday. I woke up the week before and knew I wanted something with Tilly written all over it. It's wide enough to seat her, me, and Gia—more like a small bed really—with large cushions and ropes attaching it to the porch ceiling.

I wanted something that said *you have a place here*. We've done the long-distance thing for a year, and I'm ready to start growing some roots. Even though there have been plenty of conversations about our options, ultimately, this one made the most sense since Gia and Camila are here. I would have traveled to space if it meant I got to be with Tilly, and I know she'd do the same for me.

Thankfully, Montana isn't space.

"That's for you." I step behind her and curl my hands around her waist. "Paint it whatever loud color you want."

"Really?"

"Bought a couple of samples at the hardware store the other day for you to test out."

She leans into my chest, covering my hands with hers. "You did this. You built a house, a swing..." her voice trails off. "I'm glad you waited to show me the place until now. The last time, it was a bunch of raw wood nailed together. Now...this."

There's an awe and reverence in her voice that fills my chest with helium. It gives me the confidence to let her in on the rest of my plan.

"I've got room enough for two ladies, you know."

She cranes her neck and looks up at me. "And you think Camila will go for that?"

I shrug. "Considering how weirdly close you two are, I'm sure she'd be alright with it."

"Maybe it's because we've both seen your—"

"Okay!" I cut her off. "No need to finish that thought."

She giggles and pulls out of my arms, then turns to grab my hand. "Show me the whole thing."

***

"THIS IS THE kitchen." I manually spin her around so she can see the space, then lean closer to her ear. "I plan on enjoying many home cooked meals in here."

Her voice is low. "Why do I get the impression you aren't talking about spaghetti?"

"Because I'm not."

I grab her hand and lead her through the dining room to face the living room. All the main living spaces flow into each other, offering an open floor plan that makes it feel huge. There's a fireplace wrapped in drywall, like the rest of the walls are, reaching all the way to the peaked ceiling. It'll be ready for the rough rock to be wrapped around the fireplace sometime next week.

I point at the center of the room. "I'm thinking of getting a bear skin rug to put right there, so you're warm and comfortable when I lay you out on it. Naked."

"Mhm. What if I prefer bison fur?"

"I'll get one of those, too."

She spins in my grasp to look up at me with an eager expression. "Can we get our very own taxidermied elk to hang somewhere?"

"Yes, but you know Avery's gonna want to name it."

"You're right!" She throws her head back and laughs. "Wait, if I move here that means Avery and Wyatt would be our neighbors."

I nod. "Correct."

"And we could invite them over every night."

"Maybe not every night." I raise a brow. "Sometimes I don't like to share."

I pull her flush against me and kiss her with my whole body. When I pull away, her lips are red and wet. "Let's keep going." I tug her hand, and she follows.

The whole house is one level, but I designed it so the owner's suite is on the opposite side of the house as Gia's room. Even though she'll only be here for occasional weeknights and every other weekend, hers is big enough to house her toys, and she's already mapped out the corner she wants her reading teepee. I bought her a dollhouse to go in there, too, and when Pop found out I hadn't bought any furniture to go inside it yet, he took it upon himself to furnish the whole thing. Tiny chairs, a couch, kitchen table, bed, and an armoire have been sanded and are ready for paint.

"Has she seen it yet?" Tilly steps into the empty room, running her hand along the window sill.

I nod. "She's already picked out the color."

"Purple," we both say at the same time and share a smile.

Tilly has been great with Gia. She told me up front that she wanted me to be honest if Gia ever mentioned any reservations about us or her. But all I've heard from Gia are incessant questions about when we get to see Tilly again, is she bringing her heels, will she play dress-up again. I somehow manage to get myself invited to the tea parties they host together every time.

Walking out of Gia's room and down the short hallway, I drop Tilly's hand to open the French doors to the suite, and hell if I don't add a little flare to my movements to make it even more enticing. I want this woman in my bed, my house, my family, my *life*.

There isn't much to see since it's mostly drywall still, but the tall windows along the far side of the wall have a direct view of one of the pastures. Our livelihood is traipsing around, chomping on grass while the mountains make them look like ants.

"This is our room?" she questions.

The way my body reacts just hearing her say that has me eating up the space between us and capturing her in my arms. I pick her up and spin her once before planting her feet back on the dusty ground. "Say that again."

"Say what?" she feigns nonchalance. "*Our* room."

I kiss her to let her know *our* is my new favorite word.

This house is as much hers as it is mine. The family dinners, parties, sleepovers, Saturday pancakes when Gia stays over. All of these are memories I want to start making.

Every nail I hit, I thought of Tilly sprawled across my lap as we watch a show. When sweat dripped into my eyes, I pictured the baths we'd take in the oversized tub I splurged for. The way I'd crawl up Tilly's legs in the middle of our bed, in *our* room.

I walk her backward to the wall where I envision the headboard of our king size bed would go, pressing between her legs. Her hands are digging through my hair as my hips pump forward into hers, seeking every bit of her my body can find.

She pushes lightly at my shoulders, breaking our kiss. "We don't have a bed yet."

"So?" I say. "Haven't we proven enough times we don't need one?"

"What about the windows?" she protests.

I look to the windows, panting heavily while trying to figure out why they're a problem. "What about them?"

"Someone could just walk by."

I look back at her. Those lips are my favorite color again and with my growing erection pressed tight to her center, I will find a drop cloth somewhere if she's that worried. She feels better than she did last week when I visited her and the couple weeks before that when she was here. But that's just how it is with Tilly, she keeps getting better every time I'm with her.

"The work crew is gone for the day, and my folks are in town running errands. No one is coming by here," I assure her.

Her eyes drop to my lips. "In that case. Just a quickie."

Hand dragging down my chest, she lifts my shirt and spreads her fingers along the bare skin of my hip. I shudder and instinctively rock into her. I'm impatient—she's impatient—so I reach for the button on her jeans, but have a mountain to climb first.

"I see you wore your prized accessory." I undo the belt buckle she still hasn't given back.

"Looks good with these boots."

"I couldn't agree more." I pull the leather out of all her belt loops with a whip. "But if you move in, does that mean the belt buckle is half mine?"

She pulls my hips closer. "Not a chance."

I quickly drop the belt and start on her button and zipper except I didn't account for the added time it would take to undo the laces of her boots. "Damn boots," I mutter from my knees.

Tilly's back arches off the wall. "Just rip them apart. Tear them if you have to."

Easier said.

Finally tugging them off, I yank her jeans down the rest of the way, skating a hand back up her thigh to the pretty yellow thong she has on today. "These are new."

She fists her hands in my hair, taking advantage of the fact I'm on my knees and begging for me to spend some quality time between her legs. "I bought them for vacation."

"Vacation underwear," I murmur, slipping a hand under the skimpy strap at her hip. "I like them."

She moans as I kiss my way up her inner thigh. "I knew you would."

I pause. "How'd you know?"

"Now that's a ridiculous question," she says.

I laugh against her skin, then surprise her by gripping both sides of her panties and yanking those down, too. She gasps and grips my hair tighter. "Why is that?" I ask.

"Because you love all of my underwear."

"Not true." She's so pretty like this. Bare and ripe, needy and so damn feral.

"Liar."

I lift her leg over my shoulder and dive head first, sucking at her clit until she's writhing and digging nails into my shoulder blades. We'll see if she's calling me a liar after this. I swirl the tip of my tongue as she begs and squirms, completely at the mercy of my mouth. She starts slipping under the weight of her building orgasm, and I have to push my other hand not teasing her slick core into her stomach to steady her.

Minutes or hours later, she finally releases, chasing her orgasm until she's fully sated.

"Call me a liar again." I use her discarded yellow panties and wipe my mouth with them. "I don't like your underwear when they're in the way."

Her chest heaves as she stares down at me with a growing smile. She laughs and lets her head fall back to the wall.

I stand and start unzipping my pants. "Are you going to move in?"

She watches me shove my jeans and underwear nearly to my ankles and fist my cock. Her hands are replacing mine in seconds as I knew they would. She doesn't like being left out.

"Two ridiculous questions in minutes," she says through a smirk.

I place both hands on the wall beside her head and thrust into her hand circled around me. "Just...answer...the damn...question."

She lifts her leg higher and guides me to her slick center. The tip of my cock nearly jumps early at the thought of being inside her. Slowly, she leads me home, and I rock forward watching my dick disappear inside her. She contracts around my shaft, muscles tightening as I sink as far as I can until I'm drowning inside her. I can't breathe, I can't swim up for air, but I don't want to. I want to live here, underwater, in space, on a mountain, or a valley in a house built with my hands for *my* woman.

I'm moving inside her, pounding her into the wall as she stands further on her tiptoes while her other leg wraps around my lower back to take all of me. I love this about her. How she's all in no matter what she's doing.

"Yes, yes, *yes*," she screams, and I jerk my hips faster, feeling the fullness of my orgasm ready to crash over me. "Yes, I'll move in. Yes! Always yes."

Instead of falling over the edge, I fly. I fucking soar as the orgasm rips through my body, and I pour into her. Every drop—every part of me I can give. Parts I've shared and those I swear to. I'm promising her body *all* of me today, tomorrow, forever.

My *because*.

Acknowledgements

Thank you a million-times-infinity for picking up my book, reading, reviewing, and sharing. I am so grateful to a number of people, but especially to those who have helped me harness the potential of this story. To my husband for navigating the plot and stakes. I always love talking shop, running all of my ideas by you over a solo dinner for two or in the middle of our kitchen while kids—who are not all ours—run through the house shrieking. The Fab Four for doing said shrieking and giving me some of the sweetest pep talks and delivering coffee to my cave when I needed it most.

To my fellow authors and beta readers for providing feedback on the many words I added along the way. You took the changes and challenges in stride, and I'm so glad for your continued willingness Hannah, Haley, Paige, Amy, and Ashlyn to read and critique my work. You get to see and help correct some of the roughest jokes that don't quite land. Thank you!!

And to everyone else who helped shape this book in all the ways. Erika for designing another amazing cover! I always love getting to work with you. Tracey for what seemed to be the edits that never ended, thank you for sticking with me and answering all of my questions. I owe you at least a coffee a day for the rest of your life, but we'll figure that out. All of the wonderful ARC readers that took a chance on my book and immersed yourselves in this world, thank you to the cow pasture and back. Your support is worth so much to me.

If you are interested in seeing my inspiration for some of the characters, scenes, outfits, etc. discussed in this book, you can find me on Pinterest @authorchristinahill.

I also love connecting with readers on Instagram and TikTok: @authorchristinahill. If you loved the book, please consider writing a review on Amazon and Goodreads. This is such a tangible way to help authors and for this book to reach more beating hearts.

With all of my love,
Christina

Want to read more about Wyatt and Avery?

Keep reading for chapter one of Thirst Trapp Farms.

Wyatt

"Anytime you learn, you gain."-Bob Ross

"Wyatt! Where are ya, boy? Are you going to make me come in there and find ya?"

"I'll be right out, Granny! Don't come in here, it's slippery," I say, looking down at the piles of crap lining the stall like a second skin. Leaning the shovel against the wall, I exit as she reaches the end of the row in the horse barn. "Granny."

She places her hands on her frail hips, the ones she likes to remind us are still originals. "Did you forget about me?"

I stare blankly, pulling off my gloves. "Uh, no?"

"You were gonna take me to the feed store, so I could pick up more grain for the horses," she explains. "We need a few extra salt licks for the cows, too."

She's pinning me with that hard stare of hers that's as hot as a branding iron on flesh.

"Granny, I told you over breakfast I'd go pick everything up."

She crosses her arms and shakes her head. "I don't remember agreeing to that."

She's right; she didn't agree. But she also didn't outright say *no*, either, which I considered an improvement from the ready-made answer she likes to give me: *I got it.*

Granny has spent most of her life here at Trapp Farms in Big Timber, Montana selling cuts of meat and alfalfa. Yet, despite having our farm-hand and token pretty boy, Ronny, she can't keep up with all the work this place requires. Between the cattle, horses, chickens, three barns, one house, four cabins, and one-hundred and fifty acres, it's too much even for someone with two good hips.

"You don't need to do it all on your own now that I'm here." I toss my gloves on a stack of hay and bracket my hips with my hands, giving off vibes that I can do this work, even if I only half believe it. "I just need to finish cleaning out this stall, and then I'll go."

She huffs. "I'm eighty-one-years young and have been doing this work all my life."

"And you've done a fine job, Granny." There's no way I'll tell her otherwise. "Since I'm sticking around at least for the rest of the summer, you might as well use me and these..." I kiss my biceps, and she rolls her eyes as I continue. "You've come with me every other time to pick up feed. Why don't I try it this time to see if I remember what to do?"

She squints up at me. "I guess I could call Esther to come have some pie with me. Wouldn't want it to go to waste."

I nod in agreement, though there is zero percent chance her home-made pie would ever go to waste. "I'm sure Esther would love that."

Esther is Ronny's mom and our closest neighbor. She's my mom's age but has been a good friend to Granny, especially after my Gramps died of cancer a year ago. She brought meals and pie—it's a love lan-guage—helped around the house, and organized the folks around town to take shifts working the farm to keep everything running smoothly. I owe her more than pie, but that's the only currency I've got right now and Granny's paying.

"Alright. I'll call her. But don't forget to tell Bob I said hello, or he'll think I up and died. Can't have him thinking I won't show up for Bunko and whoop his ass."

I smile down at her. "I'll stop by the house before I leave to say bye."

She nods and slowly turns to retrace her steps on the floor of dirt and hay then swivels even slower back to face me. "You might shave before you go. That thing is looking mighty shaggy." She rubs her cheeks and chin to reference my beard she's never been a fan of. "At least trim it so we can see your mouth."

Shaking my head, a laugh escapes as I rub the thick hair on my chin. "I like my beard."

"Your wife doesn't."

"Good thing I don't have a wife," I say and stick my tongue out at her.

She does the same thing then says, "It might just be the reason you don't."

This beard has been the only thing keeping me warm at night since dumping my ex. I started growing it right after I left San Francisco and a job that sucked my soul dry for half a decade. It's my emotional support beard now, and no matter what happens, the beard stays.

I pick up my gloves and slip them back on so I can finish the job, like a live-action pooper-scooper. It's the least glamorous part of the job. Actually, there are plenty of those.

"You know," Granny starts. Pausing outside the stall, I face her. That gleam in her eyes is saying enough without her having to open her mouth. "Vicky's granddaughter is coming to visit soon. Maybe you'd want—"

"No more granddaughters," I say then trudge back into the stall. I quit them cold turkey the second I stepped onto this farm two months ago and realized Granny had a list of numbers for me in her phone book.

She isn't ready to give up that easily. "Wyatt, you're gonna have to move on sometime. Might as well be now."

"Or never," I murmur. It's not like I'm anti-relationship, but more like anti-letting my Granny set me up.

"At least get her number."

I grab the shovel a little harder. "And what? Use it to wipe my—"

"Don't you finish that sentence, boy," she says with a raised finger.

That finger tells me how serious she is.

I go back to mucking. Push, lift, sling. Push, lift, sling. Farm work is repetitive, and I think that's what I like most about it. As a teenage boy during the summer months, I was forced to do the grunt work around the farm. Waking up early, flinging hay, gathering eggs, and milking the cows were torture to the younger me. The only thing I had to show for it was a mean farmer's tan and the skill of identifying different kinds of animal shit. Neither helped with the ladies.

"I'll get her number for ya," Granny says, waving a hand as she walks out, indicating the conversation is over.

I yell after her. "I'm not calling her."

"You'll want to shave that beard before your date," she calls back.

I grunt loudly, so she knows how I really feel.

That woman is a firecracker. I don't know how my dad survived his childhood. I thought relearning how to muck stalls, milk cows, and fix fences was going to be the hardest part about moving back to Trapp Farms as a thirty-year-old man. Turns out, it's getting told off by my Granny and trying to convince her I don't need a woman. Tell that to the speed dating night at the local bar she signed me up for without me knowing. I thought I was picking up dinner for us, not picking up Winnie, a girl who likes moonlit dinners and long walks on the beach—good luck with that in Montana. It's worth mentioning her brother terrifies me. He looked like a full grown man with a beard and a shotgun when we were in high school together. He's only gotten taller, and that didn't seem to bother anyone but me.

Women aside, I'm terrified of disappointing Granny, because it's not just her that I'd be letting down if my plans for the farm don't work. It's the legacy my Gramps left. It's a lot of pressure. More than lighting a match and watching my own life crumble into ruin. For all her grumbling, she needs the help, even if it's hard for her to admit.

I use the back of my forearm to wipe the sweat from my brow. There's a lot of that happening this early in June: sweat. Morning, noon, and night. A scorching hot summer in Montana is the one thing that hasn't changed since I was young. It'll only get warmer, which reminds me, I need to get a few fans for the cabins. The first guests are coming in a week, and even though we don't have the budget to get AC units, I want everything to run as smoothly as Granny's well-oiled hips.

With extra cabins sitting vacant, I figured we might as well fill them with city folk ready to do some nature bathing and marvel over birds, maybe a barn cat or two. It's all part of the rebrand I've been working on, trying to draw in folks who aren't used to this lifestyle. After my life imploded, I needed a project and Trapp Farms was it. Or, should I say, *Thirst* Trapp Farms. I haven't told Granny about all the other ideas I've got typed up in my business plan. It was hard enough for her to agree to having strangers stay on her property, so I'll have to ease her into the cow-hugging and name change later. If she wasn't so desperate to keep the farm out of the bank's hands, she wouldn't have even considered my proposal.

Trapp Farms has been the same since I was a kid, and it needs to move forward with the times. Even the rickety wooden sign swinging from the archway as you enter the farm is looking drab. Gramps probably should have used something stronger than zip ties to secure it—his solution to every problem. He used them for broken doors, bird feeders, tractor fixes, and even holding up his pants that were always too big. I still smile every time I find one. The new sign with the new name is sitting in the back of the truck, and I've just been waiting for the right time to hang it. Preferably when I believe Granny won't run me off with a shotgun, or worse, threaten me with more granddaughters.

Leaning the shovel against the stall, I use the pitchfork to toss new hay over the ground to prevent slipping. Then, I fill the water trough and feed bin, getting it ready for Axel. He's my best friend who happens to have four legs and makes me pick up his shit. I don't mind, though. He's gotten me through a lot and been my most faithful friend besides Ronny.

I fetch Axel from the horse pasture, leading him by the bridle until we reach the clean stall. "Time for a rest, bud."

He whinnies his thanks, ignoring me for his favorite snack and the welcome shade.

"Yeah, yeah. You're welcome," I say, then finish putting away my tools and gloves, and close up the barn to head for the house.

Pulling out my phone from my back pocket, I navigate to my email and wince right before the messages load. I never know what I'll find in there. Another notice? Another offer to buy the farm? Another email from my ex-girlfriend after I blocked her number? It's usually some mix of all three. But today, it's good news. I get an official acceptance for the massage therapist position I listed on social media a few weeks back. That's another thing I'll have to tell Granny about soon.

Avery Ellis her email signature reads. She'll be the first person that'll come live and work on the farm for the summer in order to start a spa complete with massages, facials, and whatever else happens involving cucumbers and mud. I may not know, but Avery, licensed massage therapist, does.

I advertised massages in the listing on Experiences R Us, a website dedicated to giving people immersive experiences in a different way of life, because I wanted people to come. Nothing says vacation like a spa. I'd started researching online how Ronny or I could get a certification in massage if we couldn't find anyone. Thank God that's off the table. Rubbing oil between my palms and laying them flat on a stranger's back is just about the most unappealing thing I've thought up. If I had to choose between feeling up a stranger or mucking Axel's stall, I would shovel crap every time.

I pause and face the wrap-around porch of my grandparent's 1920s farmhouse. It's outdated in more ways than one, but Granny won't let me renovate the *charm* out of it. One of the hinges on the screen door is currently being held to the frame by a zip tie, and the windows like to rattle every time we have a thunderstorm. But it's home.

Clicking on the number Avery has listed by her name, I listen as it rings. We've stuck to communicating via email, but now that she's accepted the job, I think it warrants a call.

"Hello?" a soft voice says on the other end.

"Hi, Avery? It's Wyatt Trapp."

She clears her throat. "Mr. Trapp, hi."

I try not to gag when she calls me this. I'm not my dad. "You can call me Wyatt, remember?"

"Okay...Wyatt."

I rub the back of my neck, feeling the dirt and grit beneath the collar of my t-shirt. "I just saw your email accepting my offer."

"Yup. That was me and not at all my friend who sent that email."

"Right," I say, lengthening the word.

I turn around and face the long dirt road leading into the farm where the cabins sit nestled beneath the shaded arbor of trees. I'm more confident at this moment than I've been all month. Maybe things are looking up.

"I'll send you the last few documents to sign, and then you'll officially be a Thirst Trapp Farms employee."

"*Thirst* Trapp Farms?" she questions.

I rest a hand on my hip. "Uh, yeah. We're in the middle of a rebrand, trying to draw in a younger demographic." There's a pause on her end of the line, and I check to see that we're still connected. We are. "So, can you be here in a few weeks, toward the end of June? I'd like to show you around the farm and get you acquainted with the space you'll be working in before the guests arrive."

"I...uh, wow. Really? Are you sure? I don't really have a lot of experience. I mean, I've worked in a spa for the past three years, so I've seen how things are done." She stops talking, and I'm about to interject when she presses on with the conviction of a Sunday preacher. "Not that I'm saying it would be easy, because I've seen how things are run. I'm a hard worker, though, and I could figure it out. But maybe I'm not what you're looking for right now?"

Picking up a stick on the ground, I start swiping at the dirt caked on the bottom of my boots. I'm not sure if she's agreeing to take the job or trying to convince me not to give it to her.

"Look, Avery. Your resumé seems solid." Ronny read it and told me so. "You're exactly what we're looking for." At this point, all we need is a human being with a beating heart and magic hands.

"Okay. Um, well, I'll need to tie things off here, but I could be there in a few weeks."

I sigh in relief. "Great. I'm looking forward to meeting you. I'll send you those docs to sign soon. If you have questions, let me know. Otherwise, I'll see you in a few weeks."

She releases a shaky exhale. "Alright, I'll see you then."

About the author

Christina is a lover of love who has been writing stories in her head since middle school. She also holds the titles of 'mom' and 'babe' and lives in Montana with her four children, husband, and cat. When Christina isn't reading or writing, she is wrangling her kiddos, home-schooling, taking baths, baking, or raising a glass into the wee hours with her book club ladies.

For more information or to sign up for my newsletter, visit www.au thorchristinahill.com